Advance Praise for *Mudlark*

"*Mudlark* is absolutely hypnotic—a page-turning tale of a dark, near-future New York, told with all the lyrical grace of the best literary fiction. I was completely swept away."

—Justin Cronin, *New York Times* bestselling author of *The Ferryman*

"Combines the spellbinding worldbuilding of *Station Eleven* with a rock-and-roll heart . . . a luscious, awe-inspiring, and gorgeously written novel about love and how it will save us, no matter what the future holds."

—Amanda Eyre Ward, *New York Times* bestselling author of *The Jetsetters*

"Intricate, propulsive, thoughtful, beautiful . . . *Mudlark* is about mothers, daughters, and rock and roll; about who leaves and what is left; about what can be saved from a damaged world that we haven't loved enough. It is an amazing book that takes readers to all sorts of depths. . . . Full of wonders [and] gorgeously written."

—Elizabeth McCracken, bestselling author of *The Hero of This Book*

"A stunner . . . audaciously imaginative, brutally tender, a love letter, and a cautionary tale. Mary Helen Specht has conjured a frightening, vivid, and profoundly humane exploration of resilience amid the ruins."

—Jennifer DuBois, author of *The Last Language*

"A tour de force, a feminist *Odyssey* through a world as dazzling as it is dark, as strange as it is familiar . . . a story about the future but also about what it is to be alive now, as a mother, a child, a person trying to find their way home on a planet that has been irrevocably altered. I churned through the pages, grateful that this marvelous book has been written."

—Louisa Hall, author of *Reproduction*

"Gorgeous, brilliant, heart-stopping . . . This book has the rock-and-roll energy of fireworks and floods. It has the style of legendary heroes who screamed out their ballads in leather jackets and cool boots. I inhaled this book and would read it again and again, would take it with me if I had to grab my things fast before the water reached the window."

—Deb Olin Unferth, author of *Barn 8*

"Richly imagined, ambitious, and propulsively written . . . a beautiful story of human relationships amid devastation, and how love and art will mend even in the darkest of times. I was captivated, terrified, and amazed at Specht's tender and brilliant imagination. This book is truly original."

—Nina McConigley, *New York Times* bestselling author of *How to Commit a Postcolonial Murder*

Praise for *Migratory Animals*

Winner of the Texas Institute of Letters Award

Winner of the Writer's League of Texas Fiction Award

"Delightfully ambitious . . . Specht perfectly captures the minute details of contemporary life in a certain social niche. . . . Novels of such scope and ambition, inspecting the way we encounter the wider world today, are rare."

—Joanna Rakoff, *The New York Times Book Review*

"*Migratory Animals* brings to the page an astonishing admixture of ambitiousness, originality, and authority that's rare among established writers and exceptional for a first effort. . . . Specht's portrait of an otherwise healthy mentally ill woman is as profound and as skillful as those found in 'depression classics' like William Styron's *Darkness Visible* and Kay Redfield Jamison's *An Unquiet Mind*. . . . Richly layered and psychologically incisive, *Migratory Animals* is that rare first novel that leaves the reader clamoring for the next."

—*The Boston Globe*

"A promising debut . . . One of the novel's wonders is the way Specht illustrates her characters—not with great globs of exposition, but with quick, economical brushstrokes. . . . So much about [*Migratory Animals*] is impressive."

—*The Dallas Morning News*

"An ambitious, highly accomplished debut . . . Specht moves among a deep cast of characters and corresponding perspectives with absolute mastery. . . . Most important, and impressive, is Specht's sure handling of the interior life."

—Ben Fountain, author of *Billy Lynn's Long Halftime Walk*

"A novel of tremendous scope and insight that succeeds both as an exploration of larger global concerns and an acute examination of the most intimate parts of our lives . . . Mary Helen Specht is a terrific writer—passionate and generous, wry and insightful. . . . A very moving debut."

—Molly Antopol, author of *The UnAmericans*

"An emotionally nuanced debut . . . The men and women of Mary Helen Specht's imagination inhabit a world of breathtaking vividness, where life's pains and pleasures ripple through to marvelous effect. . . . A heartbreaking, edifying, and resonant work of art."

—Keija Parssinen, author of *The Ruins of Us*

"In prose as quirky and elegant as its characters, Specht proves that—after confusion, missteps, even denial—a village can embrace you. . . . This big, dreamy novel flies by as swift as time."

—Debra Monroe, author of *On the Outskirts of Normal*

"A beautifully precise group portrait in which Mary Helen Specht manages to capture not just a particular set of characters but a generational mood and moment . . . Without forcing any answers, it asks a powerful, probing question: How should you behave when life suddenly gets real?"

—Stephen Harrigan, author of *Remember Ben Clayton*

BY MARY HELEN SPECHT

Mudlark

Migratory Animals

MUDLARK

MUDLARK

A Novel

Mary Helen Specht

BALLANTINE BOOKS

New York

Ballantine Books
An imprint of Random House
A division of Penguin Random House LLC
1745 Broadway, New York, NY 10019
randomhousebooks.com
randomhousebookclub.com
penguinrandomhouse.com

A Ballantine Books Trade Paperback Original

ISBN 979-8-217-09249-9
Ebook ISBN 979-8-217-09250-5

Printed in the United States of America

1st Printing

BOOK TEAM: Production editor: Jennifer Rodriguez • Managing editor: Pamela Alders • Production manager: Chanler Harris • Copy editor: Taylor McGowan • Proofreaders: Chuck Thompson, Barbara Greenberg, Amy Harned

Book design by Debbie Glasserman

The authorized representative in the EU for product safety and compliance is Penguin Random House Ireland, Morrison Chambers, 32 Nassau Street, Dublin D02 YH68, Ireland. https://eu-contact.penguin.ie

For my summer baby

Or was I in my marriage bed, stuffed with hay, or
was I in the field between the plants' burrs and hard globes
of dust in sun, or was I on the ice floor, or was I in a river
as I pushed you from my body. Once I brought you here
I could take the hood of *family,* once you drank from me,
the name of *mother.* Here I am, your animal. You have made me
flesh. I have made you to consume what the world is flurrying
even now to make. You have bound him and me together
in a ring of muscle and bone. Your hyphen weds our names. Had I
a larger tongue, I would have cleaned you myself.
I have disappeared inside your making and the joy
unbearable in its steadfast thrum. I had the low call
of it inside me always. It quakes me, rearranges
everything. Give awe your lineaments—and I will birth it.

—Sasha West, "We've Not Long Come In"

I may not tell you for certain whether he is alive or dead; it is a bad thing to babble like the blowing wind.

—*The Odyssey*

Anyone else wonder about the last drum beat?

—from Stevie Ray Vaughan notebook at Bullock
Texas State History Museum exhibit, 2017

MUDLARK

1

BURNING MAN
7 P.M.

The last time Jenny Sweet saw her daughter, the world was lashed in gold. Pastel light refracted by white sand. Dusk.

In the distance, objects were illumined against the dying sky: A temple filigreed in silver and gold, tiered like a wedding cake. An arcing set of prongs, the rib cage of a whale. A two-story Doc Martens boot attached to a clothesline—was it for the old woman who lived in a shoe? The one with all the children?

Black Rock Desert was better in photographs than in real life. Because even with her aviator goggles and the handwoven scarf gifted to her by a mermaid, Jenny felt besieged by beautiful dirt: digging in wherever cloth touched skin, fusing with the membranes of her lungs and eyes, muffling the sound of the amps.

Put on your red shoes and dance the blues . . .

The temperature dropped like a sigh of relief. Jenny looked for her daughter, to see if she was wearing her jacket. Of course not. There was thirteen-year-old Neko by the edge of the stage, twirling cords of glowing neon plastic, mesmerized by the cheap noodles of rainbow light as she danced, limbs so liquid it was as if she had yet to grow bones.

Jenny nodded at the guitar tech as he finished tuning her Les Paul Goldtop, leaning it back into the stand. The crowd hadn't recognized the band yet—everybody else on the Playa was dressed more like rock stars than they were. This gig, if you could even call it that, had been Max's idea—to promote their final album with a surprise set at Burning Man. To Jenny, it seemed like a lot of trouble for a show with no tickets, no take. For an album by a band that, unbeknownst to its fans, was breaking up. But Max got his way. As usual.

"Neko." She pointed to her daughter's bag near the tower of bottled water they'd packed in with them. "Hoodie, please." She wanted so badly to touch her, to gently slide the jacket onto her shoulders like she had when her daughter was small.

Neko frowned, clearly loathe to cover up the sequined halter she'd insisted on wearing. "I'm not cold," she said, and Jenny tried not to flinch at the hardness in her daughter's voice.

A man climbed the stage: Microphone feedback. Speaker distortion. Across the way, Max gave her the signal—two minutes to show. The man was introducing them to a surprised and gathering hive of desert people. Jenny found the candy-apple-red high-fidelity headphones and handed them to Neko, brushing two fingers along her cheekbone, smearing a patina of sand across her daughter's skin. She couldn't help herself.

Neko didn't react; despite having begged to tag along with them from New York, she was a statue erected in honor of bitter teenage self-righteousness.

"You're either *'radical or pro-parental,'*" Jenny intoned, taking off her goggles to splash the lenses with water. "Congrats on being so radical."

"Who says *that*?" snapped Neko.

"Kathleen Hanna sang that."

"It doesn't even make sense."

"Or does it?" Jenny raised her eyebrows.

"Mom, I'm starving. Did you even bring any food?"

Jenny squatted and rifled through her backpack. "Can you wait?"

Neko pursed her lips and pointed at a tent fifty yards away. "There's pizza over there."

Jenny sighed. "Fine. Straight there and straight back."

7:30 P.M.

On stage, Jenny took her place between Max and Jesse—they didn't have a front man, per se, but the audience liked to see a woman at the center, a little T & A, a little window dressing between the white guy and the brown guy, though Jenny tried not to think of it that way (dressed as she was in a plain T-shirt and billowy Thai fisherman pants). Plus, she thought, she played the axe like a killer, didn't she, and even wrote some of the songs.

The Nightjars were one of those indie bands that had been elevated to a certain level of fame. They weren't so young anymore, and neither were their fans, but they were still fucking cool. In fact, that's what people said when they spotted her or Max or Jesse on the street. *Fucking cool, man. Fucking cool.* And that's what the Burners were saying now as they yelled and swarmed, kicking up dust until their glittery faces and writhing bodies blurred. *Fucking cool, man. It's the Nightjars. The Nightjars are right there, man. They're home, man.*

The acoustics were crap, and Jenny didn't even want to think about what the sand was doing to the equipment; it was like playing a concert in a dust storm. Maybe this was just how the world was now: Dust devils in Nevada while a Category 5 hurricane threatened the whole Eastern Seaboard.

The grid of tents in the distance was like the desert base of a post-apocalyptic warlord. And people paid so much money, spent forever in a line of cars, just to be in this heat and cold and sand and thirst with thousands of strangers. *Temporary community building* was what they called it. Her brain reacted violently to the phrase, prompting Jenny's mental deejay, supplying a constant internal soundtrack to what might be called her life, to begin pumping drugged-out psychedelia, all the masters of drone.

The Nightjars opened their set with the pointillist dual-guitar odyssey they were known for, building toward crashing bar chords underpinned by Jesse on the drums. They'd never gotten around to adding a bassist, but they filled in the lower register with an octave pedal. Their technique was meticulous but their sound was messy, never cleaned up, never slick. The sonic landscape, not so unlike their personal one, was meant to sound ruinous and it did.

Despite their success, Jenny had always thought of the Nightjars as an arthouse band. But if this desert carnival was what Americans considered art these days, then maybe not. Clearly her plan to run away from all this was for the best. Then, at least, she could close her eyes to this bullshit, throw herself into the next project: a sound installation in Berlin, a Frankenstein instrument to be housed in the bowels of a church, fabricated to take advantage of its acoustic resonance. A 40K-lumen projector, lights dancing in synchronicity. A religious experience for the nonreligious. Maybe, one day, it would even impress her daughter.

After the intro, Jenny switched out her Telecaster for the

Goldtop and put the goggles back on, even though they blocked her peripheral vision: She felt like a kid looking through the cardboard tube of a roll of paper towels. Or through a kaleidoscope, colors shifting and glimmering into arrays of stained glass.

Onstage in the wind and dust, Jenny morphed into her father, who once spent a summer driving without a windshield, just goggles between him and the road ahead. She'd found his old goggles from that road trip in the attic and worn them to school every day until the hardened rubber finally crumbled in her hands. Her gentle dad, the professor of classics, who died before he ever got to see the Nightjars perform. With the goggles on, it didn't feel like Jenny was performing, but rather like she was the audience watching everything happen. A beautiful inversion. An unleashing. A letting go.

8:30 P.M.

After the set, Jenny was disoriented as she stepped down from the stage, the amp feedback echoing as she struggled to find her guitar case, tripping over a snake of cords. She'd become spoiled, accustomed to professional staff, equipment being shepherded on and off as if by punk-rock ghosts. She shivered and looked around for her leather jacket. Her skin stretched tight across neck and cheekbones. Her lips cracked and bled.

Then Max was beside her. Recently he'd grown a small paunch, partly disguised by the loose flow of his guayabera; his long eyelashes and the splash of freckles across his nose made him look younger than he was. Out of habit, she stupidly angled her head for a kiss, but instead, he leaned toward her ear. "Where's Neko?"

She bit her lip. It was so strange that her brain had to keep reminding her: They were separated. They were sep-a-rated. *I used to be your sweet mama, sweet papa, but now I'm just as sour as can be . . .*

Jenny swiveled toward the steps and the undulation of roadies and fans. No candy-apple-red headphones. No sequined halter top.

"Did you tell her she could leave?" asked Max, an edge to his voice. Lately, he was so quick to annoy. To blame her for things. He was getting his freedom, getting their East Village apartment. What more did he want?

"She went to the pizza tent. She was hungry." Jenny looked him in the eyes. They were the same height and could dance cheek to cheek, like in an oldies song. When they first met, he'd worn his curly hair long and wild. These days, his head was shaved, a well-groomed beard covering the acne scars she used to run her hands across like Braille. "I'll get her," she said.

Jenny walked languidly, not yet worried. Follow the smell of food and you'll find Neko, that was the mantra. The girl was ravenous. Jenny loved that about her.

When she arrived at the pizza tent, it was almost empty. A young woman dressed like a Day-Glo Viking said the pizza was gone, but they'd be doing another batch in a few hours.

"Did you hear they named the hurricane Frida? The one in the Atlantic? Like, after Frida Kahlo."

"Oh. Okay. Did you see a thirteen-year-old girl? Curly hair?"

"That sounds right," said the woman. "But I don't know where she went."

8:45 P.M.

Back at the stage, Jenny and Max circled, checking in with their crew, shaking off people who tried to stop them or pat them on the shoulder with "Fucking great. Fucking great."

Then Jesse was there, leaning his tall, angular body down to face her—Jesse, the quietest member of the band, the one who communicated almost exclusively in rhythm. His hair had gone gray years ago, the bones of his face grown more prominent with age. Even after all this time as bandmates, she knew only snatches about his life before they met, like the fact that he was from South Texas and his family had never owned a television or a computer, though he could rig out any piece of musical equipment ever made. Jesse always had at least two weird side projects going, and Jenny wondered if he was relieved that the Nightjars were finally breaking up, relieved to leave behind their loathsome drama.

Jesse handed her a bottle of water. "Someone thinks they saw Neko talking to a monarch butterfly."

Not a particularly helpful description at Burning Man. What was also unhelpful was the lack of cell service, which meant that even if their daughter thought to borrow some stranger's phone, it was unlikely a call would get through.

Someone left to notify security, and the rest of their limited crew fanned out in search of the missing girl. Max and Jenny peeled off in opposite directions.

Jenny remembered getting lost in the grocery store as a kid and going to the checkout counter, but Burning Man was no grocery store. She reminded herself that Neko was also no child. She wouldn't have gone far. She knew how to ask for directions. She was thirteen.

Don't panic, Jenny told herself. *Be methodical.* She scanned the nearby surroundings, trying to see them through her daughter's eyes. Sparks shot up, describing ornate designs in the night sky: fire spinners. She passed a phalanx of revelers, naked bodies covered in gold paint and elaborate feathered headdresses, and picked her way through the thick weave of people surrounding the fire spinners, whose muscular bodies glistened as they twirled blazing balls in circles and figure eights, searing the air with streaks of flame and smoke. But no Neko. No curly-haired teens in the circle of light.

She'd been explicit—*Straight there and straight back!* Why didn't her daughter ever listen? But Jenny knew that wasn't fair: No child truly understood the awesome power of a parent's worry.

Now, as she searched for her daughter in a crowd of freaks, the refrain returned, the one that had taken up residence inside her brain ever since she'd seen the extra line on the pregnancy stick: *What kind of mother, what kind of mother?*

9 P.M.

With heart racing and the coppery taste of adrenaline in the back of her throat, Jenny crossed back toward the major thoroughfares referred to as the Fallopian Tubes, weaving through illuminated bikes, spokes clattering, riders snaking through the night on their way to various parties and art installations and bars lit up in the distance. Somebody swerved a towering unicycle around her, yelling, "Darktard!"

A grove of neon palm trees up ahead. As Jenny got closer, she saw it was a dance party with a deejay spinning beats in one corner, an enormous Lite-Brite in another. She cupped her hands around her mouth and asked the bartenders if they'd seen a young girl: curly hair, sequined halter, thirteen. They shook their heads, sympathetic but uninvolved.

Inside her brain erupted a dense sound, more mono than stereo: *Born from some mother's womb, just like any other room*. Jenny remembered finding Neko wearing her Joy Division T-shirt once and laughing. "Can you name one song?" Jenny had interrogated her. "Hum even one Joy Division riff?" Neko had never borrowed the shirt again.

In the glow of the trees, a sexy cowgirl danced with a sexy samurai, a robot in a chrome corset did the moonwalk, a Tibetan monk twerked. But no Neko.

Jenny noticed an abandoned skateboard outside the bar, and she hopped on it—just stole the thing, she was beyond caring. It had been years since she'd skated, but the body remembered.

As she coasted along the road, zigzagging through the confusing layout of the place, an image of newborn Neko took hold of her mind. So small and thin that the skin hung from her body, making her look like an old man with furrowed brow. She had been born six weeks early, traumatizing them with a twenty-one-day stay in the NICU. Later, it had been important to Jenny to transform that narrative for her daughter, to whom she always said: *You just wanted to join the party early. You were ahead of your time. The doctors in the NICU were amazed when you ripped out your feeding tube. Ready to kick out the jams.*

What Jenny remembered most about the NICU was the struggle of trying to pick up their pink, wrinkly baby from the plastic warming bed without disrupting the web of tubes and sensors. That one whorl of super-fine baby hair. Stripping off her shirt behind the thin curtain, Jenny had held Neko to her naked chest—"kangaroo care," they called it—thinking: *You should still be inside of me. How can I protect you out here?*

This was also what Jenny was chanting to herself now—*you*

should still be inside of me—while skateboarding through her worst nightmare. The horror of parenthood: That anything could go wrong at any moment. That everything could.

WHEN SHE BECAME PREGNANT AT FORTY, JENNY HAD SENT OFF FOR special Yuzen paper from Japan covered in intricate patterns with names like "Chaos" and "Devotion" and "Noble Delight." Jenny's father had taught her to make origami cranes during those long flights they took all over the world for his academic conferences and endless research, and she decided she would fold a thousand of them to keep her daughter safe and lucky—anyone who folded that many cranes received one wish from the gods.

So many small steps were needed to transform the two-dimensional rectangle into a being of flight. The creases looked meaningless at first. Fold, crease, fold, flip. Each edge had to be lined up exactly. Every fraction mattered. Every mistake multiplied. This side, then the other. Symmetry that created the base square, then the petal fold, and the bird base. Only after all that did you finally make the tail and the head. The wings last of all. Fold, crease, fold, flip.

After they brought Neko home from the hospital, she hadn't resented Max's spelunking into sleep in the bed beside her because she had a purpose. Fold, crease, fold, flip. And as soon as the paper creased, the messy surf beats and fuzzy synths of her brain would slow and relax into a soundtrack of avant-garde jazz, Archie Shepp and Sun Ra.

Did the lack of sleep lead to the anxiety that led to the panic attacks that led to uncontrollable crying and shaking in a bathtub and eventually yelling for help, any kind of help? That led to a week in the psychiatric ward of the hospital, where the lights were piss yellow and the common room television always played *M★A★S★H*? Was Jenny the only one who remembered the words to the music that played at the start of each episode? *Su-i-cide is painless.*

Thank God for sleeping pills. Thank God nobody in the booby hatch recognized her, face swollen and torso caved in, bangs hanging over her eyes like a shroud. Thank God she had a sense of humor about the coloring books and crayons they pushed on the women like her, who didn't know how to knit, and about the way her milk leaked onto everything, the teenage depressives staring at the growing saucer stains on her shirt with wide, wounded eyes. She imagined everyone watching her and wondering: *What kind of mother?*

Jenny folded cranes. Fold, crease, fold, flip. But the paper they gave her was crap, and she ended up having to throw away the ones she made there.

9:45 P.M.

"I'm looking for a girl—curly hair, sequined halter, thirteen—possibly with a woman in a butterfly costume." Jenny began stopping and asking anybody she came across. "Curly hair, sequined halter, thirteen. Curly hair, sequined halter, thirteen."

They shrugged and looked at her blankly.

What kind of mother. What kind of mother. What kind of mother.

"I understand what you're saying, but can you please not use the word 'costume'?" said a man dressed like a replicant from *Blade Runner*. "A costume is what you wear when you're dressing up as someone else. At Burning Man, we wear uniforms or outfits. We are dressing up as under-supported parts of ourselves . . ."

Jenny didn't stick around to hear the rest.

Suddenly, all she felt was thirst. She *was* thirst. She stopped at a bar for water and then drank, gulped, refilled, and began again. There was a shimmery quality to the air around her, people moving in slow motion, sounds muffled.

She circled the tent, talking like one of those windup dolls: *Curly hair, sequined halter, thirteen. Curly hair, sequined halter, thirteen.*

Finally, a mohawked man about her own age held Jenny's arm and looked her in the eye. "Maybe. Do you have a picture?"

Of course. Why hadn't Jenny thought to show a picture? She held up her phone—the wallpaper on the screen was of Neko five years ago, sitting on a rock in a Vermont creek. Jenny fumbled to unlock the phone and scroll to more recent photos. Hope lit a fire in her belly.

The man looked at the photos. Neko, with her button nose and corkscrew hair so amazing it would make you lose your mind.

After an eternity, the man with the mohawk finally shook his head. "I'm sorry. I'm sure you'll find her."

Jenny took back the phone, which had returned to the wallpaper: sweet, open, eight-year-old Neko. Wet body imprint on a warm rock.

That summer in Vermont when the photo was taken, Neko's cheeks were still rounded with baby fat, goosebumps on her wet arms, and she wore a faded rainbow swimsuit, pilling at the rear where the Lycra had stretched. Her mouth had formed an expression of joy at having conquered the frigid swimming hole. She had pursed her lips, looking quickly between her parents and the boys farther down, who had been jumping from the rocks into the deep water. But the boys ignored them. Neko had splashed her father, laughing, while Jenny stared at her, trying to memorize every beautiful feature: the faint chin dimple, the shell earlobes, the unselfconscious way she held her body. Raising a child was living in a continuous state of loss, the old Neko constantly morphing into the new one. But still, one had to be thankful for these tiny losses, considering the alternative.

In that faraway Vermont swimming hole, mother and daughter had floated on their backs, fingers woven together, and Jenny had thought: *One day soon, she will leave me for the teenagers on the rocks. But not today.*

10 P.M.

The hard-packed flatness of the desert ground and the immense darkness of the sky threw off Jenny's sense of perspective—things appeared far in the distance and then, boom, were suddenly right in front of her. A massage parlor and a photo studio emerged from the darkness, then a giant neon eyeball, then a circle of brightly painted fire barrels around which people warmed themselves like at a homeless camp. She hoped that, by now, someone had "gifted" Neko a sweatshirt or jacket.

Overwhelmed, unsure of what to do next, Jenny began making her way back to their tent camp so she could get in touch with whatever counted for security around here—praying Max had had better luck and that Neko would be waiting there, annoyed at them for "overreacting."

As she skateboarded along, she heard the sound of crying. She traced the sound to a figure in the dust next to a bike. An androgynous robot sat crumpled and weeping.

The robot looked up at Jenny with pleading eyes and said, "I am so alone."

Jenny turned to leave. She felt a violent wonder that someone could be upset over something so abstract and banal when she had lost her *fucking kid*.

She opened her mouth, and she screamed.

2

JULY, 25 YEARS LATER

With the rest of the mudlarks, Neko exited the transport van to the sound of wooden bells. The men and women who clawed out a living along the Breakwater levee had begun to open their food stalls, flaying rabbits and stewing goat's milk. If you brought the children here anything—pens, candy—there was never enough, and they would tussle over it until bloody and limping. So Neko had learned to pass through like a blade.

In the world of before, her mother had encouraged her to look in the eye any beggar they passed on a street corner. She used to say that the worst thing you could do was pretend somebody's suffering didn't exist. Of course, Neko knew now that there were many worse things you could do to people.

Hillock. Rise. Rim.

The Breakwater rose up like a concrete whale. Morning light prismed off the top of the levee, the walls of which were in shadow, curving and rounded—like an enormous coffee mug. Neko's sweat had dried to streaks of salt, and she tried to imagine the grit as armor, an exoskeleton. She leaned forward, splashed water from her canteen onto her impossible hair before twisting it into two strands of a Dutch braid.

Beside Neko, Ignacio Villarreal, her partner in everything, rubbed the sleep gunk out of the corners of his eyes with a wet thumb. It was hard to tell where the dirt ended and his skin began. That beautiful face. His sleeveless black T-shirt had faded to gray over time, but he was still fearsome looking: steel-toed boots and bushy eyebrows, arms swirling with tattoos of jungle predators she'd inked for him. Here on the northeast edge of the country, it was important to look like you couldn't be fucked with, and so they'd all picked up various accoutrements to ward off thieves and organ harvesters.

Their new apprentices each had their own ways: Harriet pushed back against the prim effect of pale doll-like skin and black hair, of soft thighs and soft "bosom," as she jokingly called it, with a spiked collar and vintage military camo. Jules, short hair and lean frame, went for the blur—ambiguous race, ambiguous gender, ambiguous threat. Even her accent slipped around, as though still settling.

Muscular shoulders over spindle legs, Jules walked with a slight sway over to buy milk thistle, as she always did, from an old woman whose neck was stacked with ropes of wild garlic, and then she replaced the seeds in her amulet. She was butch and fussy, always scrubbing her hands, always straightening things and shaking out sleeping bags and using cutlery so properly, almost like a joke.

Neko bought a can of gasoline, still legal here where the electric grid was kaput, and found the vendor whom they paid to watch over their scrappy scooters. She kneeled beside her trusty machine, showering the gears and fangs with oil while watching Harriet meander along the stalls, picking up and inspecting items she had no intention of buying—ylang-ylang oil, protein paste, bracelets strung with seeds. Neko was tall but Harriet was taller, six feet. She had a small pink birthmark on her neck that reminded Neko of the rosy callus sported by the violinists she'd known growing up, the proud feature of their trade. Harriet was one of those loud, mildly annoying people with no filter, always stopping to chat up complete strangers. "This has an interesting smell. Is it cedar? My grandmother had a cedar tree in her backyard, and it smelled like this after it rained . . ."

The skinny teenager behind the table shrugged.

Harriet's black hair was pulled back in a tight ponytail. "Well, I love it."

A man standing behind an adjacent stall, tearing chicken from the bone with his teeth, stopped eating to whistle at her, leer. Jules walked over and glared in the direction of the man, her thin face getting thinner. Then, Harriet and Jules stooped to draw squares in chalk on an old strip of blacktop. "Venga, vato," Harriet called to Iggy in the shitty Spanish accent she used to try to impress him, maybe, or bond with him. Something.

They began hopscotching through the squares. Harriet clowned around, trying to elicit a reaction from a deadpan Jules. Neko watched the two women flirt, rubbing shoulders like cats, their bodies kinetic with pent-up energy, sparking. They were young and sugar-limbed and Neko tried to remember if she and Iggy had ever been that way. Yes. Sure.

THE ENTRANCE TO THE SINK WOULD OPEN SOON. THE TWENTY OR SO others waiting nearby wore headphones, eyes closed or staring off. Nervous or bored or hungover. Just another consortium of grubby mudlarks risking life and limb for a government paycheck. Nothing to see here.

Harriet purchased two small cantaloupes from a man dragging a pyramid of melons and cleaved them into halves with her ridiculous machete. Passed them around. They nibbled and sucked, the juice soothing chapped lips. Jules cut a raw onion into thin crescent moons, the smell a welcome relief from sun-baked trash. Nearby a man did push-ups, very slowly, as though in prostration.

In the early years of the Breakwater's existence, there had been a woman who did tarot readings, and though Neko had never paid for a reading herself, she liked to eavesdrop. The woman's voice had been slow and grave, even when describing the most fortunate cards—the Sun, the Star, the Ace of Cups. One day she wasn't at her small table and that was that. Years ago now.

Neko sat on a bench with her paper, and Iggy rested his head on her lap, body stretched the length of the wood. Fold, crease, fold, flip. Neko made the wrinkled scrap paper into an origami crane. Crease, pinch, smooth. The one thing everyone in their line of work learned to endure: waiting. Fold, crease, fold, flip. With each turn, she made nothing into something. The inanimate into the whimsical. If only, she thought, regret could be transformed so easily, or damage. *No, no,* she told herself. Crease, pinch, smooth.

When the crane was finished, she slid her hand beneath Iggy's shirt. His eyes remained closed but he stopped breathing for a second. She lightly moved her finger up the ladder of his ribs. They'd been together so long, and she knew his body so well, that it was almost as if she could feel the touch herself.

"Did your family call them roly-polies or doodlebugs?" he asked, eyes still closed. Her touch must have felt like their probing legs.

"Roly-polies."

"Same." Iggy blinked his long lashes and yawned, breath smelling of melon. "I would collect them on the edges of the playground to bring home for my mother."

She grunted. Her own mother would have been unimpressed.

Neko slid back on the pair of goggles that always brought to mind her one trip to Burning Man, the last time she touched her mother. Warm. That's how she remembered her mother: flushed and hot to the touch.

"Did you know people used to buy expensive tickets to camp in a place like this for a week? Dust everywhere. Hot as hell. Water brought in by the truckload. I saw it."

Iggy gave her a look.

"What for?" asked Harriet. She was so young.

"To dress up in costumes. To build crazy structures and then burn them down. To sleep all day and party all night."

"But why?" Jules's lips were thin but long and gave her a somewhat rapacious air, and her hair stuck up funny from where she'd been leaning against a wall.

Neko shrugged. "To feel free?"

Jules scrunched her brow. "Then we must be the freest people in the world."

A nervous boy—maybe twelve—approached wearing an oversized Mickey Mouse T-shirt, carrying two buckets filled with plastic sachets that refracted light like prisms.

"Filtered water. Twenty for two pints," he said.

Neko nudged Iggy.

Iggy pulled himself up, leaving a tingle in Neko's thighs where his head had been. He faced the boy, regarding him with a kind of avuncular concern.

"Ten dollars a pint is unreasonable," said Iggy. "You'll have to throw in a lagniappe." His voice was higher-pitched than his broad shoulders and fierce scowl led people to expect.

"Lanny . . . yap?"

"A gift," said Iggy. "It means a gift."

"It's filtered and it's twenty for two pints," said the boy mechanically.

Iggy walked around the kid, continuing an inspection of his wares, his outfit, his bearing. At some point, he glanced back at Neko with those wet, wise, tired eyes she loved and shook his head. She wondered if maybe, over the years, she had outsourced a general sense of compassion to him.

"Lagniappe comes from Quechua—that's a pre-Columbian society—the Inca," said Iggy. "They were lords of commerce, the Inca, until they became part of a post-Columbian society. I'll give you twenty for one pint."

"Um . . . but I said it's twenty for two," said the boy, puffing out his chest and raising his chin. Something in his bearing—the way the nascent adult and the child coexisted—reminded Neko of the skaters who hung out in the park near her apartment growing up. How she had been simultaneously terrified of and in love with them.

"There's no bargaining with you, Pizarro." Iggy pulled out his wallet. "You say this is filtered?"

"Yes."

"Filtered with the XR-20 or the new one, the XR-21?"

"It's the new one," said the boy. "The X21."

"Okay, wow," said Iggy, taking scratch from his wallet. "Can you make change?"

The boy put down his buckets, removed the money pouch from around his neck, and looked inside the little plastic purse. As he did this, Iggy pulled the boy aside in one fluid motion.

Neko could see Iggy wagging his finger at the kid, presumably telling him how anybody who said they had filtered water assuredly did not; how you should always keep change on separate parts of your person; how there is no such device as an XR-20 or 21; how to perform simple arithmetic to increase sales; etc.

They would encounter lost children like this occasionally, kids who were trying to navigate a world that conspired to annihilate them or their innocence, whichever came first. Neko watched Iggy and the boy talk, first in earnest, then she saw the boy smile and Iggy ruffle his hair playfully. She watched Iggy hand him what she could see was more than twenty, along with the origami crane she'd just been folding.

Neko made room on the bench. "Just give him our life savings, why don't you?"

"I thought you understood lagniappe," said Iggy.

"He going to be okay?"

Iggy shook his head slightly. "No."

People in their world tended to harden over time, grow a thick skin, but somehow Iggy only seemed to soften with each year.

THE SOUND OF THE PUMPING STATION BECAME LOUDER AS THEY APproached the customs portal that led over the Breakwater, its earthen floodwalls rising like a lip, sluice gates arcing open and into the Sink. They stood in line with the other mudlarks until it was their turn to show ID, scan their fingerprint, have their bags inspected.

"Neko Sweet. Ignacio Villarreal. Sign here. Harriet Heinsz . . ."

From a distance the Breakwater looked fake, the scale and proportions impossible, but here, when you got close and couldn't see the entirety anymore, it was just a vertical wall, some steps, and a dark tunnel until you reached the parapet atop the levee itself: stalls and vendors abandoned below you on one side, goats wandering like in a medieval village, and then on the other side, the skyline of Manhattan, broken skyscrapers glinting madly in the sun.

The government had employed thousands of the city's municipal workers to build the two-mile-long embankment, talking it up as this patriotic pulling-together—all very *rah, rah*. Seventeen-year-old Neko (her mother long gone, her father mentally gone) had watched on television, with her first real girlfriend, the footage of the concrete mixers endlessly lining the highway. They had come in from the rain one day, turned on the news. The girlfriend peeled off Neko's wet jeans and kissed each small mole on her thighs while the white mixers spun and spun and spun.

Neko didn't know who had named the area inside the Sink—officially the region was Decommissioned Zones 8–14. Maybe the name had stuck because the area was round and the high walls of the Breakwater made it look sunken. Or maybe because of the tides that flowed in and out, washing through, making everything damp and swampy. Maybe because it made it sound as though it were like that on purpose, a place always meant to be home to water, and not a result of the country's worst disaster of all time.

NEKO SWEET BREATHED IN THE AIR OF THE LOST. "LET'S GET CRACKing."

She rolled her moto down the slope and into the Sink before revving it to life.

3

THE THIRTEEN MILES TO WALL STREET TOOK THEM OVER TWO HOURS to traverse. They rode across the upper deck of the G.W. Bridge, watched over by the suspension towers still holding despite the temperatures and rust, mutinous weeds growing inside the thousands of niches between hundreds of steel trusses.

They rode past City College and through a deserted Harlem. It was the AMC Magic Johnson, the 28th Precinct, Bethel Gospel Assembly, the Dollar Tree, and Harriet Tubman's bronze statue, her vast skirt snaking roots behind her like a wedding train, that they used as landmarks and not the condo towers, crumpled like paper. The precinct mural with its watchful eye—who had ever thought that was a good idea?—had been graffitied to look like the Illuminati pyramid.

They passed the Hollington building, where an old guy named Jacob had been squatting for ages, surrounded by carousel animals he'd collected from around the city. Though all the mudlarks knew, nobody turned him in because he was sweet and he'd let you come inside to see them if you asked nicely. Once, he gave Neko a gumdrop, pressing it into her palm like a jewel.

They took a cratered Fifth Avenue alongside the Park, the Upper East Side's brick buildings creating a safer thoroughfare—less likely to shear and break, less likely to landslide. Early on they'd avoided Mount Sinai, a haven for squatters and junkies, but, after it became obvious that boarding it up wouldn't be enough, the government had hired mudlarks to raze the whole block to the ground. Now the foundation sprouted weeds and collected murky pools of rainwater.

They kept moving.

Most mudlark crews didn't forage south of the Garden, which was precisely why Neko's did. Smuggling for the black market was punishable by prison time and loss of citizenship, so they didn't need anyone looking over their shoulders. Each year the government paid less for the ever-degrading mudlarked materials, but there were other ways to make money. Plenty of people were still willing to pump the black market with scratch in exchange for what they'd left behind. In exchange for pieces of the Old World.

Neko had begun to sense other crews getting curious. She was worried someone would follow them, rat on them, or, maybe worse, encroach on their territory. How long could they realistically play this game without getting caught?

Jules, the crew's cartographer, took the lead as they neared Midtown. It was her job to know where flooded subways and plugged sewers had created sinkholes or caused streets to revert to rivers or undercut the foundations of skyscrapers, sections of which sometimes tumbled down with the roar of an avalanche. They stopped at a pocket park where wild garlic grew this time of year to harvest a handful to flavor the soup they would make that night with chicken bones purchased along the Breakwater.

After years as a mudlark, Neko no longer felt the wave of existential dread upon arrival in this abandoned metropolis. All that waste of human achievement. Now she could appreciate the strange beauty of decay, flushed with irises and aster and Queen Anne's lace, the initial human rank and rot slowly replaced with the unspooling perfume of wild crocuses and wet crabgrass. Her childhood was overgrown with vines. And she tended it like the grave of a beloved, which it was.

Sometimes, in her head, Neko thought about how she'd explain this new Manhattan to people on the Inside: *Imagine,* she would say, *a version of New York as it might appear in a dream, familiar but impossible. Imagine stone buildings blinding in their clarity, made sharper by the diminishment of landmarks, crumbling and shrunken, sometimes missing altogether. Imagine a place after a tornado has spun through, destroying and sparing. Imagine a city. Imagine a war zone. Look, there, the line of mold on the buildings. That tells you how far the water comes up in high tide. Over there, jump on the ground. Feel how it gives beneath your feet.*

Jules and Harriet had been with Neko and Iggy for less than a year. Usually, they hired apprentices individually, staggered so that there weren't two greenhorns on the crew simultaneously. However, they'd fired their last two apprentices at the same time for shooting up before a lark. The guys had started partying together in Fringetown—all-nighters with the border town sots who pretended to be so joie de vivre when really they were drinking themselves to death. Eventually, Iggy and Neko learned that the two were spending all their scratch on vials of morphine stolen from the clinics. She found them with needles in their arms, lips blue. She had been taken aback by how pretty the color was.

Mudlarks can't medicate the pain away and still survive it. So, they were cut loose, though it broke Iggy's heart. Jules and Harriet had been brought on as a package deal—probably only still available for hire because they insisted on staying together.

THE CREW'S HOME BASE IN THE SINK WAS AN ART DECO BANK BUILDing just off Wall Street and half a block from the new shoreline, swampy with king tides. The sturdiness of the stone superstructure and cavernous vault, where they stored scuba gear and Bunsen burners, made it a practical choice, but secretly, Neko and Iggy had also chosen it for the pretty domed rotunda and the WPA murals dulled from smoke and neglect.

When they arrived, the lock was in place, the sapphire necklace that they left as bait inside the entrance undisturbed. But as Neko's lantern scoured the floor, she noticed the layer of dust on the ground, normally thick and uniform, was feathered. Disturbed. Someone or something had been there.

She unholstered her Glock and pointed, motioning for Jules to come with her and for Harriet and Iggy to stay back, check the main hall.

The open lobby was festooned with two wolf skulls they'd found half buried together in Red Hook; fists of feldspar hung from the teller windows on translucent filament—mudlark lore had it that these mica-studded geodes brought luck. Neko and Jules softly cased each room, listening for any noise, looking for anything else out of place. They found a hornet's nest in the corner of the storage room ceiling, but everything else was as they'd left it.

"Probably just a raccoon."

"Or that cat," said Jules. "The one who brings gifts." (A slaughtered bird, wings spread, neck askew.)

"Yes." Neko admonished herself. She was getting paranoid.

The drill: Scooters were parked in one corner of the tawny marble bank hall, provisions in another, tricked-out solar cells snapped in place for battery recharges.

Iggy and Neko left Jules and Harriet and retreated to the privacy of the old manager's office. It was the day's peak heat and they lay on their open sleeping bags, limbs spread like stars. The heatwaves of New Summer always mellowed them. Taught them to be still, to expel beads of sweat like tiny blossoms on the skin. They were strummed guitars. She and Iggy were always better to each other in the summertime.

They dipped into sleep, and Neko dreamt of bird-of-paradise. She dreamt a bee came to drink, a loud thrumming, and then Neko was the petals, her lips vibrating as the bee slipped inside her mouth.

AS SOON AS NEKO OPENED HER EYES, BLINKING INTO THE DARKNESS, Iggy's hand was sliding down her arm. Their palms touched. She didn't know how he did it. How he could tell the moment she woke.

Neko turned, untwisting their sleeping bags, tucking into him. Each of his slender forearms displayed one of Odin's ravens, Thought and Memory, and she traced them with her index finger.

"I had a pet rabbit as a kid and named it Vena Cava," he said into her ear, softly, as though it were a sweet nothing.

"True."

"True. Mr. Potato Head was Aorta."

"You are so weird." She shook her head. "I wore dresses to school almost every day."

"False."

"True! So many dresses. Striped. Polka dots. Sequins. No ruffles, though. Never ruffles."

He nodded. "When we make it to the Inside, I'll get off on the noise of yard work," he said, shifting the game into the future. "Mowers and blowers and edgers."

The world was silent.

"True." She knew that one of the things Iggy was most looking forward to on the Inside was having a garden, a shed stacked with tools.

He kissed her shoulder. "True. Though Harriet says there's strict water rationing now. Our yard will probably be all moon rocks and succulents."

She opened her mouth in mock surprise. "Is that what *Harriet says*?"

The TV shows Iggy and Neko watched (news shows being too depressing—a string of weather events and shortages, political infighting) in Fringetown were invariably built around a nostalgia for Middle American suburbia, lulling them into a romanticized version of what life was like on the Inside: Fourth of July potlucks in a neighbor's yard, multicultural families pratfalling around in generic Victorians. Harriet enjoyed disabusing them of these notions.

They played this game anyway, hypothesizing what it would be like once they moved back. They had lived along the Breakwater for so long that everything else shimmered in unreality. Neko thought for a moment and then offered, "I can't wait to take the train to work." She hated to think what kind of job she would have—with a boss and rules and other people.

"False." Iggy was shaking his head. "You don't like moving vehicles unless you're the one driving."

"Well, few people have my catlike reflexes." Neko wondered if the Inside was still a place where you could buy different lotions for each part of the body. She wondered if she would stop wearing a gun and if it would feel funny, like it used to feel funny when she didn't wear a bra. She wondered if brushing her teeth would once again become an indoor activity.

Iggy would write down some of what they said in this game

in one of his notebooks. He was smart, a reader, and used to say that mudlarking was really research for the novel he was writing. All those notebooks. They were packed into a steamer trunk in their Fringe quarters, but as far as Neko knew, he never opened them again once the pages were filled.

"Let's see," she said. "I'll go to a ball game and catch the team jersey from the T-shirt gun and give it to you."

"Uh-huh." He started to unbutton her flannel shirt. "I'll go to the grocery store, win you something from the claw machine by spending more money trying to capture the stuffed animal than it would cost to just buy it."

She felt for his fly. "I'll go to Chinese restaurants and get fortune cookies whose fortunes aren't really fortunes but just random statements. Like 'Money is the root of all evil.'"

Their hands roved under each other's stiff, dirt-encrusted clothes.

Neko played this game for Iggy. He had sacrificed so much, for so many years, and now it was her turn.

This was the story of Neko's love told simply: Iggy was a light box. When she was near him, she could form no shadow. He didn't make her pain disappear, but he did make it bearable. She put her fingers in his mouth, and it seemed as though she could taste the salt herself.

4

NEKO FELT A COLD THRILL BEFORE EACH DIVE. SHE'D WORKED HARD to ensure this sector, the East Village, with its pink-red buildings and crumpled fire escapes, belonged to her crew—and her crew alone—because she used to think that coming here long after the rest of civilization had gone would be penance for her greatest sorrow.

They drove along the narrow ribbon of roadway that they'd cleared over the years, debris pushed to the sides. Neko's crew specialized in mudlarking the underwater parts of the city. And they didn't waste time. Every year the city became more dangerous—encroaching wolves and feral hogs, tall buildings battered by winds, squatters with nothing to lose. They were also constrained by the lunar calendar, by the high tides that brought a sluiceway of saltwater and mud into the street outside their door, strange fish gliding above the stripped concrete, mangy swans paddling through the silence of the Financial District.

They'd been hired to extract canisters from a submerged storage facility just past where the East River estuary emptied into the Atlantic. Rising seawaters had permanently inundated everything on that side of Tompkins Square Park. Fresh water from the river flowed on top of the ocean water, creating a salt-rich, oxygen-starved layer that pickled the underwater buildings and everything inside them like sunken Spanish galleons. Ever since Neko and Iggy had gotten into the business of smuggling out personal contraband, this spot had been a gold mine.

Incredible the objects people would pay so much money, even risk others' lives, to get back: heirloom jewelry, of course, and art objects and hard, shiny medals—they'd once retrieved an Olympic silver—but also stranger things, Barbie dolls and comic books, a glass eyeball, vintage disco platform shoes, an urn filled with the ashes of a pet hedgehog. One time, Neko's crew was directed to a stash of rare seeds for an herb called Syrian bear's breeches in a West Village cellar; Iggy kept a couple for himself as talismans. He claimed to believe in contagion and magic, that objects could hold and transfer power.

So as not to raise suspicion, Neko's crew scavenged or dove for their legitimate and illegitimate materials simultaneously. They mapped out targets in the same vicinity so that Jules and Harriet could locate and haul back fiber-optic cables, for example, while Iggy and Neko completed a shadow dive nearby, fishing for black market goods.

The crew silently traversed the maze of planks bridging the flooded streets and alleyways to their pier atop the roof of an old tenement building that put them a cozy six feet above the waterline. The housing projects towered above them, half submerged. Neko could have recognized this part of the East River blindfolded because of its smell—wet mud mingling with the metallic taint of machine oil.

Iggy poured out a splash from his canteen onto the ground.

"Why do you always do that?" asked Harriet.

"An offering?" Iggy screwed back on the lid.

They shrugged off clothes and zipped up wet suits. They

strapped on heliox tanks and walked single file down a gangplank to the floating jetty. From this spot, the water was deep and piss-colored. They couldn't see the bottom. They clipped specialized wet bags onto the descending rope line and one by one flopped backward into the water, finned feet arcing through the air, tiny dots compared to the scale of the Williamsburg Bridge spanning the sky behind them.

While never great, the visibility was best during the summer, the only season when the river didn't carry tons of sediment from upstream. They snaked around and over submerged buildings. They swam above the Formica dining table that sat upright as though waiting for a tea party and through the bob of bronze seals near the old Fire Boat House. They turned left at the Buick, right at the grand piano. They went straight over the pile of batá drums yearning for the Santeros to show up and play them. A Citi Bike covered in bivalves. An enormous bell threaded with rust. A mailbox that no longer received mail. The teredo shipworms, with their little seashell jewelry, paid them no mind and continued their work boring through the forest of wooden pilings.

From there, Jules and Harriet swam toward an office building to haul out a spool of telecommunication cables while Iggy and Neko continued on to the storage facility where they had a contract to retrieve the items from Unit 59.

Covered with a layer of mud and barnacles, the husk of the storage facility was undamaged, so Iggy and Neko entered through the only visible window, which was already broken. Being careful not to catch their equipment on the sheared glass, they swam into what had once been the front office, disturbing a school of mossbunker. There were three overturned desks in the open office layout, and the beams from their headlamps glinted off toppled photos of children alongside bobbleheads and other silly accoutrements of American work culture: *Star Wars* mugs and staplers, headphones and discount hand sanitizer. Inboxes and outboxes forever mid-task.

They passed the break room, with its yawning cabinets still filled with packages of granola bars and jars of what might have been mayonnaise, and eventually found the unit they were looking for, easily busting through the flimsy lock and jimmying open the garage-style door.

Inside, boxes were stacked along each wall. The cardboard had mostly come apart, and the only things keeping the contents together were the tight plastic bindings. They were swimming through a game of Tetris.

Neko began stripping away the mud and remaining cardboard with gloved hands to reveal cylindrical canisters that, thanks to the oxygen starvation of this layer of the river, appeared intact. Other boxes clearly contained files—waterlogged, probably unrecoverable. She took measurements while Iggy hooked hang tanks to the metal strip of the door to lengthen their bottom time on subsequent dives, when they would actually haul out the unit's contents.

Then, their breathing gas low, Iggy made the thumbs-up sign. Neko signed back, and they were gone.

It seemed like a regular job.

EXHAUSTED, THEY TOOK TURNS LEANING OVER A ZINC BOWL AS ONE of the others scrubbed their scalp with soap and water and pulled kerosene oil through their hair. Afterward, they lay on the deep steps of their building, seals drying in the sun.

Harriet told them about what it was like to be the daughter of a hedge fund family. Growing up, her parents had worked together inside the glass box of an office built in their backyard. "The transparency of the building made up for the lack of transparency in the business," she said, eyebrows arched.

Neko tried to picture all the ledgers and numbers, all the abstraction of market forces. As a kid, she'd thought hedge funds had something to do with elaborate gardens filled with fairies and gnomes.

"Might as well be the case," Harriet said, "for all the relationship they have to reality. It's really wild."

"Rich people make their own reality," said Iggy, unnecessarily.

Harriet's hair swung like a black curtain as she sat up. Her face was generically pretty until she smiled. "That's why I like this job. We're sitting right around the corner from what used to be the Stock Exchange. They pay us, but we can take the choice pieces for ourselves. What are they going to do?"

AFTER DINNER, IGGY PUSHED DOMINOS UNDER THE LANTERN, PLAYing chickenfoot with the apprentices while Neko stared at her sketchbook, working out images from the dive with her pencil: the Marilyn Monroe bobblehead, the granola bar, the milk of magnesia. She tried to draw the underwater Formica table for the twentieth time, but she could never find a way to fully capture the dreaminess of it.

Jules picked a domino from the middle, flinging a shadow onto the wall. "I never have a match for the starting double. Ever." She was nuzzling the magnificent silk scarf—an oceanic swirl of blue and green—that she'd found on a previous lark and sometimes wore in the evenings, a strange sartorial flair for someone like her.

"My grandfather in the old folks' home, he was always betting money on chickenfoot and losing his shirt," said Iggy, placing another domino.

"Gambling's illegal now," said Harriet, inserting another of her unrequested factoids about the Inside. "You know, it's funny . . ." Harriet slid a domino across the table and lined it up.

"What's funny?" asked Jules, who was in love with her.

"People used to call these things 'bones.' Even after they were made out of plastic," she said. "Used to say, *Let's play bones*. Didn't they, Iggy?"

"Yes," Iggy said in his crystalline voice.

"And now we make them out of bones again." The crew's homemade set had been carved from the thigh bones and horns of animal carcasses.

"None of these are human?" asked Jules.

Iggy gave a half smile. "None of these are human."

"Strange we've never come across a human body on a dive," said Jules.

"You haven't been doing this very long," said Neko quietly.

Iggy shot Neko a look. Back in the early days, they'd dove the East Village precisely to look at bodies. Or to look for one body in particular, though they found only others, strangers, bloated and floating along the ceilings like grotesque balloons. Though in her family's old apartment, they had found a metal tin with Neko's baby teeth inside. She'd kept it.

And then came the day—sometime around Thanksgiving of that first year larking on their own—when they'd passed the tiny, narrow rubber stamp store in the East Village. Of all the places, this was the one that did it. Changed everything. She'd loved the place as a child and remembered how she would walk into the back, no preamble, breathing in the smell of ink.

How she hovered over the old bearded man as he worked on custom designs, and how, in his gruff Irish brogue, he pretended to be annoyed. How she worshipped the twenty-somethings in high-waisted jeans and dramatic black eyeliner who worked for him, their parked bikes obscuring half the merchandise.

"My parents had the owner's telephone number," she told Iggy. "If I didn't get home from school on time, they'd call him first." Her parents had loved the store, too, because it helped them maintain their illusions of the East Village. They'd liked to pretend downtown was still dirty, still edgy, when in reality most of the other parents at Neko's school were Goldman or Fintech or Trustfund—not wacky performance artists, not eccentrics running a sticky pool hall in Alphabet City or, for God's sake, an old-fashioned stamp store.

Debris had partially blocked the entrance to the store, but Neko and Iggy were able to force their way through. This was back when it was just the two of them, before they'd begun running a full four-person crew. She and Iggy had flipped their headlamps to see in the suffocating, windowless space. Mold spackled the interior, but most of the stamp images were still legible, lined up on miniature shelves, and she photographed them: flamingo, palm tree, dancing monkey, Saturn, a toilet, a spoonful of sugar, spectacles, parachutes, missiles and bombs, Vishnu, bucking broncos, false teeth, Mona Lisa, cupids and doves, monsters of the sea, Pan with his flute, beets and walnuts and ears of corn, the Cheshire Cat, a telephone, all manner of seashell and insect and worm, a biplane, a giant octopus.

Neko picked one and stowed it in her pack: a long-stemmed cherry.

"They won't let you take it across," Iggy said. The border agents at the Breakwater were intractable. No memorabilia. Nothing. Only items on the approved list.

Neko hollowed out a space in the sole of her boot with a penknife and took it back anyway. She started a shrine to the Old World in their Fringetown apartment—in the closet, where nobody would see—and added to it each trip. Bit of a beaver felt hat from Worth & Worth, her father's haberdashery; a small box of pins from her mother's tailor on East Seventh Street; pieces of tile from the mosaic outside their neighborhood Ukrainian place (Neko was a teenager before she learned the average American kid didn't love borscht). Sometimes she felt so slippery, so mercurial: neither parent nor child, not straight or gay, not a resident of the Inside or the Sink, everything and nothing at all. She felt the need to put the pieces of the puzzle back together. To bind herself to these concrete objects from her past in order to be reminded that she was real.

Over time, as she collected more ephemera, she realized she was also creating a portrait of her parents: a bowl filled with desiccated rooibos from the Wiccan-chic tea shop on St. Mark's where her mother met one or two friends every week for years, quietly, in the back so nobody would notice them. The matchbook from the obnoxious restaurant where her father showed up in drag to belt out "The Internationale" to an unimpressed Donald Trump. The red P from the sign for the Apollo Theater, where she remembered her parents taking her to see a show, some blues band she couldn't remember the name of anymore. What she did remember was her father sitting in for a few songs with the old Black musicians, her mother staying in the audience, and how Neko had been critical of her mother's reticence and enthralled by her father's charm on stage.

As they became better at finding ways to sneak these artifacts past the border, Neko and Iggy toyed with the idea of doing it for black market scratch.

"If we're taking the risk for all this . . . stuff," he said, waving his hand toward her closet, "we might as well get paid."

Neko was standing at their stove boiling ramen noodles. Her first thought had been: *We? We are taking the risk?* But that wasn't fair. If she was caught, he would be implicated.

"Think of the money," he added. "We could save up and move to the Inside." He raised his eyebrows. "Rug rats?"

She had almost smiled then, imagining them inhabiting a normal life—or what passed for normal these days. Maybe. Eventually.

So they became smugglers. They began running a full crew. Already respected among the mudlarks for her tattoo artistry. Neko required the apprentices to choose an image from the stamp store photographs for her to ink somewhere on their bodies. "These are your options," she would say, ripping a needle out of a plastic sheath and attaching it to the machine. "This will mark you as one of us." A less than subtle way to convey: *You rat on us, and we'll find you. You rat on us, and we'll take you down, too.*

Though Neko considered herself a decent boss, she'd never managed to be much of a nurturing figure to the lost and scarred people who apprenticed for them. She'd promised Iggy this would be their last season larking in the Sink, and she wondered if the act of fabricating a child inside her own body—time was running out on that—would unlock an undiscovered maternal instinct.

AFTER THE GAME OF BONES, JULES OPENED THE LAST BOTTLE OF WINE out of a case they'd liberated a year ago, ceremoniously poured them each a small beaker of jewel-red liquid. She and Harriet sipped theirs, huddled over a book they were reading together under a wedge of lamplight—an adventure story about Jacques Cousteau. Iggy read an old magazine, licking a finger before turning each page. Neko sat, legs crossed on the floor, just content to be near them, and closed her eyes, feeling the warmth of the silence on her skin, the wine in her throat.

5

BONE SKY. NO BIRDS.

The following day they made two more dives to unload canisters from the storage facility. They sank into an Atlantis of rusty rebar bristling with snagged human detritus—tires and curtains and garbage cans—following the same steps as before: offering to Esu, then over the Formica table, left at the Buick, right at the grand piano, the mossbunker greeting them again when they arrived at the submerged building.

On the last dive, they had time to scour other units for bush meat. Most of what they found was useless or damaged, but they managed to collect a few items to sell back in Fringetown: a crystal decanter, a strand of garnets, an intact bottle of mezcal.

At the bank, they treated the goods, dipping items into baths of glycerin or spraying them with clear lacquer. Once objects were exposed to oxygen it was a race against time to preserve them. The crew began to lay out their haul and consider how they might smuggle the black market items across the Breakwater. They had bags with false bottoms and clothing with secret pockets. They sewed things between the pages of books and into Harriet's spiked collar.

Neko's crew specialized in the transportation of the analog, the physical, what she liked to think of as the Real. Occasionally an object was too big or oddly shaped, and the crew kept it in the vault until they could devise a container in Fringe to carry it back across. Sometimes clients just wanted photographs of a particular document or landmark or cemetery stone left behind, and these were the easiest jobs, though they didn't pay nearly as well.

Neko took a wire brush and scrubbed at the outsides of the canisters they'd hauled from the storage unit, caked in mud and streaked with rust.

"They'll be impossible to smuggle across like this," said Iggy.

If they opened the canisters, it would be easier to transport whatever was inside, but there was also the danger of causing or revealing damage, which meant Chaplin might try to pay them less.

The tags were laminated and Neko could still read a few of the carefully typed names under her gloved fingers: *Houndstooth* and *Red Balloon* and *Chester Copperpot.* Something tugged at her memory. Why did these names feel familiar?

Another one read *Gold* something or other. She struggled to decipher it. She scrubbed harder to reveal more letters.

Gold-ug

She cracked her neck. She turned up her headlamp to the highest setting. She yawned.

Rec—ds.

Wait a second. Goldbug Records was the name of the label that had distributed most of her parents' albums. Her stomach tightened, that feeling like dropping on a roller coaster, time streaming past like wind.

She opened the canister and Iggy, noticing this, turned and stood over her. Inside were stacks of metal discs separated by thin sheets. She carefully lifted them one at a time: master recordings for bands like Rothko's Sadness and the Housewives, labelmates of the Nightjars. Each ridged master was made of real silver.

There were at least four *Goldbug* canisters, and in the third one she found *Summer Baby,* the Nightjars' most popular album, the one that had always made it onto the music nerd lists in all the music nerd magazines. She carefully lifted the ridged disc, much thicker and heavier than vinyl, and showed it to Iggy. They stared at it together in awe.

"Why is it metal?"

"It's a master. The original recording from which all other pressings are made."

She realized why the names on the other canisters seemed familiar—they were other indie record labels from the time before. This storage cache, Neko presumed, must have come from some sort of entertainment firm or conglomerate that had once owned an interest in each of them. She tried to imagine who was left to care about long-defunct indie labels and the artists they'd put out into the world. An old producer? A descendant of one of the musicians—someone like her? Or someone who didn't even know what was in the storage unit? The recordings were probably worth a little scratch—not to mention the value of the silver itself. But why now?

"This is . . . unexpected," she said quietly. Sixteen more years until she'd be as old as her mother ever was.

Iggy reached out his arms, but she shrugged out from beneath them. *" 'Papa was a rodeo,' "* she sang quietly, without really meaning to, *" 'Mama was a rock 'n' roll band . . .' "*

Iggy's face was serious. He tilted his head. "You never sing."

"And now you know why," she sang, exaggerating the off-tune warble of her voice. During her childhood people had expected her to be musical, or to be able to identify the song on the radio, or name the members of whatever obscure band came up. "Let's just say it's awkward to grow up with parents who are cooler than you."

"Oh, please."

But it was true. It wasn't easy being the daughter of artists, to bear that pressure each time she plunked the piano or gripped the fretboard. She remembered the strain on their faces when she was practicing for her third-grade recital—the muscles so tight from pretending to be impressed. And how it had made her want to throw up, which she did, and which they'd thought was just recital nerves, but had actually been coming from some deeper well of inadequacy she didn't know how to name.

THE CREW ATE DINNER RAVENOUSLY, DUMB WITH HUNGER. THE CLICK of spoons against bowls, the flicker of light from their battery-powered lanterns. How odd it felt to Neko to do something this normal after such a discovery. Did the world not yet understand? The day had been cleaved in two, and yet here were the pinto beans, the silverware, the same needs of the body.

She gathered the dishes and walked outside to rinse the enamel plates and bowls with water from one of the buckets lined up along the edifice.

The darkness crackled with static electricity. Cicadas competed with the howls of wolves and coyotes. Here in the Sink, Neko always felt a little wild herself, her eyesight suddenly sharper, the pulse of her animal heart quickening for the hunt.

Jules joined her outside to rinse the salt water from the cables they'd hauled back from the office building. Fiber-optic cables were good finds—not too heavy but a pain for the United States to manufacture—and they provided perfect cover.

"What music did you grow up with?" asked Neko. Just because.

She shrugged. "Good music."

"Okay," said Neko, squinting at the cryptic young woman. "What was your first concert?"

"Never went to one." Jules gently dipped a cloth into a water bucket and drew it slowly along the length of cable. "What's it like?"

"Loud. My first was Lady Gaga. She came down on a trapeze dressed like an octopus." Neko nodded at the buckets. "No need to skimp. We're going to the Ice House in the morning."

"But we have enough supplies for a few more days. Harriet just did inventory."

"Don't you get tired of quoting Harriet?" she said, then immediately wished she hadn't. It was an echo from her childhood, though she couldn't quite put her finger on it. "I'm the boss, and I say we're going."

The Ice House was where they would find Chaplin, their middleman on this gig, and Neko had some pressing questions for that lovely asshole.

She looked up. At night it was important to focus on the sky, the pricks of starlight. Or else she'd begin to notice the terrifying hulk of the buildings—the dark of them, no light emerging from their orderly rows of squares, their windows smears of ash.

But above them, stars still glittered the sky like granulated sugar. Neko remembered baking cookies with her folks—

thought about how she'd spill sugar on the counter, half on purpose, so she could lick her finger and run it through. Neither of her parents could participate in an activity like baking without mocking it—sheet pans full of penis cookies, gingerbread people with severed limbs bleeding red icing. Even the cards they gave at birthdays and holidays were ironic, covered in kittens and swirly gold lettering—*God is with us every step of the way. Happy Anniversary*—with Neko forced to be the straight man, pleading with them to *be serious, for once*.

When your parents were dead, even dumb memories took on the halo of myth. And wasn't this how it always was? When you finally gave up, were finally willing to settle for what you had or to move on, well, that was when a little bit of the universe turned over and revealed its belly, like a cat. You were almost out the door, keys in hand, when it finally said: Yes, please. Here. Come.

She had spent years in the Sink trying to understand her past, trying to come to peace with it, and now that she had something she could hold in her hands, a tether to the life that had shaped this one—not her mother's body but something closer to her spirit—she didn't feel vindicated. She felt at a loss. Even more lost.

6

THE ICE HOUSE: VINES COILED THROUGH THE LEGS OF HERMES AS he perched above the clock frozen at 6:22. The Tiffany glass had been stolen long ago, but the overall glory of the Grand Central Terminal entrance remained. Neko loved walking inside the main concourse—if you didn't let your eyes focus right away, you could almost believe it was rush hour thirty years ago: people bustling under the luminous fixtures, voices skittering off the formerly blue, now algae-green plaster ceiling crisscrossed by constellations in reverse, Orion and Taurus and Gemini.

As Neko's crew walked through the still-gilded entry hall, a bird squealed overhead near the roof.

"Starlings," said Harriet, looking up. "Invasive." She explained—in what Neko thought of as her "private school voice"—that starlings were brought from Europe by an eccentric who thought Central Park should be home to each bird mentioned in the works of Shakespeare.

Then, as though not to be one-upped, Iggy told them how Tenochtitlán had had the most extraordinary aviaries in the world, full of blue-throated hummingbirds and parrots, condors and herons, egrets, wrens, summer tanagers. "Cortés set fire to them all."

Neko tried not to smile, aware of how nice it must be for Iggy to finally have someone on the crew with whom he could go full egghead. "As fascinating as this conversation is, I need food immediately."

Standing in line at Ticket Counter 3 for chickpea dogs and mugs of chicory coffee, Neko saw that Marjorie, the old mainstay who usually regaled them with scuttlebutt while waving her tongs in the air (*Guess who lost his license for hiring underage apprentices? Guess who got caught smuggling vintage video games across the border?*), wasn't standing in front of the vat of boiling water.

"She's going to have a baby," said a man with a bushy mustache and an apron that read I COOK AS GOOD AS I LOOK.

Neko tried to picture skinny, weathered old Marjorie bulging with pregnancy, like a bowling ball on a fence post. "She's about my age, isn't she?"

The man shrugged.

"Tell her we said congratulations." Iggy then turned the conversation to the petrol supply, and Neko understood that he was trying to protect her.

"Hey," shouted a familiar voice from behind them in line. "The rest of us are hungry, too."

Neko turned to see Richie, who'd apprenticed with them before leaving to start his own crew. He and Iggy bumped fists.

"Need me to cover your lunch, blancón?" asked Iggy.

Richie had left their crew after becoming critical of the risks they took for black market scratch, and he now ran a 100 percent aboveboard outfit.

Richie nodded at Jules and Harriet. "You two let me know if you're ever ready for a new gig." The pineapple Neko had tattooed on Richie's arm sprouted from his rolled shirt sleeve. She remembered how he'd almost passed out—literally swooned—about halfway through the process, and she'd held his head in the bowl of her lap.

"That would be a step down." Neko smiled, but her heart wasn't in it.

Richie ran a hand along his fade. "Straight-edge can still be cool."

Iggy grabbed Richie in a bear hug and pinched his cheek. "Good to see you, mate."

Neko paid for the dogs and gave instructions to Harriet and Jules about loading the barrels of water and supplies onto their trailers. "Nothing weird, please."

She didn't look at Richie as he left, but in her mind: the cloudy afternoon when she and Iggy had swept out of the water from their shadow dive expecting to meet Richie and Ros, their apprentices at the time, on the floating dock, just as they'd done for weeks, months, recombining from illicit pairs into a legitimate crew again before returning to the vault. But Richie and Ros were not stacking tanks and stripping off wet suits; they weren't joshing each other or tearing beef jerky with their incisors or sharing a hand-rolled cigarette as though life were long. No, they were tied up with rope, gagged, on their knees, all of their gear and haul stolen by some gang of freaks.

It was a wonder any of them were still alive.

IGGY AND NEKO LEANED AGAINST THE WALLS OF WHAT HAD ONCE been an information kiosk, sipping the bad coffee and watching the news headlines from the Inside move across the flickering screen: *UN Council Fails to Come to Agreement on Refugee Crisis . . . Water Shortages Spread to Western Europe . . . Rumi Carter Tops Charts with New VR Experience.*

Iggy tapped a nail on his mug.

"Take your time at the Pearl," she said, referring to the vaulted terra-cotta enclosure one level down that had once been a famous oyster bar and now served as a lending library.

"Another thriller?" Iggy was wearing pleated pants that were not flattering, totally wrong for him, and yet something about the awkward way he put his hand in the flapping pocket made her love him more.

"Something bloody." She tapped her forehead to his shoulder like a cat. "You know where to find me."

UPSTAIRS, AT THE STATION MASTER'S BAR, NEKO MADE HER WAY TO the cabinet where there were stacked tins of sweetened condensed milk and topped her bitter coffee with a cream swirl.

Chaplin sat presiding over a game of Texas Hold'em, wearing a wrinkled herringbone suit that softened the effect of his square wrestler's body. He saw her and said, "Hey! That's my special stash."

"Yes," she said solemnly.

Everything in the bar was perfectly appointed and maintained: a floral mural covering the walls, a saltwater fish tank stuffed with tropicals, carved wooden tables scavenged and refurbished. Chaplin, even in an apocalypse, sewed weights into the bottoms of his curtains.

A woman in denim overalls grumbled about the carbon credits she'd lost before standing and flamboyantly bowing to indicate her now-empty chair, painted a color Neko thought of as "boudoir red." A couple of people at the table looked familiar, but she didn't know any of them by name.

"We were talking about hollandaise," said Chaplin. "Are you for or against?"

"Neutral." She shrugged.

"Chaplin is arguing that a unique sauce is the hallmark of civilization," said a roughneck with a rainbow buzz cut.

"I have one last bottle of hoisin squirreled away, and I'm not sharing it with any of you flounders," said Chaplin, laying down another card. "Here comes the river."

"So, who knocked up Marjorie?" asked Neko.

Chaplin took a sip of whatever clear liquid filled his glass. "You won't hear it from me."

Chaplin was a redheaded Ashkenazi and epicurean who could drink just about anybody under the table, including Neko. He managed the Station Master's Bar and the resupply depot down below, but more important, he connected Neko and Iggy to many of their clients. So, whenever they came for resupply, she spent an hour or two trading money with him at the poker table as cover.

The East Balcony was transformed into a club near the winter holidays, and it was there that Neko had first approached Chaplin, sidling up to him on the dance floor a year after starting her own crew. Raising her voice to be heard over the garage techno pumping from the speakers, Neko had told him point-blank that she wanted exclusive access to black market gigs in the East River and rights of first refusal for anything else within a half-mile radius of the East Village. By that point in the night, he had stripped down to a ribbed tank top, the milk-blue skin of his shoulders slick with sweat. He hadn't responded verbally, but their bodies moved in tandem for the rest of the night, and they'd had a profitable understanding ever since. He was always talking shit about retiring from Sink life and heading back to the Inside, but Neko knew he never would.

After the next hand, Neko told the table, "Five-minute break." She stood. "Chaplin, help me put on some bops."

He narrowed his eyes but followed her. The off-grid sound system was perched on the counter behind the bar. She chose Metallica's *Kill 'Em All,* letting the guitar drown out the flutter of her heartbeat. Loud enough to disguise their conversation.

"Who's the client for the storage facility haul?"

Chaplin shrugged. He smelled like olives.

"Know what was in the unit?"

"No, but I have a feeling I'm about to."

"Master recordings."

He shook his head and leaned in, and she had to repeat herself three times before he understood. Chaplin opened the minifridge, taking out a tiny vase filled with sprigs of herbs. "And you're worried they're going to be too hard to get across the Breakwater?"

"Well, no. I mean, yes, they will be hard to . . ."

"Don't worry," he said. "You don't have to get them across. You just have to get them to my office in SoHo."

"Your *office* in *SoHo*."

His face betrayed nothing more.

"I'm here because some of the masters were for the Nightjars."

He closed his eyes briefly, and Neko could almost see the gears turning in his head. She knew, obviously, that Chaplin was a mercenary. Of course. But some part of Neko secretly believed he might protect her if a real problem arose, though she'd never had a reason to test this theory.

"My parents' band. The Nightjars."

He began muddling a sprig of mint in a coupe glass, his shoulders tight.

"Chap?" She was getting impatient. "The client? I need to know who wants the masters for Goldbug Records."

"I have a contact, obviously, but nobody gives their real name."

"But you can find out."

He brought his body in close, his lips to her ear. "What do I get?"

She raised her eyebrows. "What do you want?"

He dumped everything into a cocktail shaker with ice and made a racket, mouthing the words, *Have dinner with me.* He poured the drink into the coupe glass and handed it to her.

"You're funny." Neko worked hard to be in control of herself always, almost always. She pretended she only visited Chaplin in the Station Master's Bar each lark because of business. But she enjoyed it. She looked forward to it. She couldn't deny that.

"I'm very serious." He smiled his dimpled smile. "Dinner with me and I'll *try* to find the answer to your question."

"Find me the answers, and *maybe* I'll have dinner with you."

Chaplin sighed dramatically before slipping the piece of paper with the SoHo address into her back pocket. "Come tomorrow morning with the storage unit goods." Then he turned back to the stereo and clicked "Unknown Legend." *Somewhere on a desert highway, she rides a Harley-Davidson . . .*

"You did *not* just put on Neil Young."

LATER, WHEN IGGY WALKED INTO THE BAR, CHAPLIN TILTED HIS HEAD and said to Neko, "Your assistant's here."

Iggy gave him the middle finger.

Back on the concourse, weaving their way through other groups of mudlarks, they instinctually touched fingertips. Neko handed Iggy a folded stack of soft green scratch she'd won at the poker table. "Buy yourself something nice."

He laughed and readjusted his pack. "So, Marjorie. I heard

that she and Leo Press are planning to get married before the baby comes."

Neko stopped. "Oh, God. Leo Press is the father?"

"Right?"

She could tell he was trying, and failing, to keep his voice light. They rarely spoke directly about the time two years ago when Neko was pregnant, end of the first trimester, wearing her baggiest pants but, otherwise, not yet showing. She'd woken one morning to sticky wetness between her legs and the thought: *Did I piss myself?* But then her belly cramped, and she understood. A quick flash of secret relief. She'd hemorrhaged for two days before she was able to sit behind Iggy on his scooter and get to a clinic back in Fringetown. It was the only larking job they'd abandoned in their entire careers. And the main reason he was so insistent they move to the Inside before trying again.

Neko preferred to sidestep where she knew the conversation was heading—she was not interested in discussing their own domestic plans at the moment. "Chaplin has an office in SoHo."

Iggy stopped. "What does that even mean?"

"We're supposed to bring the canisters and other goods from the storage unit to fucking SoHo instead of across the Breakwater."

"Curiouser and curiouser. And what about the master recordings?"

"Says he'll try to find out who the client is."

They looked at each other in silence. Odds were that it would be another dead end, like everything else: the search for her mother's body, for the neighbors in her old building, for the people from school. All the clues and rumors over the years that never panned out. It was like her mother was intent on being as mercurial and frustrating in death as she had been in life.

When Iggy and Neko turned in to the Forty-second Street Passage, Harriet emerged and told them Jules was waiting at the ramp below with the supplies. As they walked, Iggy's handful of books attracted the attention of a group of men sitting on the ground along the passage wall.

"Come read us a bedtime story," one of them sneered.

"Be happy to put you to sleep," said Harriet, stopping in front of the one going for a throwback punk look—malnourishment and safety pins.

He nodded at the flowers on the cover of a book Iggy held tucked under his arm. "A romance novel, even."

"That's *my* book he's holding. You want to catch these hands?"

The man rose to his feet, slowly and deliberately. He looked down at his confederates and, like some kind of underland priest, beckoned them to rise by lifting his palms.

Neko felt the electricity—the attraction of opposite forces—that surged before a fight.

As soon as the three young men were at eye level, Harriet smashed the bridge of the priest's nose with her forehead. Then she was on him: jab, cross, hook. Her knuckles connected with his cheekbone before he ever had a chance to throw his arms up in defense. Even in the Sink, men were surprised when a woman started smashing things, especially faces, and it took this one a moment to get his bearings.

Iggy moved forward, but Neko gently held him back. He disapproved of Harriet's penchant for brawling. She was a cutter who needed others to do her cutting. But Neko understood there was something cathartic about going all out on another human. Harriet was tall and strong, but there was also an elegance to her movements, the cleanness of someone trained in a gym by professionals. She was so plainly a runaway rich girl trying to prove herself.

The man tried to pummel Harriet's shoulder until she threw an elbow to his solar plexus. Neko could see the man's friends finally moving to step in when the alarm came in over the loudspeakers.

BLAAAN. BLAAAN. BLAAAN. PERIMETER BREACH.

"Shit," said Iggy.

Everyone dropped their fighting stances and began jogging down the ramp toward the lower concourse. When they reached Jules, she signaled that she would stay behind and guard the supplies stacked beside her.

By the time Neko's crew arrived at the entrance to what had once been Tracks 101 and 102, the "invaders" had already been surrounded by a pack of stone-faced mudlarks. The fugitives wore coarse hooded robes that made them look like monks and carried large sacks of what appeared to be stolen supplies, their sad slingshots and shivs no match for the mudlarks' arsenal. Neko watched as their wrists were tied together and a beefcake soldier began carting them off to God knows where.

Neko shook her head. How desperate must they have been to try to steal from a major outpost with only rocks and shivs as weapons? Just half-starved "fugitives" from one of the subsistence groups that lived illegally in the Sink.

The rest of them followed the underwhelming procession back up the ramp.

"Nice work squabbling with those meatheads earlier," said Iggy.

Harriet shrugged. "You're the one with the romance novel. I was protecting your honor."

"It's Jane Austen!"

As the sad group of invaders passed Jules, who stood stiffly in front of the supply heap, one of the captured fugitives stopped suddenly, causing the others in line to stumble and jostle.

The man, all stringy arms and hollow cheeks, stared at a downcast Jules before spitting in her direction. "You," he said, like it was an epithet.

It took Neko a second to process this—the man had literally spit in Jules's face—and then she took out her sidearm and pointed it at the man. "Move along."

After the prisoners had passed, Iggy looked at Neko, and his eyes said: *Fuck this place*. His eyes squinted and blamed her, maybe not for what had just happened, for all that it meant about Jules, but for the fact that they were here to deal with it. Still. Still here. He put fingers to his throat—a tic he'd always had—pressing into the skin as though to find what was hidden there, to feel what couldn't be swallowed. "Fissure, fishmonger, funeral, fuck-up," he muttered to himself.

Jules wiped her face with her T-shirt. "I don't, um . . ."

"Leaving," said Neko, trying and failing to suppress her anger. "Now."

Jules and Harriet leaned against each other like two poles. Harriet was uncharacteristically silent, and Neko was glad for that.

MANEUVERING THE RESUPPLY TRAILERS ACROSS SHODDY ASPHALT WAS never easy, but this particular ride back to the District felt especially long.

They made dinner in silence under the smooth arches of the banking hall. Neko's arm shook with weariness as she unwrapped a wedge of dehydrated turnip. Harriet, pale face streaked with dirt, boiled water for the instant rice while Jules and Iggy unloaded the tanks of water and other supplies into the vault, their shoulders tense.

Crouched over a plate of rehydrated vegetables, Iggy, who always preferred Neko to initiate any hard or awkward conversations with their crew, ate silently.

Neko sighed, looking at Jules, face bowed over her bowl like a dog waiting to be kicked. If the man at the Ice House had recognized her, it was because he knew her from the wilds of the Sink. She was passing as a normal citizen, probably with forged papers. Neko considered how that explained the girl's vague stories of growing up on a weed farm in Montana, her general caginess. *Of course* the girl hadn't been to a concert. *Of course* she followed Harriet like a pet. Jules had been hiding the fact that she came from one of the groups living illegally in the Sink.

"We'll finish this haul," Neko said matter-of-factly, "and it should be a lucrative one for all of us. Then we'll part ways. Ig and I will help you find another crew."

"Wait," said Jules, still swallowing her food. "Please . . ."

"She can't help where she was born," interrupted Harriet, so earnest and cliché that Neko wasn't sure whether to laugh or cry.

Harriet scooted toward Jules, hooking her hand in the waistband of the woman's pants. Neko had noticed they always touched when one of them felt threatened. "She shouldn't be punished for something that's not her fault. I mean, the quotas are total bull . . ."

So she had known.

"Nobody's punishing anyone," Neko interrupted, trying to

keep her voice even. She almost wished they didn't regularly sweep the bank for government bugs so she could use the threat of surveillance as an excuse to not have this conversation. "It's just the facts. If Jules is larking under false papers, it puts us all in jeopardy. She'll be safer on a legit crew anyway."

"No," said Jules, her voice rising, pleading. "I'll never make enough scratch with a regular crew."

Neko stopped her with a look. She didn't want to know the specifics, whether Jules was in debt for her forged documents or sending money back to others or something else entirely. The details were irrelevant. She could see from the firm line of Jules's spine that the young woman was refusing to accept this turn of events.

"It's late. Let's finish this job and head back across the Breakwater." Iggy put his hand on Jules's shoulder and gave her a soft smile that seemed to say he would fix things. As though Neko couldn't see it, too. "We'll figure things out from there. Please, don't worry."

Oh, Ignacio, she thought. So fully and beautifully human that Neko was reminded every day of all the ways she'd cauterized herself.

After dinner, everyone slunk off to their own corners. The globe lantern cast a milky glow across the canisters stacked in one corner of the bank hall. Neko put on gloves and began sorting the trove of masters—more than a hundred albums from six different record labels. The heavy silver made her think of the Golden Record that had been sent on the Voyager probes to the outer regions of the solar system. She and her mother had liked to talk about it. As a child, she'd imagined a sleek alien slipping headphones over its earholes and listening to the recorded sounds of life on Earth—children's laughter, the mating song of a whale. Her mother had been easiest to connect with when talking about the things she found amazing. God forbid you ask her about her own life, though.

Neko ran her hand along the rounded edges of the discs, remembering the feeling of putting vinyl on her parents' turntable, retro even back then. This had been her main job at parties: *Hey, Neko,* her father would call from across the room, *flip the record, chickadee?* The apartment had always been filled with new people for these events, whatever young band or dance troupe, whatever wild artists or off-Broadway cast her father was suddenly into, and one thing she remembered was how generous he was to those people. Her mother might come home from some play or show saying, "That was a dog," but her father had always found something to delight in. He was always taking new people under his wing and finding promise in them. To her constant exasperation, Neko's attendance at these parties was usually cut short. Her mother liked to use Neko's bedtime as an excuse to escape, lying next to her disgruntled daughter in that little single bed, stroking her wrist as though she needed help falling asleep. She was there and not there. Or, had she been there, but it was Neko who was closed up, walled off? Too late to matter now.

Many of the albums in this cache were from bands of mid-level indie fame—not people who did stadium tours, but ones who could consistently fill club venues with hipsters and music junkies. Neko thought of her mother, guitar slung over her torso like another limb, so right and perfect, so much a part of her body. Neko had been secretly proud to be the daughter of musicians, even if their music was weird and difficult to understand, nothing like the bubblegum pop she'd preferred back then. Even if most kids at school hadn't heard of the Nightjars.

Each time she came across a master of one of her parents' albums, she put it aside in a special stack. *Wok Hei. Summer Baby.*

Darling Eeyore. She tried to imagine showing these to her own child one day. To explain life before. But how would she explain it?

Then Neko found two scrolled words that forced a gasp from her mouth: *The Wreckage*. She turned the silver disc slowly, like a Ferris wheel. Her mother's last album. Her mother's only solo album. Her mother's scream into the void.

THE WRECKAGE

Track 1: "The Warp"

The Nightjars sat in silence in the radio station sound booth. A young sound engineer, headphones circling one arm like giant bracelets, asked if they would autograph their second album, the one with the jellybean cover. "Can you make it out to Joe?"

One never knew whether an album cover was going to become iconic until after. Like the Nirvana baby, floating across *Nevermind* for all time. Max said babies were born knowing how to swim, that if you tossed them in the water, they wouldn't panic and drown but tumble and float, buoyed by all that baby fat. As if they were still partly aquatic or amphibian or alien. But surely that wasn't true. And anyway, Neko, having been premature, never had much baby fat, never grew those scrumptious thighs Jenny saw on other people's infants. None of that mattered to Max, though; he'd long ago relinquished the role of Worry to her and taken for himself the role of Sweet Abandon.

The engineer did a sound check, adjusting their microphones, asking, "Need anything else?"

They shook their heads. "We're good. Thanks, Joe." Max

always said people's names, a trick Jenny knew he used to make himself seem more approachable.

"Oh, Joe is my dad."

Jenny laughed—and was surprised when it came out sounding bitter.

Because of their weirdness and dissonance, the Nightjars always ran parallel to the star machine, never fully out or fully in. Over the years, Jenny had grown into her role as a minor rock star, faking it until the costume fused to skin.

In the early days, she and Max and Jesse had been inseparable—bandmates on tour, a songwriting team composing late into the night. She was a gearhead, experimenting with their Prophet-5 or a new sound module; Jesse found traces of melody in the midst of the noise; and Max was the showboat, the glam theatrical one, always telling reporters, "Okay, okay, I'll just tell you a little story. . . ." But not entirely self-centered. Max was also one to celebrate others.

Jenny sometimes went to the bathroom at parties just to sit on the toilet lid and shake off the stimulation. When Jenny didn't talk for a stretch of time during a band interview, Max used to place the back of his hand gently on her cheek, very obviously, as if to remind the camera that she was there, too. Sometimes he squeezed her shoulder, like a father might do before his kid jogged onto the baseball field.

This deejay, in linen pants and Buddy Holly glasses, was warm and professional and would soon recede into Jenny's memory as just another talking head.

He asked how they liked Houston ("Third Coast rap, chef's

kiss," "breakfast tacos and scratch margaritas") and their opinion on streaming and how the music industry had changed ("On our next album, I'm going to auto-tune myself to Englebert Humperdinck and we're all getting paid!"). The obligatory questions about the new album.

"It's being called 'art blues' by some critics," he said. "Does that mean anything to you guys? Was that intentional?"

"My comrades and I don't explicitly think about genre in that way," said Jesse, who liked to take the lead on aesthetic questions. Jesse always called them comrades, and Jenny used to think it was because he read too much Russian literature, but later decided it was just his way of showing affection. "But certainly, considering everything that's going on in the world right now, we wanted to capture a sense of lamentation, which is where I think the blues element comes in . . ."

The deejay asked about new bands they were listening to, and Jenny jumped on the mic to promote two women-led groups she thought deserved more airtime. She chafed against what she considered to be an unfair reputation for aloofness, for wanting to just be one of the boys rather than supporting other female musicians.

The deejay quickly looked back at his notes. "Jenny, here's another question for you. The Nightjars have been a staple of cutting-edge indie music for years, but now there's another element. How has having a kid changed the dynamics or the way you play? Is it why the Nightjars don't tour like they used to?"

Of course he'd asked her this question. As though it were a virgin birth.

Other than the fact that Jenny never lost all of her pregnancy weight—curves and breasts where there used to be boyish lines—she didn't think the band acted differently onstage after

Neko's arrival. Instead, the difference was on the tour bus. The difference was personal.

"Well, there was the increase in milk production." Jenny's speaking voice sounded airy and hollow, so different from the throaty scream people expected of her on stage. "I'd be breast-feeding her in the wings right up until it was time to go on. The crew got very used to seeing me topless. Didn't blink an eye after a while." She pictured how Max, across the way, would fiddle with his keyboard, failing to hide his feeling of exclusion from this process.

The interviewer's eyes were already starting to glaze over.

"Then, of course, she got teeth. That was exciting."

At one point on tour Neko had started to bite Jenny's nipples while nursing. Jenny had been surprised by the intensity of the pain but also by her own emotional response—the wave of rejection and disconnect. She began to cry, the baby in her arms confused and scared. Jesse swooped up Neko and tossed her in the air, chanting the words "Chomp. Chomp." He convinced Jenny it would be cathartic to write a punk song about the experience, and so she did. Soon, anytime Jenny yelped, the entire bus broke into the chorus: "Fuck you, too, baby. Fuck you!"

Jesse was a good sport, sometimes rocking a milk-drunk Neko when she had trouble settling, when Max was out micro-managing the upcoming show and Jenny could hardly stand from exhaustion. But many nights on that tour Jesse didn't come home—a woman in every port, that guy (back then, she'd thought it was only Jesse who was like that), which Jenny always found impressive considering he was an honest, decent sort with a very specific type: short-haired women with knifelike cheekbones.

She and Max were often left alone on the bus with Neko, rolling around on the floor with her as she began to interact with the world. "She's a musical genius!" said Max, when she kicked the hanging toy that played music on contact. When she began to do it more methodically, Jenny predicted, "A drummer," and Max said, "God help us."

Jenny remembered thinking: *This must be what family feels like.*

"I read something recently about how time doesn't exist in the universe at large. Not as an objective quality," she said, letting her lips graze the microphone. She was really going off the wall now—the interviewer was looking more and more uncomfortable—but she didn't care. "Instead, we are *beings* of time."

The interviewer opened his mouth, but Jesse stopped him with a hand. "Time is the scrim through which we see the world," he said, looking at her with those almost black eyes.

"Yes. And what exactly are we waiting for?" asked Jenny. "For our kid to grow up, for us to grow old?"

"For Odysseus to return and save us?"

At the mention of Odysseus, the base of Jenny's palm found her sternum. The thought of her father, a classics professor who spoke fluent Homer at home. Jenny had never felt connected to Penelope—she was always more interested in the gods and monsters—but suddenly she wondered:

What if Penelope wasn't waiting for Odysseus at all? What if that was just what she told people so as to seem like a good wife, to seem normal? What if she was waiting for her son to grow up and not need her? What if she just wanted to be left alone, and when Odysseus returned, well, the hand to her throat, to her mouth, wasn't shock or gladness but rather bits of sign language to the birds, whom she'd never get the chance to join?

The men talked, kept talking, turned back to the subject at hand, and she stopped listening.

It was not something she really brought up in interviews, but before Max, guitar had just been a hobby. She'd gone, as she liked to say, to an extremely mediocre art school and, at the time they met, was cobbling together a living as a waitress and wedding photographer.

Hanging out with Max and his roommate at the time, Jesse, in their cold-water Bushwick apartment, she'd begun to noodle around on their music. They didn't compose in any traditional way; they didn't begin with melodies but rather concepts: the street beneath the L train or the apiary at the Central Park Zoo. They experimented with noise and funky equipment. They worked to make their voices contort into a sound gorgeous and ugly at the same time—shattered china, an angel's scream.

They'd liked to joke that Jenny was like Janice from the Muppets—the hippie chick who played a sunburst Les Paul (though it would be years before Jenny could afford one herself) and was always caught telling a random story about being naked when the other puppets in the scene had stopped talking.

How long had it taken her to feel as though she owned the music as much as they did? Too long.

As she sat trapped in that studio interview, surrounded by chittering voices, an image came to Jenny, accompanied by a crooked melody, one that kind of soft-stepped around her brain: herself with her Goldtop but it was also a loom, guitar strings the warp and the weft. She was Penelope, alone in the night, alone in her head. She thought about sitting on a park bench with Neko the week before, explaining, for some reason, how she'd wanted to be an astronomer when she was a kid because she loved the stars. Then she found out you had to also be good at math. Neko had nodded and said, "I love flowers so much I can hardly stand it." The phrasing—so surprising, so unchildlike.

Her daughter, a real live person. Neko said, "Mom, I like pretty, and you like cool," and Jenny laughed.

But she'd never really thought before about making music specifically for her daughter, letting her girl come inside the shimmer and blur. And yet, was there anyone else in the world?

It would be years before she would record her own album (for herself, for her daughter, maybe for all daughters), but this was the moment she understood that music was all that protected her from what was banging at the door, from the dark future blowing through the open windows. Whatever it took, she would not let the hoards outside lay a hand on Neko. Her daughter was not for them. Penelope waits for winter, she wrote in her head.

Penelope waits for winter
Penelope waits for the quick beating wing
She tears at her cheeks with her talons.

7

A KNOCK ON THE DOOR STARTLED NEKO FROM SLEEP.

Iggy was already awake, doing Tai Chi in the corner.

"Come in." Neko unzipped her sleeping bag.

Harriet stood awkwardly in shorts and a tank top, her neck looking strangely vulnerable and exposed without the spiked collar.

Iggy's smile, always genuine, beckoned her inside.

Harriet evidently had her speech prepared. "You guys didn't back down when my parents came looking for me. Pushing their money around."

Neko remembered the mother vividly—cheeks as red as her dyed hair, Jackie O sunglasses over crocodile tears. "Yeah," she said, buttoning her pants inside the sleeping bag.

"It's not fair to throw Jules to the wolves."

"It's not about fair," said Neko, looking to Iggy for backup. Sometimes she wondered if this was what they'd be like as real parents—her the prickly disciplinarian, him the even keel.

Iggy nodded. "You were eighteen—it wasn't illegal for you to be here. What Jules is doing could end us."

Harriet shook her head. "Look, we'll have enough scratch to

buy your crew license by the end of the year. You can finish your move to the Inside to settle down or whatever. Not look back."

"We weren't the only ones who noticed what happened yesterday," said Neko.

"I appreciate that." Harriet squared her shoulders. "But if you kick out Jules, I'll go, too. Take her home with me."

"Are you threatening us?" asked Neko.

"God, no," said the girl, her shoulders shrinking back down into her chest. "I'm just saying . . ."

"You're *saying* you'll go crying to Mommy and Daddy and tell them everything."

"No, I wouldn't tell them every . . ." The girl was working hard to keep her voice steady, but she was no match for Neko.

"You expect me to believe you'll crawl back to your parents?" Neko finished rolling up her sleeping bag and rummaged for her ziplock of toothpaste. "After what your father did to you?"

Harriet's mouth opened. Then shut. Then opened. A silenced marionette.

"Look," said Iggy, softly. He put a hand on Harriet's shoulder. "We haven't decided anything. We'll find a way to look after you. Both of you."

After a beat, Harriet nodded and left.

Neko and Iggy finished dressing in silence.

"You know, she's not entirely wrong," whispered Iggy. "We could just transfer the license when we get back to Fringetown. Let them pay us back later for the difference and just get out now before any shit goes down."

"*That* wouldn't look suspicious." Neko tried to tell herself she was protecting them, protecting Iggy, and not just finding ways to put off leaving the Sink.

He put a hand on the small of her back. "How did you know about her father?"

Iggy was warmer and more empathetic than she was, that was a fact. But then a moment like this arrived and she was reminded of how men could walk through the world without seeing the threats and scars that came with being raised in a female body.

"She's not a tourist, right?" Neko felt the tough bristles of the toothbrush against her gums. "You don't trade her life of attic gold for this one unless you have a very good reason."

"You did."

"I had a good reason, too."

She finished brushing her teeth, spitting into their empty water bucket.

8

THE NEXT MORNING, NEKO AND IGGY LEFT JULES AND HARRIET TO close up the vault as they rode their scooters, the attached trailers piled with masters and the other gear from Unit 59, to meet Chaplin at the SoHo address he'd given her at the poker game. They were relieved they didn't have to find ways to smuggle the awkwardly shaped canisters across the Breakwater, but how did Chaplin plan to do it?

"Who does he know?" asked Iggy.

Neko shrugged, concentrating on maneuvering their jerry-rigged trailers around gashes in the asphalt. They followed the arteries—smaller streets, mostly—that they kept clear to help them get to and from the Ice House. The quiet of the city would have been eerie if they weren't used to it. It reminded Neko of early Sunday morning in the Old World: deserted streets scattered with soggy trash from the previous night's revelries.

Wooster Street, once cobblestoned and filled with luxury boutiques, looked bombed-out. A few places were still fronted with angry rusted grilles, but most of them were nothing but shattered glass and the ripe smell of animal dens. The address was just south of Houston: a thick metal door set into a brick wall and three concrete steps. The air was humid, and a family of beetles scuttled in the gutter over leaves and candy wrappers bleached white from the sun.

They knocked on the door, but the metal made almost no sound. Neko tried again using the butt of her Glock. Barely a ping. She didn't like being out in the open with a pile of goods, a sitting target for any scofflaws squatting in nearby buildings. Eventually Iggy pushed all the buttons on the doorplate—such a strange gesture in this place and time that Neko startled when one of them set off a loud buzz.

Beyond the door was a small cement antechamber and a narrow staircase that led to the second floor. They shut the door behind them, left the stuff there, and walked up the stairs. Neko hadn't realized it from the generic exterior, but they were at the location of a permanent art installation from before. A small hallway gave way to a large multi-room apartment with no doors, tall ceilings, and handsome walls, its interior section filled with two feet of clumpy black soil and a pleasant, loamy smell. Waist-high plexiglass was inserted across the doorway to prevent the dirt from migrating into the hall.

Around the corner, Chaplin emerged from what must once have been the curator's office. "You brought Ignacio," he noted with a dramatic sigh of disappointment.

Neko looked around with a sense of vertigo. "We came here once on a school trip." She remembered the teacher's hoop earrings, her long hair swinging as they followed her up the stairs. "It looks the same."

"I take care of the place. Water the soil. Erase my footsteps with the cultivator."

"You water dirt?" asked Iggy.

"I used to come here as a kid, too," said Chaplin. "Always wanted to jump the barrier and dive in. And now I can." He waved his hands like a tour director. "I liked the idea of having an office that looked apocalyptic. Ha, ha."

Neko set her backpack down on the floor. "I didn't know you grew up here."

"Queens. And you never asked."

Neko nodded. You never asked anyone if they were from the City. Not if you didn't want to hear all the gruesome details. Most people couldn't shut up about it, as though telling their story over and over might alter it or relieve them of it. Others never spoke a word, and that was worse.

"How do you plan to smuggle the canisters back across?" asked Iggy.

"That's an interesting question."

Chaplin led them into his office, in which there was barely space to move between all the bizarre sculptures and tapestries, paintings leaning against walls, strange and beautiful objects on every surface.

"Same way you plan to smuggle these out?" Iggy took out his glasses and began inspecting the artwork, clearly trying not to look or sound too impressed. She recognized a Mapplethorpe, a Tibetan prayer wheel, a gold clavichord.

"These are for me," said Chaplin. "And today, for you. I have more pieces upstairs that I rotate through."

Iggy stood in front of a large oil painting depicting a pale woman, a skull cradled in her lap, staring at the reflection of a bright candle flame. "Caravaggio?"

"Georges de La Tour." Chaplin moved to stand next to him. "Mary Magdalene, luminous without the pleasures of the flesh." Sensing a captive audience, he continued, nodding toward a wooden sculpture of a naked boy looking through the V of his own legs, and then to a more contemporary painting that depicted abstracted satellites coursing through blue space. "Isamu Noguchi. Sarah Sze."

"And these?" asked Iggy, crouching in front of a line of artifacts along a wall shelf.

"This is a cradleboard. Kiowa."

Neko sighed.

"And these prayer beads are made from human craniums."

"Of course they are. Can we get started?" Neko snapped her fingers as if to release the men from their pretention.

Chaplin sat down at a desk flanked by vintage computer screens and motioned for them to sit.

Neko took a load off. "Did you get the client details?"

He nodded absentmindedly, which Neko found strange, and then he reached into a porcelain bowl, took out a hard-boiled egg, and began to peel it. "You know about the bunkers, right?"

"Sure."

"Did you know there are functioning bunkers inside the Sink?"

She'd never heard this. How had she never heard this? "No way."

"Not in Manhattan, of course, but farther out. And ever since the government assigned them fugitive status, the rich fuckers have been trading with me for what they need," said Chaplin, who liked to use the word "trade," as though his business were legitimate. "That's why you brought these canisters here. They're not going across the Breakwater."

"A bunker inside the Sink ordered all of this?"

"A new client, call themselves the Cellar. They recently contacted me through the channel." He raised his eyebrows, the corner of his mouth turning upward.

"What did they say when you asked about the masters? About Goldbug?"

"They said nothing." Chaplin tapped the desk with his hand.

Neko thought she should be more accustomed to disappointment by now. What had she expected? Some long-lost music industry "aunt" or "uncle," one of the beautiful people who'd always kissed her on both cheeks?

She looked at Iggy, and he took her hand and pulled her gently to stand. "The scratch for this haul?"

Chaplin sighed and reached for an envelope. "Thing is, an hour ago another message came through the Black Channel," he said. "I'd pretended I was curious about the masters because of their financial potential. I lied and told them the stash included the master recording of Nirvana's *In Utero,* and that I could fence it for them." His words were flat, no flourish, and his voice was almost a growl. He took a breath and stared at the ceiling. "The response said it was vital all the masters arrive intact at the Cellar, but that Jenny Sweet might be open to selling some of them at a later date."

Neko stood there, stunned. Her heartbeat evaporated. Completely stopped altogether.

"Jesus," Iggy whispered under his breath.

"Not exactly." Chaplin turned to Neko. "I thought your mother died in the storm . . ." His voice was strange, and Neko struggled to parse the words, like they were in another language vaguely similar to English.

"What?"

"You told me once that your mother died."

She couldn't respond. She tried to slow her breath like she'd been trained. She tried to think. There was a strange glimmer in the air, as though she were in a computer simulation going haywire.

Finally, Iggy answered for her. "They lived east of Tompkins Square Park, so . . ."

Chaplin nodded. "You weren't at home?"

She tried to smile but it was a grimace. "By the time I got back to New York, it was over."

Chaplin looked at her with wet eyes. "I was at a friend's house in Jamaica Bay," he said quietly, "and the water moved horizontally, like you could have surfed to the Rockaways." The rumble of the generator in the corner of Chaplin's office suddenly sounded ominous, the light overhead too bright. "It was so dark and the winds so strong that his mother tied us all together with rope. Then we smelled smoke and houses began to go up in flames, seawater breaching the electrical panels, winds spreading the fi . . ."

"Stop," said Neko, closing her eyes. "Please, please, please stop."

Everyone sat there in silence. Helpless. Slack.

"It's probably a ruse," Chaplin offered. "I mean, what are the odds, right? After all these years."

Neko's whole body clanged, not just because her mother might be alive in some underground molehill, but because she might have *been alive.* All this time. And if she wasn't, why would somebody else use *her* name, of all people's?

"Where's the bunker?" she asked.

"The instructions direct me to a place at the Watering Hole," he said, referring to the northern outpost inside the Sink, "and says my people will be given the precise coordinates from there."

"Why not use drone delivery?" asked Iggy.

"There's been a drone fence over the Sink for two years."

Chaplin shrugged. "When my agents deliver the full haul to the compound, I'll have them see if she's . . . there."

The pressure inside Neko's rib cage was enormous. She'd swallowed a chain mace. "Your agents? No fucking way. You're sending us."

9

THEY SAT ON THEIR LUGGAGE AT THE CROWDED GATE, WAITING AND waiting, her mother's cell going straight to voicemail. At some point Neko must have fallen asleep, head on her father's lap, because she remembered being roused by people crying and rushing around like panicked rats. Her father tried to hold her and keep her from going to one of the televisions that floated down from the airport ceiling.

The ocean had been rising for years. Now was its chance to swarm past the city's floodwalls and stay. The ultimate gentrification. The people in all those apartment and office buildings had no time to leave for higher ground. Later, Neko would imagine that the last thing they heard was a freight train, then the bubbling of water.

"No." It was all she could say. "No, no, no."

"It's not your fault."

"But I'm why she's not here. With us."

"She'll call," her father kept saying over and over. "Cell service is down over the whole city. Once it's back, she'll call. You'll see." And the thing she remembered was that he had white sand in the spiral of his ear.

10

WHEN NEKO FIRST MET IGNACIO VILLARREAL, SHE HAD JUST TURNED eighteen, and the trail she was hiking that day wound back and forth across a creek thick with runoff. At times water seeped from the shallow banks onto the overgrown path, slicking the rocks so Neko had to pick her way carefully. Goldenrod fretted in the wind, and flies sucked dew from leaves large and flat as palms. Grasses indiscreetly spilled their seed. Back then, before the Breakwater had been completed, the border was more porous, particularly away from the old cities, and she'd crossed frequently to camp and be alone.

Neko saw him first—he was sitting on a log up ahead, staring into the creek. She reached into her pack; the pocketknife was heavy and always sank to the bottom. She took it into her right hand and pulled her hoodie up with her left. This was the thing about being alone on a trail: The dangers of bears and mountain lions were nothing compared to the dangers of men.

As she approached, he turned. His eyes were round and a bit unnerving, and he had thick black hair tied back with a velvet ribbon. His clothes were sporty and neat, and open beside him on the log was a book, spine cracked. *Crow* by Ted Hughes. She peered over his shoulder.

"Are you reading poetry on that log?" she asked. She wasn't sure why she had stopped to talk to him, or had asked him something so inane, so obvious. He didn't look particularly threatening—though she of all people should know the fault in that assumption. Maybe it was the poetry, so surprising and out of order. Or maybe orphans can always sense each other, smell the familiar scent of base grief.

He smiled. He had incredible dimples. "I *am* reading poetry on a log."

"Were you waiting until somebody came up and noticed you . . . reading poetry?"

"It's true," he said. "I've been here trying to impress someone for weeks, probably years. Now I can stop."

She shrugged, smiled. "Read something."

He picked up the book and read,

"Shock-severed eyes watched blood
Squandering as if from a drainpipe . . ."

He licked his lips. "I don't know—it's a little dreary. It said in the intro that the poet made his wife stick her head in the oven. She was another poet."

"Then what happened?" asked Neko. "Did she kick his ass?"

"One would hope."

"So what's the poem about besides bloody eyeballs?" She felt oddly unselfconscious, and for once she didn't think about her crooked nose or the freckles that had recently, thankfully, begun to recede into a pointillist background on her cheeks and forehead, or the coiled frizz of her rust-colored hair pulled back in a half-assed braid.

"That's it, really."

"Well, enjoy your log," she said, slipping her knife into her back pocket.

He blinked at her for a beat, then suddenly tossed the book high up in the air, poetry now ricocheting through branches, falling and skidding among leaves on the ground. He stood and his body began dancing, mocking classic boy band moves as he started singing the lyrics to a song about how *she don't know she's beautiful.*

When he was done with his little performance—strike a pose. She stared and he stared, clearly waiting for a reaction. Neko crouched and pinched off some snakeroot, crushing the herb between thumb and forefinger and offering it to him to smell. She had fooled around with more girls than she had boys up to that point, but Neko thought to herself: *This one maybe I could love.*

IGGY HAD ALREADY SIGNED UP TO TRAIN AS A MUDLARK AND NEKO said, fine, but only if they signed up for the Sink.

In the first year after the evacuation, before the Breakwater was completed, the government had used military trucks to extract the most time-sensitive materials from the Sink—like fresh petrol or ancient artwork from the Met. But because the city had to be evacuated so quickly after the storms flooded the subways and undermined the structural integrity of the buildings, an incredible amount of valuable material had been left behind. Mudlarks were hired to be professional scavengers of the decommissioned zones.

When she thought back on their first year, her brain played celluloid reels of Ignacio. She'd kept him locked in her gaze as though it had protective powers. The moment, lit by his headlamp, when a bat dive-bombed from the broken ceiling of a Tiffany showroom. The way he dragged his fingertips along Mason jars filled with lentils, chickpeas, brown rice lined up on the shelves of some abandoned cupboard. How he taught her to find wild edibles—garlic, onions, carrots—in unexpected patches of grass. How he said they should make a hearty hippie stew and she said, *Why not a potion?,* remembering how her mother (always something a little witchy about her) had encouraged Neko to circle mixing bowls on the floor of their apartment and pour in vinegar and baking soda, oregano and cumin and turmeric as bright as the sun, stirring with a wooden spoon. *Yes,* Iggy said, giddy, *why didn't we think of it before? A magic potion to set things right again.*

When Neko first encountered the brutalities of the Sink, it was easier to watch Iggy see them, too, as though to subsume her feelings beneath his: Iggy kneeling over an arced rib cage, white and picked clean—where had the rest of the bones gone, dragged off by some wild animal?—and the way he took in the sight with his whole body. In moments like that, he muttered strings of alliteratives—she didn't even think he knew he was doing it: *glossy, glower, gloam, the gloaming.* Sometimes she whispered her own: *gear, gobsmacked, guitar.*

Once, they turned a corner in Hell's Kitchen to encounter another mudlark, small and wiry, a can of paint at his feet, using his body to make stunning designs on a concrete wall, swoops and spirals, just as the paleolithic people at Lascaux had made cave paintings by blowing ocher from a hollow bone over hands and fingers. Negative space.

Iggy tried to befriend this man, invited him to run with them as they sifted through the city's shit for gold, but the man smiled and shook his head. Maybe he understood that too many oddballs together was asking for trouble. A lot of mudlarks in those early summer-camp-like days were just tourists, as it turned out, not cut out for the harder, darker, freer world that the Sink became.

Neko and Iggy weren't cut out for it either. Not at first.

But they were in love. They took apart engines and put them back together, hip to hip, smearing grease in parallel lines on each other's cheeks like football players before a game. There weren't small independent crews yet. The Breakwater was still in the process of being built and the roads were still good enough to send the mudlarks in on large trucks, jerry-rigged buses, and vans—in and out, so they didn't have to stay in Manhattan overnight with the cockroaches and rats, insects buzzing around them like motorcycle gangs. And nobody would have wanted to because of the smell: spoiled meat and sulfur. Hell.

Neko hadn't gotten the chance to say goodbye, so she said it every day that they rode across the crumbling blacktop of downtown, around the flooded parks where she used to play, past the burning BP station she'd never noticed was even there until it caught fire. Goodbye to the Mars Bar. Goodbye to Tompkins Square Bagels and their schmears, to Veniero's and Cafe Mogador. Goodbye to the bodegas and dry cleaners and kosher groceries that handed out candy to Neko and her friends each Halloween. Goodbye, Mercer Street Books, and to the spot near Union Square where they'd always gone to watch Manhattanhenge, the sun barreling down the street like a bowling ball. The gridiron was permanently branded in the architecture of her brain.

But what she truly wanted was to find her mother, not just to say goodbye but to say *I'm sorry*. For the big thing—but all the other, smaller things, too. Each spring, she motored past the grand wisteria on Stuyvesant—the one that had always been surrounded by film crews or selfie takers—to see if it was still there, awash in purple, and, amazingly, miraculously, it always was. It had outlasted the rest, and she thought that would have made even her mother smile.

DID HER ORIGIN STORY WITH IGGY EXPLAIN THEM ANY MORE THAN the origin story of her own parents did? Even when things hadn't been great at home, Neko had always liked to imagine the day her parents had met.

The setting: a dumpling house near the Central–Mid-Levels Escalator on Hong Kong Island. Jenny had been there for a few months, staying with friends, escaping the States after her father's death. Max had been in town to do the sound mixing for a Chinese-language film directed by Terrance Cha, whom Jenny knew from art school.

Neko begged to hear the story so many times over the years, and this is how the scene, like a home movie, had solidified in her mind:

"Wok hei," her mother and Terrance Cha called out in unison when the first plate of dumplings arrived, and her father raised an eyebrow.

"Literally, 'breath of the wok,'" the director explained to Neko's father.

"Wok hei is the spirit of the wok," Jenny added, maybe flirting.

The next day, she offered to tour Max around Hong Kong, and this part always flitted across Neko's mind like a film montage: Her mother showed her father how to light a bundle of incense as an offering at Man Mo Temple. How to move the antique wooden backrest on the Star Ferry. She took him to the Kowloon Ladies' Market and the Goldfish Market, where the tetras and bettas and butterflyfish swam inside prisms of cheap plastic bags.

It was almost Chinese New Year, and the Flower Market was bursting with cherry blossoms and mandarin trees and potted bamboo. And orchids—every color, every size. "They are the most human of all plants," Max observed. "Just look at their concerned faces."

Her mother liked this so much that she decided to take him to her favorite place: the bird market. It was where you could buy birds, yes, parrots and cockatoos and canaries lined up in big metal cages, squawking and preening. But the best part, she always said, happened along the periphery, where the old men brought their own delicate songbirds in intricate, handmade wooden cages. To show them off. To sit on benches and chat with one another. To feed them live crickets with chopsticks.

"They're taking their birds on a walk," said Max, so thrilled that he grabbed Jenny's hand without thinking. And by the time Jenny moved back to New York two months later, the two were a couple. Then they were a couple in a band.

After they recorded something he thought was good, her father began to say, "Wok hei! We captured the wok hei." So that's what they named their first LP, released by a tiny label that produced the indies of the indie world. It was seemingly just another random project in their freewheeling lives of doing and making and partying and credit card debt. They said they never expected *Wok Hei* to get much traction, certainly not to become part of the post-9/11 zeitgeist.

"I wanted to look like Ari Up from the Slits but less Rasta," said her mother once as they flipped through old photos on her phone. "New Wave really allowed us to enjoy disco again," her father explained, apropos of nothing. They said they'd never expected to become a real band that toured the world. To end up on the other side of the camera, faces on the covers of *Paste* and *Mojo*. But they had.

Neko used to believe that this far-flung origin story in Hong Kong, this unlikely rise to fame, was strong enough to weave her parents together forever, and, growing up, she'd clung to it as though it proved that the events leading up to her existence were part of something destined.

BUT NONE OF THIS, THOUGHT NEKO NOW, ACCOUNTED FOR HOW HER mother, Jenny fucking Sweet of the Nightjars, could have ended up in an underground bunker. Neko couldn't process it. All this time she'd blamed herself for the fact that her mother was in the East Village during the storm, but what if something else entirely had happened?

It wasn't as though people hadn't talked about places like bunkers in the years before Hurricane Frida, but her parents had scoffed at what they called "the survivalist wackos." If anybody in their circle had been prepper-adjacent it was Layla Wei, the manager to whom her parents attributed much of their success and who also repped other bands straddling the indie/commercial divide, bands with names that used to make Neko giggle, like Jump Frog Jump and Farmer's Almanac.

Layla Wei. Since she had so few blood relatives, Neko had been encouraged to call her Aunt Layla, and she felt a pang in her chest at the thought of her. Fun, mysterious Aunt Layla, who always treated her like a little adult and who looked more like a rock star than the rock stars—Chucks and skinny jeans, silvery jackets hanging on her androgynous frame in any weather, wild black hair when she pulled off her skullcap. She was always blowing in and out of town with new boyfriends or girlfriends, whisking Neko away to the arthouse cinema to show her films that were wildly inappropriate. Films that *will blow your mind.* At the record store, she'd shaken her head subtly when Neko picked up a *Best Of* album. Neko had never wanted to impress anyone more.

Looking back, she understood that Layla Wei's house upstate had been a disastrous hodgepodge of ethnic appropriation. But at the time, to young Neko, it had been magical: African masks in wood and raffia, terrifying and beautiful. White scrolls bleeding Chinese calligraphy. Indigo adire cloth from Nigeria and elaborately stitched rust-red molas from Panama. The kitchen had open shelves stacked with off-kilter ceramic dishes, and the furniture had all been borrowed from someplace else, church pews and tractor seats.

Neko remembered waking to the sound of laughter as a child, pressing her forehead to the window of one of the bedrooms that existed like dark pockets and seeing the adults outside drinking around a firepit. Why hadn't she walked outside and joined them? She remembered wanting to, but also being afraid. As if even then, she'd believed she had the power to break the spell of grown-up merriment.

Aunt Layla talked the loudest. "I mean it, I'm going to buy one of those Cold War bomb shelters and put it in over there behind the gazebo!" Was there a war against the cold now? Neko had wondered. Was it like the war against drugs?

And then there had been her father, talking to a woman with a truly amazing Afro, dramatic glitter on her eyelids that Neko's mother would never wear. Neko couldn't hear what he was saying to the woman, but their body language made Neko's stomach feel strange. And was it any wonder that he was having fun while her mother sat off by herself, looking up at the sky as though she weren't surrounded by people? (Sometimes Neko wondered if she hadn't actually been most jealous of her mother's own mind, that inaccessible place in her head where she seemed to spend so much time.)

Neko knew it was impossible that these were all real memories—too convenient, considering how her parents would break up; considering how in the years to come, so many rich people had bunkered up against the coming catastrophes. Surely, she thought, her brain had just imprinted future knowledge on these fuzzy childhood flashes. But still, Neko continued going over and over the flip-book of adult conversations she'd stored from childhood, looking for any clues she'd missed.

There was the school break when her parents had brought a seven-year-old Neko with them to Texas for back-to-back gigs in Austin and San Antonio. She and her mom had met up with Aunt Layla during the day—she was in Austin, too, for some reason, probably booking festival dates for clients.

"This seems kind of offensive, doesn't it?" Layla had asked, staring at a fist-sized chocolate cupcake soaked in vanilla icing. On the chalkboard menu of the sleek silver Airstream trailer it was called "the Michael Jackson."

"How's it offensive?" Neko asked before shoving a bite into her mouth. They sat on a picnic table beneath a sprawling live oak in an empty lot on an otherwise busy commercial strip. She hated it when grown-ups didn't explain things to her.

Jenny groaned at the start of a twangy song coming from the Airstream's speakers.

"Why are you always so hard on country music?" asked Layla.

"I'm not," said Jenny. "I like flattop George Jones."

A car in the parking lot had its windows down and radio on, and occasionally they could make out fragments of headlines competing with the trailer's music: . . . *Water shortages continuing to plague California and Nevada . . .*

"Why can't we just desalinate the ocean?" asked Neko, upper lip coated in icing.

"How do you even know that word?" asked Layla.

Neko shrugged. "School project."

"We can," said her mother, fingering the splitting wood of the picnic table. "It's just too expensive and time consuming. It's not enough to make a difference."

Layla held an imaginary microphone to Neko's mother's mouth. "And that has been our expert testimony from musician and amateur reader of the *New York Times* science section, Jenny Sweet."

. . . with bullhorns outside the state capitol protesting the enforced water rationing . . .

"Climate change is going to kill us all." Neko wasn't sure she believed this, but she said it anyway, testing out the idea.

"Oh, baby!" Her mother reached for her arm, the leather of her jacket as soft as the skin of her hand that gripped Neko. "Don't talk like that."

Looking back, Neko found it interesting that her mother hadn't actually disagreed with the statement. Instead, she just hadn't wanted their worst fears released into the air, as though that was what would make them real. Had her mother had secrets, even then? Plans that Neko didn't know about?

Layla lowered her head conspiratorially. "That's why we need to build our underground castle."

"Underground castle?" Neko, who had gone through a longer-than-average princess phase, liked this idea.

"Don't be gullible, Neko," said her mother, to which Layla grunted.

At some point, Neko went off to the porta-potty and returned to see her mother's head on Layla's shoulder. Grackles squawked from their perches on the power lines, traffic honked along Congress Avenue. Their bodies rose and fell together in breath. Her mother was saying something like, "The world is always ending, isn't it?"

. . . The record-breaking fifteenth Gulf hurricane this season is expected to make landfall on . . .

11

CANDLELIGHT WOBBLED ON THE WALLS.

Crease, pinch, smooth. The texture of the cheap paper made her think of shoe leather or wet leaves. Or the time she'd touched a giraffe's tongue while feeding it lettuce leaves on the zoo platform—Neko had been in awe of the animal's gleaming fur and rambling gait, the elegant megafauna. These days, in dreams, her mother sometimes took on the form of a giraffe, glorious and unknowable.

"The government doesn't issue Land Rovers to crews larking the City." Iggy's voice was hoarse.

"But they do for larks farther north."

"We've never larked that sector of the Sink. We don't know a thing about it." He slid out of bed, leaving behind a soft warmth.

"If we're not up north, what excuse would we have to go to the Watering Hole for supplies?" she asked, referring to the outpost serving the northern section of the Sink, where Chaplin had said the compound would provide the coordinates to their bunker. "Richie's larked that sector, and there aren't many crews with our diving experience. Surely he could find us a gig."

"Why would he want to help us?"

"Not *us,* maybe. But you."

Iggy kicked the baseboard electrical outlets, where the power was out. Again. "Civilization in decline."

"Nothing civilized about Fringe," she said, smiling, trying to soften him. If there was a possibility of some real connection left, anyone, she knew Iggy would help her. He loved her too much.

"Does this mean we're not firing Jules and Harriet?"

Neko opened her mouth in a silent scream. It would be harder to secure a gig with only a half crew. "But having them along will be so much more complicated." How much could they tell them about the canisters and the bunker? How much *should* they?

Iggy walked over to the enormous star chart that hung on the wall, running his fingertips through Andromeda. Not looking at her. "Why not just let Chaplin do the drop and report back? I'm tired, Neko. And you've punished yourself enough, don't you think?"

"Not as much as you're punishing me with that cliché." Not that he was wrong. Was it penance? Was it a need for closure? Was it actual motherfucking mother love? All of the above.

He let out a long breath. "I lost people, too."

Neko swallowed. She wanted to say, *But that wasn't your fault,* but instead she went here: "The more money we save before we leave the Sink . . ."

Iggy put a finger to his lips. "Neko. You've been saying that for years. The argument has lost all meaning."

She knew she should get up from bed and go to him, but she slumped farther into the mattress. "One last lark. I can't leave without knowing." An image flashed: the piano ivories of her mother's straight teeth as she perched on the edge of Neko's bed. *Get up, get up. Time to fly.*

On the other side of the room, Iggy began to stretch, rolling his body through a Sun Salutation. "Harriet and Jules are coming for dinner."

"I thought we were bringing bushmeat to the Tower tonight," she said, referring to the smuggled goods they planned to fence.

"Not until ten. I need you to get groceries. Bring Jules with you and take her by the clinic on your way."

"Why would I do that?"

"Because she has ringworm and God knows what else. Because you want me to call Richie and beg for a dangerous lark we have no business being on. Because I need to be alone, and because I asked you to."

She sighed in defeat, and he left the room.

Lying there that morning, Neko counted up the nineteen years she'd spent in the Sink, the twelve matchbooks from East Village dive bars in her collection down the hall, the two small folds of her belly. She counted the scars that crisscrossed her body, the tattoos, the meals of gruel, the shots of stupid liquor, the black market bribes and black market profits.

Then there was the kill count: Mice and squirrels roasted on spits and soaked in rum. A fetus scraped from the womb. The man she'd shot when he surprised them outside the vault, though it hadn't felt like a bullet being released from her gun but rather like a whip, like a scorpion sting—it had happened so fast. She'd found an extra pair of socks in his pocket. And what had she done then, while her crew stood with mouths open? She'd moved to her pack for the tarp folded inside and placed it gently over the body like a shroud, as though it were something holy and not just some squatter trying to steal their shit, and soon it was blooming with maroon.

Then there were the bodies she'd found, the year of suicides.

One of them they'd known and liked and so they'd left his body on a nearby roof outcropping for the hawks and wolves, the animals of the night. A Tibetan sky burial. And there was her mother, of course—a mystery. The original damage.

Over the years, Neko had been surprised to find new depths within herself: discipline and self-control, the ability to observe small changes in the environment, to repress panic and worry. She had slowly gained an entirely new relationship with pain and the engineering of her body, the steady metronome of her heart.

The danger of the Sink had been all milky adrenaline thrill back then. Once, after disembarking from a truck somewhere in Harlem, they'd stood on a crumpled sidewalk, Neko placing a mask on Iggy's face, gently, as though he were made of glass, tucking the straps around his ears, her face so close to his that she could almost touch him with her eyelashes. Then suddenly, a man, another mudlark, had grabbed her crotch from behind and then her chest—all lewdness, probably high on something—and though she'd twisted his arm until he backed away, she'd seen the look in the man's eyes.

The next time somebody did something like that to her in the Sink, she would shoot him. Iggy couldn't be turned into her protector if she wanted to keep him the way she loved him best. She would have to be his.

After that, she began to tattoo fierce creatures up and down their bodies, and soon other mudlarks lined up like supplicants, and they paid her not in scratch but in favors and small debts.

Their mudlark trainers had been ex-military, ex-commandos in some cases, and she and Iggy had been assigned to one who took their training further than necessary, requisitioning cadavers from the black market under the guise of teaching them field first aid, then giving them knives and teaching them how to carve up a body like a pig's. He was some evil shit, but it had also been fascinating to watch how he moved through the world. At the end of the day, the most useful thing they'd learned from him was how to act like a psychopath with nothing to lose. To bluff. This ability had saved their asses more than once over the years.

And that was what Iggy still thought they were doing, bluffing. But, though Neko hadn't enjoyed shooting that squatter, or any of the people she'd been forced to harm over the years, and had no particular interest in doing it again, she also didn't feel bad. Some part of her knew it shouldn't be that easy. Somewhere in her body, surely, these moments lurked. Waiting.

When the electricity came back on, Neko knew from how the ceiling fan began to whir and thump above her body, still tangled in the damp sheet.

12

NEKO SAT WITH JULES IN THE GRIMY WAITING ROOM OF A RED CROSS clinic. The window was painted with the words: SALE! MALARIA VACCINE AND HEPATITIS TEST 50% OFF. ONE WEEK ONLY!

Jules squirmed and tapped her foot against the yellowing tile. Neko pressed a hand on the woman's thigh to still her.

"Maybe we should be wearing one of those," Jules whispered, nodding to a man a few seats away in a medical mask.

"He's probably immunocompromised." Neko turned and raised her voice. "Right? Immunocompromised?"

"Selling bone marrow today. Won't get paid if I've got any bugs." The man was so thin he looked two-dimensional, like a line drawing. "They do an okay job here. Not like the butchers who bought my kidney." He lifted his shirt to show a gnarly scar on his abdomen.

Along the far wall of the windowless waiting area were plexiglass booths where machines took samples and provided readouts of various health stats. One of the booths was decorated with a cotton-candy-pink uterus.

"What are you waiting for?" Neko asked Jules. The receptionist had told her to *do the booths* before they checked them into a room. "Have you never had a gyno checkup?"

"Don't need to. I use garlic and oregano oil."

"Lord have mercy." Neko nodded to the booth. "Go on. Ovarian cancer kills."

Jules pursed her thin lips and looked away. "Come with me?"

Neko shrugged.

Inside the violently white booth, they swabbed their mouths and stretched out their arms for a prick.

"We used to have to go to doctors for this sort of information. You know, real people who shoved a speculum up your vagina."

"Yeah, yeah, life's so much more amazing these days, right?"

EVENTUALLY THEY WERE LED BACK TO AN EXAM ROOM, AND NEKO looked the other way while Jules changed into a gown and slid onto an exam table covered in crinkly paper. "This is my first time." Her voice was tight, controlled, but she looked at Neko with a kind of pleading. "To a clinic, I mean."

Neko liked Jules, she did. She wanted good things for her, but she wasn't responsible for making sure they happened. It was hard enough to be responsible for herself.

"Well," said Neko finally. "That means you won't have anything to compare it to." Cold comfort, Neko thought, but true. Iggy liked to argue that they were the saddest generation—raised off the fat of one world only to live in the hunger of its shadow. And he didn't even know about how Neko and her parents, for example, went to a doctor's office that projected its exclusivity in every detail—textured wallpaper and exposed shiplap, real peonies in a vase by the sink. She could still remember the doctor walking in with a smile, lab coat open to reveal a tailored blue suit.

"It's not like you ever asked, you know," said Jules.

"Asked what?"

"About my past. I assumed that meant you understood . . ."

"No, no," Neko interrupted. "That's how we live—moving forward. We can't afford to get sucked back into the muck of before." Neko was aware of the massive irony of this statement. She had definitely been sucked back into the muck.

"Harriet wouldn't have done it, you know."

"Stop starting conversations in the middle, as if I live inside your brain."

Jules folded her hands. "She wouldn't have taken me to her parents. Turned you in."

The statement struck Neko as convenient at best. "Threatening it—just saying it—is as bad. Worse."

After a nurse came in and examined Jules's ringworm and listened to all the beating and breathing places of the body, another tech entered and handed her an electronic tablet.

"Boss."

Neko sat up and rubbed her temples. "Don't call me that."

"The good news is that you don't have crotch cancer."

"Give me that." Neko tried to grab the tablet from Jules.

"The bad news is that you only have approximately six good eggs left. You guys better get busy." Jules made several crude hip thrusts. "I'm kind of surprised you have any left, considering. . . ."

Neko looked at the grid of numbers. She hadn't realized the gyno booth would test fertility. "Considering what?"

Jules bent over like an old lady and pretended to walk with a cane.

"You're fired."

"You mentioned that already." Jules scrolled to her own readouts. "Let's see. One hundred and fifty-seven. Want to borrow a few of my fat, youthful huevos?"

Neko had to hold the tablet out in front of her in order to read it—she needed glasses, clearly. Maybe the ophthalmologist could make her reading goggles? This made her think of a girl she'd known in school, in biology class, who said she wanted to make prosthetic eyes when she grew up, to paint them and sell them for money. And another girl, named Iris, who had claimed to be named after the part of the eye instead of the flower.

THEY WENT OUT INTO THE HALLWAY TO PAY THE BILL THROUGH A LITtle window.

"Well, if I can't give you my eggs, what can I give you?" asked Jules as they waited for the electronic receipt to send.

"Give me?"

"To stay on the crew?" Her face turned slippery again. "Reassurances? Or I could take a smaller cut? Something?"

Neko's head hurt under the artificial light and she pushed the heels of her hands into her temples. Everything felt constricted and tight.

Before she could figure out how to respond, a commotion in the hallway forced them to shrink back against the wall so a stretcher could pass, the patient on it moaning, covered in what looked to be fresh burns. They wheeled her through a door into a room with more equipment than the one Jules had been assigned. A nurse stopped a woman—crying, maybe the mother—at the door and said, "Wait here."

The woman, with short gray hair and a checkered flannel shirt, flapped her arms, hovering somewhere between shock and grief over what was to come. She smelled of smoke. She turned to look at them—through them—and said, "No water. No water."

Jules took the woman's hand and led her to a chair. "You need some water?"

"No water," the woman repeated. "The fire truck had no water."

Jules nodded. She patted her hand, and they left the woman there.

FROM THE CLINIC, THEY BOARDED AN ELECTRIC SELF-DRIVING BUS, dented like an old soda can. Fringe looked more run-down each year: corrugated tin patched the caving rooflines; voltage inconsistencies caused electronic billboards to flicker erratically; tankards lumbered along the streets delivering drinking water to residential buildings.

Neko gave Jules the window seat—she had little desire to trace the passing strip malls littered with ammo stores and psychics, cafés serving cricket fries and boiled yams, computer chop shops, windows displaying consignment AIs that claimed to clean your house or ease your loneliness. There were telegram offices for avoiding surveillance, marijuana dispensaries, nail salons that probably weren't actually nail salons. Under a perpetually half-finished overpass, a group of people worked at long tables recycling trash into things that could be resold.

"We lived upstate during Hurricane Frida," Jules said suddenly, her voice formal, as though she were giving a presentation. "I was too young to remember anything from the event itself, just worried adults huddled around a screen. The moment I remember is when our town was evacuated, when most of my friends and their families moved out of our building. We stayed, and so did the Wright-Gilmans, crazy libertarians, and old Mr. and Mrs. Sandoval, who collected stray cats until they ran out of cat food and then all the cats left or died." Jules wrapped her arms around herself as though she were cold. "We banded together for a while, taking turns going on scavenging runs, pitching in to buy sacks of rice and crates of potatoes from the black market after the stores were emptied. We used candles and battery-powered lanterns, and I liked it at first because I was a kid and it felt like camping. Like an adventure. And then when the Fugitive Law was passed, and it was no longer just inconvenient but illegal to stay . . ." Jules paused, blinked hard. "Well, I don't really talk about what happened after that."

Neko looked at her. It was the most words she'd ever heard Jules speak at one time. The woman was making an argument for herself in the only way she knew how.

AT THE BUS STOP WHERE NEKO AND JULES DISEMBARKED, THERE WAS A line of buskers. One played an old protest ballad on an acoustic guitar while the other two, wearing buckskin fringe, encouraged people to join their game of three-card monte. There was something farcical about the crumbs of culture that clung to this place, but Neko still dropped a thin roll of scratch into the busker's guitar case, failing to suppress the pull of the past.

She was in fifth grade when her father became obsessed with street performers. The best were the breakdancers. Her father had good rhythm and the body of a dancer and so, though he was older and never achieved any of the more difficult power moves, he was fun to watch. Once, on a subway platform, Neko and her parents came across a guy performing to funk on his boom box. At one point, he stopped to take a rest, lungs puffing, hands on knees, and so her father filled in. Just dropped down and started hamming it up—some simple windmills and hand hops, a quick deadman float.

Neko remembered thinking it was hilarious until she'd seen her mother's expression. Afterward, her mother whispered to him, "Do you always have to be the center of attention?" And Neko thought, *And do you always have to ruin everything fun?*

WHEN NEKO ROUNDED THE CORNER AND STOPPED IN FRONT OF THE junk store, Jules followed but crossed her arms over her chest. "Thought we were going to buy groceries."

"I need something from Shay first," said Neko.

Shay was a small Black man in his early thirties, beard already graying, whose side hustle was conserving and restoring the more delicate black market finds—items that needed wax baths or electrolysis to safely eliminate rust or other damage. He had a vacuum freezer that turned solid water molecules directly into gas without passing through a liquid stage that might harm the materials.

Inside Shay's shop, Neko and Jules walked by funky old ashtrays, blown-glass Christmas ornaments, and stacks of dusty computer parts and legacy video game consoles to find the proprietor at the counter, a clock open in front of him, tiny tools in his small hands. Without looking up, he said, "This spring right here prevents the energy from escaping all at once, only releasing it in ticks and tocks."

"A metaphor's in there somewhere," said Neko, kissing him on the cheek.

She was there to pick up a fifteenth-century incense burner they'd found in a Financial District chapel, and she had to practically pry the chunk of gold filagree from Shay's grip, which was how it always was, as though it were physically painful for him to release anything he'd worked on.

"Do you still have that old collection of atlases?" asked Neko. She and Iggy kept a stockpile of paper maps. There was no signal in the Sink and connecting to satellite could raise unwanted attention. They went analog as much as possible and always trained one of their apprentices as crew cartographer. Neko remembered barking loudly—so rare, a real laugh—when she saw that Jules had scribbled *Here There Be Dragons* off the Atlantic seaboard.

Shay pointed to a row of askew shelving along the back wall. Eventually Neko located a crinkled map that encompassed the area northeast of New York City around the Long Island Sound. It was old—from before the rise in seawater had reconfigured the coastline—but better than nothing.

"Why do you need this?" Jules smoothed out the wrinkles in the map with her palm, studying it.

"The government wants some items moved quickly from the marshlands, and they're paying extra. We might go north for our next lark." The lie came easily.

"You mean the marshlands here?" asked Jules, pointing to a spot on the map, which showed the area as it had been before, miles from water.

"You know that sector?"

Jules cocked an eyebrow. "Pretty well."

Neko nodded, taking in this information.

Back on the street, Jules said, "If you took me along, you wouldn't need that map."

"Why do you want to stay with our crew so badly?"

She grunted. "You act like it's easy. There aren't any licenses left, it's hard to find a crew that goes black, and even harder to find one not run by an asshole."

Not run by an asshole! Neko was flattered.

AT THE BEE MARKET, FRUITS AND VEGETABLES WERE THE STARS OF the show—glistening fist-sized apples, Bosc pears, onions, okra, coarse bags of coffee and cashews and flax seeds. A small crate of starfruit was displayed behind a register to discourage shoplifting, even with the armed guards milling about. Because the vast majority of pollinators were now extinct, the fruits and vegetables at the Bee Market had mostly been hand-pollinated, which was why they were so rare and costly.

Neko stopped to squeeze some half-decent-looking plums that might do well in their dehydrator. A government functionary in a military collar was hogging the aisle between stands with her Lux—a machine that was part scooter and part grocery cart—and Jules arm-checked the swivel-headed robot into a pole. The woman gave them a look that said it was exactly what she expected from border trash.

Jules pointed to a stall hawking miniature jars of jam. "Did you ever have the books about the bear who arrives in London with a note pinned to his jacket and a love of marmalade?"

"You mean Paddington?"

"As a kid I thought his marmalade was as imaginary as talking bears." Jules shrugged. "Growing up in the Sink with picture books from Before, it was hard to know what was real, what was pretend." She told Neko how piano lessons and sleepover parties were as strange and mystical to her as superheroes and dinosaurs. The idea of a zoo where you could watch elephants through the grid of a cage or see a flamingo tucking one leg beneath pink feathers was as fantastical as spaceships to Mars or schools for magicians. "And if you asked the adults: Is bubble gum real? Do bears eat porridge and marmalade and live inside houses? They would laugh at first, then get sad."

Neko groaned. "Please, stop."

Neko was thirty-eight years old. And yet sometimes, in moments like these, it felt as though she had only just arrived in this adult body, in this messed-up place. How did one make decisions or work toward a future? How had she done it all these years and why couldn't she remember? Everything suddenly felt new and impossible. Maybe this was how her mother had felt, and Neko was only now beginning to understand, now that it was too late.

Maybe keeping on Jules and Harriet would make it easier for them to get a Land Rover lark in the north or maybe not. It would certainly make Iggy less unhappy.

Neko turned back toward the stall. "For God's sake, let's buy some marmalade to celebrate a new lark in a new sector." She picked up a palm-sized jar, inspecting the handwritten ingredient list.

Jules grabbed her arm from behind. "You'll let us stay?"

Neko shrugged. "Now you know our secret, patented techniques. If we fired you, we'd have to kill you."

Jules didn't crack a smile. "But you never even let us meet the clients."

"Relax, Jules. Just razzing," she said, suddenly not so sure Jules didn't consider her one of the asshole bosses after all. Neko turned back to the tower of jam, the proprietor of which was eyeing them up and down. "If we take you along, will you help us navigate the terrain?"

"Yes."

"This has to go perfectly. Without a hitch."

"Yes, yes." Jules gently slid in front of Neko and turned to face the stall. "We'll take one of each flavor. And this lady's paying."

Neko pursed her lips. That was more than she'd planned to buy. She looked at Jules, standing there so determined. Neko opened her canvas bag to receive the bounty.

13

THE KITCHEN LIGHT BURNED ABOVE THE TINY TABLE WHERE THE four of them sat staring at the first course.

"What is it?" asked Jules, sniffing at the food.

Harriet squinted at her plate. "Think I ate this in Salento as a kid? One time my parents rented us a house that was supposed to be a villa but turned out to be this farm collective and . . ."

"Squash blossoms," answered Iggy.

The delicate, pale green and orange undulations looked both vegetable and animal, flower and squid. Neko picked one up with her fingers, savored it with her eyes closed. When she'd seen them for sale at the Bee Market she'd bought them for Iggy, even though it further blew their provisions budget. He'd told her once they were his favorite, in part because of the way they tasted but also due to the way they looked, so elegant, like dancers.

The rest of the meal consisted of dried mackerel casserole moistened with cream of mushroom soup, spiced to hide the processed cheese. Green beans from their neighbors' "war garden." Cobbler with canned peaches. Bathtub hooch.

This was the first time they'd had Harriet and Jules over for dinner in Fringe. Their quarters were cramped, filled with supplies, with Iggy's books and Neko's shrine.

Iggy raised a Mason jar in the air. "To a lucrative haul." His time alone seemed to have improved his mood.

"Hear, hear." Neko clinked her jar to his and then reached across the table to toast Jules and Harriet, ignoring the new awkwardness that silted the air like pollen.

"I've never been fired and then invited over to a nice dinner," said Harriet before tucking into the food.

"Anyway, we never officially fired you. We just said we were *considering* firing you," said Iggy.

It was the time of day when everything was in transition. Sunlight angled through the dormer window, dazzling a spiderweb strung along the corner of the ceiling. Over the years, Neko had spent a lot of energy on not getting her hopes up, but today she felt the twinge of real possibility.

Harriet nodded. "So, back into the fray, I guess."

Dogs barked outside.

"This lark is different," said Iggy quietly. "We signed a contract to move rare earth materials from an abandoned manufacturing plant that had become compromised by saltwater creep. Past Long Island."

"There a shadow gig?" asked Jules, refilling her glass with rotgut hooch, despite being on medication for ringworm and a gut parasite.

"Yes. And it's a tight turnaround. Long Island dive and then we ride out to the Watering Hole immediately after. There's a ticking clock on this one," said Neko, hoping that would be enough detail for now.

Iggy put down his silverware. "I want to be clear. You don't have to sign on to this lark. We'll still help you find a good crew if you decide to pass."

There was a hush in the room. Then Jules, eyes on her plate, put her hand over Harriet's and squeezed. "We're in."

Harriet didn't agree or disagree.

Neko was busy thinking of her own plans. Eyes on the prize.

AFTER DINNER, WHILE NEKO AND IGGY HAULED DISHES TO THE SINK, the two young women wandered around, pawing through their stuff: A calligraphy set. A Rubik's Cube, solved. A *Star Wars* Rey action figure still in its box. What narrative were they privately spinning based on the detritus of her and Iggy's lives?

Jules stopped in front of the Kehinde Wiley print Iggy had tacked to the wall: a young black man wearing camo pants and red sweatbands on his wrists, a golden cape flapping behind him as he rode a white horse in front of a rich red-and-gold background.

"I don't get it," said Jules.

Harriet stood beside her with a salad bowl perched on her palm. "I think the artist is riffing on the famous painting of Napoleon crossing the Alps? But, obviously, with a guy from the streets . . ."

There was a silence as they all stared at the print.

"I still don't get it," said Jules.

"To be honest, I don't either," said Iggy. "But I love it." He pointed to the red and gold. "When we move to the Inside I want to get this design as a wallpaper."

Harriet laughed. "Planning to lift some gold foil from the Smithsonian or something?"

"They have cool wallpaper in *One Family*."

Harriet rolled her eyes. "How many times do I have to tell you? Television is not real life. You know this."

She walked to the bookshelf. "Have you read all these

books?" She ran her hand along the row of creased and broken spines. She put down the salad bowl and began pulling tomes: *The Wretched of the Earth* and *Collected Stories of William Faulkner, Spaghetti Westerns: The Opera of Violence* and *History and Culture of the Plains Indians*.

"No, though I'm trying," he said. "The guy who runs the Ice House library, the professor, recommended most of them. They're sometimes a little much to parse on my own."

"I haven't read any of the theory, but I did read this in school." Harriet held up *One Hundred Years of Solitude*. "It starts with a field trip to see ice."

Iggy slid the books back onto the shelf. "I'll try that one next."

Sometimes Neko played out conversations in her head that Iggy and her parents might have had about Terrence Malick, about Blind Lemon Jefferson, about Basquiat and Agnes Martin. She thought they would have liked being autodidacts together.

"Did you grow up with books? What were your parents like?"

He shrugged. "My father was an engineer from a long line of engineers on Baja. Mama was a graphic designer for an advertising company."

He didn't tell them what he'd told Neko, which was that his parents had wanted different lives—his father to be a poet, his mother an artist—but they'd been raised to be practical. His mother's family had been poor migrant workers who worshipped the stable paycheck; his father's family had been wealthy back in Mexico and scorned even the whiff of bohemian tendencies. Iggy was about to start college when they died in the Sacramento Valley Wildfires.

"What did you study?" asked Harriet.

"I wanted to major in art history, maybe literature or creative writing."

"Why didn't you?"

"Well. I didn't end up going to college."

Neko tried to busy herself with the stereo, picking out a playlist, so as not to stare at Harriet and Jules as they dug around like archaeologists piecing together a foreign culture.

"I like this," said Jules quietly, nodding toward the speakers. It was the Nightjars. "What about the last album—your mom's solo thing. Can we listen to that one?"

"*The Wreckage*? No. From the master recording you have to make a mother and then use that to produce a stamper to press into vinyl," said Neko. She could still remember bits from when her mom was working on the songs. Something about how Calypso was pissed because the male gods took mortal women with impunity but she was forced to let Odysseus go free. About how the two sea monsters Scylla and Charybdis have a motivation for their rage against the humans who try to sail through their strait: They are angry at the warming of the waters, angry that they're cooking slowly like lobsters.

"Your parents," said Jules. "They were famous, right? Were you rich?"

"Enough to live well in Manhattan. But we didn't have a lot of *things*. My parents were weird about what they spent money on." Neko remembered wanting to apply to the private school where some of her friends were going and how her mother had shrugged, said fine, she could take the subway to the entrance test, but that there would be no fancy tutors. Neko had exploded—spitting about how unfair it was that she'd pay for a guitar teacher who'd recorded with St. Vincent but not tutors for her education. She'd blamed her mother even though her father had been standing there, too.

Jules shrugged. "I just can't imagine having a mother like that. So different from you."

Neko had never really thought of herself as inherently different from her mother, though maybe she was. Instead, it was the world they lived in that had changed. Jules probably imagined Jenny Sweet as fancy and art-damaged in a way that seemed so foreign to their lives as mudlarks. But her celebrity had just been a great disguise, conjured when it suited her. This is what Neko had come to understand. It was a public facade to protect her mother's private heart. Like the cracked leather jacket she'd worn on stage, then shrugged off at the apartment door.

"She wasn't some junkie diva who foisted her offspring on a nanny, if that's what you mean. She came to all my games even though she hated sports." What she thought but didn't say: *And look how I repaid her.*

"Was she pretty?" asked Harriet. "I bet she was hot."

Neko didn't know how to talk about the physical existence of her mother, especially now that she might be alive. "Kind of. I don't know."

Even though it was often how she had judged the mothers of friends, it hadn't occurred to Neko to think of her own mother as pretty or not pretty. Her mother's body was too known. Like how you can't truly see your hometown until you move away. Theirs had been a house of nakedness, neither of her parents making any effort to hide their bodies. She remembered watching her mother after a shower, toweling dry her long brown hair. Faint blue veins behind the knees, ripples of goosebumped skin as she bent down for her jeans in a pile on the floor. Her smell—always a hint of pungent soap but something else, too, some animal scent that lurked in her hair and along the nape of her neck when Neko leaned in to hug her.

What her mother had thought of her own body, she couldn't say. Her mother had never complained or preened. Neko had a vague memory of seeing her looking at herself in the long mirror that hung on the closet door, eyes sharp. But when she noticed Neko, she'd turned and flexed her biceps before lunging toward her. "Fee, fi, fo, fum, I smell the blood of an Englishman!"

What had it cost her mother to display herself without judgment?

THE WRECKAGE

Track 2: "Tales of Troy"

"Hey, Ms. Sweet," asked the preteen loudly slurping cereal next to Neko at the counter of Jenny's kitchen, "what was it like to be a rock star?"

"Was? Past tense?" Jenny paused in her job unloading the dishwasher (a luxury item in New York if there ever was one).

"I mean, like, when you were young. Did people throw panties at you?"

"It wasn't exactly that kind of music . . ."

"Why not?"

"Well, the Nightjars, we're kind of rock adjacent. You know, dissonance? No wave? Post-punk?" She shrugged. "Noise rock?"

"Not really."

"Our first album included a sitar and a chainsaw."

The things she told the girls:

The first studio where they recorded was upstairs from a pawn shop, with windows grated against the junkies roaming the neighborhood outside and a hallway that smelled of piss. It was a magical place, she told them.

Jesse was the only one who kind of knew what he was doing at that point, snaking cords to the multitrack deck. But it didn't matter. They were just pumped to be there. Cutting a record. *Cut, cut, cut,* Max yelled, swinging his Gretsch around like the axe it was. They were kids.

Early on, some critics suggested they didn't really know how to play their instruments, but that wasn't true. They just didn't know how to record their instruments in a professional sort of way. They didn't have a producer or sound engineer. And they liked the rough edges. Jenny stood on that sticky carpet and pretended to understand love and heartbreak, trying to spawn desire by singing about it. Glitter came out of their mouths like fire, that was the truth, she told the girls. When she listened to that album now, she was amazed by the amount of reverb.

The thing she didn't tell them: how she pulled Max into the back of the van before each studio session, lifted up her T-shirt, and unbuttoned his pants. He was her muse. She thought she needed to feel the heat of his skin in order to find the heat of her art. He ran his tongue along her neck, up tendons and down arteries, and something unfurled inside her, ready, for once in her life. In the studio, he whispered into her ear, "I bet you can't break my heart," and pushed her gently toward the microphone.

That sounded like a challenge, she thought. She opened her mouth and sang.

"It was like I could finally say all the things I'd wanted to say," she told the girls, washing a bowl of berries in the sink and handing it to them. "Yell them, even."

Neko's voice was quiet. "Must be nice."

Jenny's throat caught. She wanted so badly to understand what was going on inside her daughter's mind. But instead of saying what she wanted—that she loved her, that she was trying so hard—her tongue made a different shape: "Raspberries, anyone?" She looked down at them where they glistened in the bowl. "Like tiny, soft hearts."

"Yes, please," said Neko's friend, one of the new friends that Jenny couldn't keep straight.

"What are you wearing, by the way?" Jenny nodded neutrally toward the friend's Def Leppard T-shirt.

"It's my dad's. He's into heavy metal."

"Right." No reason to tell her that Def Leppard was *not* metal.

"Did you always want to be a singer in a band, Ms. Sweet? Since you were our age?"

What she told them: She told them about the clock radio she got for her birthday one year, and how there was this one station, WHAM, that played stuff the others didn't—Blondie and Devo and the Clash, Psi Com and Joan Jett, even Jawbox. How she felt as though she were tuning in to aliens on another planet. How she lay on her bed for hours listening, taped obscure songs off the radio in the middle of the night. Her bedroom was her world.

She told them that she had been painfully shy in school, but that she'd loved to sing in music class. You could be anonymous when everyone was singing all at once. Just let it all out. Let it go.

What she didn't tell them: How her father had reams of paper in his office, and how she used to steal some of it, drag it to her bedroom like a tail. The whiteness of it, the blankness. How she put words on it in pencil and then pen and then marker. Jenny wouldn't have called it poetry, exactly, but something analogous, something in the same universe.

But it didn't work. She wanted her words to light up like electricity, but they didn't or couldn't. She tore up the paper and braided the pieces, left them under her bed to rot. She looked at the power lines out the window. She listened to cicadas and the boys on their skateboards. She wished for more.

Later, when Max hooked her guitar up to the amp, Jesse stroking the drums with whisks in the background—well, that's when she found it.

And at the time, she thought Max had given it to her.

"Was it crazy when you made a lot of money, you know, when the album came out?"

"Well, the record was more of a flyer for our shows. That's how we survived back then."

"Can Neko and I come with you on tour? Pleeeease!"

What she told them: How they used to drive all night in a cramped van to get to the next gig. Sleeping on people's sofas and floors if they were lucky. All the raccoons and possums and slinking cats prowling the sides of the roads after dark. How even though they were becoming friends with a lot of the Northwest indie bands, and those guys were always trying to get them to move coasts, they stayed in the Northeast because there were so many cities with good clubs you could drive to from New York. *That's important when you're poor,* she told them. *Our first office was pretty much Max's mother's Chrysler LeBaron. The van, our first purchase with credit. And yet we were the lucky ones.*

What she didn't tell them: How it felt that night at T.T. the Bear's in Cambridge, Mass. Pulling up for sound check and seeing their name written on the whiteboard—yes, a freakin' whiteboard—under the green-and-gold awning.

In the alley before the show, they ate soggy sandwiches, Jenny pulling off slices of tomato and slinging them at Max and Jesse. Her jeans were filthy; they hadn't done laundry in forever. Nervous laughter. A set list etched in Sharpie. Inside, the stage looked like it was made from shit picked up at the dump and then spray-painted black. The PA system was the throne, the speaker cones its supplicants. The smell of beer felt like home.

Jenny took all of that anticipation, the tenderness of her head on Max's lap in the van, the shock of her father in the coffin with a carnation in his pocket, the awe of seeing Cy Twombly's Triumph of Galatea splattered on the canvas, the staticky conspiracies of late night talk radio, all the objects she didn't buy at the flea market, the rent they hadn't paid in two months. She took all of that onstage and split it open like an atom. A thunderclap. A roar. She played her guitar like she was throwing plates against a kitchen wall.

Their job was to spin until a tornado enveloped the whole dirty room, even the bartender and the people trying to play pool, good luck with that. They lit up until they burned the place down.

And the crowd went wild.

Neko yawned and stretched as though bored. "Mom, why do you only tell the stories of the crappy vans and shitty clubs?"

"Language."

Neko rolled her eyes.

"And anyway, that's the stuff that people like to hear about, it's the most interesting stuff."

"Save it for the fanzine."

Now Jenny was the one rolling her eyes.

The friend, with her chin in her palms, said, "Neko, my mom is an accountant."

Neko jumped down from the stool, tossed her hair. "Trade you."

Jenny turned back to the dishwasher so her daughter wouldn't see her face.

The things she said,
The things she didn't say,
Like two piles of marbles that grow
Until the one grows so large that it spills and clatters
and covers the floor in wretchedness

14

THAT NIGHT THE CREW ARRIVED AT THE TOWER, STICKING UP LIKE A middle finger, the one high-rise in Fringe, for the monthly "charity auction."

Neko walked into the lobby first, bringing up their invitation code on her device, while the others unloaded the goods. A hologram woman appeared and exclaimed, "Neko Sweet! Tired of being thirsty? Free yourself from water dependence and clone your brain today!" The woman wore a red dress and shimmered in unreality.

Neko froze. She'd purged her device of its identity chip, and facial recon was illegal outside of military use, but maybe even that was unregulated here.

"Imagine what it's like to be free of the need to sleep. Free of the need to eat." The ethereal saleswoman seemed to move closer, whispering in Neko's ear. "Free."

Neko could almost feel breath on her neck. "Are *you* a cloned brain?" she asked. "Out shilling for the company?"

The hologram smiled coyly. "Cloning before death means not a single brain cell or memory will be lost in the process."

"Are you a slave or are they paying you to lie in wait for anyone who walks by?"

"My mission is nothing less than eternal life."

Neko felt her face get hot. "But what is your name? You know mine. Tell me yours." She tried to move inside the hologram, but it flickered and shrank away. She spun around, trying to look the woman in the eye. "Tell me!"

Then the woman put her hand on Neko's shoulder and it felt real, substantial. Maternal. Neko yelped and jumped back.

"Hey," said Harriet, whose hand it really was. "It's just a simulation." She moved them out of the range of the hologram. People were staring. "Maybe you've been in the Sink a little too long."

Neko tried to shake a sinister feeling. All the ways in which the ghosts in her life were trying to materialize.

Harriet shuffled them toward the elevator. "We call companies like those soulsuckers. I saw a television program where they inserted a woman's memories into her clone, and the clone had a total nervous breakdown. Full-on mental collapse. And I saw an interview with a supposed downloaded brain. They had a mainframe hooked up so this guy's mind, or whatever, could answer questions."

"What did he say?" Neko wondered what else she'd missed in her years in the Sink.

"He said he missed sneezing. Funny, right? They're all such scams."

NEKO'S CREW WORKED THE BLACK MARKET FROM TWO ANGLES: straightforward jobs, often handed to them by Chaplin, involving unapproved goods specifically desired by someone on the Inside. And then there was the forgotten, the discarded—the "bushmeat," as they called it—left behind by those now dead or without the means to pay for its retrieval. They arrived at the party with roller suitcases filled with a coin collection and a flute, some jewelry, antique knives sheathed in bronze cases, the fifteenth-century incense burner, and a beaver fur coat—all to fence "for the children." Neko's watch vibrated as they entered the penthouse apartment, an indication that their signals were now being scrambled.

As they arranged their goods on the auction tables, Harriet began narrating the current Fringe fashion, which tended toward a shabby gentility. Haute couture meets the working-class dandy. "I'm seeing gabardine. I'm seeing pinstripe and puff-fold pocket squares. Hey, look, there's a fascinator."

"I feel like those are just a bunch of words you wanted to say," said Neko, though she herself was wearing a bowler hat and fake-crocodile derby shoes.

The auctioneer was in a corner of the room, talking into a headset to the secretive clientele who were, presumably, watching back at home. A camera panned over the first table of goods, each labeled with a calligraphed code on thick paper that linked it back to the seller. "The theme of the night might be dragons," the auctioneer was saying whimsically in an accent that verged on French. "I mean, look at this pair of antique brooches, their eyes rubies of the finest quality. Natural rubies, not lab-grown here, people . . ."

Neko's crew quickly backed out of the auction room, not wanting to inadvertently end up on camera.

"No brawls tonight, please," Iggy said, looking pointedly at Harriet.

In the living room, the music was loud, vibrating the floor-to-ceiling windows. Neko dragged Iggy onto the dance floor.

As they moved their bodies, she studied the beautiful couple—

well preserved and edited by the scalpels of the damned—who owned this penthouse apartment. They were extraordinarily rich—and these days, to be rich was inherently to be an asshole—and she thought of their private planes and private security details. Their spiked hair was literally tipped in gold.

"If my mother is actually there, imprisoned in an underground bunker in the middle of nowhere, someone like that brought her there," she said into Iggy's ear.

He held her tighter. "You think whoever she hitched a ride with back from Burning Man didn't take her to New York?"

"It's so far-fetched, I know, but . . . ?"

"Why would anyone do that?"

She shook her head. "The alternative is that she went willingly. Left me and never came back." She said it aloud, but she couldn't actually believe that.

Iggy flung her body away and into a twirl and then reeled her back in. They danced until sweat poured over their bodies. Until the floor became too crowded for their signature laser beams and karate kicks. Until Iggy made the sign for water, and she followed him to the marble kitchen.

"I feel guilty." He held a glass under the Pure Water dispenser.

She looked at him quizzically, pretending she didn't understand. She rooted through the hors d'oeuvres until she found a fig and held it in her mouth.

"Delivering goods to a fugitive bunker, wandering around the northern Sink. We're putting Harriet and Jules in too much danger. And, perhaps worse, they think we're doing them a favor."

"Not a favor. An opportunity," she said, gently touching his face with the pads of her fingertips. His skin was so warm. "It's symbiotic; they help us get to the bunker, and we get Jules and

Harriet more scratch than they could make in a year on a regular crew."

Iggy's face was impossible to read.

"I thought we agreed it was important to see . . . what's there."

"If your mother is there, we'll find her and bring her to the Inside with us." The tiny opal studs laddering his earlobe gleamed in the kitchen light. "I just want you to remember that there are costs. I want you to remember that your mother probably isn't there, and that other people's lives matter, too."

Neko's first instinct was to tell him to go to hell. But she knew what would hurt him more and so, instead, she turned to the room and raised her voice, bowing toward him. "Behold! The moral compass of a generation."

Then she left him in the kitchen with his water.

NEKO FOUND THE BATHROOM AND PEED IN FRONT OF TWO WOMEN—strands of tiny bells woven into their hair so they sounded like wind chimes—as they snorted blow from the countertop. They offered her a line, and she accepted. Neko could get into a good party. She was not like her mother in this way.

She made her way through the apartment, pretending to be an entirely different kind of person than she was. She danced, throwing her head around, and flirted with women in bow ties and men in velvet jackets, pretending to have seen television shows she'd never heard of and bitching about global shortages, the price of meat. Her body was a windup doll. She spun and spun like a dreidel.

Time began to bleed until she looked up and it was four in the morning. They had made a very nice profit at the auction, now over. The hallway bathroom was locked so she found her way into a guest bedroom to look for another one. Two figures were asleep on the bed, dead to the world, buried in comforters and pillows. Harriet and Jules. Suddenly Neko felt a strong urge to join them. To just lie down and sleep.

She remembered napping with her father—in her parents' king or on the floor of the living room on lazy Sunday afternoons, sunlight tracking over them like a dial. Her mother was too high-strung to nap, but there were photographs of Neko and her dad from the time she was an infant face-planted on his chest, zipped in pajamas with a heart-shaped strawberry on the butt, to when she was a gangly preteen, making the letter T with him on the floor, mouth open and drooling. Only now, as she watched Harriet and Jules sleep, shoes still on, arms flung across each other like kindling, did she realize that many of those naps with her father were too early in time for Neko to actually remember. Her mother was the one who had taken the photographs that turned into memory. She the witness to all of those moments. This world still felt like a dream from which she would one day wake up to see her mother's face. Unchanged. Unmarred by what Neko had done to her.

She pulled the door to the room shut behind her on her way out. She left the two women in peace—a rare thing in any world.

HARDLY ANYBODY WAS DANCING ANYMORE, BODIES NOW ARRANGED on sofas, making out or coming down from whatever new drug was on offer. Iggy stood at a sliding glass door, looking over the scalloped skyline. She thought of the time a gorgeous, round woman had asked Iggy, slyly, maybe not knowing he was with someone, if he wanted to come home with her. Neko could see why.

She went to the stereo and typed in the name of the third track on *Wok Hei*, and then she opened the sliding glass door and gently pushed Iggy outside into the night heat, apologizing with her body. On the balcony, she leaned into him, the sinewy chest, the sharp hip bones, the half-moons of dirt beneath his fingernails as his hands reflexively rubbed up and down her arms. She knew she should tell him about her eggs, but she didn't know how.

"Ignacio Villarreal." The poetry of his full name, the way it floated through the mouth, no edges. "*'Please, please, please, please . . .* '" she sang along, loving how her father's voice pulled the word apart until it encompassed everything and everyone that ever was and ever would be—it was a balm. It was an electric prod. It was a loss.

Neko remembered when they'd gone to the Air and Space Museum and her father was handed a space rock for the first time, so much heavier than it looked, and how he'd cried. How he'd held it out to her and said: *This. This.* He'd worn glitter nail polish, and his fingers had shone when he lifted up the meteorite and offered it to her. An incandescent power chord. Then she thought again of the burned girl from the clinic that morning. Raw and flayed, flesh glistening. And of how fire didn't just burn human atoms into air but also left a residue behind, like the juice from an orange. Without gauze to protect her, would the girl stick to walls and chairs, the inner layers of her body unable to differentiate her from the objects she touched? Neko hoped the girl was alive and suspended in a bath of ointment, in a pool of tears, so that nothing could touch her where it hurt the most.

THE WRECKAGE

Track 3: "Violets and Wild Celery"

For years, Max was the air Jenny breathed. Until Neko. When their daughter was born, they became a triangle, a new kind of geometry that was more beautiful than the line they'd been before. But not simpler. Life became a Kate Bush song, baroque and exquisite and brutal.

Counterintuitively, motherhood made social life a little easier for Jenny. People assumed a baby cramped one's style, especially in New York. But not for her. Before the baby, when they weren't on tour, Jenny often canceled plans last minute with outlandish excuses because she really wanted to stay home and read mystery novels or listen to LPs, lying on the floor with her legs up the wall, chatting with Max or monologuing to the houseplants. She didn't mean to be a flake. Gallery openings, walks along the High Line, late-night sushi dinners—all sounded good at the time she was invited. But as the event neared, social anxiety grew like a strangler fig.

After the baby, Jenny was actually more out in the world, particularly once Neko began shedding naps. When they ran out of things to do with her in the apartment, they'd strap the girl into a complicated modern baby carrier and walk from park to park or meet friends for lunch or get lost for hours in the Museum of Natural History. Jenny felt ambivalent about motherhood but never about being Neko's mother. *Look at these, my childbearing hips. Look at these, my ruby-red ruby lips . . .*

Jenny was pleasantly surprised to find that carrying a baby on her chest was the perfect disguise, an invisibility cloak—nobody recognized her when she was out with Neko. On the other hand, Max was a spectacle when he carried the baby, maybe even more so, and he basked in the special attention lavished on fathers who perform the most basic tasks of parenthood. Looking back, Jenny could see how they'd mistaken the growing affection they felt for their daughter as a growing affection for each other, holding hands as they stepped out on the town, nuzzling the baby and each other as though they were one three-headed beast. Back then, she could never have imagined how spectacularly it would fall apart.

Jesse began to stop by the apartment for non-band reasons, holding the baby while Jenny showered and made herself food.

"Swiss chard and artichokes," he told her, explaining what he was going to grow in his new community garden plot. "Sage and lavender and maybe Icelandic poppies."

"You aren't, like, *on* any Icelandic poppies right now, are you?" Jenny rooted around in the cabinets for *herbes de Provence,* which she put on pretty much everything. She was only partly joking. Jesse was the kind of guy who refused painkillers at the hospital because opioids were "so addictive," but had also been seen slinking off to public housing dens as though he were William Burroughs.

"Don't be crazy." Jesse sat on a stool, Neko tucked into his elbow like a football. "Opium poppies are totally different."

Jenny rolled her eyes. "Tell me again how you managed to get this plot? I know people who have been on the waitlist for years in the LES." She put the water on to boil. They no longer had time to make fancy pour-over coffee in the morning, and Jenny had come to like the crystalline way Nescafé glinted when she opened the canister. And though she couldn't claim the instant coffee was good, it reminded her of being young and abroad for the first time. As though motherhood were also another country.

"The Chinese ladies," said Jesse.

"The Chinese ladies."

"The ones who dance in that park in Dimes Square."

"Yeah." Jenny tilted her head. The old women met there in the mornings, moving their arms and hands in sync to the music on someone's boom box, some sort of Asian square dance. She and Max stopped there occasionally with coffee and a bagel on the weekend to watch. "What does that have to do with community gardening?" Jenny flipped an egg in the pan, butter browning and sizzling.

Jesse yawned. "Everything. They have the inside track to all the gardens around there. I started joining their dancing a few mornings a week, and I think they gave me a garden plot just to stop me from coming around."

"Jesus Christ."

He pretended to nibble on Neko's belly. "My plants will be as tender as this here tender babe."

Jenny slid the eggs onto plates and looked up at her friend. They didn't say more. In his arms, baby Neko began to cry.

It sounded silly to admit, but when Neko was an infant, Jenny considered them to be close.

She remembered those early "conversations," where she explained to Neko that for some songs you actually wanted old strings on your guitar, ones that were nice and muted, because new strings could sound too twangy. And if you played one note for long enough you could hear a pattern of subharmonics that might actually be the voice of God. How nineties hip-hop was the best—"N.Y. State of Mind," "Life's a Bitch"—because it was more minimal, contained fewer strains of R & B. *Neko, darling, here is an old rotary phone, see how you turn the numbers like a wheel? You can't call anybody on it anymore, but there was a time. And phone books! Don't even get me started on phone books. And, look,* she would whisper into her daughter's ear, *don't tell your father, but I'm actually a huge fan of Brian Eno. Huge.*

Back then, when she passed the East Village store owners pulling up their metal grates and hauling boxes from the sidewalk cellars, or druggies huddled on stoops, or cigarette butts and other flotsam and jetsam of the night, she thought about how the baby's biological detritus now littered the passageways of her own body. Her daughter's cells circulated through her veins and always would.

As a toddler, so slowly it was hard to pinpoint when it fully crested, Neko began to show a preference for Max. She ran to him full tilt when he opened the door, shoving her body into his grinning like mad. She endured the company of Jenny but preferred her father for games, for bedtime, for most things. In the middle of the night, when Jenny went to rock her back to sleep after a bad dream, she would cry forlornly: "Daaaddddy." It was a type of pain Jenny wasn't prepared for—rejection, insecurity. She tried to expand her personality—funny voices, silly dancing—but one-upmanship was impossible with someone like Max, a natural-born performer.

Jenny hadn't grown up with two parents, so she had no internal model for how one might love two people in different ways. And she'd grown up without a mother—dead in childbirth—so she wondered, naturally, if she wasn't doing it all wrong. She began studying the other women at the playground, trying to copy their moves—the ways they scolded, or comforted.

It was Max's mother, Dilly, who reassured Jenny that the phase was normal. "Honey, that's how they work you. On again, off again. You just gotta wait it out. Kids take their mamas for granted, but kids always need their mamas." And Dilly was right. Neko came back around.

Max was close to his mother, adored her, so Jenny began studying her, too, in the hopes of learning what it *meant* to be a *good* mom.

In this case, it meant cooking the food your son loved as a child every time he visited. It meant letting him take you for granted. It meant insisting on the manners you'd taught him, no matter how antiquated, and it meant putting all the attention you'd once lavished on your progeny into your plants after the children left home.

And Dilly's garden was *gorgeous*. She specialized in roses, despite the fact that they were so much trouble and bloomed for such a short period of time. Jenny loved listening to her talk about her flowers: damask, gallica, hybrid perpetual, floribunda, Sutter's Gold and Blanche Mallerin and Neige Parfum, rose hip and rose musk.

"You know," Jenny told her, eating leftover chicken standing up in her mother-in-law's kitchen, "Hip and Musk would be a good band name."

"Honey, come sit down," said Dilly, laying out napkins in seasonal napkin rings. "This is what dining tables are for."

"Sorry," said Jenny, fork half raised. Chagrined.

Growing up, she and her father had slurped bowls of saucy

pasta at the kitchen counter, listening to his Dolly Parton and Steely Dan records. Somehow it had felt less lonely standing up. (Maybe that was why Jenny loved food trucks—Korean, Mexican, Middle Eastern, whatever. Some of the trucks in their neighborhood had loyal followings, usually men who hung about, sitting on the curb, eating and waiting for some sort of delivery gig. She liked to give one of them cash and ask them to order her something. Jenny never sat with the loyal following to eat—wouldn't dream of imposing—but she'd sometimes raise a taco or whatnot in thanks, the way you might tip a hat.)

At one of Dilly's sit-down dinners, which Jenny learned to enjoy, Dilly went on and on about planting a row of cabbage roses—it was all she talked about.

"I even found the most stunning rabbit head when I went to dig the hole for the last bush. Some fox, I assume, left it for . . ."

Jenny imagined the cabbage rose must be a rather sad and quotidian variety. "'Cabbage rose' sounds kind of homely," she mumbled. Something about the word *cabbage*.

Dilly corrected her with vehemence: "Lord, no, sweetheart! One cabbage rose is worth five other roses. Literally." She told Jenny that's why they were so rare, even in wedding centerpieces. They were called cabbage roses because they were perfectly round and dense with petals. "A perfect fist of a flower . . ."

Listening to her go on, Jenny smiled and thought: This was what it meant to Dilly to be a mother. It meant being entrusted with the care of the cabbage rose. Understanding its potential even when there were no blooms. Tending it. Tender. Tend. Leaving it to grow in the soil for others to admire. Leaving it to the elements when you had no other choice and praying against a hard freeze. Remaining optimistic that the work would be worth it.

Jenny thought about Calypso's garden in *The Odyssey*—

verdant grapevines, rills of water, lavish blooms—and it reminded her of Dilly. Years later, she wrote the song "Violets and Wild Celery" as a gardening guide for goddesses, the lyrics borrowed from conversations with her mother-in-law.

When Dilly died suddenly of a brain aneurysm, the cabbage rose was not in season. How Jenny would have loved to scatter the old woman's grave with those flowers, which she'd come to love, too, thick as peonies and more fragrant.

When Neko began to pull away from Jenny again, Dilly was no longer there to reassure her. Neko was old enough now to know better than to say she preferred her father, but it was obvious in the way she orbited him like a moon. Went to him for help with homework, for fashion advice. Snuggled with him on family movie night. Made fun of him and chased him around the kitchen with a wooden spoon, laughing maniacally. Before each basketball game, he'd say to her, "I bet you can't break my heart."

Neither Jenny nor Max gave two shits about sports, but he was better at faking it, one of the benefits of growing up in a world where sports were a main currency of male friendship.

After a playoff win against a prissy private school, Neko met Jenny's high five with a limp palm. Still, Jenny tried: "You were like the Mailman, you really *delivered*."

Neko ignored her.

"You know, like Karl Malone." Jenny looked at Max for confirmation. "He was called the Mailman, right?"

"That's right, hon. That's right."

But he and Neko were already moving away down the bleachers, discussing the pros and cons of zone defense.

Jenny had always been happy to let Max have the spotlight in terms of the Nightjars, even preferred it. When the fans flocked to him, fine; when their only daughter did, it broke her heart. *What kind of mother?* The refrain was always in her head. How long did Jenny hold on with tight fists out of fear that, if they split up, Neko would choose him? How long did she spend waiting for things to go back to how they'd been before? Waiting to feel like a family again?

And if I wanted I could
I'd tender them up
And I'd give the violets faces

15

STANDS OF BLACK POPLARS AND LOBLOLLY PINES STOOD BLEACHED and blackened—ghost forests, killed from the roots up by the advancing salt water. Velvety tufts of cordgrass and black needle-rush were snaking their way through, taking over everything. Neko felt there was something worse about the wild decay out here—as though the entire planet had been abandoned.

They had to stop frequently to remove brush or navigate roadways rippling with the roots of sweet gum and sugar maple, and, even with four-wheel drive, the Land Rover was slow and jostled like mad. Neko drove—Iggy or Neko always drove, since Jules and Harriet had been born after the ubiquity of self-driving cars. Iggy had taught them how, but they both white-knuckled the steering wheel, making everyone nervous.

IT WAS JUST AFTER NIGHTFALL WHEN THEY CROSSED INTO WHAT HAD once been Connecticut and arrived at the inland side of the channel where they would dive the next morning. In the distance was an old electronics manufacturing plant and storage facility, the loading docks and entryway already underwater.

Their official gig was to rescue the rare earth minerals left inside the carcass of a building, haul back whatever was salvageable before it was entirely inundated.

Westchester County had always been a different world from Manhattan—Yonkers, the Rockefeller Estate, dickhead commuters with more money than God—and Neko always forgot how close it really was, just up the FDR to I-95, just northwest of Long Island Sound.

They set up camp in a parking lot of what was left of this "bedroom community" (*Such a funny term,* thought Neko) to avoid the sticky marshland. The three women sat around a trash can fire while Iggy slept stretched out on a sleeping bag nearby. The rotary machine purred quietly as Neko carved out a two-headed snake along Harriet's triceps, occasionally wiping off the extra ink with a paper towel soaked in green soap. Harriet wore only a bra, revealing the first tattoo nestled between her shoulder blades: a floating jellyfish, chosen, she'd said, because it looked spectral but delivered a sting you could feel. Neko silently admired how classically beautiful the young woman was—the undulating muscles of her back, the curve and flesh of her hips, the long tendons of her neck.

"Next," said Neko, removing the needle from her machine. She gestured for the two apprentices to switch places.

Harriet stood, inspecting the snake, ringed by inflamed skin. But Jules didn't move. The idea had been for the two of them to get matching ink.

Eventually, Harriet noticed Jules's immobility. "It's all right if you're not ready."

Jules nodded. In the soft flicker of firelight, she resembled a shy child, with her boyish haircut and almond eyes. This was not the first time Jules had backed out of a crew tattoo. Surely, thought Neko, she wasn't afraid of the needle. Maybe it was a fear of being marked. Of the permanence of it. Or the fear of being tied to someone else.

Neko could understand that.

She also knew that if you wanted a mudlark's history, tattoos were one way to get it. On her thirtieth birthday, she'd had a cake tattooed on her thigh rather than eating one and, a year later, when she became anemic, a juicy, marbled steak on her forearm. A history of hunger.

DURING THE NIGHT, IT BEGAN TO RAIN, AND SO THE CREW MOVED from the parking lot into the cramped vehicle, an acrid smell rising from their bodies as the hours passed. Neko's talent for being able to pass out anywhere was rewarded on nights like this, though several times Iggy had to nudge her to change positions because she was snoring.

By early morning, they were awake, restless and sore. Iggy, sitting in the front passenger seat, passed a sleeve of jerky to Harriet and Jules in the back, and Neko, feeling chilled, shifted her cold hands to between his legs to warm them. The emerging patter of birdsong signaled dawn, and they put out the solar cells to charge their electronics, then began.

The dive groundwork took longer than usual because they didn't have a prepped dock or rope lines. Harriet and Jules were quiet but precise, as if they might prove their worth by doing everything right. Harriet's perfect penmanship marked routes to the targets on the maps. Jules operated the laser level and surveying rod to estimate the best placement for their jetty.

To Iggy, Neko complained: "This is an annoying detour."

"It's the closest lark I could find at short notice. We had to have some reason to deliver to the Watering Hole, and this is it." The look he gave her stopped any further complaints.

EVERYTHING WAS READY.

Neko was usually able to clear her head before a dive, but now her head was swimming in the past. When Neko finally free-fell into the frigid ocean channel, she thought of an afternoon from her childhood at a cold spring-fed pool. She remembered standing at the edge of the natural pool, paralyzed, her mother beside her, holding her hand as they leapt forward. The cold, liquid shock had taken her breath away at first, but then she'd swum. Neko's mother had mostly taught her things it turned out she had no need for—how to write a thank-you card, how to name her emotions, how to kick a soccer ball into a net. But she had also taught her this: to close her eyes and jump.

Beneath the surface, the crew allowed their belt weights to take them below the current. Like a flock of birds, they mimicked the person in front, turning and kicking in near unison, crossing over the crumbling remnants of a snaking coastal road, floating above the ravaged roofs of seafood shacks or whatever these buildings had once been, eventually swimming through the underwater bay doors and hauling themselves up onto the concrete steps in the center of the manufacturing plant.

The windowless facility was dark. They popped on their beams. Neko kept double-checking the names on the list because they all sounded the same: samarium, terbium, scandium. The minerals were sought after as components in all sorts of things—catalytic converters and monitors and magnets and rechargeable batteries—so the government had mudlarks scouring every possible place where even small quantities might still be stored.

An hour later, struggling with a case of lanthanum disks, Harriet groaned. "This fucking blows."

Neko tried to wipe sweat from her eyes. "Do you have to say aloud everything that crosses your mind?"

Iggy, who was sorting bottles of neodymium granules nearby, clucked like a mother hen.

"Did you guys notice the underwater flock cables we swam past?" asked Jules. "On the other side of that bridge? I figured Harriet and I could grab them on the way back if you guys are good to lug out this mess."

Flock cables were valuable finds. Neko and Iggy shrugged in agreement.

After zipping the rare earth materials into waterproof neoprene bags, the crew strapped on their tanks. Neko and Iggy attached the bags to leads on their wrists while Harriet and Jules kicked off west to retrieve the cables.

Iggy and Neko descended, engorged dry bags floating behind them like wraiths, and about halfway across the channel Neko checked her oxygen gauge—it read only 5 percent full. Had they spent longer than planned underwater?

Neko signaled to ask Iggy his levels, and he signed back a number four times what her needle read. *Shit,* she thought. There must be a leak. She showed him her gauge and then unhooked the dry bag from her wrist, handing it off to him—she needed to reduce her drag—and looked up to the distant ripple of light on the surface. They would have to ascend where they were instead of swimming back to their entry point.

Bodies upright, Neko and Iggy began kicking. They faced each other, and she focused on Iggy's eyes, framed by the mask. She pictured the way he squirmed when he was being tickled. She pictured the chubbier, baby-faced version of Iggy she'd first seen on that hiking trail two decades ago, before his body hardened into lean efficiency. She used these images to distract herself, to slow her breath. But fear is its own runaway train, and soon she could detect the thinning of the breathing gas.

Iggy pulled her closer, maneuvering their bodies so as not to become tangled in the lines to the dry bags, and then he held out his demand valve. They began to share air, handing the mouthpiece back and forth like a dance. They rose alongside their combined column of air bubbles.

Breathe. Pull. Slow.

Don't panic.

The light. Almost there.

At the surface, Neko barely had time to take in one fierce gulp of air before being forced to swim hard against the water that threatened to push them toward open ocean. They moved parallel to the current, trying to avoid the eddies where nails and shards of glass and other debris gathered and swirled.

Iggy was falling behind. Neko turned and realized that the full dry bags were making it too hard for him. She reached out to take one from him but couldn't get close enough to unclip it. She took her Z-knife and cut the lead. Neko tried to wrap the rope around her arm, but a sudden wave slapped at her face and pushed the dry bag into the main force of the tide.

"Shit, motherfucker." The bag floated out of reach.

After she and Iggy managed to pull themselves onto a protruding rooftop, they used beacons to signal their location to Harriet and Jules, and then they waited, the sun bludgeoning them as it turned toward the horizon, the shimmering ocean spinning away, roiling and unmistakably wild. She felt the urge to jump back in and do it all over.

Despite all that had gone wrong, despite the chest still gasping for air and the muscles shaking from strain—or maybe because of them—Neko felt alive. She looked at Iggy and wondered if he would miss this, too.

THE WRECKAGE

Track 4: "The Floating Island"

At the "teen adventure" campsite, Jenny forced herself to make small talk with the other parents while Neko and the rest of the girls banged pots around in an attempt to cook dinner.

The fire looked sallow in the dying light, the air wet with midsummer humidity. The food, when it was ready, was mush, and Jenny pushed it around in the bowl, decided to have beer and mango for dinner instead. In the half-light, she watched a pair of loons touch down on the pond and couldn't help wondering what Max was doing back in the city. But she knew.

The other parents talked about the lack of funding for public education in the city, about volunteer opportunities involving Mandarin and college admissions exam prep companies. They talked about not actually caring where their kids ended up as long as they were happy. Oh, yes. Of course. Happy.

Other people ruined the experience of being in nature. Jenny had wanted to bring Neko camping, just the two of them, but Neko was at the age where she desired the gaze of her peers. When Jenny tried to force the issue, Neko had tossed off: "I don't need to spend two days pretending to be homeless." It was what Max always said about camping.

"Don't you ever get tired of quoting your father?" Jenny had replied, but she'd kept looking for a way. The brochure for this trip had claimed it would teach girls survival skills. And that was what Jenny wanted more than anything: for Neko to survive. Happy, sure. But what was happiness if you weren't strong enough to endure it?

Jenny tried to convince herself that her relationship with her teenage daughter was normal: Maybe the best mothering was invisible, she told herself. Maybe the best mothers were central to their children's lives even though the children would hardly realize it. Weren't the mothers people anguished over after leaving home—the ones dissected in a therapist's office for years—the mothers who made it all about themselves? Their dramatic dance numbers by the living room piano, their lipstick and statement jewelry, the way they lavished you with attention and secrets and then disappeared, always leaving you wanting more. The way they wormed themselves into your friendships, desperate to know everything; the way they took you clothes shopping as though it were a rite of passage. The way they mooned over boys with you, mooned over girls. The way they pretended they understood.

Of course, Jenny got most of these ideas from movies and television and books. What did she know about having a mother?

Jenny had never pined for a baby. She'd been on the pill for years but had become lax as she'd gotten older, feeling less fertile or maybe just lazy. She wasn't sure what had made her walk into the drugstore and buy the pregnancy test—she hadn't had any of the classic symptoms yet, nausea or sore boobs. She just felt wrong. She felt like a Brontë sister lost on the moor.

The baby was due in the summertime. A summer baby made it seem as though God didn't even understand Jenny's basic disposition. She liked to bundle up against the world. To nest and cuddle and eat soup in restaurants built of dark wood. To walk in the snow under lamplight. A summer baby implied sweat in all the creases. It implied arms out, open wide. Unfurling. Jenny had not felt ready to unfurl.

Max was thrilled with the idea of a kid—he didn't share her shock and puzzlement—and so immediately set to trying to cheer her up with giant cups of shave ice. His excitement seemed to have no room for doubts, no room for questions about whether he was fit or whether he even wanted to stay with her for the long haul. They were in Hawaii on tour, and somehow this made things worse, the sun blaring even in autumn, yelling at her to be happy.

One of those mornings she left before dawn for a hike by herself, a trail where she had to pull herself up by a rope in the dark. The little pillboxes on the hill left over from the war were painted in pastels that glowed when the sun rose, and even this was an affront. Nobody and nothing had understood the feeling in her body. Even nature shrugged.

After dinner at the campsite, Jenny and one of the dads were rinsing the dishes.

"I hope it doesn't rain." He nodded toward a guitar case leaning against his tent and then gave her a look. "Thought I'd play some songs for the girls."

Shit, thought Jenny. She'd been identified.

"You play?" he asked, offhandedly, but then he laughed, unable to keep his cool. He was cute with his trimmed beard and toothy smile.

"Sometimes." She rubbed damp hands on her jeans. She couldn't help but smile.

"Maybe I could teach you a few things." Now he was bent over with giggles. The guy was kind of charming, she had to give him that.

"God, let's hope so."

"I'm Brent," he said, reaching out a hand.

"Jenny."

He nodded. "Yes."

As it darkened, everyone sat around the campfire and the trip leader asked them to share what they hoped to get out of the girls-and-parents adventure weekend. There was so much flannel, Jenny felt like she'd been transported back to a Nirvana concert circa 1992. People said the usual things: Change of pace. To learn how to navigate without technology, learn how to set up camp. Confidence. Fresh air.

Jenny tried to catch Neko's eye, but her daughter's face was a mask of practiced indifference. "Bonding," Jenny said when it was her turn, which was part of the truth.

The nice dad, Brent, said when it got to him, "Trees. I spent my childhood surrounded by trees, and I miss them."

Later, while the girls huddled around flashlights, alternating between shrieks and whispers, Brent guided Jenny into the trees. The branches shuddered in the stark moonlight. He reached into his pocket and drew out a marijuana vape pen, offering it to her in both palms.

"This stuff is called Purple Haze."

It felt nice to be flirted with, actually. It felt nice to be offered something for free. Just because. She placed the plastic between her lips. She tried not to think about Max and whether or not he was alone. She didn't really want to know.

The night felt too loud for the woods.

"Can I tell you a secret?" Brent took the vape pen and flipped it through his fingers like a miniature baton.

Oh, no, she thought, this was when he would tell her that he was in a band, actually, and did she want to hear some tracks, or worse, that he was the Nightjars' number one fan or, worst of all, that he had this huge crush on her in the early aughts. You know, when she was young.

But as he leaned in to whisper whatever it was he had to say, there was a sharp crack of twigs, a rustling of leaves. Jenny turned to see her daughter in the glow of a lantern. The glare Neko gave her was murder, and Jenny realized the situation looked bad. But what was she going to say? *No worries, we're just smoking chronic over here*?

"Mom, where's the bathroom case?" Neko held up the lantern, shining it into Jenny's eyes, blinding her. "I need to brush all this meat off my teeth."

"Right. Yes. All that meat."

They walked together to the tents, and as Jenny shuffled through the duffel bag, her daughter grunted with impatience, and maybe some other emotion that neither wanted to name, and said, "God, Mom. Seriously."

In a moment she would always wish she could take back, Jenny snapped. "You know, Neko, your father isn't perfect. There's a lot you don't know about him. There's a whole hell of a lot you can't see yet."

Neko took the bathroom case and stalked off.

The trees swayed in the wind as though laughing at Jenny, left behind in the dirt.

In their final birthing class at the hospital, the nurse had gone over basic newborn care, asking the class, *Why might the baby be crying*? Hunger. Check. Wet diaper. Check. Jenny had raised her hand and, making one of those ill-advised jokes Max hated, said, "The effects of climate change?" Nobody laughed and the nurse nodded. "Okay—maybe the room is too hot or too cold."

One Sunday after playing a show, later in her pregnancy, Jenny had taken the fetus on a second hike. It had been spring, the nearby creek full and clear from snowmelt and the recent rain, turtle bellies slapping at the water as they slid off rocks for a swim. The trail ran near the edges of a burgeoning suburb, the echoing din of human progress woven into the patter of birdsong. Things she hadn't appreciated as a young person: the smell of trees and water, the comfort of strong sun on skin, the crackle of leaves underfoot. Jenny had vowed to take the baby here again after she was born so she could see it with her own eyes. She had hoped they were not bringing the girl into the world just to watch the fall of the planet, the human race skittering like ants. She had hoped there would still be some beauty left.

Wanted wind at our back and
The god gave it wrapped in a bag
We mistook it for gold, let it out
Smoked a fag
As the floating island burned

16

IT BEGAN TO SEEM LIKE THE LARK WAS CURSED.

It was early afternoon by the time Harriet and Jules rescued Neko and Iggy and brought the remaining goods back to shore.

"What happened out there?" asked Harriet.

Iggy inspected Neko's equipment as she took it off, eventually holding up the regulator. "The O-ring is fucked."

Neko took it from him. *Shit.* In her rush to pack for the lark, she must have grabbed the wrong regulator. Thank God one of the others hadn't used it, she thought. She had enough to feel guilty about.

"Well, we didn't get the flock cables either." Harriet shrugged. "They were too trashed."

They packed the Land Rover with boxes, tying some to the luggage rack up top. Neko stopped to look at their handprints left in the dust on the side of the vehicle, and then she thought about how Iggy made fun of her for using the word "vehicle," too formal or technical or something.

As she rounded the side, she slipped in a puddle of water.

"You've got to be kidding me." On the ground was their water cooler, totally empty, having gotten knocked over somehow while they were gone.

"That was supposed to last us until the Watering Hole," said Iggy.

"Water, water everywhere," said Harriet quietly, surveying the saltwater marsh surrounding them, "and not a drop to . . ." Birds screeched and flapped away in the trees.

Jules went inside the Land Rover and brought out the map. She pointed to a freshwater creek about a mile and a half north. "If we head out now, we should be back before nightfall."

"Do we all need to go?" asked Harriet.

"You have other plans?" asked Neko.

"I thought someone should guard the materials."

"Water's heavy," explained Iggy. "If we're to make good time, we'll each have to help."

THEY SECURED THE LAND ROVER AND SET OUT IN THE DIRECTION OF the creek, bushwhacking their way through overgrown semi-marshland. As they walked, it began to rain again, and they pulled ponchos over their heads and kept moving. Neko marveled at how animals never showed any misery when it rained. Cows and deer in a field, crows lined up on a branch. Did it not bother them? Was there a thin, indiscernible membrane protecting them from the harsh realities of their physical world? A place inside their animal brain to which they retreated?

It reminded Neko of walking through the kitchen in their apartment growing up, her mother holding a chef's knife like a sword in the air. Frozen in a spell. Then she would reanimate and smile at Neko, continue making supper, though sometimes only after scribbling on a scrap receipt to remind herself of something for later. Neko had told herself she wasn't invisible. She had told herself that was just what it meant to be an artist.

Sometimes when Neko listened to her parents' music, the music they'd made together and the music they'd made apart, she tried to place when in her childhood they might have written that song or lyric or melody. And as she rewound the image of her mother in her mind's diorama of their apartment, open kitchen and long, thin living room, zooming in and zooming out, she wondered: Was she coming up with the song about when the earwig met the dung beetle? Or working out the tricky chord change in the second verse of the song about bumper stickers?

Or the image of her mother sitting straight-backed on the uncomfortable bench that lined one wall of the studio. Mouth turned down so she looked a little hangdog. If Neko concentrated, as she'd had time to do over all the years that had passed since then, she saw her mother's eyelids twitching, saw how she was mentally tracing notes on the staff, winding them up and down like Penelope at the loom, as she would say.

But no matter how hard she tried, she couldn't rewind those scenes to find the moment where her family unraveled. Did it have something to do with those awkward family trips to Vermont? Or that time she'd caught her mother messing around with some dumb dad in the woods at her scouting retreat? Had it happened in a language she didn't understand? Or so slowly that it never registered? Maybe that was why its discovery had been such a shock to her. Had made her so angry that she wanted to punish them. Maybe that was also how her mother ended up with so many secrets—a finished solo album, a bunker. Another life?

———

HONEYSUCKLE SCATTERED ON DIRT. BRIARS SCRAPING LEGS. A FOG of gnats.

Neko didn't see the ravine in front of her until she'd stumbled over the ledge, poncho ripping on a branch as she fought to hold on to a dead tree trunk, boots slipping in mud, trying for purchase, for traction. Iggy grabbed one of her belt loops, pinching the wind out of her, and eventually her crew negotiated her splayed body back onto solid ground.

Neko felt her cheeks turn hot. "Fuck this place." Her bones suddenly felt like they were pressing toward the ground, as though gravity had increased its force.

Jules just pulled out the wrinkled antique map from her pocket as though it were no big deal. "We might have to detour another half mile or so to get around this crevice."

Neko seethed but she followed.

A cloud skidded in front of the sun and the light turned amber. A giant trunk towered above the tree line up ahead—not a tree, but one of those old cellphone towers dressed to fit in, albeit poorly. Then, thunder overhead. Sharp cracks of it.

An hour later, they arrived at the creek just as the rain finally let up. After the quixotic hike and the effort needed to filter the water and seal it into the drums, it had gotten late.

"We'll make camp here," said Iggy, and, despite the damp conditions, they each nodded, disappointed but also lacking the energy to haul water in the dark. They splayed out their ponchos and slept. Neko dreamt that she was cold and, when she pulled a blanket to her chest, it crumbled into dust.

NEKO WOKE TO A GROWL—SOMETHING ANIMAL NEARBY. SOMETHING out of place. The overpowering scent of licorice.

She felt chilled and her intention to jump up while sliding

her gun from the holster was hobbled by strands of knotted hair caught in her shirt button. She had to yank herself loose, the adrenaline causing her to do it too hard. She fumbled and lurched, bleary-eyed.

In the swampy, mote-filled light, she saw that the growl had issued not from a wolf but from three white men who looked like wolves, encrusted in dirt and buckskin, hair matted.

Everything was surreal: Three men leering. A light mist slicking the ground and beading across Neko's cheeks. Squirrels scampering through the leaves like dervishes. Her unlaced shoelaces socializing with the weeds.

How long did she stand there dumbly? It felt like forever, her mind oddly blank. As though the fog had erased her years of training.

Neko was flanked by Jules and Iggy, both with heads bowed in submission. Then she saw Harriet, off to the side, camouflaged by shadow, a knife to her pretty throat. Her canvas pants looked ripped and there was blood, or was it mud? What was happening?

Shit. Shit. Shit.

One of the wolf men spoke in rapid-fire patois and Iggy lifted his head, standing in such a way as to block the fact that Neko had a gun half cocked, and with his arms in the air, he walked to the tree where some of their supplies hung and pointed. "There." She tried to figure out how Iggy understood what they were saying, what they wanted.

One wolf man grabbed the supply bags from the cradle of the trunk, dragged them across the clearing. The effort he put into it seemed excessive, so maybe he was weaker than he looked. He glanced inside one of the bags, nodded to his companions, and then strapped the packs onto his own back. Neko's eyes were obsessed with the fold of his hands. Nobody else seemed to notice, but her brain noticed everything. Yet she did nothing. An errant leaf fluttered down as though giving up.

Another of the wolf men took Harriet's device from her wrist—with an odd gentleness—before tossing it into the underbrush. So, they weren't planning to give her back.

Neko's brain ran through simulations—if she shot, would they still hurt Harriet? How quickly could she leap to the hand with the knife and would it be fast enough? She was a dumb cow snagged in barbed wire. A rabbit caught in the hunter's trap, wondering how to gnaw off its paw.

Nothing Neko could think of to do would help. Helpless. She thought she sensed smoke, but maybe it was her own fear.

"Take the stuff, but leave her," said Iggy, entreating. He was pale, blunted.

The men ignored him.

Jules's mouth opened and closed; her feet shuffled oddly, like a windup toy's.

"Harriet," Neko whispered, willing the girl to look at her, and she did, eyes wide and wet. Her face was a pasture. Neko didn't try to console her—that wasn't their way. But something imperceptible crossed between them like static. A deeper well. A shoring-up.

Then Harriet and the wolf men were gone.

17

THEY DISGUISED THEIR WATER DRUMS WITH A LAYER OF BRUSH. THEY suited up. As they stalked through the woods after Harriet and the wolf men, Neko's body took over. As long as they kept moving, she wouldn't have to think about what might be happening to their young, pretty apprentice.

They moved forward in quick bursts, Neko pointing to the next rendezvous point, each of them scurrying forward and then crouching in stillness as they listened for any sign of human movement. Again. And again.

Eventually, they figured out that the men were trying to throw them off the trail by crossing back and forth across the creek, though they must have been too concerned with their speed to notice Harriet was dragging one of her boots though the mud.

At one of their listening stops, Neko leaned in to Jules's neck. "Any idea where they might be heading? Any water holes or settlements nearby?"

"You think I know . . . ?"

"You said we wouldn't need maps if we brought you. That you were from here."

"Not *right* here," she said.

The sky grew dark with clouds and the rain began again. They hadn't found any footprints in some time, so they circled back, looking for torn branches, for any sign of movement in the alien terrain.

"Here," said Jules finally, and they all took a deep breath.

They moved alongside a copse of beech trees where the tall grass had been flattened. Neko figured this meant either that they were getting close to the men's camp or that the kidnappers had stopped bothering to cover their tracks. Despite the sort-of trail, it was slow going in the rain as they ducked branches, slid through sharp undergrowth.

Neko was in the rear, keeping an eye behind them, which was why she didn't notice that Iggy and Jules had stopped until she almost barreled into them. She grabbed Iggy's arm to keep herself upright until she could see what they saw: a lambent ghost.

No. A white deer. An albino. The insides of its ears and the watery rims of its eyes were a delicate pink. It was a young buck, its antlers still covered in velvet despite it being late in the season, and several yards behind it, mostly hidden by brush, were two does.

"This is a sign," whispered Jules. Her expression was flat and strangely lacking in panic.

"What?"

"For the Lenape, an albino deer means wisdom is coming."

Neko shook her head. "The only thing this is a sign of is our stupidity." Her voice, at its regular volume, released the buck from its trance, and he ducked and darted away through the arbor of branches. "This is a trail used by beasts to get to the water. Not the men, not Harriet."

The gaze of a wild animal—even if it wasn't rare, even if it wasn't white—might have appeared to convey some wordless truth that humans had lost. But like so many lovely and transient beings, they were just alive. Just wild. Just like Neko was wild and alive and would die and there was no meaning in any of it.

Neko looked at her watch, which had recorded their movements, and quickly began to backtrack toward the stream. This mistake had cost them too much time, and Neko slowly began to entertain the possibility that they wouldn't catch up to Harriet. They wouldn't be able to stop the men from doing whatever they planned to do with her. For the first time since she woke to the wolf men, Neko pursed her lips and zagged through the underbrush like the animal she was.

EVENTUALLY THEY HAD NO CHOICE BUT TO REST—OTHERWISE, THEY risked destroying the real tracks with their circling, or drawing attention with their headlamps. They crouched together in the cloudy, foggy dark. An occasional slip of moon illuminated their immediate surroundings: grass glistening like wet straw, spirals of honey-flecked lichen, the trunk of a downed pine split to reveal its heartwood. A shrike called out in the distance.

"Maybe they'll just let her go," whispered Jules. "Maybe they just want leverage. And food." She slapped her own cheek, hard. "Why didn't they take me . . . ?"

"Do they plan to ransom her?" asked Iggy. "But how?"

Neko didn't respond, too busy with her own silent self-flagellation: Why had they risked camping in this swampy shithole? How could they have slept through the men's approach? What had they gotten themselves into by moving into the northern Sink, where they were strangers who understood nothing?

"There used to be an orchard here," said Iggy. "See there." He pointed to a short line of trees on the other side of the stream. "Some of the apples have already dropped."

Neko shone her light and saw them scattered over the ground, hard little fists nicked by claws and beaks. Funny how things like these—heirloom apple trees and flowering dogwoods, ornamentals planted by humans—could outlast the things humans built. The apple trees continued to fling their fruit every year. Confetti at a party where nobody showed.

AS SOON AS IT WAS LIGHT, NEKO AND IGGY AND JULES WORKED ALL THE angles. They even risked digital detection to download a more current satellite map of the area, but the only potential campsite they found had been abandoned for weeks. They sprayed black light anywhere it might pick up fluids and used their animal whistle to try to signal Harriet, elicit some sort of response. But nothing. Just dense woods and soggy ground. The overgrown ruins of quaint HOA-compliant "barns" and collapsed A-frames, the twisted metal signs for big animal vets and horse boarding. A flock of geese migrating south.

In the middle of the afternoon, with still no leads, they stopped. Neko crouched and opened her mouth and screamed. Iggy knelt next to her and said nothing.

Jules stared at them impassively, and then said, "Though I don't know this exact patch . . ."

They stared back at her and waited.

". . . I may know people who do."

Iggy slowly walked over and put his hands on her shoulders. "What people?"

"Nearby." She removed herself from his grip. "They'll help us if they can."

Struggling under the weight of the drums of water, they hiked back to the Land Rover.

"I hope we can find them with less than five gallons of gas," said Iggy, after checking their supplies. "Otherwise, this thing won't be getting us out of here."

Neko reached for Iggy's hand. They wouldn't leave Harriet behind, but they also were not equipped for a long-term search and rescue in unfamiliar terrain.

As they hastily packed the Rover, Neko felt a sourness in the pit of her stomach. She felt bad for being so hard on Harriet, but mostly she felt bad for dragging them all into this. If they didn't make it to the Watering Hole by next week, they would lose the gig to the bunker, and she would deserve that and much more.

JULES SPOKE ONLY TO DIRECT THEM DOWN VARIOUS SMALLER ROADways, and eventually Iggy began asking the questions Neko's mind should have formed but hadn't.

"Who are these people?" His naturally high voice always made any interrogation seem friendly.

Jules swallowed. "Friends from before."

"From growing up?"

Jules nodded, and Neko realized that she hadn't told Iggy the details Jules had shared about her childhood. When had she stopped sharing every facet of her life with him?

"How big is this group? Why do you think they'll help us?"

"Turn left at the garden center on the corner." Jules didn't speak for a moment. "It's hard to explain. You'll understand when we get there."

They passed collapsed storefronts and hollowed-out gas stations, the occasional abandoned strip mall and school playgrounds rusting in the sun.

Iggy wasn't giving up. "What made you run away from . . . here?"

Jules's face was subdued, thoughtful. "I didn't run away." The thing about a vehicle was that it was easy to just look straight ahead, not face anyone. "I just grew up."

Eventually, they came to a sign that said *Dis-il—ry*.

"There," said Jules. "We'll stop there."

"Why?" asked Iggy through his teeth.

"Trust me."

"Tell us why." Neko wanted to shout but managed not to.

"You'll see. I promise."

Iggy looked at Neko, who shrugged, feeling strangely borne along by the circumstances. He steered the vehicle off the road.

Everything felt oddly silent as they trudged to the door—no birdsong, no breeze. It was miraculous that the building, covered in peeling red paint, was still standing. Inside, the darkness was split by shafts of smoky sunlight. There was a long wooden bar, still intact, though the stools were splayed and broken. It looked as if the place had been colonized and then abandoned by a series of rodents, their droppings calcified in the corners.

Jules began knocking around in some cabinets. Neko stooped behind the bar. There were rows of dusty bottles of rye.

From the next room came Iggy's voice: "In here."

She immediately moved toward his voice and took in the scene: A room with what looked like antique furniture. Cobwebs fluttering from the ceiling like veils. The decayed bodies of two people still sitting upright in chairs, their exposed jaws grimacing, but otherwise—otherwise it was as though they'd died of boredom. Died just waiting. But for what?

Suddenly Neko felt overwhelmed by her sense of smell. It wasn't coming from the bodies—they'd been there too long, stripped of organic matter by the passage of time. Maybe it was the odor of a decaying house, of wild animals nesting in old quilts, of their own ripe, unwashed human bodies moving through a place that didn't belong to them.

Why was this place—so easy to see from the road—still here and stocked with liquor? Despite the dust, the building was in surprisingly good shape. No water damage on the ceiling. No mold devouring the gypsum boards or floor joists. Dead bodies undisturbed by predators or scavengers. She turned toward Jules and said: "Something's not right . . ."

But it was too late. Shadows emerged from the doorway and turned into two men with shaved heads, carrying rifles. Where had they come from? Neko and Iggy moved back-to-back.

"No." Jules stepped between them and the strangers. "Everybody relax. It's okay," said Jules, first to them and then to the two men. "These are sentries. This place is the entry into our land."

"Why are they pointing guns at us?" asked Iggy.

The men were stone-faced, saying nothing, but reluctantly they lowered their weapons.

Jules's voice was unhurried. "We'll walk from here."

The distillery, Neko realized, was a spiderweb. "What about the Land Rover?"

"It'll be secure." Jules put on her pack and ducked through the back door of the distillery. She beckoned to them. "I want to find her more than anyone. This is the best way."

Neko felt herself balk, but when she looked to Iggy for confirmation of the fact that this was crazy, his eyes were on Jules, his eyes were curious and willing.

JULES LED THEM THROUGH A PINE STAND, THE GROUND SOFT AND forgiving, blanketed with rust-colored needles. They kept walking, deeper and deeper into the woods, though they were not following any path that Neko could discern. They were walking blind.

Neko had always believed she and Iggy were at the top of the food chain. Natives of the crumbling land. Veterans of the wild. For maybe the first time in her mudlarking life, she thought: *This must be how it feels to get cut down to size.*

They walked so long without coming across a road or any sign of human civilization that Neko thought they must be in what used to be a state or national park of some sort. As though reading her mind, Jules said, "Centuries ago, this was reservation land. The natives grew an enclosure of black oak and box elder and drove their game into the pound until they needed it for food."

When the sun set in earnest, they switched on their headlamps. Neko was eying her watch, trying to trace their path, when Jules came to an abrupt halt.

"We're here."

Neko peered through the dark. "I don't see anything."

Jules put her hand on Neko's shoulder. "Look up."

They tilted back their headlamps.

Iggy gasped. "Dios fucking mío."

18

TREE BRANCHES HIGH ABOVE THEM WERE THREADED WITH TINY lights, faint like distant stars. The beams of Neko's headlamp jerkily illuminated a settlement: wooden structures cantilevering from the trunks of trees, ropes and pulleys strung like spider-webs, and, perhaps most spectacularly, thick limbs dripping with enormous spheres, hives for a race of fantastical beings.

Neko's first reaction was to squat in a protective stance, one hand skimming the ground as though to ensure it was still beneath her. A rustle in a nearby tree, and a rope ladder unfurled. Jules grabbed the rope and began to climb. Iggy made as if to follow, but one of the so-called sentries shook his head in the negative.

Jules looked down at them, suspended on the swinging rope ladder. "Give me a minute." Her right eyelid flashed, and Neko thought: *Did Jules really just wink at us?* Maybe Jules was a great actress, a liar, but even so, she had to believe that Jules loved Harriet and wouldn't have brought them here if these people couldn't help find her.

They stood beneath the web of twinkling lights for what felt like hours but, according to Neko's watch, was just under twenty minutes. The air held a strong perfume that Neko couldn't place. The men with the rifles said nothing until suddenly one gestured for them to climb the same ladder that had taken Jules into the canopy.

AT THE TOP, NEKO PULLED HERSELF ONTO A PLATFORM AND FELT a sense of wonder that people lived here—in treehouses. Like a childhood dream.

The platform they stood on was only the first "story." At least two more levels were built above them on the same trunk, and the floor space was crowded with sacks of potatoes and beets, wheels of twine, and cardboard boxes with medical-sounding labels. Two peahens, each tied by a clawed foot, were strung up over the edge to drain beside one scrawny rabbit, damp with blood, so fresh its eyes still shone topaz.

Up here, level with the hanging teardrop-shaped burrows, Neko saw that their thatches were woven from plastic packaging strips. Each of the structures had a side opening, like the nests of the weaverbird. An engineering marvel. She would soon learn that to spend time inside them—performing any activity, any movement—meant getting accustomed to the subtle sway and shift made by the colossal aeries. Like getting your sea legs, or riding on the back of a motorcycle, it required a looseness of the body. A willingness not to fight the world but to move with it.

"I feel like this is a video game," whispered Iggy, "and we just leveled up."

There was a whistle and then a flashlight signaling them from a nearby platform, and when they redirected their headlamps, they saw Jules gesturing toward a zip line. They took turns, awkwardly gripping the bar, trying not to slip to their deaths.

Jules handed them each a makeshift harness, and Neko awkwardly fumbled with the buckles, wondering why in the world these people had built their settlement in a place so difficult to traverse.

"The U.S. government has seismic detectors that look for large patterns of activity on the ground," Jules said, as though reading her mind. "So we became trapeze artists."

Neko considered the word choice—"trapeze artists" sounded so whimsical and Old World. And then there was the word "we."

"What about satellite footage?" asked Iggy.

"When the leaves fall, we use . . ."

"Something proprietary." A petite woman emerged behind Jules. She was stout, her dark hair streaked with gray, maybe a few years older than Neko. "Welcome to the Hive."

Jules introduced her. "This is La Jefa."

"Jules said you could help us find someone," said Neko, unsure how much the woman had been told. "Our crew member, Harriet."

"Yes. Julieta told us." She went on to say they had an idea as to who might have taken her. "We'll handle it."

"Ayudaremos," said Iggy, smiling, his Spanish so natural and fluid and yet also out of place.

"No," said La Jefa lightly. "We've already sent scouts. Descansen. You must be exhausted. My daughter will show you where to bed down." Her voice was raw and formal, like someone who didn't have the need to speak often. "We want you to be comfortable here."

Neko almost said: *Daughter?* In Fringe, when Jules had told her about growing up in the Sink after the hurricane and ended with, *I don't really like to talk about what happened after that,* Neko had assumed her parents were dead. All the fugitive groups they'd ever encountered were made up of ragtag libertarians or naïve adventurers or mud-encrusted urchins with nowhere else to go. Neko had never seen a place like this before.

JULES LED THEM TO ONE OF THE HANGING NESTS, WHICH WAS JUST BIG enough for Iggy and Neko to lie side by side in their sleeping bags, with hooks along the walls for their things.

"Te llamas Julieta?" asked Iggy in the throaty voice he used when his feelings had been hurt. "You *never* told us."

Jules shrugged, looking chagrined.

"What is this place?" asked Neko, thinking there were more important questions than what Jules's birth name was.

Jules's voice was quiet. "The Hive. Home sweet home."

"I mean, how . . . ?"

Jules sighed. "That's why I didn't tell you before. Every answer leads to more questions. I'm sure you can see why we protect the secrecy of this place with our lives." Jules stood incredibly still for a moment before turning to leave. "Get some rest. We'll talk more tomorrow."

NEKO AND IGGY BURROWED INTO THE NEST, USING THEIR BACKPACKS as pillows. Outside, the heavens wheeled.

"They bring us in at gunpoint and then expect us to sleep," said Iggy.

She lay on her back. "We'd have done the same."

Iggy rubbed his eyes. "Ella habla español this whole time and never told me."

Neko looked at Iggy as though he had a fever.

"Their accent isn't Mexican," he added. "It's something else." Iggy stretched and yawned. A leather jacket had never fit a man as well as Iggy's leather jacket fit him, thought Neko, watching him shed it and fold it beside him. Neko couldn't help but see that even in moments like this, even when they had to be soldiers together, he was *so beautiful*.

"And Jules," he continued, "being raised out here in the wild."

Neko laughed, though it came out more as a bark. "We live like this every time we cross the border. And without a city in the trees to protect us."

Iggy slid her shirt away and kissed her shoulder, softly. Sweetly. It felt exquisite and excruciating at the same time. He said, "But to be a child in the Sink is a whole different thing. That's why we don't have one yet. That's *why*."

Neko admitted what part of her had already known: Iggy's thwarted paternal impulses had been channeled into their apprentices for too long.

An owl began to call from its own nearby nest, and Neko, inside her thirty-eight-year-old body with only a few lingering eggs, had nothing to say to that: no words or even distinct thoughts. Instead, a series of sensations bloomed inside her solar plexus: Emptiness. Numbness. A deep bowl of grief and fear.

She tried not to think about what Harriet was experiencing at this moment. If this was a preview of parenthood, what torture, she thought. What fucking torture. At times like this, she wished they'd never taken on apprentices at all. It was too painful being this intimately connected to other people, making choices that affected them.

"Should one of us keep watch?" asked Iggy eventually.

A moth thumped its bulging thorax against the holster of Neko's Glock. "We're so outnumbered, what good would it do?"

Even as she said that, Neko didn't think she'd be able to fall asleep. But the nook was warm and dark, and she was depleted from days without rest. There was a kind of relief in having someone else be in charge for once. Plus, she was Neko, and she could sleep anywhere. So she did, dreaming about the time a man taught her how to put a bit in a horse's mouth—pressing the gap in the gums like a combination lock. Click, open. Metal, sinew.

THE GRUNTS OF SQUATS AND THEN PLANKS AND THEN SQUATS AGAIN. There were thirty adults of varying ages, races, and body types exercising beneath the swaying branches on a lower platform, shaking the bowels of the tree. She and Iggy watched from their nest as the group responded in unison to a barrel-chested man's commands.

Neko and Iggy stared at this display in confusion and awe. Then a black-haired teenager, maybe fourteen, appeared, hanging from the zip line in front of them. "Your colleague—they've found her. Follow me."

The young man, dressed in green camo, let go of his carabiner and went flying back down the line.

Neko and Iggy looked at each other, eyes slit. They latched their harnesses and stumbled behind like clumsy oafs.

He led them to a crowded platform, and they ducked back and forth, craning their necks—Neko suddenly anxious that they had misunderstood—but no. There was movement down below, and from the underbrush a small group of people emerged and in the center: Harriet. Standing with elbows tucked to her sides like wings, eyes focused on something in the middle distance. The sunlight through the trees dappled her skin. Her body was ramrod straight, as though she were in a military lineup.

For a moment, the thought flashed across Neko's mind: *Who are these people, and what are they really doing here?* Then Jules was there, pushing her way to the top of the entrance ladder. When Harriet climbed up into the canopy, hardly seeming to register the crazy structures surrounding her, Iggy and Jules both rushed forward, knocking into each other to get to her. Neko hung back.

"Are you all right?" they asked in unison.

Harriet was motionless, not rejecting or returning their affection, not making eye contact with either of them, and then she said, "Something like that." Her shoulders suddenly crumpled.

Almost everything that had occurred since they left Fringe had surprised Neko, but maybe nothing so much as what happened next: Harriet slid past Jules and Iggy and fell into Neko's arms, which she hadn't realized she was holding open. They said nothing. They held each other with muscle and bone.

19

IN THE PRIVACY OF THEIR NEST, THE FOUR OF THEM STILLED THEIR bodies to try to prevent the aerie from swaying. Iggy had the first aid kit and was checking Harriet's vitals. Her face was covered in a faint sunburn that made her look flushed. "How do you feel?" he asked. "Where did they take you?"

Harriet didn't flinch when he pricked her with the monitor that took a white blood cell reading, a hemoglobin count. "I don't know."

"You don't know where they took you or you don't know how you feel?"

Neko shushed them. "Stop hounding her." Ever since the hurricane, she'd come to expect that when things took a bad turn, it would only get worse from there. She'd forgotten this feeling of grateful relief when something was even partially righted.

Iggy squinted at the readouts. "Slightly elevated cortisol, but everything else is within normal range."

Of course, that didn't mean Harriet wasn't damaged in other ways, ones they knew better than to ask about. At least not yet.

Neko squeezed Iggy's arm and nodded at Jules and Harriet. "Let's give them some space."

He nodded and stood. The nest swung; they groped for balance.

"No," said Harriet. "Stay. Please."

Iggy sat back down. Neko hesitated and then slid next to him.

Jules's hands shook noticeably as she pulled Harriet's head into her lap, threading fingers through her impossibly fine hair. "You're really okay?" she asked, voice plaintive.

"It's over," said Harriet.

It wasn't over—not really. But they sat together, and the rhythmic pulling of their breath felt like a comfort.

Jules told them the wolf men were stragglers, starving and desperate, and that her people had apparently been keeping a wary eye on them, which was why they'd been able to locate Harriet so quickly.

Harriet lifted her hand as though to conduct an orchestra but then brought her fingers to an iridescent beetle that was climbing its way up the side of the nest. She let it sit on her knuckle, antennae quivering. "Your mother, I met her when they found me," she said. "Is your father here, too?"

Jules shook her head.

Harriet cocked her chin.

"Died of scarlet fever. Years ago, before we found a source for procuring antibiotics." She looked at them and sighed, and it seemed to Neko that she was once again lamenting the fact that each answer provoked more questions.

For Neko, the air in the nest felt still and soft. Robust. It felt as though she could sense the machinery inside each of them recalibrating to this new reality. Her own brain felt arrested, paused, gears preparing to turn in the opposite direction.

"My family's from Chile," said Jules, voice husky and large, as though it were the beginning of a fairy tale. "My parents were recruited by the U.S. government after the brain drain. They worked on the Mississippi levees and later the Great Lake floodwalls."

"What you told me in the clinic," interjected Neko, "was *any* of that true?"

"Sure. I just left out some details." Jules picked burrs from Harriet's clothes, like a monkey grooming her companion. "After Hurricane Frida, my parents did refuse to move to the Inside, that was true. Chile had already splintered, and there was no going back there either. They stayed in the Sink and eventually built this place. The Hive is an open community dedicated to starting over. Better."

Neko sensed this story was a gift—even Harriet's eyes sparked with some life again.

Staring out the opening of the nest, Neko caught sight of a cottontail twitching in a bush down below, its fur tobacco-brown. She wondered if it would end up feet in the air, blood draining, like the one they'd seen yesterday.

"The Hive," said Iggy, turning it over in his mouth like a pearl, or like a puzzle he wanted to unlock. The nest swung slightly as he repositioned himself.

The nest fell into shadow as clouds obscured the sun.

Jules looked at Iggy. "Last year, the Inside destroyed our permaculture beds with a drone attack. Luckily, we built a ways away and they didn't find this place."

"I thought there was a drone fence around the Sink," said Neko.

"Not for them."

Jules said saltwater encroachment made it nearly impossible to grow food hidden in the brush anymore without drawing outside attention with tilled or raised beds. She said that when she was young, there were sweet potato vines winding and smothering the bushes near the creek where she played. Kale and chard bending among the tents where they lived back then. Cherry tomatoes like rubies.

Jules lifted her palms into the air, linked them like wings, and made a shadow puppet against the nest wall. Then the shapes condensed and slithered. "Neko," said Jules quietly. "I'm ready for the ink."

Neko studied Jules to see if she was serious. To see if she really meant she wanted to stay with the crew, to tattoo herself with the mark. Here, Jules was a different person, older and more sure of herself, and maybe the old skittishness had been an act all along. Or maybe the gears inside her body were changing, too, recalibrating to what was ahead. Neko had figured that this would be the end with Jules. Now that she was home.

"My works are in the Rover."

Jules pulled her hands through Harriet's hair, and Neko closed her eyes and imagined lying in her own mother's lap, how her mother's fingers had played her scalp like a piano.

THE WRECKAGE

Track 5: "Sirens"

On the subway ride to Red Hook to see Loretta Lynn play Pioneer Works Jenny pretended not to listen to Neko and one of Neko's friends talk about their favorite bands, the friend saying she went to see Adele last year with her father, then asking what Neko's first concert was.

"Lady Gaga," said Neko. "She came down on a trapeze."

Jenny couldn't help it. "Technically, your first concert was the Nightjars."

Neko and the friend both looked up, as though surprised to find a parent with them at all.

"When I was pregnant with you, I had to switch to a smaller-bodied AE guitar and angle my stance to get to the microphone. But, bet your pants, I made it work."

Neko rolled her eyes. "That doesn't count, Mom."

"You want me to tell you about how I breastfed you backstage and then traded you for my guitar when it was time to go on?" At the time, she'd tried to hide the ache, the maternal feeling of wanting to stay with the baby. She was a rock musician, for fuck's sake.

"And now you're forcing me to go see a geriatric lady play country music."

"I'm not forcing you. You could have chosen to babysit for Kathleen in Jersey."

"What a choice!"

"And have some respect. Women like Loretta Lynn made your lives possible. Opened doors for you, made space for you." Jenny thought about the anodyne music Neko and her friends listened to on their fancy earbuds. When Jenny was their age, she was ordering cassettes and CDs from the Kill Rock Stars catalog, headbanging to punk music with so much tube crunch that she finally felt allowed to be angry. "When I started going to shows, it was this very physical, masculine energy everywhere. Mosh pits and girls getting bloodied up and shoved out of the way. Female musicians were the ones who fought against all that, who made sure girls like you could be at the front of the stage without going home with a concussion."

"Yes, I'm sure Loretta Lynn was very much like, 'Girls to the front of my mosh pit, please.'"

Jenny sighed. "You know what I mean."

Neko began to sing "Stand by Your Man."

"That was Tammy Wynette."

"Well, if Loretta Lynn is so great, why didn't Dad want to come?"

Jenny swallowed and moved so that a young couple could slide past her out of the subway car. "Too intimidated, I guess."

Onstage, Loretta Lynn wore the most amazing sequined turquoise jacket. She was eighty-four years old and had to sit on a stool rather than stand, and someone else played lead guitar because of her arthritis. But alongside the pedal steel, her voice soared, shocking Jenny with its deep warble and steep ascents. Even Neko, sitting beside her, seemed begrudgingly impressed.

What kind of old woman might Jenny become? The kind who ordered brioche at the café each morning, wearing a wide-brimmed hat and red serape? (She wouldn't mind this, honestly—she rather loved the sound of dishes clattering, of cups on saucers.) The kind in beige slacks and orthopedic shoes? Certainly not the kind in pearls and sweater sets and pumps. Absolutely not. Sometimes musicians were allowed to stay cooler longer, but it was dangerous to hold on to it too desperately. Could she walk around the nursing home still in a leather jacket?

Jenny remembered how her father had kept a few pieces of her mother's clothing—her wedding gown, a sequined shift dress worn one New Year's Eve, a pair of bell-bottom jeans. As a teenager she tried on the sequined dress and the jeans sometimes, standing in front of the full-length mirror, conjuring the ghost of her mother. The clothes had never fit perfectly, her mother having been shorter than Jenny, her hips rounder. Jenny was no replacement, no replica.

Her father had never pulled out old photo albums, but he hadn't gotten rid of them either. She liked to look through them when he was out of the house, poring over images of her parents, their arms full of yellow flowers in a small, tasteful chapel. She'd learned from a book about how the Aztecs kept small bouquets of marigolds, occasionally pressing them to their faces, because of the odor of the blood-soaked priests and then later the stench of the Spanish.

Neko had never asked to borrow her clothes, but maybe

Jenny should set some aside for her. Just in case she changed her mind one day.

The crowd at the Loretta Lynn show was a bit hipster, a bit country. Jenny literally put her hand on her heart when the old woman sang "Blue Kentucky Girl." On this evening, the crowd was united despite everything. One of those rare shows where everyone feels they are standing in the flow of history as it whooshes by. Here, and then gone.

Jenny felt around in her jacket pocket for her notebook and began to sketch an idea for a song where all the sirens were dressed like old Loretta Lynn in sequined jackets and they sang to her daughter, *We are one,* and they even half meant it. She'd been writing songs lately that she hadn't been sharing with Max and Jesse, that didn't feel right for the band.

She'd always thought Max was her muse, the one who made her voice—her career—possible. But maybe he wasn't a muse. Maybe he was a siren. Every time she let her guard down, it was Jenny who was smashed against the rocks.

Max had brought music to her, like a boy with a giant conch shell on the beach, and maybe she'd confused the two, blended them together in her mind.

But she could make music without him. In fact, why even let him be the siren? She would make new sirens. And what if these sirens, the wise women in Loretta Lynn jackets, were calling out for a different kind of destruction? For the old ways to be bashed against the rocks, maybe. For Jenny's old life to be taken down to brass tacks. A man-eating mother.

What if these sirens were like a fire engine's red sirens, blaring a warning to get out of the way as it rushed through the streets, trying to save the world from burning? Why does a siren have to be false just because it destroys? Maybe her album wouldn't *do* anything the way a whip did something to a horse's back, but that didn't mean music wasn't a power to be respected.

How many times do we have to say?
How many dollars of equal pay?
We are the sacred ground, give us the f—ing crown

20

NEKO WAS ANXIOUS TO GET GOING. SHE DIDN'T WANT TO ARRIVE AT the Watering Hole behind schedule and give Chaplin any excuse to send a different crew to the bunker, but Iggy convinced her to give Harriet a few days to recover.

The Hive treated them with a combination of generosity and reticence: They were given extra rations and unreasonably soft blankets; they were swatted away when they tried to help.

"Everyone is so *nice,*" said Harriet, as though she were saying *too nice*.

"Hospitality is one of our guiding principles," said Jules, her voice hovering in the space between mockery and sincerity.

Neko watched with fascination as Jules tried to draw out Harriet, who snapped in annoyance at her efforts, shrugged off her affection. Jules seemed to accept this shift in attitude, but Neko didn't understand why Harriet wasn't directing her anger at Neko and Iggy. For dragging her into this new wilderness with new, unknown terrors. For letting her be taken. For not getting her back for almost three days.

"Jules," said Neko, trying to mend things between the two the only way she knew how. "I got the tattoo machine from the

Rover. If you can find me a place to recharge it, I'll give you the two-headed snake to match Harriet's."

Before Jules could answer, Harriet did. "No. That design was never right for you."

"I want to do it," said Jules, quickly, her voice a hi-hat.

Neko watched as Harriet, knees pulled up to her chest, brought a hand to the snake on her triceps as though protecting it—or erasing it.

Neko made the decision to take a side. "Pick a different image. Your own."

AFTER HARRIET WAS FOUND, IGGY BECAME GREGARIOUS, WALKING around and introducing himself to people and quizzing them on the water collection method, the terrace architecture, and the hypocaust system they used for heat. Neko seethed with frustration over the delay, but he still managed to drag her to one of the platforms to show her the box flues that lined the tree trunk and, in the winter months, drew hot air upward from the furnace, heating the various levels as it went. "They use a woven canvas to tarp over the platform's canopy," he said. "It's brilliant."

Neko inspected the square pipes to see how they kept the trees from going up in flames and saw they were coated with ceramic tiles.

"Where do they get these?"

Turned out they made them themselves. She was invited to clamber down the ladder to watch Richard, the head potter. The brick kiln was the only structure built on the ground, and as she ducked through a trellis, she found Richard working to the sound of trap music on a battery-powered speaker.

"An engineer who's also a potter—impressive."

Richard didn't look up from the long bench where he was

wedging a handful of wet clay, kneading it, removing the air bubbles. Using the meaty part of his left hand—his right slowly squeezing water from a sponge—he centered the clay on his wheel. Finally, he glanced up. "Nah. I'm not an engineer." He had glossy dark skin and a shaved head. He might have been older than she was, but it was hard to tell. "I just hooked up with this cabal of math nerds when I left the Inside."

"Why's that?"

"How could I resist the revolutionary spirit?"

Neko was intrigued. "Revolution against . . . ?"

"The Babylon system," he said, mimicking a Jamaican accent. He smiled. "Don't listen to me. I was tired of living in a world ruled by fear." He looked at her. "How long's it been since you were there?"

She shrugged. "Long time." Neko thought of the last time she'd traveled beyond Fringe—to sell her father's things, transfer his savings into crypto. At that point the place had still been a facsimile of the country she'd grown up in, though it sounded as though change had been steady and insidious since.

She asked what he made other than the box flue tiles. "Coffee mugs and knickknacks?"

He smiled. "I make the trade tokens." He reached into a bucket and handed her an orange ball of hard glazed clay, like a marble but rough to the touch. "We call them sun coins."

She rolled the ball between both hands. "What about counterfeit?"

"Sang de boeuf." He told her about the oxblood glaze used on Chinese court porcelain and how it had taken decades for a Western ceramicist to finally re-create the rich red color. To find the perfect balance of copper. "Let's just say this orange glaze we use on our tokens would be equally hard to reproduce without the secret recipe." He put a finger to his lips. "Snips, snails, and puppy-dog tails."

THE LAST TIME NEKO AND IGGY ENCOUNTERED AN ILLEGAL GROUP IN the Sink anywhere near as organized as the Hive had been just after they became licensed mudlarks. Because of some poor weather, they'd ended up stopping for the night on the way back to the Breakwater and had stumbled upon a group of young, dreadlocked white people embracing the philosophy of "rewilding." They wore bone earrings and belt buckles made from elk antlers, and they showed Neko and Iggy how to make warm beds from pine needles and how to tan a hide using the hump bone from a bison. They said they were glad the Sink was in collapse; they said they were ready to return to the earth. They cut felled tree trunks into moons and half-moons. Their yurts smelled of rotting fat.

Deer carcasses were useful: Their toes could be rattles and fishhooks; legs could be shivs and boning knives. Their tendons could be rendered into glue, their hides into clothing. But even knowing all of this didn't necessarily save you in a place prone to violent storms and floods, to debilitating tick-borne diseases and prowling wolves. The next time Neko and Iggy visited, half of the members were dead and the other half starving. It took more than dilettante wilderness savvy to survive entirely cut off from the modern world. What Jules's Hive—or whatever they called themselves—had achieved seemed too good to be true.

"IT'S TOO GOOD TO BE TRUE," SAID IGGY.

Neko was changing clothes after a much-needed bath when

Iggy slid into the nest and began rifling through their medical kit.

"I need to show you something." He asked her to bring some paper and follow him.

She tucked her sketchbook into her pants, strapped on the harness. On a platform farther down the zipline, they stopped in front of what looked like a gossamer sail, and Iggy pulled back the flap.

It took a minute for Neko's eyes to adjust to the dim lighting. Inside, the floor was a layer of woven raffia, upon which four small children lay on pallets.

"This woman is going to show you how to make an origami crane," he told the kids, who sat up slowly and circled around Neko. She saw that one of them had a prosthetic limb. "While she does that, I'm going to do a few quick tests."

Up close, she could see the raccoon rings around their eyes, the yellow of their skin. They were listless but curious, and she wished she had real origami paper—bright colors, intricate gold leaf.

She was no stranger to suffering, but Neko fumbled with the origami anyway. Her fingers felt like light. She couldn't get purchase. She redid the base square three times before finding a rhythm with the petal fold. Crease, flip, pinch.

If only she had saltwater taffy, a brick of marbled halvah, a honeycomb, she would give it to these children, sticky sweet. But all she had was this silly paper trick. Still, they studied her as though it were something amazing, so she made another crane, and another. They didn't cry when Iggy slid a needle beneath their skin. They didn't smile either.

As Iggy was finishing up, a woman, long hair twisted into a bun, opened the flap, surprised to find them there.

"Can I talk to you for a minute outside?" Iggy asked softly.

On the lip of the platform, Neko watched as Iggy showed the woman the readouts, lips pursed, and explained that the children were severely anemic and that at least two of them had beriberi.

The woman sighed. "Jules brought some vitamins and antibiotics. We've already started them on a round of treatment."

"They need citrus and legumes . . ."

"We all do." The woman's face was fierce. "Now, excuse me while . . ."

"Look. What I was going to say is that studies show increased carbohydrate intake augments the thiamine requirement . . ."

Neko handed each child a paper crane.

MEALS WERE DISTRIBUTED ON TREE TWO, AND IGGY AND NEKO LINED up with the rest for rations: a protein packet and a bowl of oatmeal. Off to the side, two people were churning butter. Neko heard people speaking English, Spanish, Québécois, all dressed in shades of green or brown to blend in with the trees.

As Neko walked to join Iggy at the railing, Jules's mother appeared with a hand on her shoulder. "Neko, the mudlark." She wore corduroy overalls and her neck was encircled by a blue-green silk scarf that looked familiar—the one that Jules had kept at the bank vault.

"You found Harriet. We're grateful."

She nodded. "Thank you for taking care of my Julieta."

"Jules takes care of herself mostly." Neko wasn't very good at regular conversation, but they were guests, so she tried. "You trained her here?"

The woman shrugged, looking at the two dozen people milling around them on the Tree Two platform. "We teach one another what we can."

"Are you the leader of this . . . place?"

"Facilitator. We have no leader. La Jefa is a nickname." The smile on her face looked strained, as though she'd lost practice using those muscles.

Neko wasn't sure she believed this, but she nodded.

"I wanted to give you these," La Jefa said, handing Neko and Iggy a bowl of fat pecans.

Neko's mouth watered. "How did you wrangle these?"

Jules's mother spit off the railing. "Same way we do everything else."

Neko looked around at the other people, who were eating their breakfast quietly, trying not to stare. She felt Iggy's body tighten beside her. "We don't need special treatment."

"We want you to feel at home." Her palms were upturned.

"These should go to the kids who are sick," said Iggy.

La Jefa's face went blank. "They are being taken care of."

"Children need more than expired vitamin pills to thrive." He was trying, and failing, to keep his voice soft.

La Jefa's hands retracted into her deep overall pockets. "We have a solution in the works. Don't worry your precious head."

AFTER LUNCH, NEKO RETURNED TO THE NEST FOR HER SKETCHBOOK and found Harriet completely naked and hunched in the corner. The woman's hands were tucked under her body like a broken bird, her back rounded, knobs of bare shoulders.

With each shudder, the nest shook slightly.

Neko just stood there. It was not yet midday, and here was her apprentice's face against the green of the nest's weave. Weeping.

"Harriet," she said, and the young woman froze as if she could be camouflaged by stillness. "Harriet."

She began to moan softly. Neko tentatively moved closer,

said "Harriet" once more, and then placed a palm on her bare shoulder. Harriet did not stop shaking, but she raised her chin from her chest, as if it took the greatest effort to do so. Her face was pink and wet. Her lips swollen.

"Don't touch me unless you're going to fuck me."

Neko's hand retracted.

Then a shard, a howl, from somewhere deep inside the woman: Harriet laughed. She said, "Leave me alone. Please."

NEKO WANDERED THE MAIN PLATFORMS, PRETENDING TO LOOK FOR something, trying not to make eye contact with anyone. Eventually, she heard arguing coming from a nearby nest. Because the conversation was in Spanish, it took her a moment to realize the voices came from Jules and her mother. Neko wasn't perfectly fluent, but she understood enough to pick out some words and phrases: *too dangerous, the Breakwater,* and several times the word *stay*.

Great, she thought. Harriet was cracking up and now Jules would stay behind with her people. How would they explain the disappearance of their apprentices when they returned to the Breakwater with the rare earth materials? Everything was getting too complicated. She needed to find Iggy.

When she did, it was in the sick tent with the sick kids, where he was animatedly teaching them how to play chickenfoot dominoes. From where she stood at the gap, peering in, she could see that, despite his long-winded explanation, the children were rapt. Neko loved him more now than she had when they were younger, than she had when she understood him better. And so she let him be, retreating again to the long wooden balcony, wishing there was some place to go in this godforsaken city in the sky.

Neko knew—she couldn't help herself from knowing—that living in the trees like this was a fairy tale, a delusion. Even if these people were true engineers, exponentially more prepared than the amateurs they'd met before, there would come a time when it wouldn't be enough. New permaculture beds would be flooded or razed just like the previous ones. The platforms would rot, need to be constantly repaired. Once the government realized an organized group of fugitives was living here, they'd capture them or drive them out. This was not a dream that could last.

"It's only a matter of time for these people," she had said to Iggy, when they were alone in their borrowed nest earlier that morning. She had been sketching images from their sojourn: the oblong nests, the wooden bathtub, the dizzying fairy lights in the trees.

Iggy had looked up from where he was mending a rip in the seam of his shirt. "Maybe they'll get lucky. I'm rooting for them." He tied off the thread. "Despite everything, this is the best place I've been in a long time. Don't you think? I kind of wish we could stay longer."

Three blackbirds lined up on a branch directly in front of where she now stood on the balcony, staring at Neko as though she had something they wanted. She opened her hands to them. Nothing. They flew away.

Neko wasn't here to worry about Jules and her family. Rather, she was here to find her own mother. If her mother was alive. If. If.

If her mother were alive, had she lived these years like the people here? Free? Or in a cell underground? She hated to imagine the latter, but if it was the former, that brought up a different, harder question: Why wouldn't she have reached out to Neko?

When they were in Philadelphia, in those liminal few years after the hurricane but before her father died and she left to become a mudlark, there had been one moment, as she sat on the sofa with him, when he'd asked the question about Burning Man that must have been floating through his mind for months: "Why did you have your friend send that text?" His voice soft, not holding any blame or anger, though the words themselves had been tiny bullets that hit Neko like bird shot.

"Because she was breaking up the family."

Her father had let out a long breath. "I did that, not your mother."

Shaking the memory from her head, Neko felt tugged downward, the sadness that resided in the pit of her stomach spreading. She needed something—a little shock to the system, a deposit into the account of secret moments that kept her going. She swung herself down the zip line toward the storage platform and slipped her body between the boxes and bags of foodstuffs, rooted around in the produce. Next to the leeks, gritty with dirt, was a small sack of bright yellow lemons from their Land Rover. Iggy had convinced her to leave their produce behind for the kids. She peeled one lemon with her thumbnail, ripping off the bitter pith, the soft white of the underbelly pitted with divots, an entire miniature world. She bit into the fiber-laced flesh of the lemon and let the juice seep into the back of her mouth—sharp and wondrous and tart as hell.

She looked up to see a sentry, still with his rifle, staring at her. She ate the lemon in its entirety. She smiled at the man and felt a small lift, a little morsel of light sliding down her soft gullet.

"WE'RE HEADING OUT TOMORROW," SAID IGGY, THE CREW GATHERED around him in the nest. "When we return the Rover and factory minerals to the Breakwater goons, we'll tell them there was an accident with Jules. That she didn't make it back. And Harriet, you can lay low at the Watering Hole while Neko and I complete the last leg of our lark."

"Lay low?" Harriet raised her voice for the first time since her return. "You're not going to use what happened to me as an excuse to cut me out of the crew. Or out of the payday . . ."

"When you say last leg of the lark—what does *that* mean?" interrupted Jules.

Iggy gave Neko a look that meant he was handing it off to her. His profile was encased in sunlight from the nest's opening.

"Well, we're delivering goods to an underground bunker." The cotton on her shirt snagged on the nest as she stood, thread pulling a fissure along the sleeve. "You know. As one does." Everything unraveled in the end.

"What? Where?"

"We don't have the exact coordinates yet."

Harriet asked if it was legal.

"Definitely not."

"I'm coming, too," Jules butted in. "I never said I wasn't."

The aerie rocked from their movements, and they held on until it stilled, staring at one another in a confusing standoff.

"I overheard you," said Neko. "Your mother wants you to stay."

Jules grunted. "My mother wants me to stay in Manhattan. But she doesn't get to decide. I want to go with you."

Flustered, Iggy shook his head. "But how can we trust you?"

"What do you mean?"

He rubbed his eyes and lowered his voice. "Were those raiders at the Ice House from here?"

Neko sucked in air—it hadn't yet occurred to her that the

"raiders" that day who'd recognized Jules must have come from here. But of course.

Jules sighed. "A couple of them used to be. They left the Hive years ago."

"How can we be sure?"

"Why would that guy literally *spit in my face* if we were part of some grand conspiracy together?" Jules's face was flushed. "When we came on this lark, you already knew I was using false papers. It's not my fault Harriet was kidnapped, but you could argue it's my fault that she's back safe." The young woman made an effort to look them in the eyes. "This is my home, but I left because I want something different."

Neko realized that she still didn't know what that something really was. She tried to read Harriet's face, but her eyes were far away.

Jules changed tack. "Look. You don't know this part of the Sink like I do. With me on your team, you have allies. As you can see, that's not worth nothing." There was a beat of silence, and then Jules said, "Isn't this where you tell me, *You can come, but no more monkey business*?"

Neko didn't smile, but she nodded at Iggy.

"You can come," said Iggy, squeezing Jules's shoulder, "but no more monkey business." And then he began hooting and squatting like a chimp.

THAT EVENING, NEKO MADE IT A POINT TO SEEK OUT LA JEFA.

"I'm sorry to steal your daughter again."

"I'm sorry, too."

Neko nodded. "Is there anything we can do before we leave?"

She shook her head. "No, no." She looked up toward where

a group of people was gathering, beginning to clap and make a fuss over something. "Later, though." Jules's mother turned, eyes unblinking. "There may come a time in the future when we need a favor."

"Excuse me?" asked Neko, not understanding.

"I'm sure we can count on you."

Neko realized that she and her crew would leave in debt to these people—the worst kind of debt because the cost was unknown. But this was the way of the Sink, she supposed, though she was beginning to wonder if there was more going on in the Hive than *an open community dedicated to starting over.*

"But now," said La Jefa, "we're celebrating." And she drew Neko into the crowd, which circled around a pie aflame with candles and held by a shyly smiling Jules.

"It's her birthday?" whispered Neko.

"Well, no. But we've missed her last three, so . . ."

Everyone began to sing.

IT WAS FUNNY WHICH REMNANTS OF THE OLD WORLD—LIKE CANDLES and birthday parties—survived. Neko was born in June, so there had never been a school party—usually just gorging on cake with her parents in a city that had largely emptied out for the summer.

In fact, the Nightjars' song "Summer Baby" had been written about Neko's birthday. According to the story told to her, the band had been in Hawaii for a music festival when they found out her mother was pregnant, and for some reason, the thing they all couldn't get over was that the due date would be in August.

"I always figured I'd have a winter baby," her father had told her.

"Winter babies. That's why we're so *cool,*" joked her mom, born in February.

"Reserved," her father piled on, "a hoarding of the harvest."

"Wet wool. Musk."

"We are definitely musky."

So they'd written a song about it, and it had ended up being the closest thing they ever had to a *Billboard* hit. Neko had loved it, of course. She'd loved to hear the story of it—the lemony Hawaiian sunrise; the shave ice; the wonder over the baby, who at the time looked like a little shrimp in the sonogram photo—and so she was always asking them to play it, though it was not a lullaby, not even close, the jangling of minor chords and non-melodic, non-rhyming choruses belted out and merging with guitar crescendos so that if you didn't already know the lyrics, hearing the song probably wasn't going to elucidate them for you.

Sometimes her mother had tried to pick up the old Alvarez leaning in the corner of the room, but Neko would wail, "Noooo."

Her mother would laugh before carrying Neko into the studio where the Les Paul stood on its stand.

Summer baby. Sun glare. Red skin. Summer baby, of long days, of nights warm enough to sleep in the fields, covered in dew. Of swelter and languor. Fireflies. Summer baby. The sound of wooden bats. Thock, thock. Boredom and empty afternoons. Summer baby. Scorched. Abundance and dry lips. Shave ice with chili guava. Thock, wooden bats. Thock, thock. Sunscreen. Salt. Sweaty hair at your neck. Summer baby. Summer baby. Summer baby.

THE WRECKAGE

Track 6: "Say Cyclops"

"I'm not running around again." This was what Max had told Jenny the previous week when she said she wasn't sure she wanted to go to Vermont this year.

"What are you doing, then?"

"I don't know how to articulate it in words." As though words were the problem.

Jenny had fiddled with the strings of her pajama pants, covered in tigers. "Well, paint it, then. Or dance it. Or act it out like charades. Hieroglyphics?"

Max's face had convulsed between laughter and disgust. He'd picked up a knife from the dish drying rack and looked at it as though he were contemplating slitting his wrists.

But she wouldn't feel sorry for him. She wouldn't give in to his theatrics this time.

She thought about how Neko asked to try her coffee once a month or so, each time torquing her face at the taste. But she kept asking. As though she already understood that growing up was about learning to love that which is bitter.

At the ramshackle Vermont farmhouse they'd rented for the month, Jenny and Max unloaded groceries and talked about what to make for dinner. As though their marriage wasn't tender and teetering after Jenny had forgiven him—had she, though?—for the affair he swore was finished. For good this time.

"Pancakes for dinner!" declared Neko.

"For dinner?" asked Max. Jenny could see that he was torn between wanting to be the fun dad and his new obsession with healthy living.

"French toast, then."

They laughed at Neko's idea of a compromise.

"Waffles?"

"Waffles and chicken," said Max. "At least then we'll get some protein."

While he cooked, Jenny and Neko rummaged through cabinets for place mats and tea light candles.

They sat down together under a funky old chandelier, Neko drinking water from an enormous wine glass.

"Are you guys getting divorced?"

Neither of them answered right away, looking at each other, processing this question.

"Why would you ask that?" asked Max.

The girl was staring at her food, turning it over, as though it were a fascinating, newly discovered species.

"Technically, baby, your mom and I can't get divorced," said Max.

Neko's face scrunched. "Why not?"

"Well, baby, we never officially married."

"What!"

"I mean, we're basically married. Just not in the eyes of the law. And divorce is a legal procedure. We always thought marriage was unnecessary and, to be honest, kind of bourgeoisie."

Jenny wasn't sure whether to laugh or cry at this explanation. "Don't worry, Nekester," she said, resorting to a refrain from her daughter's infancy. "The important thing is that you're safe and you're loved."

Neko finally looked up at them. "But are *you*?"

Jenny stared at her daughter, trying to comprehend those words on those heart-shaped lips. Was her daughter just mimicking? Reflecting back? Or could she see right through them?

"We are a family," Max said, as if this answered the question. "We'll always be family."

After dinner they played gin rummy in front of the fire. Jenny didn't believe in letting kids win at games; it wasn't good for them to think that life was that way. But Neko was naturally lucky at cards. She won, not always, but often, without them ever throwing a game on purpose. Maybe it was an omen for her daughter's future. Auspicious? That was the word.

One of their early albums had been titled *Auspice*, but from Jenny's perspective now, she thought, *What rot.* I mean, how young and stupid had they been to think they could prophesy the future? That they could interpret the signs of a world gone mad?

People would always assume it was the infidelity. But the truth, as usual, was more complicated. Maybe Jenny should have left him years ago. Maybe it would have been easier for Neko, for all of them, to adjust if they had pulled the trigger earlier.

The first time they'd gone to Vermont, after the first time things had fallen apart and their therapist suggested they escape the city, Neko was seven. They put the band on hiatus, not the marriage—the argument being that the marriage needed to heal and survive on its own terms, without the constant pressure of their livelihood. What did it mean that she found it easier to stay in the same bed as Max than on the same stage? Maybe the only reason she had been the faithful one was the lack of opportunity.

It was a platitude to say that people changed. Of course they did. But Jenny felt as though nobody ever mentioned how change wasn't the issue so much as the *rate* of change. Max's omnivorous, voracious curiosity was one of the things that made him such an interesting artist, but it also made him hard to grow alongside.

There was the Las Vegas phase, where he learned all the complicated odds for Texas Hold'em. Then, almost as soon as Jenny became comfortable at a poker table, he swore off gambling. "Go if you want to," he would say, shrugging. Then it was basketball and the Spurs—he was obsessed until the day he decided television was rotting his brain and melodramatically tossed it onto the sidewalk. There was the washboard and bluegrass phase and the classic car phase. He even got into knitting for a while. In a television interview once, he said, "I was a Taoist on Tuesday, a nihilist by Friday. Most of my life has been like that."

The thing was, she was open to *his* new interests, but he never followed hers. So, over time, Jenny became wary of getting too involved in his manias and hobbyhorses. She tried to focus on her own things: paellas, genealogy, political activism of a sort. The fact that he'd cheated on her—sure, it didn't help things. But there hadn't needed to be another woman for Jenny to feel like a runner-up in Max's life. To feel like an audience member at the Max Show—which as time passed had also become the Max and Neko Show.

The band's hiatus did ease tensions—their fraught emotional situation had been freed from the added strain of artistic and business complications. But as time went on, the new space between them grew maybe too large. What did normal couples, who didn't work together, talk about?

She read in some stupid advice column that indifference in a relationship was worse than anger. So Jenny tried to care more. About everything. When he put the dishes into the dishwasher all wrong, she didn't just redo it as she usually would have—she called him out. "Come on, grown man! Surely you can anticipate how concave shapes left facing upward will fill with water." He smiled, saying, "You always had the engineer's mind." When she told him he couldn't just give Neko heaping bowls of ice cream every night, he said, "Okay," and started buying vanilla, which Neko didn't care for.

Years had passed and they were back in Vermont. Was it a prison or a refuge? Jenny now sat on a wooden balcony at sunset where, even on the third floor, one could catch only slivers of pastel, the trees like spikes flush with leaves, hemming them in. She worked on her solo album:

Say ceiling, say civilization, say civilities,
Say sorry
Say roundabout,
Say rover, rover, let the lotus eaters come over
Say Cyclops, Circe, Calypso
Scylla and Charybdis
Swiss chard for the bard

She was happy. Max was miserable. He was a born collaborator, but Jenny had come to realize she liked working alone. Though, technically, she wasn't working on her album entirely alone. Jesse was going to produce it. Her own dirty little secret.

"We should do a live album," Max said at one point, peeking his head through the doorway.

"Yeah?" Jenny was wary.

"Most live albums are so phony, you know. Overdubs, stupid fake crowd noises. Ours would be pure." His eyes were wide.

Jenny knew nothing they did could be pure, but she nodded noncommittally.

Through, the rural stillness, heady and thick after more rain, there was one bird whose call she heard over and over, and the image that came to mind was cut quartz. She wondered if she could re-create the sound on her Moog.

A few years ago, Jesse had read some dense linguistic book about musical cognition and how different languages describe acoustic range. He'd told them it wasn't always done with spatial metaphors like up/down, as in English. The example that he kept mentioning—in increasing awe of it—was the Zimbabwean musicians who referred to low pitches as "crocodile" and high pitches as "those who follow crocodiles." As a band, they began to come up with their own peculiar ways to describe sound, at first as a joke, but then some of it stuck, a private language. "Kimchi" had to do with drums, when they were both crisp and spicy, taking over the flavor of the song. Sometimes Jenny pleaded for the vocals to be more "sloe gin fizz" and less "lavender hand lotion." And with basically every song they were trying to achieve "wok hei." Like dragon's breath. Here in Vermont, working on this track, Jenny wanted lo-fi but with less distortion, less fuzz. Less "dragon's breath" and more "dragon's gold." The buried treasure greedily hoarded for its sparkle and shine. That was what she was going for now.

Jenny heard the screen door bang down below, the clack of

a plate on the picnic table—Max and his vice, blowing the smoke from his cigarette into the steamy air, and his virtue, giving her the space to be up here for a while. She couldn't see him, but she could hear the flick of the flint. Two cigarettes in a row. Neko must have been inside reading manga because he tried not to smoke in front of her. Apparently quitting smoking wasn't a priority of his new healthy lifestyle—paleo something or other, where you ate like a caveman. Faintly, she could hear that he was listening to one of the early mixtapes she'd given him, the one with too much Joy Division. She heard him say under his breath, "I love G. I live for G." She wondered if he was talking about the note or the chord. Or something or someone else entirely.

Writing songs by herself was like solving a puzzle box. Everything was intricate, miniature. Her Moog Grandmother was like the magnifying glass that allowed her to see into the dollhouse rooms of her past. She twisted the decay dial, pressed down the keys, and turned the spring reverb: magic.

Today, she plugged her tenor electric into the Grandmother and played about the first time they'd come to Vermont, damaged but more hopeful.

Gold
Goldenrod
Gold band
Dark
Darkest
Darkness.

Back then, they'd stopped at a barn advertising maple syrup. The woman inside let them taste three types and, as she handed them tiny paper cups, explained how they were produced by collecting sap at different times of year: golden, amber, dark.

Jenny watched her daughter, never before allowed to take syrup straight into her mouth, no cheap box-mix pancake to dilute the sweetness. Seven-year-old Neko was in heaven.

The three of them were giddy with sugar.

When they had to decide which type to buy—beige plastic jugs lined up along the wall—it was Max's idea that they count to three and each say their favorite at the same time. One, two, three. Jenny said, "Dark"; Max and Neko said, "Golden." *Gold. Goldenrod. Gold band. Dark. Darkest. Darkness.*

In the decision of the maple syrup, Jenny was outvoted, and they bought the golden—so tawny and light that it almost disappeared when you poured it on anything. The opposite of Neko's "gold" bracelets that she refused to take off, and that turned her skin a sick chartreuse.

Jenny had thought: *For most of my life I have been free and done exactly what I wanted—I wish that for you, child. I wish for you to drink the world like a cup of golden syrup. No napkins.*

Gold
Goldenrod
Gold band
Dark
Darkest
Darkness
Helios warns us not to eat the cows but he's just the sun
What does he know about flesh, anyway?

21

AT THE WATERING HOLE, A SECURITY GOON INSPECTED THEIR PAPERS as they waited in line for fuel.

"You've been out four days past your time allotment," he said.

"Blown head gasket," explained Iggy, going for a man-to-man tone of voice. "Took us a while to find some sealant and motor oil to fix it."

"Four days?"

"This is a Land Rover, mate."

"Why didn't you contact us on the satellite?"

He had their lie ready. "Last time we did that, the agency sent another crew, and those assholes stole the whole gig from us. Not doing that again."

The goon grunted and nodded them through.

THE MUDLARK BOARDINGHOUSE WAS LOCATED IN AN OLD MANSION built around a central courtyard. Each of them was issued a hammock to hang from the hooks that studded the walls, swinging above broken and mangled Saltillo tiles, mouse droppings swept into the corners. Harriet wrinkled her nose at the bathroom's yellowing porcelain and mildew smell.

They showered and left to procure supplies. Neko felt bleary-eyed and exhausted in a new way, deep in her bones.

FIRST STOP WAS AT A PLACE THAT HAD ONCE BEEN A VAST PARKING complex, now home to a freewheeling gray market—not exactly illegal, but products that went unregulated by the government and purchases that were nonreturnable, caveat emptor. The darkness of the tunnels themselves was permeated by the warm rectangles of lantern light emitted through each opening.

They walked along the crowded thoroughfare, past storefronts hawking questionable dietary supplements and shady technology add-ons, past kiosks displaying taxidermied foxes with haunted glass eyeballs and brightly colored diamond kites, until they eventually found Sacred Moon. The sign was small but easy to spot—the only one hand-painted on plywood. Inside, shelves were lined with crystals and jars of dried plants. There was a mossy quality to the air and soft trance music on the sound system.

As they walked toward the back, Iggy stopped to inspect a large chunk of quartz while Neko approached a woman who stood behind the counter staring into a microscope. "We're looking for something special."

The woman glanced at them and shrugged as if to say, *Why else would you be here*? Purple asters were tattooed down her cheek and neck.

"Mountain ginkgo."

"Kyoto ginkgo is FDA approved. You can get it in any pharmacy." But she was studying Neko more closely now, waiting for something.

"Hawaiian mountain ginkgo."

The woman didn't flinch. "That plant went extinct a hundred years ago."

"Is that so?" Neko hoped she had her lines right—she'd memorized them with Chaplin, which felt like a hundred years ago.

"Look here," said the woman, turning the microscope toward her.

Once the lens was in focus, Neko could see tiny worms on the surface of a dark leaf. She let Jules and Harriet take a look next.

"What are they?" she asked.

"This particular herb only works if the parasites are alive. If they die, so does the leaf's power to amplify the female orgasm." She took the microscope back. "Nature is amazing."

Neko looked at Iggy, who was blinking rapidly in an effort to keep a straight face.

"Come back in one hour."

THE CREW WALKED ALONG THE DANK ARTERY OF THE GRAY MARKET. The mudlarks at this outpost, which served the northern Sink, tended to be younger since rural gigs were less desirable, and they sported retro trends—punk and goth, war-grunge, and K-pop. Some of them wore masks sewn to make their faces look like skulls or flocks of butterflies or dragons breathing fire.

The crew window-shopped: Vials of unregulated blood coagulator. Anti-aging pills that may or may not have been carcinogenic. Night vision contact lenses. Cell scramblers. Military-grade muscle enhancers. Runes and smudge sticks and votive candles made of ambergris.

Neko bought a small carton of goat milk from an automated fridge.

Jules turned to Neko and asked, "How do they know we don't just want the actual Hawaiian mountain ginkgo?"

"It's code," said Iggy, more gently than Neko would have.

"Yeah, but what is it code *for*?" asked Jules, insistent.

Iggy and Neko looked at each other. All the information they'd been given thus far: *Get to the Watering Hole and ask for the Hawaiian ginkgo plant at Sacred Moon in the gray market.*

"The coordinates for the bunker?" Neko drank from the diamond spout of the milk carton and then nodded at her bag, where she had the master of her mother's album. "I need to find the music chop shop."

"I'll come," said Harriet.

Neko shrugged.

"Me, too," said Jules.

Harriet pursed her lips strangely, and Neko could tell she was nonplussed. "Stay with Iggy. I've got a list of supplies I need you guys to procure."

WHEN THEY WERE OUT OF EARSHOT, NEKO TURNED TO HARRIET. "ARE you ready to tell me what's going on with you two?"

Harriet let her smile fall. "I just need some space."

Neko's parents had used a similar phrase when they told her they were separating. As if the problem were a matter of geography.

"How'd you know Iggy was the one for you? You know, when you were young?"

"I thought he was hot, and then suddenly a decade passed." Neko shrugged. "It's hard to explain."

"Personally, I'm attracted to the strong, silent type. You know, the mysterious ones with dark pasts." Harriet paused and her voice changed, lowered a little. "But now I'm starting to think I just choose them so I can project onto them what I want to see. Know what I mean?"

"Maybe."

"Do you tell each other everything?" Harriet continued. "Do you keep secrets from him? Is it sometimes a drag running a crew with your hubby?"

Oh, God, thought Neko. *Kill me now.* "Do we need to find a therapy kiosk?"

"Would you ever sell your crew license to one person? Like, to just me?"

Neko looked at her, trying to figure out what Harriet was really asking. "It's easier with a partner."

"Sure." Harriet moved in front of her as they wove their way through strangers, so Neko was staring at the sinews of her long, thin neck.

Neko felt an urge to reach out and touch her. "Hey, have you ever thought about a tattoo on that swan neck of yours? Maybe a sugar spoon? Or a Gila monster?"

"Did you know that Gila monster venom is an ingredient in weight-loss drugs . . . ?"

Neko and Harriet found the sound shop at the end of the tunnel, its walls lined with earbuds meant to be surgically implanted in the ear canal.

She took the master, encased in a foam sleeve, from her bag. "Can you take this and make a mother album?" she asked.

The ponytailed proprietor took the silver disk and inspected it. He sighed deeply as though she were asking a huge favor.

"I'll pay."

"Yes, you will." He typed something into his computer. "Also, we have a special today on embeddables . . ."

WHEN THEY MET UP WITH THE OTHER TWO, JULES WAS CARRYING A bamboo cage with a songbird inside.

"Oh, God." Neko had asked them to buy something mildly illegal—something punishable by a fine—so that if they were stopped by the authorities while moving Chaplin's materials to the bunker, it would serve as a red herring. She hadn't meant something living, though. Something that made noise and needed to be fed.

"A lilac-breasted roller from Tanzania," said Jules.

"*Bellissima,* no?" asked Iggy.

The bird, feathers bristling and cheeks puffed out, looked as though it had been dipped in kindergarten paint. Lilac breast, yes, and a yellow-and-green head. Its back was streaked with orange that led into two forked tail feathers. Neko had to admit, it was lovely.

"You two are in charge of taking care of that thing."

AT SACRED MOON, THE WOMAN BEHIND THE COUNTER HANDED NEKO a small tincture bottle. Unsure what to do, Neko stood there holding it in front of her.

"Why don't you smell it?" said the woman sweetly, as though she were now a department store perfume lady.

Neko unscrewed the top, sniffed, then handed it to Iggy. It was an incredible smell—sweet and floral, but also a little lemony, a little earthy.

"What is it?"

"Hawaiian ginkgo."

"You said it was extinct."

"There are clippings from the last one in the Harvard Herbaria. We've extracted the DNA and re-created the olfactory experience."

The scent was so wonderful that for a moment Neko forgot to be annoyed and confused. Then she remembered why they were here. "What am I supposed to do with this?" She had assumed when she asked for Hawaiian gingko that she wouldn't actually get Hawaiian gingko.

The woman shrugged. "You said you were looking for something special." She nodded at the bottle. "I'd close that up if I were you. So it doesn't dissipate." Then the woman turned her back as though to dismiss them.

Neko stood there trying to interpret the words. She could tell from Iggy's face that he was pissed.

"Oh," said the woman. "I almost forgot. I have passes to Club Kindred tonight that I can't use. Why don't you go?" She handed over an envelope. Inside were four tickets and a handful of pills. "It'll be the bee's knees."

22

AS THEY WAITED IN LINE OUTSIDE THE ENTRANCE TO THE "CLUB," Harriet brought one hand out of the pocket of her jacket to reveal the four tiny pills lined up on her palm like a row of buttons.

"So, Jules, what do you know about the lotus-eaters?" Harriet presented the pills to Jules with a sacerdotal gesture; Jules reached for one with her thumb and forefinger, but Iggy's hand got there first, covering the pills and Harriet's palm. He shook his head. "This is a job."

Harriet frowned and put the pills back in her pocket.

Club Kindred was situated inside an old public library, and the line snaked up the massive steps. The night was muggy, a gibbous moon sagging in the sky.

"Private party," said the bouncer, oddly slender and thin-boned for his position, though the gnarly scar across his face was likely intimidating enough.

"We have these," said Neko, handing over the passes.

Inside, the building vibrated.

On the mezzanine, Neko tried to make sense of a water-damaged mural that unfurled along the hallway: women in robes reaching up and holding something—branches? scarves?—and floating above what had probably once been grass or heather but was now black with mold spores and latticed with the flashes of white lights.

Benches were blanketed in people in various stages of passing out; rooms branched off to either side with deejays spinning UK garage and trance. Some people wore goggles, interacting with spatial audio and elements only they could see. With a nod, the crew split, snaking their way into separate rooms.

Neko slid onto the dance floor inside what had once been a reading room, though any oak tables or quaint green lamps were long gone and a flood of bodies writhed in their place as speakers hanging from the rafters banged out maniac thumps from an 808. The plaster of the impossibly grand barrel vault ceiling was cracked and the shelves that lined the walls were warped and bookless, though Neko saw that people had filled some of them with old coins and paper notes and bundles of sage. Offerings to the gods of pleasure and forgetfulness. A waitress coated in body paint to look like a flamingo walked around wearing a tray of shots like an old cigarette girl, and Neko bought two.

The music felt like it was entering her body in little electric shocks. She stood there and let herself enjoy the feeling, let herself be seen. *Here I am,* she thought. *Come and get me.*

"Nice ink," said a voice.

Neko turned to see a middle-aged man, way too muscular. He pointed at her tattoo of a pair of dentures—those beautiful, gummy chompers featured prominently on her upper back. They were a tribute to her grandmother, who used to take out her false teeth to scare young Neko, grinning with a gaping maw. Neko would run from the room, screeching, before immediately turning back. Just one more look. The push and pull of horror.

When visiting her grandmother, after her bath, Neko had been allowed to open the jars of thick white creams smelling of bergamot or rose and slather them over her body until she could have slipped down the drain. She'd gone to sleep encased in a moist film of love, and in her dreams, her limbs had bloomed into all the flowers and fruits that lent their essence to her grandmother's magical balms. She'd felt protected. If anyone came for her in the night, she was sure her grandmother would take out her dentures and roar.

When the man in the club reached out to touch the tattoo, Neko roared at him and kept moving.

EVENTUALLY, SHE FELT A TORSO AT HER BACK, PRESSING INTO HER lightly but too completely to be accidental.

Chaplin.

She smiled. From behind, he put his fingertips on her hip bones, and they started to move together, as vipers might weave back and forth to ease the digestion of swallowed prey. Oh, Chaplin.

His breath on her neck. "Ignacio?"

"Somewhere around here."

"Shame."

Neko's left hand was in the air. She felt Chaplin's fingertips run down her body, wrist to thigh, and something ached inside her. She was a tree and the sap was rising. They danced so as not to draw attention to themselves. At least, that's what Neko told herself.

When she turned to face him, she noticed he was wearing a ridiculous jumpsuit and contact lenses that turned his eyes an eerie milk white—probably meant to trick the facial scanners.

"Didn't expect to see you here."

"The bunker ordered a lot of goods, not just the canisters. I decided to bring it all myself," he said, "so I could see you." He handed her a key to the locker where everything was stored. "You're not wearing your new perfume."

"About that . . ."

Leading her farther into the mess of the dance floor, he explained that the scent in the vial was the passcode. "From here on out," he said, "it's how the right people will recognize you as also being the right people."

It was hard to hear him over the pounding of the music.

"We show up at the bunker wearing perfume, and they let us in?" Neko asked.

"You wish it were that simple." He said they would travel to coordinates deep inside the Sink, and, from there, someone would recognize their scent and give them directions to the final location.

Almost to herself, she wondered, "Maybe I should leave the apprentices here at the Watering Hole."

"No." He shook his head. "You will need a full crew."

The music transitioned into a new track, this one more languid, keyboards spiraling against the drums. They swooned. His elbows felt like sandpaper. Neko welcomed the sweat, something slick to keep her body from sticking to his. Her body wanted to stick. She looked up at the arched ceiling—at least fifty feet above them—and eyed the one remaining plaster rosette. She would have liked to take it with her.

As they danced closer to the deejay, they had to dodge flinging bodies and whipping glow sticks. "You don't have to go through with it," Chaplin said. His mouth was up against her ear. She couldn't see his face. "I can't protect you out there."

She danced harder; she swung her head back and forth, curls plastered against her forehead, and knew her neck would be sore tomorrow. She and Iggy had partnered up when they were so young.

Chaplin stepped away from her and spun. "Come back with me. I'll get someone else to do the drop." He began doing the running man, arms moving back and forth, turning his words into a chant timed with the music. "Come *with* me. Come with *me*."

She laughed and the hurt on his face was a flash, like a lightning strike, there and then gone.

He composed himself and smiled more coyly. "Come with me for *one* night then? Just one little tiny night?"

The only time she'd ever betrayed Iggy was back when they were training to be mudlarks. And, afterward, the poor one-night stand—some woman from Hoboken—had mooned over her for months, making Neko feel even guiltier. She thought of her father and his longing for a woman who was everything her mother was not. She thought of all the things people want, or think they want, and how impossible it is to know the difference.

"Not tonight," she said, breathing him in.

"Being with you is like falling asleep in a spot of sun only to wake in the cold dark." Chaplin then told her to check the unisex bathroom, third stall, after the phrase *I wanna fuck you like an animal*.

"Subtle," she said, "and classy."

He cupped her neck with his hand, and then he started to move backward into the crowd of dancers, away from her. She almost reached out. She almost said, *Wait*.

She turned back to the crowd and rode the wave of the music.

NEKO LEFT THE THIRD STALL, HAVING WRITTEN DOWN THE LATITUDE and longitude numbers scrawled among the crude bathroom graffiti, and was surprised to find Jules waiting for her in front of the row of sinks. Her eyes were glassy and wide.

"Do you feel okay?" Neko asked, wondering if she and Harriet had taken the pills after all. She found a paper towel to wet. "Where's Harriet?"

"Picked a fight with some guy who whistled at her. After she clocked him, he challenged her to a game of pool and now she's running the table." Jules accepted the damp paper towel, pressing it to the back of her neck. "I saw you dancing," she said.

The light fixtures along the mirrored wall were brass contraptions that gave off a muted glow. A jewel box.

"That's the game," she said.

"I just . . . worry about you guys, that's all," said Jules, looking straight ahead into the mirror. "I wouldn't want Uncle Iggy's feelings to be hurt." In the sweetness of her voice, Neko detected something off.

"I'm more worried about Harriet. What's going on between you two?"

Jules let out a long breath. "I want to help, and she doesn't want my help." Then Jules's face shifted back into something Neko couldn't read. "Chaplin is a black market profiteer," she said. "He's just another tool of the system, you know."

Neko turned on the tap and splashed her face. She noticed her teeth were yellowing. "Welcome to the Sink, sweetheart."

As they made their way through the bathroom door, back into the noise and light and denial, Neko remembered the time at the poker table when she'd told Chaplin she and Iggy might pack it in, move to the Inside. He'd laughed in her face.

"What? Think I'm too wild for life on the Inside?"

He'd shaken his head and smiled. "You don't like to do what

you're told." Later, after the poker game was over, he'd turned to her and said quietly, "You know mudlarking is not really wild, right? You know that we're all working for the Man."

AS NEKO WAS LOOKING FOR HER CREW SO THEY COULD LEAVE, HARriet appeared, grabbed her forearm, and pulled. Neko thought she must be taking her to Iggy or to the exit, but no.

The thump of the bass receded as they wound their way up a small staircase, and a different, softer sound emerged as they approached a small, round stage where a striking older woman was dancing, the bells circling her ankles and wrists jangling as she moved. A traumatized music box ballerina.

Neko's palms tingled. It was hard to do anything but stare.

"I wanted you to see this," whispered Harriet.

The dancer twirled through the thick, smoky air. She wore a red leotard, and the outsides of her thighs were spackled with bruises.

"I made a ballerina sculpture in art class once," said Harriet. "Out of wire and papier-mâché. I painted her black and strung her with orange blossoms."

The woman in the red leotard twirled like her life depended on it. There was something both sad and admirable about her, the jangle of her bells and the circling of her wrists.

Eventually, Neko and Harriet turned back. The staircase was narrow. Their hips touched as they descended.

"Don't you find this hard?" asked Neko quietly as they moved. "This life? Maybe it was fun at first—the danger and adrenaline—but do you really want the license? Do you really want to stay?"

Harriet stopped and turned. Her eyes were as brown as tree bark. She was so young.

"When I was a kid, we went to Harvard to see the only Le Corbusier building in America," Harriet told her. "There are photographs of my parents and me in front of it when I was little, and I'm pointing up at the cantilevers. They liked to say my first word was 'see.'" Harriet turned back around, jacket tied at her waist in the heat of the club, shirt scooped in the back so that Neko could see her scapulae, three small moles like Orion's Belt.

"Okay?"

"I like not feeling the pressure to be something special. In the Sink, there's satisfaction in achieving the basics: survival, money, the occasional beauty."

Neko nodded, noting how Harriet had elided the other side of the coin: hard beds, hard bread, squatters with knives. Though maybe they were not so different from fathers who knocked their daughters against walls.

"Look what I won at the pool table," said Harriet, smiling, opening her bag to show Neko a string of dried chilies, a tin of petroleum jelly, a clutch of bangles.

Neko, now having to yell over the techno music, said, "Those bracelets will turn your wrist green, you know."

Harriet laughed. "Good."

THE WRECKAGE

Track 7: "Hades"

The land stretched in every direction as though nothing else existed, gold in the morning light. It reminded Jenny of *The Odyssey*'s oft-repeated chorus: *rosy-fingered dawn*. How Homer claims Poseidon goes on a trip to visit the Ethiopians who live at the ends of the earth, some near the sunrise, some near the sunset.

The driver had turned from the two-lane highway onto a dirt road, though the passengers would hardly know it because the tricked-out Hummer practically floated. Up ahead: a brutalist metal dome. Wind turbines sparkled in the sun. Max began singing under his breath, "'. . . *upon the fields of barley* . . .'" His a capella was extraterrestrial.

"I hate that song," whispered Layla. "It makes me cry."

The realtor, if one could even call him that, had insisted on the early hour so they could "see it in the best light," as if anyone bought a condo in a refurbished missile silo because of how it looked during the golden hour.

Jenny and Max and Layla tumbled from the Hummer. They followed the Asian family from Vancouver who had just exited the first vehicle toward the entrance to the Hades Survival Complex. A sharp wind threatened to take off Jenny's X-Ray Spex trucker hat.

"The monolithic dome is built to withstand winds stronger than an F5 tornado," said the realtor, Paul Something-or-Other. He wore ill-fitting camo and carried a leather briefcase. "If only Dorothy'd had access to a bunker condo when that storm hit, am I right?"

Max went wide-eyed.

Layla Wei had convinced Max and Jenny to come with her to tour the facility, where she claimed to be seriously considering buying an "apartment." She'd told the developers that they were "her associates" because only people who provided documented proof of the ability to purchase a two-to-four-million-dollar unit (liquid, because no bank would finance such a thing) were allowed to tour the bunker and learn its location.

Despite the wind, which threw dirt into their faces, Paul didn't immediately let them inside. "I think it's important for me to mention," he said, looking serious, though looking serious might have been a permanent condition for Paul, "our clients are not the 'survival nuts'"—he used air quotes—"you hear about in the media. They are educated and informed. They want to make sure their families are protected in an uncertain world."

Max whispered in Jenny's ear: "Unlike poor folk, who prefer to feed their children to the wolves."

Jenny's face agreed with him, mirrored his disgust, but inside she felt slightly more ambivalent: Was this what it meant to be a good parent these days? A bunker in your back pocket?

"Vancouver is not close by," said the patriarch of the Vancouver family, as though unsure if Paul was aware of this geographic fact. "If there is truly a disaster, how will we get here?"

Paul nodded vigorously. "We have three emergency plans for each family to ensure passage to the facility in the event of *any* catastrophe."

"Asteroid impact?" whispered Max. "Nuclear winter? Yeti attack?"

"What sort of plans?" asked Layla, pinching Max into silence.

"We can't disclose the details until after you've provided the down payment." Paul turned to the fingerprint scanner and let them inside.

They were carried belowground by an elevator cast in an eerie red light. It seemed to take forever to deposit them at the model condo.

The woman from Vancouver, dressed in what looked like something from a designer safari collection, turned to Layla and said something in Chinese.

Layla looked chagrined. "I don't speak Mandarin."

The woman sighed and turned to dig around in her purse, which was almost as big as she was. The couple's two college-aged children were blank-faced, clearly wanting to be anywhere but here.

Inside, the model looked like any generic high-end apartment except for the lack of natural light. Fake windows displayed glossy static photographs of fields and streams, which to Jenny was somehow creepier than just having a blank wall. At least there was authenticity to a blank wall.

Paul told them that full-floor units could house up to ten people, half-floor units five. "There is redundant air filtration, including nuclear, biological, and chemical."

"Animal, vegetable, mineral." Max continued his whisper campaign.

Jenny felt as though she were watching Max, performing like always, from a gaping distance. Why did he feel so far away?

"As you can see, high-end stainless appliances and Kohler fixtures throughout. And each unit comes with a five-year food reserve!"

Across the marble kitchen counter, the patriarch of the Vancouver family peppered Paul with questions. "Will there be a medical doctor in residence?"

"Depends," said Paul. "You're not one, are you?" He laughed. "No matter who is at the facility, there is a fully outfitted medical first aid center. The equipment is so advanced, I could probably do surgery on you if I had to."

At this, the man wrinkled his forehead. "You don't own a unit here, do you?"

For a moment Paul's face froze, but then he recovered. "No, no I don't. As it mentions in the paperwork, we screen all of the buyers of these units. Background checks. Resource checks. Good people all around."

A moment of silence fell. Jenny felt bad for the guy, resisted the urge to pat him on the arm like her childhood doctor used to do. *Pat, pat, pat.* The best medicine. She thought of playing doctor with her daughter, who loved to diagnose Jenny, picking up the plastic tool—what is that one called, not the stethoscope but the one that looks into your eardrum?—and saying, "Oh, no, Mama, you have mosquitoes in your ear." Neko gave her peanuts for medicine, placing them gently in Jenny's hand, and, in that moment, they did more good than all the Xanax in the world. When their cat, Tootsie, died the following week, Jenny had taken out the peanut jar, echoing Neko as she placed the nuts in her daughter's damp palm, hoping it would help. Hoping she would understand that this was her way of saying everything would be okay.

"Let's continue. I can't wait to show you the pool level."

From there, the tour became even more surreal. The pool had a waterfall feature made from fiberglass rocks and a domed ceiling that provided "a sense of sky" and it all gave Jenny the feeling of being inside a dollhouse or maybe a dream, one where the objects shimmered and tried to communicate their needs.

"I'm changing my mind about this place," said Max, tapping on the fiberglass and creating an echo. "There's some real potential here."

There was a dog park, basically a room covered in Astroturf. A floor for aquaponics and aquaculture food production. A library (shelves empty except for two copies of Kahlil Gibran's *The Prophet*), an arcade (*Ms. Pac-Man*), and a classroom with desks lining the wall.

Max put his arm around Layla, who raised her eyebrows in annoyance. "Imagine a music video set here. We could have Astroturf on the ceiling, the rooms getting smaller and smaller, the fake windows displaying images of Mars."

"Down, boy," she said.

"Would be very *of the moment*, don't you think?"

The last stop was the indoor shooting range. They had to crowd into the small space, which to Jenny looked like the shooting galleries on cop shows, the outline of a body attached to a retractable hook.

"The purchase of any unit at Hades Survival Complex comes with mandatory weapons training. Everyone must be prepared to participate fully in the protection of the community."

Jenny felt the tension in the room rise. "Protection from what?" She would like to imagine protection from evil, from solar winds, from extinction. But these kinds of weapons were meant to be used only against other animals, ones like themselves.

"That is, of course, dependent on the circumstances."

Jenny tried to figure out why the developers had named it Hades—had they really wanted prospective investors thinking of the place as some version of Hell? Then again, she thought, in *The Odyssey,* the dead who live there tell their secrets only after being given the blood of the living. Blood currency.

"Your website said there is military-grade security?" asked the patriarch.

"We have protocols in place for every possible danger."

Max mimed taking one of the guns from the glass case and shooting himself in the head.

Layla asked, "What kind of protocols?"

"We can't disclose the exact nature of our strategies before down payment." The realtor shrugged apologetically.

Jenny wondered if "military-grade" security guards would actually stick around to protect a bunch of rich people after the world had gone to hell. More likely they would turn on them. More likely they would abandon these people with their freeze-dried beef jerky. And who could blame them?

She thought about the violent magic of ripping a baby, blood of iron, out of her own body, something from nothing—although that wasn't entirely true because the fetus had also sucked from Jenny's own teeth and bones, taken what it needed if it was there to take. But still. The baby was not there in the world and then, one day, her body had produced it. Jenny wondered what else her body might be able to transfigure out of thin air. A boulder. A tree. If she closed her eyes and concentrated hard enough, would something begin to gestate in her collarbone? She put her hand on her chest and wondered if it already had. Then Jenny went home and wrote a song on her tenor electric—about blood currency, the only currency that actually mattered in the end.

The cat died, glassy eyes
My daughter didn't cry
She asked if the cat spirit would get wet outside

23

USING THE GRAFFITI NUMBERS FROM CLUB KINDRED'S BATHROOM stall, the crew plotted the latitude and longitude degrees on a paper map, then stood over it in silence, committing to memory the precise location and various potential routes.

"This isn't a regular shadow job, is it?" asked Harriet eventually. "This isn't just a big payday."

Neko looked at Iggy but said nothing.

"I mean, is it just a coincidence that the first time we take a gig outside Manhattan is immediately after you find your parents' master recordings?"

Neko forced herself to stare into Harriet's eyes—the blinking of her brown lashes. Harriet, pushy and smart, privileged and also wounded by her upbringing. Not so unlike Neko had been once.

"Yes," said Neko, and then she rolled up the map and torched it with her lighter.

Harriet stuck her finger into the birdcage to stroke the songbird, which they'd named Siouxsie Sioux. "Canary in a coal mine, baby girl. That's what you are."

AT ONE POINT, IGGY STOPPED DUCT-TAPING CRATES OF MATERIALS destined for the Cellar. "Speaking of masters, was the chop shop able to press it for you?"

"They were able to make a mother but not the stamper to press it directly into vinyl."

"We should pack it separately from the master." Iggy felt around behind him for the scissors.

"Actually, I gave the master to Chaplin to take back with him. Didn't want to risk having both on my person."

Iggy rolled his eyes.

Neko tried to make her face neutral. "You know what the Hive potter said? That he left the Inside because he was tired of living in a world run by—"

"Don't do that," he interrupted, putting down the roll of silver tape.

"Do what?" she asked, though she knew.

"Pretend your reluctance to move is because you want to protect me from the Inside."

She tried to put her hands on his shoulders, but he shrugged them off.

A LONG TIME BEFORE, MAYBE FIVE YEARS INTO THEIR MUDLARKING life, Iggy had been offered a job on the Inside by one of his old high school buddies. It had been a strange time for them: They were smuggling more and more for the black market and their most recent protégé, Richie, had just left to start his own crew.

"The gig is in Kansas City," said Iggy one day, after coming back from the market loaded down with food: turnips and yams, goat-milk yogurt. "Thought I'd put together an application."

She was lying on her back on their kitchen table, listening to Beach House on her headphones. She always felt listless when they were "home" in their flophouse apartment, at a loss for what to do with her body.

Neko swung her feet to the floor to help him unload perishables into their half fridge. "Kansas City," she said, nodding. "Wholesome Midwestern schools."

He held up a purple Cherokee tomato to show her that they were finally in season. "Neighbors who pour you sweet iced tea from a pitcher."

"Amber waves of grain."

"A normal life."

They were talking to each other in words but their voices were flat. As though, if they made no sudden movements, what they *said* they wanted might settle into Neko's rib cage and become what she actually wanted.

Before Iggy submitted his official application to travel to the Inside for the interview, Chaplin came through with the most lucrative black market job they'd been offered thus far. They decided to put off Kansas City.

"Is that okay?" Neko asked. "There will be other jobs, right? Other cold glasses of sweet tea?"

But, of course, there wouldn't be.

THE OUTPOST CHECKPOINT WAS HOUSED IN AN OLD NATIONAL PARK visitor center, and through the illuminated glass, Neko could see a diorama of a taxidermied brown bear rearing up on its hind legs. She stopped the Rover at the window that used to be the place for rangers to check camping reservations but what was now essentially passport control. Because their vehicle was packed with boxes of illegal goods destined for the bunker, Chaplin had arranged to bribe this particular security goon, and so Neko double-checked the name tag (WAYLON) and handed over the prepared envelope stuffed with carbon credits and scratch.

"Price of entry has gone up." Waylon had a big round head topped with shaggy blond hair that made him look more comical than intimidating.

"Since when?"

"I have a partner tonight." Through the dim interior, Neko saw another agent sitting with his back straight against the wall. "He wants a cut."

"Give him a cut of yours," said Neko, willing to play chicken with this meathead. Beside her, Iggy was using one hand to press down on her leg as though to keep her from jumping out of the vehicle and strangling the man.

Waylon shrugged and held up his radio as though he might call them in. He raised his eyebrows.

"Wait." Iggy turned in his seat to scan their supplies. "Maybe we have something else you might want? Almonds? Penicillin?"

"Don't be stupid."

Neko felt her eyelids twitching, the taste of copper in her throat. They could fight their way out, but if they did that, they'd have goons on their tail.

"Ignacio." Jules's voice rose up from the back seat. Her voice said his full name with a perfect accent. "Aquí."

Neko kept her eyes on the agents, but she heard rustling from behind her as Jules handed something forward. Then Iggy was opening a small cinched bag the size of a fist, catching three of the Hive's ceramic discs—sun coins—in his palm. The orange glaze flashed in the Land Rover's interior light as Iggy handed them over. Waylon let out a low whistle. He waved them through.

Neko put the car in gear and slid back onto the road. She felt her breath coming in small shallow sips. "Why are you carrying sun coins? And why did a government outpost guard want them?"

"We're not some backwater nobodies. We have connections—I tried to tell you."

Neko turned to look at Iggy, who was clearly trying not to laugh.

From the back seat, Jules said, "Aren't you glad you brought me along now?"

There was a pause, a quick beat, before Neko said, "Best keep quiet."

And she did. They all did.

NEKO DODGED POTHOLES AND BRANCHES AND TRASH. THEY STAYED north of the old New Haven line, parts of which, along with I-95, had already been swallowed by the new coastline. The crumbling of the smaller roads required constant backtracking, which meant it took two full days to close in on their coordinates. Eventually they had to park the Land Rover, cover it with brush to protect the goods, and hike the rest of the way on foot.

Before heading out, they sprayed themselves with the ginkgo perfume, Jules coughing in response to the sweet, heady cloud of particulates. "Mother*fucker*."

The hike was painstaking, skirting what had once been some sort of planned community, collapsed houses and rippled fences. Velvet cattails and luna moths. At one point, Neko saw something sharp in her peripheral vision, and she dug it out of the mud with calloused fingers. A bronzed baby shoe.

She used spit and her shirt to shine the surface, held it up to the sunlight. It was made such that, though it was plated in hard bronze, the sides of the shoe undulated so she could almost feel the soft leather and looped laces. Her mother had had one coated in silver that sat upon her dressing table in their East Village apartment. Neko didn't really believe in signs, but it felt fortuitous nonetheless. Some sort of confirmation that they were moving in the right direction.

Her hunt was drawing to its end, she could feel it. Each hour it became harder to suppress the physicality of her emotions, the dread and anticipation like dueling guitars. Neko closed her eyes. She thought of the bite of a crisp apple. She thought of the sound of a mandolin. In her head, she heard the first few bars of a Cat Power song: *Mo-ther . . . I know your face.*

"Can I tell you a secret?" her mother had asked once. They were sitting at the square table, the one with the black-and-white checkerboard design, languidly eating oatmeal; it must have been a Sunday morning. Neko skimmed brown sugar with her spoon.

"Sometimes I get an overwhelming desire to lick you like a cat. Like a mama cat wetting her kittens with a rough, pink tongue from head to paw. A full tongue bath."

"Gross," Neko said. She knew how to act the part of teenager. But she remembered this, even now, because secretly she was pleased.

As a teenager, everyone is embarrassed by their parents, embarrassed by their periods, embarrassed to be called out in class. Embarrassment is the underground spring that runs beneath everything. But what Neko remembered most was being embarrassed by the power of her feelings. By the love she felt for her parents, despite everything. It was why she was so angry when they finally split.

"I think I'm a hedonist," she told her mother. It was probably not the same morning, but in her memory the two conversations melted together.

"Oh?"

"Don't laugh. I know you're trying not to laugh." Looking back now, what she probably saw pass over her mother's face was panic. But they were a family that liked to pretend everything was a joke.

"Is that why you've written the word 'whore' on the sole of your tennis shoe?" Her mother was slicing a banana, coins of yellow fruit sliding into her bowl.

"They can't call you one if you call yourself one first." She was baiting her mother. She wanted her mother to talk to her about sex, but hadn't wanted to have to ask. Or to admit out loud that she didn't understand the prickles of desire and shame. The urge to take off her clothes and be judged by the world. To be wanted.

"Who would call you a whore?"

"Maybe I am a whore."

"Don't say that."

"Don't be such a prude."

Her mother offered her the rest of the banana, but Neko didn't want it.

Now an adult herself, Neko had come to understand this wasn't unusual, this dynamic between teenagers and their mothers. Most people had the opportunity to repair the relationship in the years that followed, but Neko had never gotten the chance to tell her mother she was sorry, or admit how warmly she remembered the days her mother let Neko play hooky from school, when they would spend the morning fondling the merchandise at fading West Village record shops—complaining with the proprietors about the bratty NYU kids—and then eat butter beans at some old-school café with a tattered awning, sit side by side at a countertop with bronze foot railings and jacket hooks and mounds of silverware rolled up in napkins.

One time her mother had been excited about a Nina Simone album they'd found. "She was your grandfather's favorite. He never got sick of listening to 'Sinnerman.'"

At the time, Neko had shrugged, not really caring that she hadn't had the chance to know him. But now, she wondered when the ghosts in her life had begun to outnumber the living.

AFTER LOSING HER MOTHER (OR SO THEY'D ASSUMED), NEKO HAD FINished high school in Philadelphia, where her father had grown up, though his family was all dead by then, too. He let her go to school online, never protesting the fact that she barely left the house. He was too numb to do anything but make room for her on the sofa as they watched television.

It wasn't until her mother was gone that Neko realized how much she'd held together their little family. Wasn't that how it went? Enamored of her father's flare, Neko hadn't noticed it needed fuel, someone to write the grocery lists and call the repair person and sign her up for karate. Someone to pay attention. To witness. Maybe in a regular world, her father would have risen to the challenge, but in the world they found themselves in, he never recovered. He began repeating himself, forgetting things. He began to liquefy.

When she thought about the house in Philly, after the hurricane, before the evacuation, she remembered lying in a narrow bed, the sounds of screech owls and flags from neighboring porches whipping in the wind. She'd missed the East Village, but she'd also known she couldn't have lived there without her mother anyway. So. There was that.

She remembered the metallic jangle from the ring of keys her father had taken to keeping on him, like he was a night watchman, and how, when she'd laid her hand on his to still the noise, she could feel the tiny lines of his knuckles, and how those lines made her want to cry. Disaster had made him ordinary. Before, whenever her father was home, there had been loud music, loud talk, glitter streaking the countertops of the bathroom. Not anymore.

When she pictured his "new" girlfriend, Aimee, it was the outline of her body standing at the fridge, staring into the portal of light as though something amazing—plums or pineapples or a time machine—might appear if she waited there long enough. Aimee had liked to tell Neko random facts that she'd read, and the ones Neko still remembered were about seahorses—how they mate for life, twisting their tails into knots, and how they dance for each other every morning, and how they aren't actually good swimmers but they are good drifters.

That was what they'd all been doing that year—drifting. When the electricity became erratic, they strung a clothesline and the clothes fluttered and whipped like the porch flags, and Neko would weave among the shirts and dresses and let them fall around her like a shroud or maybe like a veil to protect her from the harsh gaze of the sky. People were upset about what was happening, anxiety and panic everywhere as the evacuation deadline approached, but what did Neko care about that when she had already lost her home, her mother?

Aimee was the only person who seemed to notice how lost she was. Of course, considering the circumstances, Neko resisted the woman in almost every way, even her gaze. But she accepted her gifts of expensive colored pencils and thick art paper. Neko gave up basketball, which up to that point had been her *thing,* and took up the only hobby that allowed this new ocean of grief and guilt to leak onto the page—a small, brief release.

After the hurricane, Neko barely spoke for over a year. She wasn't technically mute—her mouth could form words and did so if absolutely necessary, though she preferred gestures and nods. But she didn't engage in conversation or use language to express herself or say anything at all, ever, to the therapist her father took her to see. Letters, syllables, sentences were obsolete. Vestiges of a time when things made some sense.

One afternoon, she was bumming a cigarette off one of the drag rats along Preston Street when she heard an insistent hum coming from an abandoned hair salon. When she poked her head through the broken window, there was a teenager tattooing her own leg. Haley.

"You know, like the comet," said the girl, shaking a bottle of ink. "Neko like the singer?" she asked when Neko mumbled her own name. Neko nodded, though she wasn't sure if Haley was referring to the right singer—the redhead, not the blonde.

Haley had dreadlocks, was pretty in a gangly way, and ground out her cigarette stubs on the sole of her boot. She didn't seem to mind that Neko rarely spoke.

After hanging out in Haley's parlor for a week, poring over the girl's collection of "borrowed" art books, Neko pointed to the image of *The Great Wave off Kanagawa,* and Haley tattooed it on her lower back, just above the sacrum. The pain was the first pleasure she'd felt in months, the needle the first way that Haley touched her.

"You're from New York, aren't you? I can tell," the young woman said as she worked. "I'm from the Rockaways. Our front porch was sheared off by the wind, and my dad was digging dead bodies out of the garden the day after the water receded."

As soon as the tattoo was done, Neko said, "Teach me." She'd spent months sketching with the pencils her father's girlfriend had given her, but there was something different about carving an image onto skin. An alchemy. A penance.

Haley taught her how to hold the machine, about hand speed and needle depth and voltage. Neko practiced tattooing fruit skins, and the first image that came out to her satisfaction was an illustration from a strange children's book about Death becoming friends with a duck: an image of the duck lying on top of Death to warm him after they'd swum in the pond. The book said, "Nobody had ever done that for Death before."

Haley let her tattoo a clock on her back to the left of her spine. "Feel the vibration in your stretching hand," Haley told her. "That's how you know you've hit the sweet spot." Lines and then shading and then color. It was terrifying at first. "Don't ride the tube. Float the needle in the skin."

This is how they worked: needle cartridges and rotary machines and vials of ink laid out like instruments of torture, fingers and palms finding their way through the image. This is how they loved: a bottle of cheap sake and afternoons in the backroom, fingers and palms finding their way through the body. Everything smelled burnt, singed. And Neko's mouth began to make sounds again—moans at first, then words, the names of the inks: Robin's Egg. Butter Beer. The Walking Red. Gangrene. The images on Haley's body reminded her of the ones from the stamp shop of her childhood: Opera glasses. Shaving brush. Crystal doorknob.

Haley had the slightly haunted, slightly frantic eyes of the newly sober. And she had a sweet tooth. Neko brought her gifts: honey, popsicles, a bottle of grenadine. "You'll rot your teeth out," she would say, but smile, handing over each item like an offering. Sometimes, when Neko showed up, Haley would be hosting what she called a "spirit party," starting with her tarot deck, the cards soft and damp, and ending the night with a hand-carved Ouija board, laughing at the strange messages channeled from the other side. She played old punk music on the stereo and never asked why sometimes the chord progressions made Neko cry.

Neko had never seen Haley step outside the building; she was clothed and fed by the goodwill of those who came for tattoos or spirit parties or to look through the collection of books. What if people stopped coming? What would Haley do then? Neko realized that maybe she wanted to take care of this person more than she wanted to be taken care of by her.

Then, one day, Neko found an injured bird. She wrapped it in a cloth napkin and put it in the pocket of her trench coat. She arrived at the abandoned parlor and Haley was tattooing a beautiful sun-kissed blonde. Haley looked at her and shrugged, and Neko understood that the love affair was over but that she could take the art with her. The bird in her pocket made no sound.

BY THIS POINT NEKO WAS SEVENTEEN AND HER FATHER'S EARLY ONSET dementia had begun to steal so much from him—his dancing, his long shaggy dog stories, his desire for the spotlight, and even his music, all sunk into his boggy brain. The thing that stuck with him longest was knitting. Maybe because he didn't have to think about it; muscle memory just turned the yarn into cloth. The funny thing was that *what* he was knitting constantly shifted—sleeve or scarf or the contours of a hat—until the cloth became part monster, part abstract art.

Because he had money and a semi-famous name, the facility to which he was assigned had lemony walls, framed photographs of Yosemite. The food was fine, though her father lived for the ice cream. There was a large black mat in front of the doors to the outside because apparently dementia patients wouldn't cross it. They couldn't tell the difference between the dark floor and a deep hole into which they might fall.

After her father had lost most of his speech, Neko would sit on the opposite side of his bed from Aimee, who brought necklaces to dangle in the sunlight. Neko was seventeen and technically supposed to be living with her, but instead she was couch surfing with friends.

One day, Neko asked the question. "Was Aimee the reason you and Mom broke up?" The way the girlfriend had so gently and effortlessly inserted herself after the hurricane was suspicious.

Her father just stared at her. He said nothing, but tears began to gather in the pink corners of his eyes, catching on the long, thick eyelashes that graced his drooping face until the end. She didn't wipe the tears away, but she took out a bag of peanuts and fed them to him one by one—the same thing her mother used to do for her when she was a kid and upset. It helped.

When she got the call that he had died, she didn't go to the nursing home. She didn't go to the funeral. She hadn't seen her mother's dead body, and she didn't want to see his. In that way, they still lived inside of her. Maybe this was why she was able to hope, to believe, that one of them was still alive. Somewhere out there, warm to the touch.

24

WHEN THEY ARRIVED AT THE COORDINATES, THEY FOUND A SMALL clearing with split log benches lined up in rows. Some sort of meeting place. The benches were sanded and in good repair. They heard nothing but the high-pitched chitter-chatter of Siouxsie Sioux in her cage.

The crew made camp a half mile away among towering black oaks that gave the forest a gloomy feel. Jumpy and nervous, they waited. Were they supposed to hide? Or reveal themselves like sitting ducks?

ON THE THIRD MORNING, AS THEY RE-APPROACHED THE CLEARING for another day of staking out the coordinates, they heard voices—a loud, ringing male voice that was answered by a chorus. Neko crept forward on little cat's feet, peering through the underbrush.

Today there were people sitting on the log benches, and at the front, a woman was standing waist deep in a large stock tank, shivering, arms crossed submissively in front of her chest, a look of abject terror on her face. A tall man in a cowboy hat was holding her by the shoulders. Suddenly, he pulled her down toward the water, her mouth gasping.

At the sight of her head going under, long hair reaching out like tentacles in the water, Neko's heart began to pump as she tried to calculate whether or not they had a chance to extract the woman without getting themselves killed. Maybe she could use her Glock to hold the man hostage, she thought, stepping forward.

Then the woman rose from the water, sputtering and smiling, propped up by the man in the hat, who said, "Praise the Lord."

Neko stopped short. She and Iggy exchanged looks.

The baptized woman at the front, clothes soaked, arms lifted above her head, began to sing slightly off-tune. Everyone on the benches stood and joined in. It was a gospel song, vaguely familiar, though Neko had only ever attended church when visiting her grandmother. The congregants wore canvas overalls and work boots and animal pelts.

Maybe her crew was losing their edge, after too long in this whole business. Or maybe these people, who lived God knows how in the far reaches of the Sink, had developed animal-like senses, but the entire back row turned in synchronicity to look at Neko's crew crouched behind the scrub brush.

So much for the element of surprise, thought Neko.

The strangers beckoned to them, moved down to make room on the last bench. As Neko and her crew emerged into the clearing, Iggy made a contrite gesture toward their mud-splattered attire, mouthing apologies for being late.

"No dress code for Cowboy Church, sweet pea," whispered a woman with white hair that looked as if it had been cut with a machete.

They stood when the others stood to sing, and sat when they sat. They did the only thing they could—they played along.

AFTER THE SERVICE, NEKO WATCHED CURIOUSLY AS JULES APPEARED to search her pack, as though looking for something to add to the crate where folks were leaving an array of donations: eggs, batteries, sachets of vitamin powders, some scratch. Jules's hand emerged with a pack of stickers, which Neko recognized as short-range trackers.

As people came up to greet them, welcoming them to "Cowboy Church," Jules was affectionate, smiling and patting backs—and, Neko noticed, surreptitiously attaching the stickers.

"We learned about this place from John," said Neko when asked, making up a name. "Don't know his last name, no, but he said it was worth the hike. Sorry we were late."

When she tried to suss out where people were living ("You all nearby? We just moved camps ourselves . . .") people suddenly became less forthcoming. None of them looked like rich people living in a bunker.

"You're not a doctor, are you?" one man asked, and when Neko shook her head, said, "A pity," before moving off.

The preacher himself approached. He was a middle-aged white man, the only person Neko saw who was fully dressed in an actual cowboy costume, down to the spurs on his boots and a horse tied up nearby. "You don't smell like you're from around here," he said.

They stared at him. Was he talking about what they thought he was talking about?

"True," said Iggy.

"That's okay, that's okay," the man reassured them, as if it was something about which they might be embarrassed. "Y'all are welcome."

Iggy reached out his hand to shake, and the preacher said he hosted a service in this spot every Sunday morning. They nodded, waiting for what came next. The man smiled, but didn't offer anything more.

Neko looked at Iggy. They were in the right spot. The man had mentioned their smell. What else were they supposed to do?

Neko nodded at his outfit. "This isn't exactly ranching country."

The man smiled. "Rounding up souls, not cattle." He rummaged around in his literal saddlebag. "Does one of you read? Let me give y'all a copy of *The Cowboy Apostle*. We're nondenominational, but this gets at the heart of our philosophy." He pressed the book into Neko's hands. "I've been praying for new members and had almost given up hope—especially for more women. Two women, to be exact."

"Two women?"

"Yes. There isn't much time." There was something in his expression that eluded Neko—it wasn't quite panic but something near to it.

"Much time before what?"

He looked at them hard. "Before the Lord comes for what is his. Not much time *at all*." He walked along the aisle, straightening benches. "I've always found the chapter on prayer to be the most useful. You might start with that."

The preacher looked around, noticed that the rest of the parishioners were gone. "Two women only. *Two women*."

"Our crew rides together," said Neko.

The preacher quickly slid the rest of the books back into his saddlebag and brought out a box wrapped in paper and twine. "It can be hard making the move out here. Let me give you some of my chokeberry preserves to sweeten the journey."

He handed them the jar and swung up onto his horse.

AS SOON AS HE WAS GONE, JULES QUICKLY BROUGHT OUT THE FLIMSY tracking pad that showed where the stickers were heading. "Cheap pieces of shit," she said. "Only three of them are actually working."

"Why do you have tracking stickers?" asked Neko.

"Bought them at the gray market," she said, as though that were a reason.

"What's the deal with two women?" asked Iggy. "They can't really expect . . ."

"Maybe they have limits on the delivery crew," said Harriet.

Neko shook her head. "But Chaplin insisted we needed a full crew."

Jules had her pack on and was heading toward the edge of the clearing. "Unless you want to split up right now, you're coming with me to find out where these people homestead."

"Is that an order?" asked Neko, sharply.

Jules's face softened. "Please. We'll be out of range of the trackers soon."

THEY WERE FORCED TO FORD A SHALLOW MARSHLAND AS THEY FOLlowed the trackers. When the blinking transmissions began to weaken, Jules went ahead to get eyes on one of the groups.

As they waited, Harriet flipped through *The Cowboy Apostle*. "Don't you guys want to say a prayer?"

At the chapter the preacher had referred to, she wet the tip of her index finger, turned each page slowly. She showed Neko and Iggy an underlined sentence with the words *Monday, 5am, Kensico Dam Plaza* scribbled beside it in the margin. The marked sentence read: *Each prayer is a message that flies like a starling through the sky to the nest of Our Lord.*

Neko rubbed her red hands, stinging from all the sharp edges of wild brush. What had her life come to? "Monday is tomorrow."

Eventually Jules appeared between the trees, and as they hiked back to their own camp, she told them that people appeared to be bivouacked in a ravine. "Maybe fifty of them? Kids, the whole shebang. And if there's an official church service each Sunday, that means there may be similar groups nearby."

"That's fascinating, but we have something else to deal with right now."

Jules nodded. "Sure. Totally."

Neko turned around to see Harriet digging into the jar of chokeberry preserves with her fingers and then putting them in her mouth.

"Delicious."

THEY DECIDED NEKO AND HARRIET WOULD PRESENT THEMSELVES AT Kensico Dam Plaza, less than a mile from their camp, and Iggy and Jules would trail their movements from there. If they became separated at any point, the plan was to meet back at Cowboy Church the following Sunday.

"Why Harriet?" asked Jules. "Maybe I should go with you instead."

"No," said Neko, not feeling the need to justify herself.

"But . . ."

"You must be out of your mind if you think I'd take you."

Jules looked to Harriet for—what, support or sympathy?—but she just turned and walked away.

"Harriet, wait," said Jules, following her at a fast clip. "Babe?"

Neko walked in the opposite direction and found a small incline. She squatted to pee but Iggy had followed her. "Cool, cool. Who needs privacy, anyway?"

"I don't like this," he whispered.

She pulled up her pants. "If we don't go along with the instructions . . . well, where are we? Wandering the Sink illegally with a Land Rover full of black market goods?"

"We could dump the goods and go back. We still can."

"Everyone would be out for us then." She reached for his hand and fumbled.

"If I'm honest," he said eventually, "this feels more and more like your personal quest. Like I'm being left behind."

"No." She struggled with how exactly to respond. "No, no."

Dusk was falling, the air picking up a chill. They stood there for a while, holding hands but not looking at each other.

"Something is changing. Maybe for the best, maybe not. I don't know."

She pursed her lips. She felt pulled apart by love and anguish. "You mean more to me than . . ."

"Stop." Iggy slipped his hand from hers. "I just want you to remember that I'm not your support staff. I have my own desires in life. One of them is you, Neko. But it isn't the only one."

25

SUGAR STARS AND A GRAPEFRUIT MOON.

The grass plaza was overgrown, but the three-hundred-foot rock dam still rose above them in defiance. They parked the Land Rover on the flattest section they could find, unsure whether they would be taking the vehicle with them.

Fifteen minutes after the designated time, a man emerged from the shadows at the foot of the dam. He had a hoverboard, which made Neko laugh. Hover technology was not new, but it took a very strong, very expensive battery to power, so Neko had never seen it used in the Sink.

"Nice to meet you." Iggy held out his hand, but the man—short brown hair, plain brown clothes, about as nondescript as one could get—just nodded curtly. He motioned for them to help load the goods onto the floating platform.

"Do you talk?" asked Jules.

"Whatever doesn't fit on the hover," said the man, "put in these." He held out three large hiking backpacks.

They did as they were told. The night crackled with static electricity.

Finally, everything loaded and tied, the man looked Neko and Harriet up and down and said, "Follow me. No lights."

Neko reached out a palm and briefly placed it on Iggy's chest. She clicked off her headlamp, eyes slowly adjusting to the dark, and left Jules and Iggy behind.

The guide, who wore military-style night goggles, led them away from the dam, steering the hoverboard through the foliage in a zigzag pattern, stopping periodically to check a readout on his watch.

Neko had run her own operation for so long that it felt strange not to be in charge. Her arms and legs tingled, as if vulnerability was sensed in the cells of the skin.

After an hour, the trees turned to weeping willows, and Neko realized they were moving toward the reservoir. Near the edge of the water, their guide fumbled in the overgrowth. He brought out what looked like a black beach ball from a pit in the ground and used a tool from his pack to inflate it. In less than ten minutes, they were holding a raft big enough for all three of them and the goods.

Before they pushed off, Neko splashed her face. She felt so stupid for not having anticipated the possibility of an aquatic entry, which would make it difficult for Jules and Iggy to trail them. Water lapped the shoreline like a tongue.

THEY ROWED ONTO THE VAST BODY OF WATER, A SHEET OF HAMMERED tin, the wind fighting against their muscles and broad oars. In the morning light, the lake was a sickly green, overtaken by an algae bloom unfurling beneath the surface. Their guide—they were never given his name—directed them a little this way, a little that, as they sailed west.

"Why is your navigation so specific?" asked Harriet. "Do a few meters left or right matter if we're just rowing to the other side?"

The man didn't turn around. "They matter."

They spent the morning traversing the wide expanse of the reservoir to where it narrowed into a finger inlet. Eventually, their guide directed them to dock in a small cove where it was shallow enough to disembark. They were bone-tired; it was only early afternoon.

"Don't tarry," said the guide. "We need to get out of view as quickly as possible."

"Who still says 'tarry'?" asked Harriet.

The small rocky beach onto which they dragged their aching bodies was adjacent to the remnants of a pier, now green-slimed and rotting, behind which was a series of cabins set back from the shore—probably an old rustic summer resort.

While the guide was deflating the raft, not paying her any attention, Neko took the bird in its cage and crept toward the crumbling pier. She gave Siouxsie Sioux extra food and hung the cage on a pole magically still standing along the crumbling dock. She hoped Iggy and Jules would find it and know that this was where they'd landed. Her own trail of breadcrumbs.

WHILE MAKING CAMP THAT NIGHT—HEATING UP A NUTRITION packet, stamping down the ground where her bedroll would go—Neko's nerves clanged. She and Iggy never slept apart. Never.

Neko's parents had been touring musicians and so lived parts of their lives separately out of necessity. But even among normal couples, even among the mudlarks and border trash, she and Iggy were unusual. They didn't take solo jobs or go on trips.

They were like conjoined twins. Sometimes she wondered if she and Iggy never had a kid in part because there was no space for anything between them.

Until now, she thought.

For once, Neko couldn't fall asleep. She thought of their psychopathic ex-commando from the mudlark training camp, and how he'd once tried to demonstrate the importance of maintaining complete control over one's emotions by taking a pregnant rabbit, slitting open her belly, and stabbing the tiny, gummy fetuses one by one with his switchblade.

Lying in her bedroll alone in the dark, Neko thought: That pregnant rabbit and her progeny existed in a long line of living beings that she had failed to protect. She had protected herself, yes, and Iggy. She had taken pride in protecting her crew until recently: fast asleep while Harriet had a knife put to her throat. And then convincing them all to chase her own past to find the first person she'd ever put into harm's way—real harm's way. Her own mother.

All these years, she'd thought she'd driven her mother to her death. But maybe, instead, she'd driven her underground—and which was worse? If her mother was alive, had she been bewitched into some cult or worse? Would she welcome Neko's intrusion after all this time?

The words came unbidden: *We shared a body.*

Her mother had said that to her during the first summer they'd spent in Vermont. Neko must have been about six or seven, and they'd gone to the nearby village to see a Prince cover band. Food trucks hawking German pretzels and pita wraps circled the green, where hippies (and their children and their many, many dogs) lay on blankets and rolled joints.

Her father was going on about how the biggest difference between being onstage versus in the audience was the olfactory experience—how crowds were flush with odor, body odor and hashish and green tea and burnt cheese and toe cheese and grass and patchouli and hairspray and coffee breath and beer breath and sage and dirt and wet fur and honey. Sweetness.

"What about onstage?" someone asked.

"Smells like adrenaline," said her mother.

"Smells like burning dust," said her father.

Neko remembered the pleasure of eating cheese fries from a paper sleeve and watching Aunt Layla kick around a strange ball with a few of the roadies.

"Nobody hacky-sacks anymore," her mother yelled at them.

"What's a hacky sack?" asked Neko.

"See?"

During "Raspberry Beret," her mother dragged a pleased Neko to the open area in front of the stage. They danced. Silly-danced, flapping about and tossing their hair in the air. There were other people dancing, too, and soon a girl with a prickly shaved head, maybe nine or ten, grabbed her by the hand and began twirling her in fast circles.

Neko didn't like it, but found herself unable to speak up. There was something off about the girl, something aggressive about the way she gripped at Neko's arm, pulling them toward the margin of the dancers. Eventually, Neko lost sight of her mother altogether, but she didn't fight or scream, though she was scared. She remembered thinking that maybe this was what big kids did—flee from grown-ups into secret places. Her arm hurt where the older girl's fingers dug into it; taller people blocked her view.

Finally, Neko heard her name and her mother's panicked face appeared above her. Something in her mother had shifted, and she pushed the older girl. Literally pushed a child onto the ground. Her mother froze, eyes wide, as though shocked at her own actions, and then the next thing Neko remembered was her mother picking her up and running into the parking lot. After she stopped, breath coming hard, they sat on the curb, her mother hugging her tightly. Too tightly. "We shared a body."

THE WRECKAGE

Track 8: "Athena Is Overrated"

The day Jenny saw Max with that woman again was also the day she finally cleaned out their storage unit with its broken pieces of furniture, never to be fixed or reupholstered, and the last boxes from her father's house.

In one of the boxes she found stamps. The woodblocks-and-ink kind of stamps, at least a hundred of them. They were old, and she seemed to remember that they originally belonged to her grandmother who had taught school for a few years during World War II, before Jenny's grandfather returned and she became a housewife for the rest of her days, amen.

The images and letters on the stamps were a fascinating window into what that age had deemed important to teach children—*Lincoln, igloo, toothbrush*—or maybe what words had been considered most likely to be used in a sentence—*mother, milk, wolf*. And offensive ones, too, like *Jap boy,* decked out in a tiny kimono, his eyes exaggerated. There was no German boy, no American boy. Jenny had loved her grandparents but found them impenetrable, too. Something about that generation was foreign to her orientation and experience, and her father seemed to feel this as well. He had escaped inside the ancient world and she inside the arts, and neither of them ever fully considered if or how they brought their own ancestors with them into the present.

She wondered if Neko would feel that way, too.

Jenny took the whole lot of them, wooden cubes and rectangles, slung in a grocery bag, to Randy at the stamp store across the park, two blocks from their apartment. It was a windy day, and her long hair whipped into her face and eyes.

Randy was there, working behind his desk in the back, and his gaze, always half closed, as if his eyelids were weighted, took her in and then the bag and its contents.

He didn't go in for pleasantries, so she just stood silently while he looked through them. *Tiger, light, taro, father, little, farm, butterfly.* She wouldn't have guessed the one that would make him laugh: *comb.*

"I make stamps." He put his palms over them. "Don't buy other people's stamps."

"I know."

He looked away. "They're in decent shape. A little soap, and they'd be good as new."

Jenny shrugged. She didn't want to have to say aloud that bringing these big and tiny blocks of physical, concrete language, of word units—what was it called, langue or parole or something else?—was more like an offering. An erasure of the past.

She poked around the shop for a bit, careful not to knock anything over with her blue-jeaned hip. It didn't take long to make the circle. When she returned to his desk, he had his half-moon glasses on, inspecting the stamps again.

"I'll take them off your hands," he said. He gestured toward a glass pot of sludge. "Coffee?"

"No, thanks," she said, which she hoped he knew meant thank you.

On her way out, feeling a little lighter and looser—which was saying something because she'd felt so heavy lately—she saw him. Them.

Max had said he'd stopped seeing her, but there they were, walking, not hand in hand but bodies close, his head angled her in toward her. In the East Village, no less. In Jenny's own neighborhood, as though he could care less. Or wanted to be caught. Or maybe was just stupider than she'd taken him for.

Was there a stamp for *asshole*? For *heartbreak*? Was there a stamp for *fool*?

On their weekly stroll, which they referred to grandly as *walking the earth,* Jesse told her that he'd bought a house on Long Island.

"Why?" Jenny asked him. "I mean, Jesus."

"I'm tired of how the trees in Manhattan are so small." They were walking down St. Mark's, and he pointed to a sad little thing, spindly and half covered in browning leaves.

"Well, the roots have so little space," she said, picturing what she'd read about how a tree's canopy mirrored its root base. "What do you expect?"

He gripped her upper arm as they walked, as though he were old or as though they were entering a ballroom. "More," he said. "I expect more." He looked at her sidelong. "Don't you?"

She didn't answer. They waited for the light to change, and for a moment she rested her cheek against his shoulder, feeling the windbreaker material against her skin.

"I have a recording studio I want you to check out, by the way," he said. "It's in Jersey City. It might be perfect."

The light changed and they walked across the street toward the bodega spangled in fruit and cheap carnations and boxes of cigarettes lined up in rows. She picked up things and held them to the light before letting them fall into her canvas tote. She knew Jesse was watching her, but these apples and tampons and Red Hots were not for him. Let him go to Long Island. Fine. They were all going somewhere.

One thing that had made Max and Jenny right for each other, and then later wrong: She liked meeting in the dark, and he was drawn to neon light, preferably the old-fashioned kind shaped like a tipping martini glass. Why hadn't she fallen in love with Jesse instead, who in many ways was more like her?

But there were reasons. Two quiet people weren't always meant to be together. And maybe she'd sensed, even at the beginning, that the drugs held a stronger sway over him than they should.

Once, he'd told her that when he was growing up, the house across the street from his had a tall chimney where a small colony of bats roosted. From his bedroom window, he'd watched them flush themselves out at dusk. And Jenny hadn't thought the bats in her own chest could handle that sort of gaze. Max's distraction had given her space of a sort. For a while.

As they left the bodega, she said, "You see, when Owl finds a new house for Eeyore, whose house was washed away in the flood, it's actually Piglet's house. But Piglet is too nice or embarrassed to say so, and so Piglet leaves and goes to live with Pooh."

Jesse nodded as though this story made sense. "The world is deeply weird."

Was she the Piglet of her relationship? Jenny wondered. Too shy or frozen or lacking self-confidence? Just letting another woman take her house? Not believing that she deserved it any more than anyone else?

Fault was a tricky thing. Fault lines. Cracks that spread until it was too late.

The following week, the Nightjars played San Antonio's Majestic Theatre, a few blocks from the Alamo.

Jenny didn't know why she waited until that moment before the encore to bring it up. But he had his excuses, of course.

"I just ran into her at the record shop. I was buying more albums we don't have room for, Sonic Youth's *Sister* and the Make-Up's *After Dark* . . . She just happened to be there, too."

They already owned *Sister,* and she was pretty sure Max knew that. She was also pretty sure that Jesse, who had an alarmed look on his face, was only pretending to adjust the laces on his sneakers.

"Yeah. The record store."

"You have to trust me."

Actually, she didn't have to. "I'm done bashing myself against the rocks."

"What rocks?"

"It's over."

His neck was blooming red. "No. Not over."

The sound guy gave them a nod. She walked back onstage to the roar of a grateful and impatient crowd.

It was an early show—done by ten—and Jenny wanted to take in the River Walk. Neko declined with a grunt. Their daughter had recently cut her hair short, and her curls stuck out from the sides of her headphones as she listened to the *Hamilton* soundtrack.

However, when Max came out of the hotel bathroom wearing his civvies and wanted to go along, Neko changed her mind, letting her headphones slide down her sinewy neck. The three of them descended the curving limestone staircase that led down to the river, which was really more of a canal, lined with walkways on either side and brown brick buildings fronted by wrought iron balconies. The oxbow of the river was crowded with people and chain restaurants and bars serving pitchers of margaritas.

Max stopped and looked Jenny in the eye. "Not over."

In a wide stairwell off to the side, an old man was playing a squeeze-box, slowly and mournfully, and, as if on cue, Max gravitated toward him like a magnet, crouching at his feet like a supplicant. Jenny kept walking, more slowly, and Neko, surprisingly, stayed alongside her.

Someone hawked roses "for the lady," and chubby middle-aged couples in khaki shorts and bedazzled shirts jostled with the university frat boys. But there was a more local element, too—San Antonio teenagers who apparently used this as their drag, smoking cigarettes and eyeing one another, young girls in spaghetti-strap tank tops and boys in white sneakers like glorious boats. Just a little older than Neko.

At one time, Jenny might have found this sociologically interesting, perhaps inspiration for a Nightjars song—culture clash in modern America. But now she only saw the menacing undercurrent. How many of these young people, strutting and laughing, had a future in this messed-up country? For which ones was this the best their lives would ever be? Would any of these girls be assaulted tonight in a dark corner of this garish tourist attraction—pressed against a historic mission wall until they could hardly breathe? How many, for any number of complex reasons, would unhook the straps themselves?

In a shadowy corner a boy—man?—was gripping the upper arm of another teenager, whispering into her ear; Jenny found the slit of his eyes suspect, the expression on the girl's face too still.

Without thinking, she moved her body into their space. "What, you worried she'll escape?" she hissed at the boy. "Let go of her arm."

The two teenagers looked at her, surprised, and then loud laughter tinged with mockery escaped their gaping mouths as they moved away from the crazy lady. Her.

Neko was clearly mortified—her gaze seared Jenny. "This is why I *hate* hanging out with you, Mom."

Jenny sucked in air. "You know, Neko, I never got a chance to know my mother."

Her daughter looked at her with predator eyes. "Lucky you."

Jenny turned and hissed.

And then the girl was gone, too, drawn back toward Max, who was now trying out the street performer's squeeze-box, oblivious.

Jenny pressed her hands to chest and neck. *If only I'd thought of the right words, I could have held on to your heart.*

The path became less crowded, quieter, the bars classier and farther apart, the vegetation on either side lush with rosemary and flowering vines. As she walked, she wondered how long it would take before this River Walk flooded, before the dam that controlled the water levels of the city could no longer hold its own against the frightening forces that were building around them. In that moment Jenny felt sick to her stomach with love and horror, helplessness and shame.

Milk, mother, wolf
Athena, such a bitch, watching over him
And what am I?
Just milk, mother, wolf

26

THE NEXT MORNING, THE GUIDE LED THEM NORTHWEST UNTIL THEY eventually reached a tall mesh fence topped with concertina wire. They skirted the metal webbing until the man abruptly stopped, rolled up a section that had been surreptitiously cut, and motioned for them to duck through one by one. Neko dragged the heel of one boot to create a slash in the ground outside the perimeter for Iggy and Jules to find—not that she really expected they'd be able to track them across the lake. In all likelihood, she and Harriet were on their own.

A mound appeared in overgrown grassland. Steel doors were tucked into bedrock, and a faded sign informed them that this had once been a munitions depot. Their guide typed a code into a box along the outer wall, and the steel doors opened with a loud clang.

Neko and Harriet followed the guide into an empty barrel-ceilinged space. The doors closed behind them, and they heard the sound of locks clicking into place. A small red light illuminated the antechamber, and Neko saw there was a real live elevator, silver and shiny and waiting for them. Neko wasn't sure what she'd find down there, but she opened her palms wide, standing before a moment that yawned with possibilities.

AFTER THE GOODS HAD BEEN TAKEN BELOW AND THOROUGHLY searched and probed and cataloged, Neko and Harriet were escorted into what looked like a conference room lined with shelves.

Neko studied the books, entirely free of dust and lined up inside this beautiful and horrifying time capsule. Most of the tomes seemed related to survival, and Neko pulled down a hardback medical textbook, feeling the rough sandpaper of the brown cover. Her finger traced the diagram of the circulatory system, the ribbons of blue and red branching into smaller tributaries: subclavian, jugular, iliac, radial. There was a certain beauty to the map of the veins and arteries, thought Neko. Unlike the diagrams of muscle—gummy pink, pulled tight into a landscape of constriction.

"The most elegant machine ever made."

Neko turned around to see a man, maybe in his sixties, nodding at the book she'd opened. He was dressed like a Wall Street businessman from Before in a gray suit and striped tie, cuff links that caught the light.

Harriet, who had been running her fingers along the books' spines, tilted her chin, voice sickly sweet. "I'm Hannah and this is Nora."

"Michael." He reached out to shake their hands, and Neko wasn't sure she'd ever felt skin so soft. "Welcome," he said warmly. "You can't possibly imagine how welcome."

Michael was not exactly good-looking, but he had that visage of gentle refinement some men achieved as they aged—deserved or not.

Neko shifted from foot to foot, muscles sore from rowing across the reservoir. "Are you the one in charge, Michael?" She tried to turn on the charm (did she have any?) because she needed to find a way to stay past the drop-off.

"Please, sit down. You must be exhausted." He pulled out a chair at the table and motioned for them to do the same. "I'm chairman of the board," he said. "But we're all equals here."

"Everywhere I go these days, people claim to have no leaders," said Neko, offering the sort of observation she would normally keep to herself, except instinct told her that a man like this would respond best if she was openly skeptical. If she played hard to get.

"Everywhere you go?" He leaned back, his body language encouraging her. "I'd love to hear about that."

Neko forced herself to smile. "We're just couriers. Nothing special."

"Couriers for Asher Chaplin must lead extraordinarily interesting—and dangerous—lives. We're starved for stories here." He sighed and his blue eyes watered. "Tight security means we're usually on satellite blackout."

Neko sensed an opening. If her mother was here under protest, Neko couldn't ask about her directly. She needed an in. "Maybe security is something we could help you with—there are new advances. Why don't you let us stay a few days and inspect your system? See if we can help you upgrade. The government won't let you remain here forever unmolested."

"And you would do that for us?" He sounded amused.

"It's in our interest to keep you a happy customer."

"We're already grateful. You're the first guests we've had in years."

"How's that?"

"We usually have goods delivered to our people at the dam,

then transfer everything back ourselves to keep our location . . . private."

Neko was taken aback by this information, but before she could figure out how to diplomatically ask why they were an exception, Michael's face and tone changed dramatically.

"Your offer to help with our security is interesting considering Chaplin's current . . . troubles." He raised his eyebrows, his mouth a severe line. "So, he made it out of the Ice House alive?"

Neko processed his words without letting her face show confusion. She had no idea what troubles he was referring to and that made her nervous. And worried. "You know a lot about current events for someone living in blackout."

"We have informants."

She pressed her hands into her legs to keep them from shaking. "It was a setback, but Chaplin—and the business—is fine. You know how the media likes to blow things out of proportion." She really was winging it now.

"Must have gummed things up."

She kept her face blank, hoping it read as though she were keeping professional confidences in check rather than emotions. "The Ice House is not our only point of operations."

Michael nodded, his body relaxing. "We were surprised it happened there first. For two years, our sources have been predicting an uprising farther north." He stopped short, appearing to regret his disclosure. "There's a guest room I hope you'll both find adequate. I'll talk to our head of security about a consult, as we'd already planned for you to stay a few days, of course."

Neko tried to smile.

"And I insist you join me at dinner."

INSIDE THEIR QUARTERS—NARROW AND LINED WITH BUNK BEDS—Neko and Harriet stared at each other.

"What the . . . ?" started Harriet.

Neko put a finger to her lips and pulled Harriet into the tiny bathroom, where she ran the faucet. She put her hands under the water, and it felt good on her raw, dirt-encrusted palms. Neko thought again of the man who had stopped and deliberately spit in Jules's face in the Ice House and wondered what she was missing.

"Will we still get paid?" asked Harriet. "If Chaplin's . . . gone?"

Neko shrugged. She wished Iggy were there.

"Why did they expect us to stay a few days? And why do you actually want to?"

"Recon."

"But why?"

Neko paused. The bathroom was so small she was basically straddling the toilet. "I might know someone who ended up here."

Harriet tapped the counter with one fist. "Fuck." She let the door slam on her way out.

ONCE HARRIET LEFT THE BATHROOM, IT FELT SMALLER, SUFFOCATING. The longer Neko spent as a mudlark, and the more weeks and years she accrued tripping through the wild spaces of the Sink, the more the entire concept of a dwelling felt strange: A box. A box with different corners meant for different activities. A box, a cage, inside of it a wheel, a feed trough. Humans orbiting the place like stations of the cross. Like the leopard at the zoo who wears down the dirt with her mad pacing.

She cupped her hands under the faucet, drenched her head and neck. The mirror in the tiny bathroom was one of those grubby metal plates like the ones you find in mental hospitals. Neko stood in front of it, water dripping from her face and hair. It felt true that aging happened slowly and then all at once.

Neko wondered if her mother would recognize her, practically middle-aged, baby fat burned away by life in the cauldron. Would her mother be disappointed it had taken her so long to find this place—or about something else that she couldn't predict?

She remembered when they told her they were separating. How they'd taken her to a beautiful place to do it, as though that could ameliorate her suffering. As though it wouldn't ruin that place for her forever.

"Magenta," whispered her father.

"Cotton candy," whispered her mother.

The James Turrell light installation, built into a grassy quad, projected a light show each dawn and dusk on a floating concrete ceiling that contained a square open to the sky.

"Mom, obviously," said Neko. They played a game where each time the color changed, her parents had to name the shade, with Neko giving a point to the description she thought superior. She'd always loved the names of colors—when they got her the 120 Crayola set, she'd made them read the names of the crayons over and over: *Eggplant, Blue Bell, Macaroni and Cheese, Inchworm, Fern, Timberwolf, Denim, Fuzzy Wuzzy, Sunglow, Bittersweet.*

Sitting there on the cold concrete, Neko was enthralled by the intensity of the pink saturation, made entirely from projected light. The idea that something so physically insubstantial could look so real—it was maybe as close as she'd ever come to a religious experience. A few college students sat across from them, their eyes heavy, probably still up from the night before. The light shifted to a cloudy blue-green.

"Algae," said Max.

"Periwinkle."

"That is not periwinkle, Jen."

"Okay, mallard."

"Point to Daddy."

"Are you just throwing me a bone?"

"No, algae is right. So gross it's pretty."

The color of the actual sky through the aperture was now changing as rapidly as the projected light—from midnight to royal to a pale, glassy blue. Did sunrise happen more quickly than sunset?

Though they'd already been there an hour, Neko was disappointed when the show was over. Another day arrived, steam rising from the grass of the hill outside the structure. They sat there for a moment as if suspended.

"We have something to tell you," said her father finally, putting his hand on Neko's leg, looking grim.

"About the band?"

"In part."

Neither of her parents looked at each other.

"Mom already told me," said Neko, yawning, suddenly wanting to be anywhere but there. "She said there might not be another tour for a while."

HAD SHE FELT SAD AT FIRST? MAYBE. WHAT SHE DID REMEMBER WAS how quickly the grief, or whatever soft emotions came first, had been transformed into the hard edge of rage. How quickly the desire to stop it from happening shifted into a desire to make her parents sorry, specifically her mother, whom she blamed more.

Maybe because her mother seemed more eager to tell her the news. Maybe because Neko believed her mother hadn't tried hard enough, hadn't been fun enough, game enough somehow to keep her father's attention.

The obvious thing was to run away—not forever but just long enough to make them feel pain. But that was easier said than done in New York. Neko's parents had always encouraged her to be independent—she was comfortable riding the subway and finding her way around the city during the day. But it frightened her to imagine joining or competing with the gangs of feral teenagers that frequented the tunnels and piers at night. There would be no way to hide what she was: fresh young meat.

So she put it off, pretended everything was as normal as it could be for a family breaking apart. Eventually, she thought she might pull the trigger while her parents were at Burning Man. Initially, she told them she didn't want to go, didn't want to pretend. Then she told them she did want to come after all. She told them maybe it would be fun—ha, ha.

27

NEKO AND HARRIET WERE LED TO A PRIVATE APARTMENT FOR A DINner hosted by another member of the board, a woman who introduced herself as Gloria when she opened the door, dressed in an indigo kimono.

"Come, come." She ushered them inside with a dazzling cheerfulness. "New blood! We've opened a bottle of the good stuff." Gloria hugged Neko and Harriet like they were old friends.

Neko was suspicious of what it would do to a person to live underground for so long, but aside from the over-the-top affection, everyone they'd met so far appeared surprisingly normal. Healthy. Eccentric, but in the way one might expect from anyone rich enough to be in a place like this.

The apartment stood in stark contrast to the guest bunk where they were staying—the walls here were covered in tapestries and modern art framed in crisp gold, and shining copper pots hung above the kitchen island like open mouths. Probably the best offerings of a mansion squeezed into a three-bedroom flat. Neko ran her hand along the beautiful woodwork that lined the walls.

"We had our yacht designer do the interior," said Gloria.

There were ten people in attendance for dinner, including Gloria's husband and grown children; Michael; a couple everyone called Mr. and Mrs. Zhang, who sported almost-matching puffy, snow-like hair; and a stone-faced man who might have been part of the security detail. Not Neko's mother.

She studied their faces for clues. Neko looked to the mouth, which she believed could reveal, in the twist of a lip, the show of teeth, what the owner may wish to hide: hesitation, complacency, resentment, secrets.

The spread included delicately sautéed shiitake mushrooms over poached fish, Roma tomatoes, artichokes, sour cherries in syrup. She had expected extravagance of the canned and freeze-dried variety but not this.

"Wow," said Harriet, mouth parted in anticipation.

"They're impressed," said Michael to the others. The table barely fit them all. "Look at their faces."

"You two look fairly healthy," said Gloria, appraising them. "I take it food supplies haven't gone entirely to hell out there."

"We're okay."

"Any diseases, chronic or otherwise? We can do bloodwork."

"I said we're okay." Neko tried to smile, but it turned out more like a grimace.

"Well, here. Have some fish—it's good for the brain." They slid slick fillets onto Harriet's plate, then passed around an enormous bowl of nuts.

"Walnuts. Good for heart health. Ovulation. You really can't get enough."

"I bet they didn't expect to eat so well," added Mrs. Zhang, whose gray cashmere sweater screamed *quality,* though Neko noticed scars where an amateur had stitched up tears.

"Probably thought we were all succumbing to deaths of despair. Or living down here like *Lord of the Flies.*"

"Like *The Road.*"

"Yes, like *The* fucking *Road.*"

They all laughed uproariously, and that's when Neko began to sense the cracks—the off-kilter laughter, the strange unison of it.

Neko was about to ask how long they would go on talking as though she and Harriet weren't there, but then one of Gloria's adult sons turned to her and said, "Video-game downloads. And a new console. Can you get them for me?"

"Drake, honey. Not right now," said Gloria, as though he were fifteen and not closer to thirty.

"But I thought they were here to get us things?" He stuck out his chin.

"I could, I can," said Neko, looking at him directly. Maybe he was a weak link.

"Son," said Gloria. "We negotiate as a team, remember." She looked at Neko and mouthed, *I used to be a CFO,* and Neko wasn't sure if the comment was intended to be informational or intimidating. "We'll continue to contract with her group only if the deal is advantageous. And secure."

Neko leaned forward. "And if it passes a vote."

They turned to her with confused faces.

"If it's advantageous, secure, and if it passes a vote," she said. "Michael explained how everyone at the Cellar is an equal partner."

"Indeed," said Mr. and Mrs. Zhang.

"Indeed," said Michael.

"Indeed," said Gloria's husband, whose name Neko had already forgotten.

"Speaking of the rest of the *partners,*" said Neko. "Where are they?"

"We call ourselves 'the root vegetables,'" said Gloria.

Neko blinked. "Cute."

"There are sixty people living in the Cellar . . ."

"And counting," said Mrs. Zhang with pride.

". . . Right. So, as you can imagine, we couldn't fit everyone in here for dinner. We're a community, not an army with a mess hall."

Semi-hysterical laughter erupted again.

As the others began discussing "community-building" activities, Neko turned to Gloria and praised the meal, but the woman didn't smile.

"Part of me has so many questions about what's going on out there, about your life," said Gloria, mouth leaking sadness. "But the other part of me doesn't want to know." She looked at the ceiling. "Quiet mind, quiet heart."

AFTER DINNER—ELLA FITZGERALD ON THE SOUND SYSTEM, ANOTHER round of cocktails crossing the lips of the increasingly loud and chatty cabal of bored alcoholics—Neko decided to see what she could find out from Drake.

She maneuvered him into a corner of the living room and got him talking about video games—all the ones he'd beaten over and over again by this point.

"I even managed to defeat the final level without the gun implant!" He was thin and clean-shaven, not bad-looking, really, despite his stunted maturity.

"Is that so?"

"I had to engineer my own headset after the original chip got fried."

"Cool."

Eventually, she asked if there were other venues of entertainment at the compound—filmmakers or musicians, other creatives in residence?

"Not really," he said, unhelpfully. "Mostly just money people."

"You mean people from the industry?"

"I guess. Laurence Cole supposedly produced movies, some arthouse ones nobody's heard of."

"What about music? There were some pretty fantastic master recordings in the haul we brought you." Neko kept her voice low.

Drake squinted. "There is one woman—she's on the board with Mama. I think she was a music person back in the day, but down here she's director of the future." He rolled his eyes.

Neko's heart fluttered. "What's her name?"

"Oh, I don't think I'm supposed . . ."

"Is it Jenny Sweet?" She could hardly hear the music over the beating of her heart.

"No . . . um . . ."

Harriet appeared and perched herself on the arm of the chintz loveseat where Neko and Drake were sitting. "Sorry to interrupt, but I need to talk to my boss for a sec."

Drake shrugged and walked back toward the kitchen before Neko could tell him to wait.

"Did Chaplin tell you about the eggs?" whispered Harriet.

"What eggs?" Neko kept her eyes on Drake to make sure he wasn't leaving the party altogether.

"Of course he didn't." Harriet shook her head. "Damn it."

"*What* eggs?"

"I was just talking to Gloria and, *apparently,* Chaplin promised them three good eggs."

"I still don't understand what you're saying."

"Human eggs. For Drake to fertilize and his mother to carry. That's why they allowed us to come here and why they wanted two females. Our eggs, Neko."

AS NEKO MINGLED AND TRIED TO MAKE NICE DURING THE REST OF the party, underneath she seethed with anger. *Chaplin better be dead,* she thought, *or I'm going to kill him.* She supposed the generous interpretation would be that he did it to get her inside the bunker, but why not tell her beforehand?

Eventually, Neko managed to corner Drake again. "So you're going to be a father."

His eyes grew large. "We need more kids here. Mama says we're getting too old."

"No special someone here for you?"

He closed his eyes briefly and shook his head.

"In my world, there are a lot of women who would be interested in a handsome, educated man like yourself. A lot."

"Mom says that girls aren't interested in video games."

Neko nodded toward Harriet on the other side of the room. "Some *women* are." She looked to make sure nobody else was eavesdropping. "But I need you to tell me more about the person who might have worked in the music industry."

Drake shrugged. "She works on the aquaponics floor. She's . . ."

"Her name, Drake."

He hesitated. "Real names are only for the community, Mama likes to say."

Neko forced herself to touch Drake on the arm. "I'm more interested in what *you* have to say, Drake."

He looked frightened and suspicious. "Mama wouldn't . . ."

"Mothers don't have to know everything, do they?" Neko closed her eyes as she said this, the irony not lost on her. "And what they don't know won't hurt them."

28

THE SIGHT OF HER UNRAVELED SOMETHING INSIDE NEKO.

As soon as the elevator door opened, Neko felt an urge to huddle against the woman she'd known since birth, as close to family as it came in her world. To sob into her arms for all that they had lost.

But she didn't. Cameras. Eyes everywhere. Instead, she walked over and lodged herself next to an enormous tank of shimmering fish, body blocking the view of her palm pressing hard into the palm of Layla Wei. Hand on hand on glass.

She hadn't seen her since before the storm, since she was thirteen years old, and now Aunt Layla was old. Because her father had never been able to get ahold of her after, they assumed she died in the hurricane.

"Who in the . . ." Layla looked up—surprised, confused.

Before she could call out or sound the alarm, Neko whispered, "Wok hei."

Layla stared in that gape-mouthed way that confirmed she hadn't known Neko was larking for Chaplin. Hadn't known any of it.

"It's me."

Layla began to cough, a smoker's rough cough, and tears formed in the corners of her eyes. "You're all grown up. You're alive."

"So are you."

"What are you doing here?"

Surrounding them were tanks with plastic buckets and tubes connected to a vegetable bed sprouting lettuce and tomatoes and cucumbers. Aquaponics used the fish waste to fertilize produce, and produce to clean the bunker's water for reuse.

"Can we talk here? I have so many questions."

"Yes. The tank pumps drown out our voices." She picked up a sieve and a bag of pellets to begin feeding the tilapia, who circled, eyes as skittish as Layla's. "How did you find me?"

"I mudlark for Chaplin." Neko squinted, trying to figure out if this was truly news. "When he said Jenny Sweet claimed to be here . . ."

". . . you came to see for yourself." She grunted. "Now I understand why he asked about Goldbug." She studied Neko. "Look at you. I always knew you were a tough cookie. Like your mom."

"My mother isn't here. Is she?"

"I always loved the way her hands could dismantle bread." Layla continued to feed the fish.

"What?"

"I used to come here to sing where nobody could hear me, and now I raise these little guys."

Neko had never known her to sing. Aunt Layla had always been a caretaker of music, not a producer of it. "My mother." Her inflection was intentionally a statement, not a question.

"I know," Aunt Layla said, softly.

"You know?"

"I know how I look."

At this, Neko stepped back to take her in—as though it might provide a clue. Unlike the group at the dinner party, with their fake tans, Aunt Layla looked sallow, washed of color. Always thin, now she was skeletal, and she wore a pressed and tailored suit with a Mao collar, gunmetal-gray hair pulled back in a chignon. She looked like Layla Wei dressed in a costume for a play set in some freakish alternative future, which Neko supposed was more or less the case.

"My mother."

Aunt Layla took a small net and swept it through the water, capturing one small fish, an anchovy. Without gloves, she wrapped her hand around the silvery scales as it wriggled, took a knife with her other hand, and cut into it.

Neko stared while her Aunt Layla—or whoever this new version of her was—sliced the fish into thin strips and then ate each piece, one at a time, tossing the head back into the water to be swarmed by its old colleagues.

"Why do you think fish float to the top of the water when they die?" Layla licked her fingers and returned to feeding the rest of the fish their pellets. "As though that bright spark of soul was only *just* heavy enough to give them equilibrium in the . . ."

"My *mother,*" said Neko again.

Layla stopped feeding the fish, closed up the feed bag. "It's the same with humans, though. Dead man's float." She cocked her chin.

Neko began to feel sick. From the beginning, she'd tried to leaven her expectations, always aware that the message might be a mirage, a trap. But she hadn't considered the possibility that her mother had come here, been brought to this horrible place, and then died here, too. The possibility that Neko was too late.

"The message said she was here."

Layla's voice brightened. "Yes! Forever."

"Forever?" The word was sandpaper. "You have her body?" Neko's voice came out like a hiss.

"Well, I . . ."

It was hard to breathe, suddenly. The air in the room was too warm—Neko felt her chest heaving, but no oxygen was reaching her lungs. "What, in some freezer? A plastic baggy of ashes? *What*?"

Aunt Layla became very still. She thumped her heart. "You brought her to me."

Neko wanted to yell at her, to scream, but she didn't have the breath. She wanted to loosen her clothes; she wanted to rip off the buttons and zippers.

Layla tapped her fingers on her sternum. "*The Wreckage*. It contains her consciousness. You brought it, and now she and I can be free."

Neko's heart in her rib cage: pummeling, pausing, pummeling again.

"That album contains your mother's consciousness, her brain waves. It's complicated." She began to ramble about how it contained the "bright spark." The part that allowed the body to sink. "I've been waiting so long, you have no idea. I'm the director of the future, for God's sake."

The colors of the tubes connecting the tanks tortured Neko's eyes: the primary blue, the sickly yellow, the shade of emergency red. "How crazy *are* you people?"

Her thoughts involuntarily returned to the living room, the one in their old apartment, where she used to picture her mother's final moments, where her mother met a wall of water after the seawall busted open and a storm surge flooded the East Village. Ever since Chaplin had told her of the bunker's message, since the beginning of this quixotic quest, that room had drained, like a film reel moving backward, restoring all possibility.

Neko sank to the floor to keep from falling. She put her head between her knees. To gasp. To hide her face.

"Get up, get up." Layla's hands were on her shoulders, pushing at her. "They'll come for you."

Neko didn't respond.

"Everything is ready," said Layla, pleading. "I have plans you don't understand."

Neko looked at this woman, whom she knew so well and didn't know at all. Whom she loved and despised. "Do you know what I risked to come here?"

Layla gripped Neko's arm too tightly and leaned down over her, spittle spraying her face. "I'm going to set her—us—free."

Neko wrenched her arm away and then: sharp noise and bright lights. The elevator opened and a security guard was suddenly beside her, stepping between her and Layla. "Director Wei. Is everything all right?"

"Oh, yes, Harrison. Fine." Layla's voice was brittle, formal. "This courier came down to see how our aquaponics system works, and it seems she got a little disoriented. Poor thing looks anemic."

The security guard pulled Neko up by her armpits, and she let him.

THE WRECKAGE

Track 9: "Tiresias Foretells the Future"

Soothsayers speak of journeys
They speak of other realms
Where women do not know the sea nor mix their food with salt and Chablis

Jenny Sweet had always been attracted to what she referred to as arcana. She told people she'd inherited this from her father, who spent his spare time "practicing" the divination system of the *I Ching*.

After touring the Hades bunker with Layla, Jenny and Max had somehow ended up on an "exclusive" mailing list aimed at rich doomsday preppers. The couple was bombarded with ads for everything from cryonics to "executive extraction insurance" to investment opportunities for potential moon colonies.

They laughed, Max posting the most ridiculous ones on social media. But secretly, there was one email Jenny kept—she dragged it over to her starred folder, opening it every few days, finger hovering above the RSVP button, until one day she clicked. She told herself she was doing it for research for the new album. Because it was the arcana of their age.

"It's like a Tupperware party." Jenny had struggled to explain it, sitting across from her manager in the dark, sooty tea shop in Hell's Kitchen.

"A *Tupperware* party?" Layla Wei fondled her porcelain cup. "You're not really selling it."

"You know, somebody hosts a private party to show off the product. They probably get a discount for doing it or whatever. Like a Tupperware party."

"The product?" Layla poured mossy-smelling tea from the pot at the center of the table. "You can't even say it."

Jenny ran her finger along the graffiti carved into the wooden table. "I went to the middle of nowhere to see that bunker with you. This is only Central Park West."

"Do I have to wear a garter belt and smoke Virginia Slims? Can I bring a bottle of my mother's little helpers?"

Jenny smiled, relieved she wouldn't have to go alone. They chatted—music industry this and that—and Layla gave her a thumb drive with some new tracks from a band she'd just signed. They tried to remember the lyrics to Veruca Salt's "Seether" but kept getting tripped up.

At one point, Layla put a hand on her collarbone, looked sideways at Jenny before whispering, "You could just say the Nightjars were on hiatus again." They'd recently announced to her that the band was breaking up, that this would be their last album. She didn't like it.

At the table next to them, a man was putting wedding invitations—red with two white bicycles—into envelopes.

Jenny took Layla's hand in hers. "You know how Odysseus spends years as Calypso's lover on that island?"

"Oh, God. What is it with you and Homer?"

"And then he comes home to Penelope, who's been waiting for him all that time, and it's a big fat happy ending?"

"Is there about to be a moral to this story?"

Jenny shrugged. "I'm working on an album—a *solo* album—based on *The Odyssey*."

Layla tried to pour more tea but the pot was empty. "That's so pretentious."

"Right!" Jenny laughed. "I'm turning the sirens into nags. You know, 'We want equal pay! We want affordable childcare!' And Odysseus and his crew just don't want to hear it, you know?"

Layla shook her head. "I love you almost as much as I hate you right now."

"The truth is, I've been working on this album for years. But I don't think it's just an album—I think it's bigger. Part tomb, part womb." Jenny laughed at herself as she said it.

"This is getting worse and worse."

"I want you to help me find a place, somewhere not in New York, a museum or space where I can use this album to make something more experiential." They put cash down for their bill like old people. "You know, Layla, I have ideas, too."

Layla stood and stretched, a cracked pillar. "Have you noticed the Nightjars have been with me longer than my other clients? A lot longer."

"Other bands moved on to better management, did they?"

"Ha, ha." She crinkled the bill in her palm. "I like discovering the next thing. I like change. I like the new."

"Yes, and Max is new every week."

She looked at the ceiling. "I took on the Nightjars because of Max. But I stayed because of you. You are a badass, Jenny Sweet. Did you know that?"

———

At the party there were twelve kinds of mini quiches.

"Do you think these are the frozen kind from Trader Joe's?" Jenny whispered, inspecting the diminutive crimped crusts.

"I think these are the kind made from scratch by an undocumented brown woman sleeping in a closet." Layla did not bother to whisper this.

"A lot of judgment for a woman throwing money at a survival condo."

The party was at the San Remo, cherrywood wainscoting and mid-century mod everything. The apartment wasn't the penthouse—apparently Bono owned that—but the views were incredible, above the park with its bucolic green-gold treetops swaying like one gorgeous organism.

The host worked in private equity, which made Jenny feel guilty for assuming she was a Stepford-type housewife—there was something about the fierce blond highlights and ruffly pantsuit. Her husband was not in attendance, and, in fact, almost everyone there appeared to be female.

"Women are the future" was the first thing the host said after clinking her glass for attention. Her voice had a slight British lilt—cultivated, Jenny suspected. "For centuries, men have chased the fountain of youth and power. One could argue that, in doing so, they have brought us here, to the brink of destruction." The art deco chandelier winked as the sun hit it. "If things are to be different going forward, women must participate more fully in the new technologies that could save us." *She walked like a woman but talked like a man . . .*

The host went on to explain that the consciousness-preserving technology currently in development was technically available to anyone, but that she had made it her personal mission to ensure that at least 50 percent of down payments came from individuals who identified as women. "We will not be exterminated while they live on." The host told them to get something to eat and find a comfortable place; the company's CEO and the head of research were here to answer their questions.

"So, she's saying that uploading your consciousness so you can live forever is a way for women to *lean in*?" Layla slurped an oyster from its shell. "At least with the bunker I'm not pretending my selfishness is part of a feminist revolution."

"But you're in a bunker. This way, you'd be freeeee . . ." She made her hands into a bird.

They sipped Bloody Marys from tall glasses. Good, peppery Bloody Marys. "We should day-drink more," said Layla.

"You day-drink all the time."

"Not with you."

They looked around, quietly speculating about the other women in the room. There was a generic quality to most of them, and they seemed to know one another, probably part of the same philanthropic rich people circles. The only person they recognized by name was Milla Sandoval, a sculptor who also lived in the Village. Milla nodded at them, her face flushed with what Jenny read as embarrassment at being caught here among the lip-filled, botoxed faces that surrounded them.

Jenny had decided to age "gracefully"—just a pot of drugstore face cream and weights twice a week at the cinder-block boxing gym. Not because she was immune to vanity, but because she didn't like pain. A friend had taken her for a "treatment" once, and a woman in scrubs had aimed lasers at her face, zapping her over and over. The smell of burnt peach fuzz had made her want to throw up. It reminded Jenny of when she'd gotten a tattoo after high school, an ill-advised "tribal" design on her lower back, what people used to call a "tramp stamp" before they learned to keep such things to themselves. Jenny had hated that experience, too. Never wore crop tops after that, nor did she ever get another tattoo.

Layla gently elbowed Jenny in the ribs. "I listened to those samples you gave me. Of your solo stuff."

"And?"

"Artsy-fartsy as fuck."

Jenny shrugged. "I don't care if it sells."

"I do, but look, I'm not asking you to make it more commercial. Who's producing?"

"Jesse."

She raised her eyebrows. "Figures. Do you still want to treat it like some high-end performance art?"

Jenny nodded. She wanted space and light and sound and movement. She wanted it all.

"I found this church-turned-museum in Berlin with tons of money, and they're looking to fund an artist-in-residence. You could take all that equipment you're always dicking around with and re-create the album in the catacombs there. Odysseus goes to Hades or whatever. It's not going to help us sell a lot of albums, though."

Jenny tried to take this in. "When?"

"After Burning Man. If you want it, you'll get it. If you won't let me make you a middle-aged rock icon, I'm at least going to make you a middle-aged art dame. Though I can tell you which one pays better, and it ain't that."

"How long?"

"In Berlin? You'd have to stay for at least a year."

Layla looked at her, and Jenny could see that she understood what this meant. If she moved abroad, equal custody of Neko would be impossible. She'd be the holiday mother.

"Jenny Sweet. Oh my God." They were interrupted by a

man with a buzz cut and bulldog eyes who introduced himself as Chance Morris, a name that sounded vaguely familiar, though Jenny couldn't place him. He wore jeans and expensive sneakers, and he shook her hand gently. "I can't believe you're here." He started humming the chorus to "Summer Baby."

Jenny tried to smile. "This is Layla Wei."

"A pleasure." He managed to appear thrilled to be in their company while also scoping out the rest of the room with his peripheral vision. "My parents are going to *die* when they find out I met Jenny Sweet in person. You cannot imagine. Die!"

"Well, that seems extreme," said Layla. "Especially considering their son's occupation." And that's when Jenny realized that Chance Morris was the CEO of the Fourth State.

"Hmm." He danced on the tips of his shoes, casting a glance at the hostess. "Speaking of which, it looks like I'm on. Wish me luck."

Chance Morris walked over to a sideboard and pulled a string to light up a neon sign in the shape of a brain, and the room went silent. "What if I told you this was all we needed to live forever? Plasma. The fourth state of matter." He smiled and looked at his partner.

The head of research, a fellow at MIT, was a small, scrappy-looking guy with a peg leg. Not a fancy prosthesis but a metal limb that he told them he'd fabricated himself from a baseball bat and two lamps. "It also functions as a bong," he added before Chance Morris hurried him along.

"We've known for a while that alpha waves signal synchronous activity of the pacemaker cells . . ."

". . . essentially a relaxed state of mind . . ." inserted Chance Morris.

". . . while beta and gamma waves reflect desynchronized brain activity . . ."

". . . busy thinking, or problem-solving . . ."

"Yes." The scientist nodded and went on to tell them about a new brain wave that had been discovered—"We're calling them zeta waves"—that appeared to be the by-product of human consciousness and expressed themselves on the same scale as sound waves.

"Zetas are like the waves on the surface of the ocean of consciousness." Chance Morris's voice was eerily calm, like a meditation app. "But if these waves are captured in a pure quantum state, we think they can be used to reproduce, or reverse engineer, the precise consciousness that created them."

"In a quantum supercomputer, we can generate pairs of qubits that are entangled." The scientist was getting excited. "Changing the state of one instantaneously changes the state of the other, even if they are separated by very long distances."

"What Einstein called 'spooky action at a distance.' Schrödinger's cat is both alive and dead."

"Kind of," said the scientist with furrowed brows.

"Well, in layman's terms," said Chance Morris. "But the problem is that nobody's been able to build a quantum supercomputer large enough. And we aren't going to 'build'"—he made air quotes with his fingers—"one either. We are going to harness what is already all around us." His fingers flickered back to the neon sign in the shape of a brain. "Essentially, we will turn the plasmasphere surrounding the globe into a quantum supercomputer and use your zeta waves to translate your consciousness inside."

Most of what the scientist explained next made even less sense to Jenny—she learned that neon signs and lightning were both examples of partially ionized plasmas. Neither liquid nor solid nor gas, plasma was apparently a magical substance, its behavior dominated by electric and magnetic fields.

"And inside the plasmasphere," said the scientist. "We can *theoretically* release your consciousness from the body. *Theoretically* forever."

Chance Morris clearly didn't like the emphasis on that word and was quick to add that they were already in human trials, which caused a gasp from the room. "In fact, I've just had my zeta waves recorded for the proof of concept."

Milla Sandoval raised her hand. "Would you still have access to your memories?"

"That's the million-dollar question, isn't it?" The scientist laughed inexplicably. "Each time you access a memory, your zeta waves are involved, we know that. Our hypothesis is that it will all be accessible, but we're still building out the specifics."

"And this is a good reminder of why the sooner you have your zetas recorded, the better. Your brain physically degrades as you get older. This technology allows you to live on *and* remain young."

"And, ladies," added the blond host, holding up the celery from her Bloody Mary. "Keep in mind: You only have to pay half when you record your zetas. The rest isn't due until the technology is ready and able to project you into the plasmasphere. This is your opportunity to lock in a price now."

After the presentation was over and people had begun socializing again, Jenny and Layla walked out onto the balcony without saying anything. Layla took the olive from her glass and sucked on it quietly. Later, Jenny would look up the company's scientist on the Internet and find that, in addition to his work on brain waves, he was also known for recording the vaginal contractions of ballet dancers and sending them into deep space. Oddly, it made her like him more. The humanness of it, maybe. The offensive whimsy.

"Crimson and Clover" was playing on the stereo, and though

it was basically a ballad, Jenny noticed how you could still hear the rock 'n' roll underneath, there in the bottom of Joan Jett's voice. Watching the trees down below, suddenly so still, so arched, Jenny imagined the power in not dying. The power in a mother just waiting. She wondered how different her life might have been if her mother had lived. She remembered how as a baby Neko had said the word "moon" like a prayer. Moon. In awe that it was there. Again. Still.

29

SHE WOKE IN LAYLA WEI'S BUNKER APARTMENT. NEKO'S WHOLE BODY felt sore, gut-punched. Her chest ached. Her heart hurt. She couldn't be sure where emotion ended and the physical part of herself began.

She had already lost her mother, but the trauma, released from wherever it had been stored, was on the rampage again. Wreaking havoc. Neko lay stunned and wilted atop a small bed.

Layla was across the room, writing at a desk, but she turned once she realized Neko had come to. "How do you feel, doll?"

Neko shook her head. Words stacked up in her mouth. "My mother."

"Chin up," said Layla, nonsensically. "All is not lost."

The apartment was spare—maybe only a dozen identical items hanging in the open closet—more like a hotel room than a home. Like Layla was afraid of taking up too much space. There was an antiseptic, institutional smell that reminded Neko of visiting her father toward the end. Wholly unlike the "Aunt" Layla she'd known growing up.

"What do you mean?" Neko thought about getting up, but didn't.

"My body is falling apart. I'm ossifying. Yours will, too."

Neko rubbed her temples. Sipped air.

"We're containers of sloshing liquid. An organic colostomy bag. Life is just an endless loop of shitting and pissing and bleeding and wiping . . ."

"Jesus Christ." Neko shook her head. "This is supposed to make me feel better?"

"I'm going to transport us into the plasmasphere."

Neko swallowed. Tried not to blanch. "Us?"

"Your mother and me."

"Aunt Layla." Neko's throat finally loosened. "Remember how you asked me to call you that?" Maybe she couldn't get her mother back, but at least she could get some answers. "I need to know how you ended up here. And what was really going on with Mom and those master recordings."

Layla turned around and smiled. There was a slight asymmetry to her lips, her mouth hovering on a leer. "After they catalog the goods, they'll give me *The Wreckage*. Then I can *show* you."

Layla clearly hadn't realized that the album wasn't among the goods. Neko had sent the master back with Chaplin and kept the other one—the mother she'd had pressed at the Watering Hole—in her own things, wrapped in a wool sweater and buried at the bottom of her and Harriet's supply bag. After all, it was *her mother's*.

"Explain it to me now, Aunt Layla."

Over the next hour, Neko tried to piece together a narrative from Aunt Layla's meandering exposition. Apparently, there had been some company claiming to be able to use sound waves to capture the signatures of individual consciousnesses. Layla and Neko's mother had been told that later, even after death, presumably, the sound waves could be played into plasma, the fourth state of matter, and that they could have a second, disembodied life in the plasmasphere. "Your mother called me right before the hurricane and said that her brain *was* her solo album. The master must contain her consciousness in sound waves, understand?"

"Not really."

"It's just like Jenny to use her own brain as performance art."

"Is it?"

After the hurricane, Layla went on to tell her, she hadn't been able to get in touch with the company. Poof. They'd disappeared along with their technology. So she'd spent the years researching and building a machine herself that could transpose sound waves into plasma. "Like a starfish, a part of you might be cut off, something gone, but you're still here. Regenerated, in a way."

"Why didn't you retrieve the master before now?"

"Oh, I tried. Believe me. It took me some time to find out exactly where it was, and then I had to wait until the rest of the board agreed to go to Chaplin."

They sat on the edge of Layla's bed.

"I want *you* to be the witness, to watch it happen." The woman was practically giddy. Her breath was a hothouse. "To take care of the machine once we're free."

For a moment she considered not telling her, but what good would that ultimately do? "It's a scam, Aunt Layla. I'm sorry."

Aunt Layla's brow creased and she shook her head. "You don't believe me." She squirmed, pulled at the sleeves of her sweater like a little girl.

"There are all sorts of scams promising extended life. Soulsuckers."

"Soulsuckers?"

"Yes."

Aunt Layla's face, puffy and pink, shifted slowly into an emotion it took Neko a moment to place—something practically ancient, a remnant of the old days, when people could still be surprised by the world. Neko felt bad for inspiring it, but she felt worse for herself.

"No. This one is real. You just want your mother for yourself. You and your father never understood her like I did."

Neko tried to breathe out all that was inside her but that she could not say. She refused to cry or yell or shake Aunt Layla hard. "Well, maybe I'm wrong. I'll take you to the Inside, and you can find out everything for yourself."

"But the Inside . . . is a hellscape."

Neko reached to touch her mother's old friend, but the woman shrank from her. "Aunt Layla, you live in a missile silo."

Some of Layla's steely hair had escaped its bun and was sticking, sweaty, to her temple. "You think your life is so great? Dragging yourself through the Sink looking for scraps? It's me, here, that found a way to save your mother, not you."

"What is your deal?" Neko's frustration grew. "Why are you so obsessed with her? She wasn't *your* mother. Why not just plasmasphere yourself or whatever?"

Aunt Layla's eyes widened. "I have my reasons. I can't tell you."

Neko turned away, touched the wall for strength. She had wanted to believe she might see her mother again, though maybe what she'd really wanted was for her mother to understand what had happened at Burning Man, to forgive her, to see what she'd become. "Well, I'm not giving you *The Wreckage*."

"What do you mean?"

"It's not with the rest of the goods."

"You didn't bring it?" Her voice was incredulous. "Even though you thought your mom was here?"

Neko didn't respond. Was she protecting Layla or punishing her? She wasn't really sure.

"You have to give it to me." Layla licked the corner of her mouth. "Do I have to kneel on glass or what?"

"If you want it, you'll have to come with me. I'm not leaving it here." Neko consciously softened her voice. "I'll take care of you."

Aunt Layla's face closed in fury, eyes focused just above Neko's head. "Jenny was going to take off, you know."

Neko opened her mouth, not sure if she wanted her to continue.

"Before the hurricane, she'd already accepted a residency in Berlin. She was planning to leave you behind with your father and fly across the ocean and live there. Her art came first."

Neko felt a hole punch through her chest, cleanly riven. "Why are you telling me this?"

Layla shrugged. "Maybe don't waste your whole life trailing after a woman who was running away from you."

30

THEY WANTED EGGS, BUT NEKO SAID THAT WAS A HARD PASS. "I TRAFfic in a lot of things, but human organs are not one." At least in this, she could protect Harriet.

"Trafficking! Who said anything about human trafficking?" Gloria was apoplectic. "I just want to be a *grandmother*."

Neko still couldn't figure out exactly how Chaplin had thought he would get away with this. Had he believed she'd throw one of her apprentices under the bus to save his relationship with the Cellar? Or had he just promised these people random shit to seal the deal and then assumed Neko would talk her way out of the eggs altogether?

"Please," said Gloria. "What do you want? I can give you what you want, can't I?"

Neko laughed at this so she wouldn't cry.

Harriet, who had been silent up until now, broke in. "We want to take the outstanding payment with us. Physically."

Michael and Gloria shook their heads. "Everything is already arranged. We have the digital transfer standing by."

"Chaplin's operations are intact, but he needs to lay low, stay off the Black Channel for a while." Harriet was nonchalant. "If you want my eggs, you'll give us the rest of the payment in scratch."

"No," said Neko. "No eggs."

Harriet pursed her lips. Her T-shirt had bunched up around her flanks, and she pulled it back down. "Give us a minute."

IN THEIR QUARTERS, HARRIET SAID NOTHING AT FIRST. INSTEAD, SHE went into the bathroom, filled a basin with water, and motioned for Neko to sit in a chair.

"Your hair is a tragedy."

"You mean 'travesty.'"

"Both." She unraveled the Dutch braids, pushing Neko's reluctant head back into the bowl until the tangled curls ran with water, gently working fingers through the knots.

"Harriet, I probably don't have any good eggs to give." Neko told her about the Red Cross clinic readouts.

"I'll give them mine . . ."

"You won't give them anything!"

"Shhh. Just listen." Harriet squeezed oil into her palm—where had she gotten it?—and ran her fingers along Neko's scalp. "I'll give them some silly eggs if they give us the scratch. *And* if you give me sole control over the crew license."

Neko's mind integrated the various streams of information coming at her—Harriet's words in her ears and the warmth of the woman's finger pads running along her temples. "Does this solo bid have anything to do with the Ice House? Do you know what Jules's people were doing there?"

"I used to think I understood her, but she's a cipher." Harriet shook her head. "She knew the whole time."

Neko sat up, accidentally knocking the basin. "About the Ice House?" Wet hair dampened the back of her shirt.

"About my kidnapping." Harriet pressed a towel into the spilled water on the floor. "When her people came to collect me from the men, there was no real confrontation. The men were almost . . . deferential."

"What happened before that?"

Harriet shrugged. "I was too scared to sleep, became delirious. I watched them play cards and piss on trees."

Neko looked at her—Harriet's chest and neck were ruddy.

"Fear is its own trigger. And if I let you all assume it was something worse, maybe it's because I wanted to get back at Jules. Wanted to see if I could make her feel bad for all her secrets."

"Why would the Hive have you kidnapped?"

She shook her head. "I'm not sure. Ransom from my parents?"

"Why didn't you tell me?"

"I'm telling you now."

Neko reached out a palm to Harriet's cheek, and it was so warm. "If the eggs work, they'll become your biological . . ."

She put her hand on top of Neko's. "I know."

HARRIET WOULD PROVIDE THEM THREE HEALTHY EGGS. THE CELLAR would hand over the final payment in scratch.

Harriet took the hormone injections that they'd unwittingly brought with them. Then they waited the requisite days to have her eggs harvested. Neko paced like a caged animal. Circled and waited and circled again.

THE NEXT EVENING, HARRIET, TIRED AND CRAMPING, WENT TO BED early, and Neko decided to accept Gloria's invitation to "Women's Tea." She imagined plates of cookies and mahjong, but when she showed up at Gloria's creepily opulent apartment, there was a circle of meditation cushions on the Turkish rug, mossy incense and chanty music in the air.

A half dozen women were tightly huddled around the kitchen island whispering to one another, backs turned—Neko recognized Mrs. Zhang from her sharp-angled blunt haircut. As she neared the kitchen, they all turned around at once, each holding some sort of dried stem or stick. To her surprise, Aunt Layla was there, and she gave a small smile that Neko couldn't read. Regretful? Awkward? Warm?

"Welcome to the coven," said Gloria, wearing so much sparkling makeup she looked irradiated.

"Um."

"She's joking," said a Black woman with diamond studs, Bantu knots in her graying hair.

"What are you holding?"

"Whoever draws the short stick leads the guided meditation." Gloria's voice was brassy, performative. "Lucky for us, Layla drew it tonight."

Neko debated leaving, but what the hell?

At first there was hemming and hawing over the seating arrangements, and Neko tried to make her legs bend and fold on her cushion in a way that wasn't entirely excruciating. Then there was breath work, some *om*s. She felt painfully self-conscious.

"Let's say you're on an airport runway," Layla started. She had her eyes closed, palms on her thighs, and was seated almost directly across from Neko. "Let's say it's one of those planes where you have to walk up the stairs, like you're the president. Or maybe a rock star. Let's say you do walk up them and soon you're in the clouds. Watery and gray. Occasional flurries of light streaking through. The windows in this airplane are connected like a long glass ribbon."

Everyone else had their eyes closed tight, but Neko kept hers open slightly. She watched Layla, studied her inscrutable face, as she told them how the flight attendant was passing around a cardboard box with a slit in the top, telling them to write down their biggest desire and slip it inside. "*What* do you *desire*?" Layla asked. She repeated the question.

"Let's say you desire to leave this place underground. Let's say you could take flight into the clouds like this airplane. Where would you go? Would you go with someone you used to know back to a place where you used to live? See if there's something there for you after all?" Layla's eyes opened, fast and hard. Blink. She looked at Neko and smiled.

Neko nodded, thinking she understood. Relieved. Anxious. Layla was agreeing to come back with her after all. She tried to imagine how Iggy would react.

Mrs. Zhang took over from Layla, leading them in what she called Tonglen meditation, where they breathed in the suffering of the world and breathed out the antidote to that suffering. By the end, Neko felt weak. From the breathing or the suffering, or both.

When it was over and they began to line up for tea, Neko tried to talk to Layla, to confirm that she'd really understood, but her aunt had pulled Gloria into the hallway, was saying something in the host's ear, then giving a quick wave and exiting the apartment. Neko moved to follow, but Gloria slid in between her and the door.

"Please stay," she said. "I need to show you something."

Reluctantly, Neko waited. One woman was going on about phosphorus, about its importance and scarcity, how it was "life's chemical bottleneck" on Earth. Another rocked her teacup back and forth but didn't take a drink, gently singing under her breath, and someone else said, *Remember how television could make a person glow blue? How you could see it when you walked by a window at night? Remember that?*

Neko listened, munching on salted nuts and raisins, until eventually the rest of the group members washed their own cups in the sink, said their goodbyes like a mantra, and left.

Gloria put a hand on Neko's shoulder and mouthed, Stay. Then she took a canister from the cupboard, opened it. "We move from the symphony to the encore," she said, holding a perfectly rolled joint in one hand and a lighter in the other.

Neko reached for it. "Now you're talking."

The two of them sat beside each other on the kitchen counter, passing the joint back and forth.

Gloria turned on the exhaust fan over the stove and exhaled into it. Up close, in the bright light of the kitchen, her hair was the color of beets. She kicked one foot out, using it to point to a photograph hanging on the wall in front of them. "My grandmother in Cusco," she said.

In the sepia image a dark-haired woman was standing on a cobblestone street in a smart wool suit and black pumps. "My grandmother missed a connecting flight to Peru once—in the era before cell phone ubiquity—and yet her uncle knew exactly when and where to pick her up. It was how she realized he probably wasn't really a cultural attaché."

"Ah. Generational wealth and power," said Neko lightly.

" 'And you may find yourself in a beautiful house, with a beautiful wife.' " Gloria didn't act offended. *" 'And you may ask yourself, Well, how did I get here?' "*

Gloria snuffed out the joint in the sink. "How do you know Layla Wei?"

"What makes you think I know her?"

"We're like the blind around here. Take away one of our senses and the others grow stronger."

"I've known Layla Wei forever."

Neko slid down from the counter and walked into the living room, drawn toward the jawbone on the mantel, which she didn't remember being there at the dinner party. Her parents had owned one for a while, when her father was collecting strange instruments, and she remembered him trying to convince her it had come from a mountain lion he'd hunted and killed. But she'd known it was from a horse—she had the Internet—and she used to try to play it, rattling it like a tambourine. Like the jaws of death, come to dance you to the other side.

"Why did you want me to stay?" asked Neko, running her hand along the bone. Her head swam pleasantly from the weed. "What did you want me to see?"

"Oh. Well. I was going to have you send a message from me to someone on the Inside," she said from the other room, her voice straining. "But I changed my mind. It's probably too late to matter anyway."

Neko walked back to the kitchen and watched Gloria splash water on her face at the sink before turning back around. "I know that I didn't do the best job with Drake. I didn't understand what I was getting into with this place when he was young. I was depressed." She rolled up her sleeves, slowly, deliberately. "But I understand how things work now. If these embryos make it, I'll take good care of them. I promise you."

Neko noticed Gloria's left forearm was dappled and dotted, and instinctively, she reached out to touch it with her fingertips, to say, *The mosquitos must love you*. But as she did, she realized her mistake—no mosquitos down here. Scar tissue in little perfect circles. Cigarette burns, a dozen of them at least. Neko touched them, the softness of the tissue, and Gloria let her.

They said nothing for a long time.

"Is Layla . . . well, crazy?" Neko asked quietly, finally.

Gloria looked at her. She slowly took back her arm and then walked over to a closet door in the corner of the kitchen. When she opened it, a stack of paper toppled onto the floor. Hundreds of thick sheets covered in swirls of watercolor streamed into the kitchen, all various shades of blue.

"Only as crazy as you have to be to live here. As crazy as we all are." The woman began to pick up one rectangular paper at a time. "Turquoise, baby blue, periwinkle, midnight, Klein blue, Pantone 292, royal blue . . ."

ON THE NIGHT BEFORE THEY WERE TO LEAVE THE CELLAR—AFTER A woman in gloves scraped Harriet's ovaries—Neko went back to Aunt Layla's apartment.

"You're not packed."

"No," said Layla, at her desk again. She turned in the swivel chair. "The machine would be too awkward to travel with—and what if it got damaged?" She smiled brightly. "I can't imagine having to rebuild it, can you?"

"What?"

Layla turned back to her notebook and began scribbling again.

"You're staying in the bunker?"

"I need the tech we have here to power the machine."

Neko could sense what she was up against: Delusion. Fear. The ways the mind conspired to hide from reality. She had watched it all with her father.

Neko gently scuffed the leg of the bed with her boot. "I thought you wanted to be *free*? Isn't that the whole point of the machine?"

Layla kept writing for a minute and then released her pen. Without looking at Neko, Layla picked up a glass bottle from the table and swallowed a pill from it with water. "But there's too much to do, too much."

Neko crouched and tried to look her in the eyes. "I'll help you. You won't be alone."

Silence.

"It's hard to give up your pretend power and depart for the unknown. Believe me, I know how that is."

Layla was writing again, furiously. "I was remembering how you ate a fistful of glitter as a toddler and, later, your diaper was like the inside of a Tenderloin disco!"

Neko closed her eyes. Disappointment was the air she lived in now.

AS HARRIET SNORED LIGHTLY ON THE BUNK ABOVE HER, NEKO WISHED she had her ink works with her. Instead, she took out a pen and began to sketch.

She thought about how when she was eight years old, Aunt Layla had visited her family at their vacation rental in Vermont, and the two of them went berry picking. There were raspberry bushes growing wild along the road—scraggly with jagged leaves surrounding spikes of soft red fruit. But the blueberry patch had been planted by the owner and was fenced in, multiple varieties lined up in orderly rows. Neko loved how everything about a blueberry bush was round, even the mild leaves and the gentle swell of the soil at the base, the berries growing in clutches.

Neko remembered walking behind Layla, bent over with her

long fingers skidding across the tiny globes, searching for perfection. Neko understood the ripest ones were deeply, entirely blue, but it was hard to pass up the ones in transition—psychedelic swirls of purple and fuchsia. Layla looked in Neko's bowl at one point and said, "Those aren't ready. You're picking the wrong ones." Neko couldn't stand to be embarrassed in front of Aunt Layla, so she shoved a handful in her mouth, claiming to prefer the taste of the not-yet-ripe ones, the sour mealiness.

Layla accepted this explanation, and began handing over any of her own blueberries that weren't quite soft. It was the first time Neko realized what it meant to have a secret life churning beneath the surface, one the adults didn't suspect, zipped tight inside the body. Even so, it hadn't yet dawned on her that the adults in her life held layers of existence to which she wasn't privy. And how much of her future would be dedicated to peeling those layers away.

Neko needed to focus on her own life again. She had to hope it wasn't too late to salvage a future with Iggy. To finally make a clean break.

By the time Neko had filled the page of her sketchbook, there was an anchovy, like the one Aunt Layla had killed and eaten, swimming downstream along her rib cage. Frozen in the current of time. Blissfully unaware of its fate, or hers.

THE WRECKAGE

Track 10: "Turning Pigs"

The warehouse studio in Jersey was a rough-cut gem. No plush rugs or espresso machines, just the things that mattered: a mixing console with automation, a beautiful vintage condenser and ribbon mics, proper monitors, and acoustics to die for. Jenny had always preferred to record analog, old-school, but Jesse had forced her to at least try his new digital software, and now she was kind of obsessed with how they could tweak a rim shot on a snare with insane precision.

They showed up at seven in the morning every day for two weeks to cut *The Wreckage* like it was their job.

"Let's see what happens with a different guitar," she said. "There's too much quack."

"Try the bridge pickup," he said. "It bites harder."

She played it again. And again. And again. The lyrics were taped to plastic folders so they would stay on the music stand without rustling. The microphone was off-axis, near the cone but kind of hanging off the side to allow some air in.

Jenny had always thought her singing voice was too angular, no vibrato at all, and didn't merge easily into harmony. So she used its force and range like a cudgel, a primal release. She liked to think of it not as screaming at somebody, but as screaming *with* them.

"How was that?" Sweat beaded on her temples.

"Let's play it back through the monitors. The monitors tell the truth."

She loved watching Jesse work at the consoles. A fucking magician.

"Where did you get the idea behind this track, by the way?" he asked. "Who's the pig? Or do I want to know?"

In the early weeks of pregnancy, Jenny had felt horrible—nauseous, yes, but also depressed. Nothing gave her pleasure. One afternoon before a show, she walked along the frozen creek running through the city of Boulder, Colorado, a lone grocery cart caught in the middle of the white ice like an apocalyptic human fossil. She called Layla on her cell and cried.

"When I imagine my future, it's like there's a haze over everything. There's nothing to look forward to."

"Whoa," said Layla. "Hold your horses. That's just the hormones talking."

"I never dreamed of being a mother."

There was a pause. "Maybe accepting motherhood is the same thing as accepting your ambivalence about motherhood."

Jenny's breath emerged like smoke. "Shit. Where did that come from? Are you drinking?"

"Bourbon."

"I thought you were cutting down."

"Next week."

It was a stereotype that pregnant women wanted to klatch with new mothers, others who had been through it. But Jenny preferred confiding in Layla, childless Layla. Layla, who would always remember that Jenny was a woman first, an artist, not just a mother. Layla, who wasn't distracted by her own maternal plot line.

"Tell me a story," said Jenny.

"What kind of story?"

"My father used to tell me Homer."

Joggers ran by Jenny along the creek trail, bound in black thermal like Arctic researchers or cat burglars.

"I can do that," said Layla, voice dropping, glass tinkling. "We begin in the middle of things. On an island—I don't remember the name, but it's not important. It's owned by Calypso, a powerful witch. She wants Odysseus for herself and has turned the last of his men into pigs and trapped him on her island for, I don't know . . . five to seven years, let's say. They have tons of sex, but Odysseus would really like to go home again."

"Wait. How did he end up on this island?"

"You'll find out later. I told you, we start in the middle."

"It was a different witch, Circe, who turns some of his men into pigs," said Jenny. "When the story begins, his men are all *dead*." Since she'd become pregnant, the concept of death had taken on new meaning for Jenny, or perhaps it was more accurate to say *less* meaning. It was more transitory, more provisional. It had become a question mark, returning her to the days of teenage existential inquiry: What did it mean to be dead, anyway? Or, for that matter, alive? "Why wasn't Odysseus turned into a pig?"

"Good question."

There was a pause on the line. Jenny tightened her scarf around her neck.

"I don't remember." Layla sounded sheepish, which almost made Jenny smile.

"Hermes gives him a special herb that protects him against Circe's magic."

"Fine, fine. I feel like you're not interested enough in the sex part."

The next week, Layla sent her a care package with ginger lollipops and DVDs of feminist horror films. Jenny didn't have any siblings, so she would encourage her child to call her friend Aunt Layla. A found family was still a family.

Circe turns the men to pigs
Says, forget your home
Forget your land
And Hermes has a charm for me
Black roots with flowers white as milk, ginger lollipops

31

IT WAS DAWN WHEN THEY LEFT THE BUNKER, AND NEKO FELT BOTH lighter—the goods now off-loaded, replaced with a thick roll of scratch—and heavier, her future like a yoke.

There, on an overcast morning outside that human anthill, wind blowing loose hair into her mouth and knee-high grass clutching her calves as the guide rolled up the wire mesh of the sliced perimeter fence, Neko was painfully aware that she was entering a world of unknowns. Was Chaplin dead? Was there a war on? And most important: Where were Iggy and Jules?

Neko and Harriet followed the same nameless man as before to the crumbling summer resort and the reservoir, dappled in shadow. As the guide used a pump to inflate the raft, Neko pretended to go for a piss. She found the birdcage where she'd left it and, inside, Siouxsie Sioux on her side. Cold, stiff, faded in the wan light. Iggy and Jules had never trailed them this far. Because of the egg extraction, she and Harriet had missed Cowboy Church, and now it would be five more days before another Sunday.

They rowed across the twisty lake in silence. A family of homely brown ducks skimmed the surface with their wings.

Neko pushed down the anxiety and longing that threatened to spill from her mouth. She had wrenched Iggy out of the life they'd made, the life where they'd understood the rules, and for what? To discover a loony old aunt living underground? To follow a dead woman who, if the loony aunt was to be believed, had always planned to leave her behind?

WHEN THEY RAN THE RAFT ONTO THE BANK, NEKO WAS SURPRISED TO see Jules standing on a rock in the open with one hand shading the sun from her eyes, waiting.

Greenish clouds gave the air an eerie light that meant a storm was coming.

They scrambled up the rocks, but the guide stayed on the raft, giving a loose salute before using an oar to push off the bank, rowing back across the still water.

"Where's Iggy?"

Jules grinned, and something inside Neko loosened in relief. Jules motioned for them to follow her along a deteriorating blacktop. "He would have come, but he was needed for calf wrangling."

"What does that mean?" asked Neko.

Jules looked sidelong at Neko. "Bunker drop went off?"

Neko nodded. They passed a mailbox, bent catawampus and painted with the words *Love Letters Only*.

"What was the place like?" asked Jules. "Aquaponics system still up and running? Do they have a lab to make their own antibiotics?"

"Yeah. Sure."

"We lost Siouxsie Sioux," said Harriet. She looked nervous in Jules's presence. Contained.

"What took you guys so long, anyway?"

Neko stopped Harriet's open mouth with a sharp look. Neko wasn't providing more info until she saw Iggy herself. "We can debrief later. Where are you camped?"

Jules didn't reply at first. "You remember that ravine with the settlement?"

"For Christ's sake."

ALONG BOTH SIDES OF A GENTLE EMBANKMENT, SHELTERS HAD BEEN constructed with milk crates and blue plastic tarps, clotheslines crisscrossing back and forth. There were plastic drums set up for water catchment, a rusty bike leaning against a tree. A man in baggy jeans and a hooded sweatshirt was boiling something over a campfire, and he looked at them with wide brown eyes as Jules deposited an armful of firewood at his feet.

"Meet Xavier," she said. "The guru of lichen soup." The cauldron of moss looked like something out of a fairy tale.

Neko thought she recognized him from Cowboy Church. "And Iggy?"

Jules pointed past the tents to where a maple was trying to turn color, the New Summer having watered down the foliage until leaves barely flushed anymore.

To avoid walking directly through the camp, Neko went up and along the top of the embankment. As she approached, she could see Iggy through the lattice of branches, surrounded by seven or eight raucous children in ill-fitting clothes.

They appeared to be playing a game of tag that involved crawling in figure eights around Iggy's legs. His height, his riot of black curls and exaggerated mouth, all made him look like a beautiful Muppet. In a game whose rules Neko couldn't quite discern, he would stand stock-still for a moment as the children slithered through the triangle of his legs, and then he would run, boys and girls chasing after him, screaming bloody murder. She'd forgotten how loud children could be. Freeze. Run. Freeze.

This must be calf wrangling.

What kept Neko standing there longer than she'd intended was his expression. It took her a minute to place the emotion—she had so rarely seen it cross his face. Joy. Iggy was covered in pure joy. Smeared in joy. It had nothing to do with her, but there it was. He'd found joy all on his own. And when he saw her, he brought it with him, smiling with his eyes and running toward her and picking her up, but the incline pulled them off balance until they lay on the grass, looking up at the anxious, curious faces of children bending over them like beanstalks.

Iggy put his mouth on her ear and whispered, "Your mother?"

Neko shook her head in the negative, and he reached for her hand. The children wandered off, leaving them splayed on the ground.

"Storm's going to be brutal," he said, nodding up at the clouds.

Her chest was bursting with bitterness and love. "Let's leave right now."

Iggy sucked in a breath. "Oh," he said, voice strange. "Right now is tough."

WHEN THE CREW GATHERED INSIDE A TENT TO DEBRIEF, NEKO learned an explosion had taken out the Ice House and probably Chaplin, and there were reports of the Breakwater going into lockdown. The government had called back all mudlarks from the field immediately.

Neko nodded. "Once we get back to the Land Rover, we'll make good time. Assuming nobody's stolen our fuel."

There was a brief silence as everyone stared at Neko.

"What?"

"And these people?" Jules hesitated. "They need our help."

Neko tried not to roll her eyes. "If you want to leave some supplies, fine, but we have to get going to make it to the Breakwater before we're locked in. Before the storm." Neko was tired and hungry and wanted a bath.

"Neko," said Jules softly.

"Not my circus, not my monkeys."

"The Hive wants to help these people survive, and I'm here to make sure that happens." She paused, then, almost under her breath, added, "My mother wasn't sure I was ready for this, but I'm ready. I'm staying."

If Neko still felt any guilt for bringing them into this mess, it evaporated in that moment. "Why are you so interested in them?"

"Part of our mission. Finding new communities, new allies."

Neko looked at Iggy, but his eyes were on the ground. None of this was news to him. "Allies for what?"

"The revolution."

Neko suddenly saw the roots that had been running beneath their lives for the past year. Jules's plan was much bigger and more premeditated than Neko had understood. She quietly asked, "What was your endgame?"

Jules raised her eyebrows. "Endgame?"

"Why were you sent undercover to mudlark with our crew?"

Jules didn't answer.

"Once you had your false papers, you could have stayed on the Inside," said Harriet, her voice so quiet that Neko could hardly make out the words. "Helped others from your community get over."

Jules abruptly grabbed Harriet and kissed her on the cheek. "What makes you think our goal is to get to the Inside?"

Jules told them the Hive was made up of loosely connected groups. "Safer to not know the details of what other factions are doing." The man at the Ice House, the one who'd spit in her face, had recognized her, she said. "He assumed I was a traitor."

A booming came from outside the tent where they all squatted in a semicircle. It sounded like a fighter plane going low—like war—but it was just thunder closing in. Neko looked down to see that she was gripping a towel, the rough and nubby one she kept tied to her pack, sweat-stained and gross.

"If this is such a sophisticated organization with its own sleeper cells, why did you send those people into the Ice House with nothing but shivs?" asked Harriet. "To be slaughtered for recon?"

Jules blinked. "They had their role to play. Just like we do."

32

THE LICHEN SOUP TASTED LIKE DIRT. NEKO ATE IT ANYWAY.

Later, Iggy took her by the hand and led her through the camp as people caked in dirt secured their belongings ahead of the storm. A wild-haired child, pulling a cart of yams and tubers, looked at Neko sideways, stuck out his tongue. Three young women in ratty sweaters and ski caps walked abreast, arm in arm, whispering to one another. A thick-necked young man played a harmonica under the roof of a plastic tarp.

Iggy's breath tickled her neck as he leaned in. "These people were living on two connected farms farther north but were run off their land by a rival group. They've spent the last six months trying to survive by foraging, but winter is coming."

Neko stopped and sat heavily on a rock outcropping. She wanted to sleep for a year. "So you want to help them, too."

Iggy sat down beside her. "I'm tired of being a bystander." He looked directly at her with an expression of longing—but not for her. Longing for something else.

"So we stay, risk our careers trying to shore up their lean-tos and create a better water filter for a bunch of strangers?"

"Yes!" The exasperation in his voice surprised her. "I know

it's different from what we did before—risking our lives to retrieve inanimate objects for rich people." He closed his eyes, rubbing his knuckles across his whiskers. "Jules and her Hive help people build real communities in the Sink. What have we ever done?"

She closed her eyes, trying to understand how their dumb little choices had taken on such large-scale import. "If the government finds out we're helping them, we'll never get back in. We might never leave the Sink."

He didn't answer at first. He softened. "Maybe so. Maybe it's a stupid idea."

There was something strange about the inflection of his voice, the tilt of his face, and it took Neko a minute to place it: Iggy sounded just like she used to sound. Unconvincing.

Part of Neko wanted to grab hold of him and tell him she loved him no matter what, but it also felt like the wrong time. Like there was no time. Like time had exploded in her face.

SHE FOUND JULES HELPING TO TEAR DOWN THE CAMP'S MAIN COOKING equipment.

"Meet Geo and Frankie," Jules said, pointing to two middle-aged men helping her pack. There was no rancor or worry in her voice. Like it was just any other day.

"Hey," said the one whose salt-and-pepper hair was tied into a low ponytail.

Neko reluctantly shook their outstretched hands. "Can you give us a minute?"

When they were gone, she crouched beside Jules, talking low. "It won't be enough. Even if you stay."

Jules continued to take apart a camp stove. "That's where you're wrong." She struggled to fit the pieces into a burlap bag.

"Mudlarks exist because the government pays us to. When the scratch runs out, so will we. It isn't mudlarks diving into a lost civilization who will survive. The future is these people living on the knife's edge." She paused. "Dying on it."

"You act like I'm the enemy."

"Are you?"

"You've been convincing Iggy of it."

"That's not fair." For a moment it almost looked as though Jules was going to get upset, but she brought her face back under control. "I love Harriet. And I've lost her because of my work for the Hive. But I loved her, love her."

"Right."

"I don't care if you believe me. But I've sacrificed, too."

"True believers are so annoying." Then something flickered across Neko's mind—the image of Jules standing by the reservoir with her hand over her eyes. Of the soldiers from her community walking them toward the city in the trees. Of the failing O-ring on the dive and the mysteriously emptied cooler, pushing them toward Harriet's kidnapping. "How did your people know we would be arriving that day? At the old distillery?"

Jules looked up without saying anything.

"Considering your limited access to resources, it's amazing the advanced technology your group has developed," she baited.

"We liberated some military supplies, including chips that can send long-range signals for, I don't know, years. They implanted one when I left to join the mudlarks." She tapped her skull.

"And how did you know we would be coming across the lake yesterday morning?"

Jules opened her mouth and then shut it.

"Do I have one, too?" She gripped Jules's arm so it would leave a mark. "Did you tag me like a fucking cow?"

"No," she whispered, shaking her head. "But Harriet . . ."

Neko felt so stupid for not realizing it earlier. All the ways they'd been played.

"For safety," said Jules quietly. "We do it for safety."

"All for our own good?" Rationally, it made no sense for Neko's feelings to be hurt—but they were. Neko wasn't surprised by what Jules had done—that certainly wouldn't be the word for it—but, for a reason she didn't fully understand, she still felt betrayed. Again. As though some part of Neko was letting her do it over and over.

"We were able to save Harriet when she was taken. And you. We knew where to find you when the two of you split for the bunker. I *protected* you."

Neko spit on the ground. "Or maybe you put Harriet in danger precisely so you could save her."

NEKO FOUND HARRIET AT THE CAMPFIRE, PICKING AT A MEAGER DINner. Smoke dispersed into the twilight.

"You talked to Jules?"

"I told her I'd be taking over the crew license alone." Harriet looked stoic. "She accepted it."

"I need to show you something," said Neko. With one hand on Harriet's shoulder, she fingered the woman's hairline until she felt a bump—something hard beneath the skin. "Do you know what this is?"

Harriet touched the spot. "A bug bite or something."

"Nope."

Neko took out her thin penknife, disinfected it in the fire, turned Harriet's neck toward the firelight, and then pressed the tip of the slim, scalpel-like blade into her skin. Harriet inhaled sharply but did not cry out. Neko held up a tiny metal wire, like a beetle's leg, and pressed a rag to the tiny puncture wound with her other hand.

Neko dropped the tracking bug into Harriet's outstretched palm. The woman studied it for a moment and then tossed it into the fire. "Jules?"

Neko nodded. "To protect you."

Harriet snorted.

As they sat there in silence, Neko thought back to when Harriet had first joined their crew—so quick to laugh and to offend and to pretend she could do more than she really could. This woman now sitting next to Neko was a coiled spring, which meant Neko and Iggy had done their job, though it was hard to take pleasure in that.

"You know how you guys used to make fun of me for correcting you about the Inside?" asked Harriet, voice soft and distant.

Neko nodded robotically—that seemed a lifetime ago.

"I never told you the whole story." Harriet cleared her throat. "How things degenerate so slowly that it takes a minute to recognize what's happening. That delays in services won't get shorter but longer, that the blackouts won't get better but worse, building materials more scarce rather than less. Poorly maintained roads make traffic worse, ancient vehicles waiting in lines at endless checkpoints—and then there are the stalled trains, grounded planes, the shortages of everything."

Neko squeezed Harriet's hand harder, to comfort her or make her stop talking, she wasn't sure.

"For a while, having money softens the blow, makes you think you're protected. But even we need city services. Even our stately houses eventually submit to indignities: the plumbing makes noises like ghosts in the wall, we close off whole floors, let the landscaping wither."

Neko pictured young Harriet, all knees and elbows taking up space, surrounded by threadbare New England luxury, as she came to understand that her parents could not shield her from the spreading shadows. Part of Neko longed to hug that girl.

"And the outrage—this is America!—turns to bitterness and then to a passive acceptance." Harriet's voice rose and then fell again.

Neko didn't reply—what was there to say, really?—but she understood what Harriet was trying to tell her: There was no going back.

"Things are over with Jules," said Harriet. "Obviously." She finished her soup in one gulp and stood. She took a handful of kindling and threw it onto the fire. "The thing is, I even believe in her vision of an independent Sink. Her revolution. But she was willing to sacrifice me for it."

The fire crackled and sparked, crackled and sparked.

THAT NIGHT, NEKO AND IGGY LAY IN THEIR TENT, LISTENING TO THE ambient noise from the camp: snoring and sighing, children whispering and being comforted. Iggy held her tightly as she finally told him about Aunt Layla and the master recording and the soulsuckers.

"She thinks she and my mom can be angels together in the plasmasphere or something."

"Oh." His breath was warm. "Yikes."

Neko closed her eyes. She could hear raindrops on their tent as an early band of the storm moved inland from the Long Island Sound.

Neko liked the feeling of the word "sound" in her mouth, the way it rounded and hollowed out her head. And the meaning, too—all the ways water penetrated the dry world: finger inlets, rivers, fjords, sounds, channels. Sinks. She thought of her mother's body, blasted by seawater. Her physical form would have broken down quickly, bloated and then digested by sea creatures, bones worn by the tides and the sand.

She tried to imagine what it would be like to have a mother without a body. Just an eye in the plasmasphere. Just a screen of lights. Blinking out a message like Morse code. Not pretty, not *not* pretty. No blue veins on the backs of her knees. No goosebumps. No tiny white scars on her knuckles. No animal smell at the nape of her neck.

A ghost. A nothing. A mother who moved away to distant lands, only appearing once in a while, a fuzzy picture on a screen. Hardly any kind of mother at all.

Iggy stroked her arm as she nestled into the nook of his armpit. "You knew your mother in real life," he said, softly. "She helped make you."

"She was planning to abandon me." Only with the words in the air did Neko recognize she still had the capacity to be hurt retroactively. "Layla said my mother was planning to move to Europe. Leave me behind."

"That was so long ago, mi vida." Iggy sighed.

"But I dragged myself through the East Village all those years like a gravedigger. Thinking I was the worst daughter of all time."

"Neko, Neko." His voice wasn't warm. "She never made you do any of that. She was dead."

"We should have had a family by now," said Neko.

Iggy looked at her like he didn't know her. He turned away, burrowing into the sleeping bag, closing his eyes. She pulled herself taut along his back.

"What?" she asked, trying and failing to keep a sense of pleading out of her voice.

"Selfishness isn't a good look on you."

Neko felt stung. But she resisted the disconnection the only way she knew how—with a stupid attempt at humor. "Since when?"

They lay there in stillness and heartbreak.

"For the first time in my life," he said, "I don't know what I want."

Neko felt the scampering feet of desperation in her belly. "I'll make you happy. I will."

"You have."

Something about being beneath the small dome of the tent, the interiority of it, made her think of her emptying ovaries, bright like silver moons. If the moons broke in two, she wondered, what would be inside? Would it be sticky or hard or would it spill fast like water? She said the words before she could change her mind: "I don't have many good eggs left. I haven't known how to tell you."

He didn't say anything for a minute. "Lots of kids need parents. It doesn't matter if they're genetically related to us." He stroked her head. "Go to sleep," he said. "We'll figure it out tomorrow."

But Neko wasn't tired. She lay there watching shadows.

She tried to imagine a life with Iggy on the Inside, tried to picture herself in pleated slacks, pushing a shopping cart down the aisle of some grocery store filled with boxes and cans. Or in a house, a baby crying out in the middle of the night, or—what? Even before the hurricane, she'd never had a normal life.

She couldn't animate a narrative in her mind. Instead, the image reel that finally unspooled was this memory:

Bethesda Fountain, Central Park. They were young and still had a chance to do things differently. Almost a decade ago now. It had been the first warm and perfect week of what was otherwise a soggy spring. They had finished their dives and would cart everything back to the Breakwater the following day—but that afternoon, they were free. The asphalt paths of Central Park were overgrown, the once-sweeping lawns now waist-high grasses filled with brambles, young trees obscuring the metamorphic rock formations and sucking the ponds dry. Home to wolves and snakes and all manner of wildness. But the large plaza around Bethesda Fountain, with its intricate stone carvings and grand staircases, still retained a vestige of civilization. Several crews, including theirs, set up a fire and smoked guinea pigs on a spit. "Put the beer on ice," somebody said, though of course there was no beer, no ice. Someone went around collecting donations of smuggled liquor to concoct a disgusting punch. Richie, their apprentice, rigged a speaker system to play dubstep and hip-hop and whatever tracks anybody had that people could dance to. A crescent moon of battery-powered lanterns perched along the southern lip of the fountain. Iggy was busy for much of the day with a secret project, and Neko herself began drinking early, ordering everyone around until Richie finally said, "Come on, boss." She laughed and danced, letting her limbs tangle with the other bodies moving in a circle over the herringbone brick of the plaza like it was a country dance floor. She flung her hair back and forth and refilled her thermos, not caring if she would pay for it the next day. Darkness fell. And then. Just when she was starting to worry: Iggy arrived. The man was literally aglow. He walked toward them from beneath the arches of the Terrace Arcade, throwing light onto the faded panel paintings along the interior. A loose cape draped his shoulders, and it appeared as though it had been cut from the night sky. It twinkled. Blinked. The lights were there, and then gone. Everyone turned. They watched as he began to twirl slowly and then faster, and the lights became more erratic. Iggy had caught dozens of fireflies and trapped them between two loose pieces of muslin, some crazy idea he'd gotten from a poem. Neko danced with her love, in awe of him and his cape of stars, which enveloped them, their bodies sparkling with the light of the living, also the soon-to-be dead.

33

WHEN NEKO WOKE UP, IGGY WAS GONE. SOMETHING WAS DAMP BEtween her legs—her period. She found her menstrual cup, wet it, and put it in before more clothes got stained. There was something about the coppery smell that made her feel real.

She rummaged through her things, reorganizing in preparation for leaving. But where was the mother for the album? The wool sweater at the bottom of the supply bag was wadded up, nothing wrapped inside it. She tore apart her bags and the tent.

Nothing. Gone.

Outside, she looked for Iggy. Dazzling morning light reflected sharply off the wet grass and gaping pools of rainwater. There he was, and she went swamping through the puddles to get to where he stood over a table with Jules and Harriet and a few others.

"Have you seen the album?" she whispered to Iggy.

He blinked at her and shook his head. Everyone had stopped talking.

Harriet came over to Neko, put a hand on her arm, and said, "You'll never believe this." She nodded at Jules. "Tell her."

Forearms leaning into the table, Jules acknowledged Neko

with a nod before launching into her "new, exciting plan" to commandeer the Cellar, along with its medical supplies, firearms, and, most important, its sustainable food sources: the aquaponics system and aquaculture.

"It's the clear next move," said Jules with her new, annoying tone of conviction. "Neko, you said my staying won't be enough. But maybe this will be."

Jules told them the Hive could use the bunker as a central node for a settlement. She would act as "facilitator" and use the Cowboy Church to find more people and bring them into the fold. "We don't want power. We want community. But I need your help."

"Everybody wants power," said Neko. "You'd have to use force, and while they're idiots, they have a lot of guns."

"If we took everyone here with us, it wouldn't be impossible," said Jules. "To push our way in, to convince them there was no alternative."

Two tiny white butterflies lifted up from a spray of dandelions, and everyone turned toward the fluttering creatures for just a second. And Neko thought briefly, *Even beauty is just a dumb distraction now.*

She looked at silent Iggy—why wasn't he helping her dissuade Jules from this stupidity?

"You and Harriet exchanged contact info with them on the secure channel, right?" Jules brought them back to the business at hand like the general she obviously wanted to be. "So, help us figure out the best way to trick them and breach the door. You owe us. Remember?"

In a better version of this world, thought Neko, one might encounter herds of elephants escaped from old zoos or trees full of fat, ripe figs just when you needed something sweet. But that was not the world they'd ended up in.

"Did you just say that *I* owe *you*? Is that what you just said?"

Neko and Jules stood inches from each other; everyone else faded into the background. At their feet, red ants poured from a mound like skidding drops of blood.

"Maybe you listen to old-school hip-hop and maybe your skin is tanned leather from years in the Sink, and maybe you don't live on the Inside anymore." Jules's voice was an anvil. "But you carry its systems inside you." She pointed to the camp, her chin held high. "These people need the antibiotics and aquaponics systems from the bunker."

Neko's brain searched for something on which to land. It was hard to argue with Jules outright because maybe it wasn't the worst plan, at least in theory. The Cellar was valuable and being wasted in the hands of morons. "But when the Hive takes things by force, people die." She thought of Aunt Layla in her small apartment, old and vulnerable. Of Gloria. "Like Chaplin died."

Jules's face broke for a moment, briefly showing its youth. "He was your friend, and I'm sorry. But he was also a war profiteer, an arms dealer . . ."

"Nobody is innocent in all of this," said Iggy, interrupting. "Including us."

The look Jules trained on him in response was difficult for Neko to read—it said, *Of course,* and also, *What does it matter?* "My point is that we had to take the Ice House. As long as the government maintains militarized outposts inside the Sink, communities like ours will never be safe to grow, to establish our own leadership and economy. We had to show them that bringing the Sink under control would cost them too much time, money, and life." Jules moved closer, and Neko could see the tiny scar where she'd had a nose ring, the one they'd had to cut out with pliers when it became infected. "We are not the bad guys. *They* are the ones who blew up our food source and drove us from our homes. *They* are the ones who must learn they can't act with impunity. You said it yourself, they'll never leave us alone, not unless we force them to. This is a war to control the Sink, and it's time for you to choose a side."

Wind cycled through the trees, leaves luminous with raindrops. Tall thirsty grasses surged around them as though to whisper something important. Neko clapped. "I just love rousing speeches." She turned to Iggy, trying to find their private language, trying to connect with his eyes. "You're not on board with this?"

Iggy looked at her with a hardness she wasn't used to, could never get used to. "This was my idea."

"What?"

Iggy pulled at the studs in his earlobes, dark circles under his hooded eyes. "Last night I couldn't sleep and started thinking about how to really make it work. Neko, I told you I was tired of being a bystander."

Harriet gently inserted her body between them. She turned to Neko. "Look. I don't care what the situation is here, but you need to get me to the Breakwater and to the license. We had a deal."

Neko's gaze stayed on Iggy. "I know." She pulled away from Harriet. "I hear you. I need a minute."

ALONE WITH IGGY, SQUEEZED INTO THE LAND ROVER, NEKO LIT INTO him. "You just went and made this decision? Without me?"

"You've been making your own decisions for a long time."

Neko's first impulse was to call bullshit, but she decided on a different tack. "If we are caught, or identified as being part of a bunker coup, there will be no more larking for us, no more Inside."

His face softened. He put his fingers to his neck, pressing into it in that way he did, so familiar and heartrending. "Look me in the eyes and tell me you really want to go to the Inside." His words were like feathers floating aloft, taking an eternity to reach her.

"It's what we've always wanted."

"I used to believe that deep down you wanted a family with me but were trapped here by the guilt over your mother. I don't believe that anymore."

She protested, but her voice felt small. "I'm done with my mother."

Iggy returned her gaze, his face eerily neutral. "It's like you still think you can make her sorry. Like you never really grew up."

"But you love me." This was as close as she could come to begging.

"Sure." He said it with a voice that was both soft and faraway. "While you were gone, Jules and I talked a lot about her community, about the world they're establishing here. If the Inside will just leave them alone, they can build oyster beds along the coastline for food, protective wetlands and dunes to fight erosion. There's a place for me. I want to help create something not tainted by the shit smell of history."

"Everything is tainted by somebody's shit."

Iggy reached for the door handle. "Whatever."

Neko tried to stop him. "You're just doing this because I can't have a child. Because I told you I'm out of eggs."

He blinked. He shook his head. Neither of them believed her, and they both knew it. "You can still make it to the Breakwater. If that's really what you want. But I'm with the Hive."

Then Iggy was slipping out of the space between her body and the world. The door swung open and the car's ceiling light went radiant. Neko opened her mouth, but she didn't know how to tell him that she didn't know how to live without him as witness to her life, or without being witness to his. Then the door clicked behind him and she was alone with the dashboard and steering wheel, with the dimming light and the fruity, chemical, acrid smell of plastic. She was heartbroken. She was relieved.

NEKO SAT OUTSIDE HER TENT, THOUGHT ABOUT *THE WRECKAGE*. SHE had been so stupid—letting Gloria keep her behind at the Women's Tea, smoking the lady's dope like she didn't have a job to do, and all the while Layla had clearly been rooting through Neko's things. Stealing the one object that had started this whole thing. Back to zero. Except not really, because Neko had even less than she'd had before.

If she stayed in the Sink, she would be committing to this silly life as a fugitive, storming underground bunkers and taking orders from self-righteous young people. But if she left with Harriet in the morning, she'd never get the mother back, and would never get a chance to warn that remarkable, brutal, frustrating aunt of hers about what was coming for her.

Neko thought about how different her life had turned out from the one her parents had imagined for her. But the thing was, she had actually loved this life. She had loved being a mudlark. She had told herself that she did what she did as penance, as a way to hold on to her past, but maybe that had never been entirely true. Maybe that had just been a grand excuse to spend each day on a motorcycle, or on a deep dive in her own wreckage, riding the wave of endorphins. Pretending she was free.

"Miss Neko." A little girl bumped her head into Neko's legs.

"Hey, be careful," she said, thinking of the Glock holstered on her thigh. "And don't call me 'miss.' In fact, don't call anyone 'miss.'"

The girl, her brown hair matted and dirty, carried a small, beaten guitar. She tried to pick at the strings.

"God, that's out of tune," said Neko. "Give it here." She took the guitar and began adjusting the tuning pegs.

"Can you teach me how to play?"

Neko sighed. "I don't really know how."

34

BURNING MAN
10 P.M.

At Burning Man, Jenny rode the skateboard through smaller "streets" lined with tents and yurts of various sizes and shapes, some of them gathered into theme camps. She passed glowing signs declaiming ALIEN LOVE NEST AND SPOCK'S MOUNTAIN RESEARCH LAB; the Elvis camp was blaring "Hound Dog," and Barbie's French Revolution was surrounded by an installation of beheaded dolls; there was even something called Mom Camp, whose sign claimed they offered "nonjudgmental motherly advice doled out with lemonade and cookies."

The semicircular temporary city of Burning Man was arranged so that each street radiating from the Man was named after its respective position on the "clock" and each curving cross street after the theme—this year "decomposition." And how appropriate, thought Jenny, the way everything in her life was falling apart: her marriage, her band, and her relationship with her daughter, her most beloved.

By the time Jenny arrived at their camp located at 5 o'clock and Fester, her body was coated in a thin layer of white alkali dust, as if she'd been dipped headfirst into a bowl of flour. Their manager, Layla Wei (who had refused to come herself, calling Burning Man "white tribe shit"), had arranged for them to stay in a yurt at an already constituted camp, the theme of which was College Cats. As Jenny stumbled through the assembly of tents, the first people she came across were dressed, of course, like fucking cats. One was lecturing the other about Malthus.

"His principles are misunderstood. As the population of mice increases . . ."

"Is Neko here?" Jenny interrupted. "My kid?"

They looked up, squinting at her.

"Or Max?"

"Meow," said the shorter one, nodding, and pointed to the corner tent.

10:30 P.M.

Inside the tent, she found Max listening to a man and a woman dressed in canvas pants and safari hats, holding walkie-talkies crackling with static.

". . . Ranger Danger has sent out an alert to all organizers and vol—"

Jenny butted in. "She's not here?"

Max shook his head, arms crossed, shrunken. "The Black Rock Rangers are the security force, apparently. They say they have a system for finding wayward children."

"Wayward?" Jenny was living the worst nightmare of her life—why did it also have to occur inside some alternate reality where the safety of one's child was in the hands of a group of Indiana Jones lookalikes?

"Ranger Danger is our leader and the legendary protector of the Playa," said the man earnestly. "Imagine all the lost, fucked-up people at Burning Man each year. Finding them, reuniting them with their people, is what we do."

"Neko is not fucked-up," said Max. "She's thirteen."

They nodded vigorously and handed Max and Jenny a radio. "We'll be in touch via the code word *nightjars*. I'm guessing you guys won't be able to sit tight, so why don't you head to one of the community areas to help search—Center Camp Cafe or the Esplanade."

After they left, Max finally looked at Jenny, face contorted in the raw expression she associated with his love—though it reflected love for Neko, not for her. His eyes were red, and Jenny was reminded of how, soon after their daughter was born, he'd come home weeping when he couldn't find preemie-sized diapers at any store in their neighborhood. She was reminded of how he'd taught baby Neko to point—*Hey, you*—and how she would giggle when Max pointed back, their fingers touching like "E.T. phone home," like God on the ceiling of the Sistine Chapel. *You said I was your blue, blue baby,* he would sing to her, *and you were riiiiight*. The diva and the doting father.

"She's smart enough to have found us by now," he said. "To have found someone."

Jenny wasn't ready to face the implications of that. She put her backpack on the ground and began repacking it with water bottles and warm clothes for Neko. "I'll go to this Center Camp place," she said, her heart aching but her voice steady. "You check the Esplanade. Take the radio. We'll meet back here in two hours?"

Max rubbed his eyes, zipped up his jacket, and nodded. "Young girls are never safe. Did we make that clear enough? Or did we let her believe the world is a better place than it is?"

If someone had taken her, or taken advantage of her, it was

their fault, that's what Max was really saying. And he was not wrong.

11 P.M.

Jenny borrowed a College Cat's beach cruiser to make her way to Center Camp. As the night wore on, the partying had become more intense, and it felt like riding a bike inside of an enormous speaker vibrating with a relentless EDM beat. She approached a cube of stained glass lit from within, filled with fist-pumping dancers, but as she got closer, she saw it was constructed not from glass but from plastic. That was the thing about this place—everything that appeared magical was actually made of trash. And this was what kids never understood, thought Jenny, as she tried to imagine what—or who—had lured Neko away: glittery costumes and loud music and older teenagers? All those shiny things with cheap, sharp edges.

Jenny passed a nude Jesus strung atop a cross on wheels and an art car dragging a toilet on which a man sat reading a book. It had all stopped registering. The rangers had given Jenny a purpose—get to Center Camp Cafe—and she clung to that. She tried to trick herself into believing that if she went along with the process, everything would work out. The rangers had said they found lost people all the time, hadn't they? And surely people didn't come to Burning Man looking to steal children. It was going to be *all right,* she told herself, despite the low warning of Grace Jones behind her temples: *Waaarm leatherette . . . waaarm leatherette.*

When she found Center Camp Cafe—an enormous big top like at a circus—she parked the bike next to a life-sized chessboard with various bodies standing on squares in a way that made it unclear who was actually masterminding the game. Inside the tent, people lounged on dusty sofas and raffia mats, drinking coffee and reading actual physical newspapers under faux gas lanterns. The headlines were all about Frida swirling off the Atlantic coast, hundreds of miles away.

A dozen people were flossing their teeth with one extremely long thread. Beneath the oculus of the tent, there was a small stage where an Indonesian shadow-puppet battle was playing out, intricately designed animals fighting each other with tiny swords.

Jenny took out her phone again, opened it to what she had decided was the clearest photo of Neko, and began making rounds. It was crowded in the tent, and she tried to move from left to right so as to be sure to cover the entire space. The acoustics created an intense background murmur, and at times it felt like being in another country where people spoke a language she didn't entirely understand—words like "MOOP" and "obtainium" and "nose tators" and "sparklepony." And if she heard another person say, "Welcome home," she was going to vomit.

Eventually, someone wearing armor made from forks and knives said, "You should ask Indigo Girl." He seemed excited to be able to help. "She'll know where your daughter is."

Too flustered to ask why that might be the case, Jenny just followed his pointing hand to a tall, imposing woman wearing nothing but blue body paint from head to toe, pubic hair shimmering with some sort of lapis glitter. Jenny's brain immediately tuned in to Gal Costa singing tropicália.

Jenny showed her the photo and asked if she'd possibly seen her daughter. "Thirteen, about this tall, maybe wearing a halter top?"

The woman grabbed Jenny's hands and pulled her down onto a nearby sofa. "What's her full name?"

"Neko Sweet." Jenny suddenly understood that this was pointless.

The woman closed her eyes, still holding Jenny's palms between hers, and began to hum. Jenny tried to pull her hands back, but they were gripped too tightly.

After an eternity, Indigo Girl clicked her eyes open like a doll. "I am an embodiment of the Hindu goddess Kali. Destruction is transformation in disguise."

"Fuck," said Jenny, standing.

Indigo Girl pulled her back down. "It's not uncommon. Thinking you can escape all that is difficult by leaving. Hiding like a snake in its den. Hibernating like a bear in winter."

Jesus Christ, thought Jenny. "So, you're saying my daughter ran away to hibernate like a bear?"

Indigo Girl smiled, but there was a challenge in her expression, too. "I'm talking about you. *Your* plan to run away."

Jenny was suddenly aware of all the things touching her body—the hair on her cheek, the neckline of her shirt, the rings that circled her swollen fingers. "How did you know about . . . ?"

"Ironic, isn't it," whispered Indigo Girl. "You planned to disappear and now, instead, your daughter has gone and done it first." Then she closed her eyes and began to hum again.

There was so much Jenny wanted to say to that. Max and Neko knew that she planned to move out, but it was true that they didn't know how far she planned to go. Not yet. But that wasn't the same as running away. Why hold your family back once they've stopped needing you?

"Your daughter," Indigo Girl said eventually, "has a strong aura. You should be proud. Sharp like a porcupine."

"Have you actually seen her, though?"

The woman pointed to her forehead, her third eye. "Go to the Temple of Bone. The Playa will provide."

11:30 P.M.

The Temple was the last structure before the open desert—possibly the sort of thing to attract her daughter. The idea was a stretch, but her daughter wasn't at Center Camp Cafe and Jenny didn't have many options left.

A barista at the Cafe suggested Jenny get there via one of the art cars that made their way into the Deep Playa at this time of night.

"Welcome to the Ghost Ship," said the skeleton pirate as he directed her to the ladder inside the bowels of what looked like a two-masted Spanish galleon.

Jenny climbed to the main deck and, shoulder to shoulder with a line of shouting revelers, watched the changing landscape as the galleon/bus made its slow march away from the camps and into the Playa.

She watched people playing golf with burning rolls of toilet paper next to a fiberglass tiger head and a row of open coffins. A submarine emerged nose-first from the sand, frozen in time. A long strand of balloons arced into the sky until she couldn't see where it ended.

Everything gleamed with the surreal, and Jenny began to feel dizzy. Momentarily disconnected from worry and panic. It almost felt like she had been drugged, and she had to remind herself to take water from her backpack and drink. To keep searching for any sign of her daughter—leggy and button-nosed and beautiful—in the groups of sparkling young people.

The Man—a five-story stick figure that would be burned like a pyre on the final night—was positioned in the middle of the Playa. Once the ship cruised past him, everything became darker, quieter. Without neon lights or flashy sculptures, the desert floor itself became the dominant feature. A chalky, desiccated lake bed, cracked like pottery glaze. Dust devils spun up into the black sky like dervishes. The Temple glimmered up ahead, the only shape on the horizon. *Like the portal to a subterranean civilization,* thought Jenny.

She imagined the sound installation she was planning to build underground for her album, once she left for good. A guitar the size of a crypt. How she wanted the harmonics to reverberate, how the speakers would make the space feel bigger, the air a veil of luminosity, all connected to the root system that spread out from her decaying body and into the world.

Maybe she was not so different from the Burners after all.

MIDNIGHT

As the Ghost Ship advanced, others on the deck began rapidly whisper-chanting, "Temple of Bone, Temple of Bone, Temple of Bone." All the words associated with this year's theme now made Jenny's skin crawl: "bone," "ghost," "decomposition." Waiting for the fake boat to stop and let them off at the fake temple, Jenny heard the sudden sound of rapid machine-gun fire. But no. Not gunfire. White, fizzy fireworks were raining from the largest of the temple domes.

She looked desperately for Neko in the crowd outside. She had no idea how much time had passed—surely she wouldn't make it back to the College Cat camp by the time she and Max had agreed on. But she was here and so she would do the only thing that mattered: find her girl.

The Temple was made up of one tall cylindrical dome surrounded by four shorter ones connected to it by suspended walkways. Everything was white and had a vaguely Indian feel, like a kind of mishmash Taj Mahal. She was funneled into one of the smaller structures, where the walls were made from intricately carved wooden panels—they were lovely and looked as though they would break at the slightest provocation.

There was a more subdued mood here—no dancing or screaming—and more families, which gave Jenny some hope. Tranquilizing sounds emerged from a series of gongs, which appeared to be operated by a mechanical timer. Low notes reverberated long after the high ones. In the science of sound, one had to choose between brightness of feeling and how long that feeling could last. *Kind of like life,* she thought.

Having confirmed that Neko wasn't in this first space, she climbed the walkway toward the larger, central cylinder, which rose at least four stories. Inside, she found herself on an interior balcony that circled the floor below, where people sat meditating. Among them she recognized Julio Smithson, who had directed the music video for the Nightjars' song "Hard Honey" and had recently become a medium shot in Hollywood. She considered going down to him, but she didn't think he'd ever met Neko.

Attached to the railing were hundreds of strips of white cloth. Jenny knelt and looked more closely to see that they were inscribed with names.

"Who are these people?" she asked a woman beside her.

"The dead," the woman said. "We leave tributes here to those we've lost." The woman handed Jenny a piece of cloth and a pen. "You look familiar," said the woman. "Do I know you from somewhere?"

Jenny's eyes were drawn to the names. Maybe she knew that the longer she put off finishing her search of the Temple, the longer she'd put off not finding Neko there. Maybe the papers held some clue. Mostly people had left first names—*Maya, Jen-*

nifer, Hillery, Jill, Dalia, Deb—or what might have been nicknames, Playa names—*Rocknut, Socknut, Gigger.* Other people had written down things like *glaciers, civility, hope*.

Jenny looked down at the white strip of cloth in her hand. What name should she write? Her father's? The Nightjars? Her marriage? She almost laughed. Instead, she took the pen and wrote: *Jenny Sweet*.

12:30 A.M.

The night was so long, and Neko was nowhere to be found.

Jenny had begun to feel frantic again—each time she searched a part of the Temple, it had to be searched again because what if Neko was there now? Or now? Or maybe now? What if they were spiraling around each other, entering when one exited, exiting just as the other entered? It felt like being trapped inside an M. C. Escher painting—walkways and stairs and people so strangely dressed they looked alike. And that incessant gonging, which had begun to sound like *What kind of mother, what kind of mother.*

The next time Jenny was on the outside balcony of the center dome—the tallest point on the Temple—she began to notice something strange. The stars looked muddy, smeared across the sky. Black Rock City and the Esplanade appeared farther away, their lights dim and pulsing. A dust storm.

Everyone else was moving inside to escape the enveloping cloud, but Jenny couldn't make herself leave. Couldn't even make herself lift her bandanna to cover her mouth. Something in her welcomed the blurring of the world, invited the tiny particles that entered her lungs like needles. A comforting obliteration. A physical pain that almost mirrored the deeper one. The electronica of Nine Inch Nails.

Soon Jenny couldn't see her outstretched hand. She was all alone. The whole world was muffled. Which was maybe why it took her a moment to realize her phone was vibrating. She thought she must be imagining it—there was not supposed to be cell service here, but when she looked at the screen there was one bar. The Temple of Bone must've been high enough to pick up some faint signal. There was a text message. Not from Neko, but from Neko's best friend back in New York. Jenny would have cried if in its dehydrated state her body could have made tears.

> *Neko called. I thought you should know she's okay. She's coming home.*

JENNY KEPT LOOKING AT THE TEXT TO CONFIRM IT WAS REAL. AT FIRST she felt a sharp sense of relief—someone somewhere had heard from her daughter. She hadn't entirely disappeared into the ether like a desert djinni.

Then, confusion. The text was from Neko's best friend, Greta, in New York. How had Neko gotten cell service to talk to Greta, and what did she mean when she said she was going home? Jenny tried to call and text Greta and then Neko and then Greta's mother, but all she got was *call fail, fail send, call fail, fail send*. The faint signal that had let this text through was mercurial—probably a distant echo from one of the camps where tech billionaires and real celebrities stayed in a sort of luxury, including their own Internet hot spots.

If Neko had been able to use her phone, then Jenny needed to get somewhere with a signal, too. She took the spiral staircase two steps at a time to the ground floor of the Temple of Bone. Julio Smithson, the director of successful indie films and once-upon-a-time music video impresario, was, thank God, still sitting with his eyes closed, hands cupped in zazen mudra.

She bent over and pressed on his shoulders, more forcefully than she'd intended. His eyes snapped open. His pupils were enormous. "Jenny fucking Sweet."

She tried to smile, but her face wasn't obeying her anymore. "I need your help," she said into his ear.

JULIO WAS NOT STAYING IN A CAMP WITH "JUICE," AS HE CALLED IT, BUT he knew people in Dior Camp, which had everything. He said he would take her there. His white linen suit was somehow free of dirt and wrinkles.

"My daughter's in trouble. I need to call her."

He nodded. "The Playa will provide."

"Not you, too."

He laughed as though Jenny was hilarious. "Susan is staying at Dior Camp, too. Have you seen her? Her entire outfit is in bloom."

Jenny didn't know what he was talking about or what he was on. "Susan?"

"Sarandon," he said, raising his eyebrows conspiratorially.

Outside, Julio began waving a handkerchief—did he really have a silk handkerchief?—to flag down an art car tricked out to look like a silver UFO from *War of the Worlds*. The dust storm had abated and the lights from Black Rock City twinkled in the distance.

Jenny had to practically sit on Julio's lap to fit into the crowded car, a Volkswagen bug beneath the silver saucer. As the vehicle plowed across the desert floor with pure recklessness, a sudden realization compressed Jenny's rib cage with further panic: If Neko had contacted Greta, then Neko wasn't truly lost. Neko hadn't been kidnapped or lured into a drugged-out party with adults who now held her captive. Neko had chosen to leave.

"So, honey," said Julio. "Who's getting custody?"

Jenny let her head fall on his shoulder. "You've heard."

"A dagger to the heart." He patted his chest. "I always said, if you two could stay together this long, it proved it could be done."

"Sorry to disappoint." Jenny tried to breathe through her mouth because the human odor was so overwhelming. "I think my daughter ran away."

He nodded as though he heard this all the time. "When Jill and I got divorced, you wouldn't believe all the shit Coco tried to pull. Trashed the house while we were out of town. Stole her mother's Xanax. Stole my Xanax. Joined the marching band, for fuck's sake." He started coughing, hacking up a lung. She handed him her water bottle.

1 A.M.

The car stopped momentarily near an enormous mound of ice—a huge ball of melting snow in the desert. Inside were clocks: old two-bell alarm clocks, oversized pocket watches, the standard circle clock that adorned every American classroom.

"That's what I want," she said. "To turn back time."

Julio sighed, following her gaze to the ice sculpture. "A little on the nose, don't you think?"

"I wanted to be a good mother, but I just didn't know how to do it. So the answer to your question: I'm taking on a project in Berlin to make things easier on all of us. Maybe she'll come for the summer." Did she think Julio Smithson would be impressed by her stoicism, by the way she looked at the situation with dispassionate objectivity?

The car's radio was tuned to one of the Burning Man stations and someone was giving a "weather" report: "The tsunami is imminent. I repeat, everyone put on your Nevada-issued snorkels immediately."

"Berlin . . ." Julio didn't say anything for a minute, searching through his numerous pockets and eventually pulling out a tin of petroleum jelly.

"I'm doing a sound installation in the catacombs beneath the Uber church. For a year."

He sighed.

"Men do it all the time. She'll probably be relieved I'm gone."

"Ah! The passive-aggressive martyr. Nice one." He jabbed his finger into the tin of petroleum jelly. "Look. Teenage girls and their mothers butt heads. It's a truism. You can't take it personally."

"You sound like my mother-in-law."

"Soon to be ex-mother-in-law."

"She's dead."

Once they arrived at the Esplanade and exited their art car chariot, Julio kept stopping to show her things: "Look, it's Dr. MegaVolt," he yelled, pointing at a man in a robot suit with ducts for arms using a Tesla coil to shoot out sparks.

"Don't worry," said Julio. "My suit is fireproof."

She turned him to face her. "Where is this camp?"

He stuck his pointer finger in the air as though testing the wind's direction. "Behind the red chandelier," said Julio.

She had no choice but to follow him, Alice and the White Rabbit. They cut through bars and tents, eventually borrowing a motorized scooter that Jenny insisted on being the one to operate, which meant taking directions barked out by Julio at the last possible minute: "Left *now*!"

Just as Jenny was about to give up on him—to find someone who could take her to the Rangers instead—they cruised through an elaborate pergola trellised with flower lights. Through it was a giant chandelier on the ground, lit red from within. It was twice Jenny's height and covered with looping rococo metalwork. The sculpture lay on its side, as though it had fallen from the ceiling of the sky, one end made to look like a ripped section of drywall and the other end trailing luminescent electrical lines.

"Here," said Julio, picking up one of the lines and handing it to her.

She took it from him, and it gave her a brief electric shock. *Fuck this place,* she thought. She dropped the "interactive art" and followed Julio through a small warren of professional-looking yurts to an unremarkable door.

Inside, a man stood behind a small podium, like a maître d' at a fancy restaurant. On a long table was laid out an extraordinary buffet of hummus and tabbouleh and about seventeen types of olives; the ground was layered in plush rugs and fluffy poofs. A Bedouin lifestyle tent.

Julio was sobering up, and he found her the hot spot password and a relatively quiet corner table.

"You don't understand," she said before he turned to leave, still feeling the need to justify herself. "She loves *Max*. She will be *fine*."

He just stared at her for a minute. "Then why did she run away? If she was getting what she wanted?" He looked up and around. "Like Burning Man itself. Full of people searching for something they don't have."

He showed her how to connect to the Wi-Fi, patted her arm, and left.

She sat there, calling Neko and then Greta, but each time it went straight to voicemail. Jenny's phone had bars, had a signal finally—so why were their phones now off? She sent texts, too, and they went through. But no response. Her heart was beating so hard she thought it might jump into her throat. She lay her head on the table.

Julio's words in the art car had shaken something loose in her, some shameful recognition. If Neko had run away, well, that was the territory of teenagers. A truism, he called it, and he was right. She was trying to tell Jenny and Max something. To communicate her anger and pain.

As she thought about this place, the swirling phantasmagoria of it all, she realized, with a sort of self-loathing disdain, that this was where people came to live out their childhood fantasies—playing dress-up and participating in their utopian gift economy, a place with no bedtimes, no strangers, all glitter and magic. But she was no better. Her plan to move to Berlin was no less childish. She'd told herself she was looking out for Neko, but maybe she just wanted attention, too. Maybe, deep down, she just wanted them to be sorry, to realize that they needed her and beg her to come back. After all, even she knew good mothers didn't run away.

2:30 A.M.

"Here you are."

Jenny looked up to find Jesse standing above her. He was wearing a hoodie and carrying a messenger bag. He looked exhausted.

"Any news?" she asked.

He shook his head and sat down beside her. "Everyone's looking. We'll find her."

"She ran away." Jenny showed him the text, practically shoving the phone into his face. Jesse reached into his bag for reading glasses and out slipped an album, strangely wrapped in lined notebook paper rather than a sleeve.

Picking it up from the floor, she held it at the edges, raising her eyebrows at him as she handed it back.

He shrugged. "It's for you. Was going to give it to you earlier, but then . . . well, Neko . . ."

"What is it?"

"*The Wreckage.*"

It felt to Jenny as if the entire day had been engineered to break her heart. "How?"

"I knew you'd want to listen to it this way, not just digitally, so I had our guy at Goldberg Records press it from the master."

"From the master?" She smiled. "Look at you." Every copy degraded the master, which was why one basically never used it to press directly into vinyl.

"I know. But just one." He nodded. "Take it."

At that moment, someone young and impossibly thin ran through the tent, yelling, "I lost my glow stick. Has anyone seen my glow stick?!"

Looking up, Jenny noticed a small group of men—or, on closer inspection, a man and his entourage—filling their plates from the buffet. There was something familiar about the man, but she couldn't place him at first. Music industry? Some pseudo celebrity she'd seen on television? There was something about the way he held his shoulders.

Then the man, with his buzz cut and bulldog eyes, looked up at Jenny, a carrot stick held between his fingers like a cigarette, and Jenny knew who he was: Chance Morris, boy CEO of the Fourth State.

"Hey, Jesse," she said. "Give me a minute, okay?" And she left him there and walked over to where Morris and his crew were sitting down.

The bodyguards dropped their pita pockets, bodies tightening into alert.

"It's okay," he reassured them. "Ms. Sweet is a potential client." His eyes searched hers, and he seemed to sense her distress. "Are you okay?"

At any other time, this conversation would be laughable, thought Jenny. "I think my daughter may have left," she said, struggling with how to convey the context and gravity. "How does one get out of Burning Man? I mean, from the middle of it? Without a car?" She was still trying to do the math in her head. How was it possible for Neko to be on the way to New York? And, if it wasn't possible, why would Greta lie?

Chance Morris shrugged. "The same way I'm about to leave. There's an airstrip. My plane should be landing about now."

"You have a private jet."

He stared at her as though that were a stupid statement. He finished chewing and then said, "I have to get back to Manhattan. Investor meeting."

Jenny felt as though she'd lost the script of her life. "Can I get a ride?" She didn't have any idea if this was the sort of thing that people asked of a person with a plane, but if there was a storm bearing down on the East Coast, she didn't have a large window of time.

"Yeah, okay." Hummus gathered at the corner of his mouth.

"We're leaving as soon as the plane gets clearance. I need to get home before they close LaGuardia."

"Thank you." Jenny felt her heart squeeze. The ceiling fans of the Dior tent whirred above them.

Chance Morris said he would pick her up there in his golf cart in ten minutes to take her to the airstrip. "My parents are going to flip when they find out Jenny Sweet was in my baby plane."

SHE RETURNED TO JESSE, WHO WAS LOOKING ANXIOUS, AND BEGAN TO babble about how, since there was a chance Neko had left on a plane, she was hitching a ride back to New York. Jesse and Max should stay here and keep looking. In case it was all a misunderstanding. "Tell him to keep looking," she panted, as though Max would ever stop.

"What about the record?" Jesse whispered.

She looked at it in his hands. "Hold on to it for me."

He put it gently back in his messenger bag, and looked her in the eyes for a beat too long. Then he was gone.

She picked up her phone and tried again. Voicemail. Jenny felt strange leaving, but it also felt right. Divide and conquer. They didn't need to be a couple to help Neko. To raise her. Her breakup with Max did not require her to break up with Neko. She was Jenny's child, not a partner or lover. She was her baby.

LATER, AS JENNY RODE ALONGSIDE A TECH MILLIONAIRE ON A tricked-out golf cart toward an exclusive airstrip at Burning Man, she reached her hand out into the dust. She knew that

Layla would be pissed when she turned down the Germany gig. But that was okay. No matter what, she and Max and Neko would always be a family.

And when she found Neko, she would find a way to make this clear. To make her understand what kind of mother she was.

35

RAIN LASHED DOWN.

Neko had contacted the Cellar through the secure channel they'd previously arranged, told them that her and Harriet's transport had broken down and that they needed a few tools to fix the engine. She left the encampment in the middle of the night, telling no one. Not even Iggy.

It was dark and miserable. Skirting the reservoir rather than rafting across took longer, was harder. The wind shifted slightly, driving rain directly into Neko's face.

Trudging toward the bunker, Neko tried to untangle the knot, inspecting and naming each strand of pain: Disappointment at not finding her mother. Bitterness at being a pawn in Jules's scheme. Confusion over the changes in Iggy. Even the fact that she would never see, or touch, Chaplin ever again—everything about him blown into a thousand little pieces, including her mother's master recording.

But the mother recording was still out there. If she could get it back.

As she walked, she thought about Burning Man. She remembered how the noise-canceling headphones muffled most of the sound, which had made it more surreal to watch all those people moving their bodies, jumping and twirling, diaphanous wings and glittering muscles, feathered masks and unicorn horns. Two women dressed as butterflies, or maybe moths, had grabbed Neko's hands, and soon they were all spinning in a circle, laughing.

She remembered strobe lights and a pyramid. She remembered stealing a cookie from another table without asking when there was no pizza left in the tent—her mother had told her that everything at Burning Man was free—and how this theft had made the people nearby widen their eyes and cover their mouths. The cookie didn't taste quite right, but she'd eaten it anyway. Liking the attention, she'd reached for another one, but a ladybug stopped her.

"Those are magic cookies," the ladybug said, smiling. "One is enough, trust me."

Suddenly the attention on her felt uncomfortable. "Why is everyone here so white?" This was something she'd heard her mother say earlier in the day and it came to her in this moment.

"Ha! There's a question!"

"This girl doesn't pull any punches."

"Burning Man isn't about what's on the outside, little one, but what's on the inside."

"Technically, I'm one-eighth Cherokee," someone said.

There was a moment where Neko looked around and couldn't see the stage with her parents on it, a brief moment of panic, but then everything softened, and she began to feel like she was floating.

The ladybug was back again, but now there were two of them. "Are you on an adventure?" one of them asked her.

"I'm on a quest," she said, which was partly true. She was in search of something.

"What are you looking for?" asked the second ladybug.

And in that moment Neko said it aloud. "Something that will make my parents sorry."

And later, when she found a cell signal and asked Greta to send the stupid text about her going home—it was just to buy time. She didn't think her mother would leave. She didn't think things through at all. She didn't think.

"YOU'RE SOAKED." DRAKE WAS THE ONE WHO OPENED THE DOME, RAKing her body with a flashlight.

"Cats and dogs," said Neko.

He squinted at her in confusion.

"Never mind."

It was a relief to be out of the deluge, but the air was sticky, the clamminess of wet cloth and hair. As the dome closed, Neko felt her lungs working harder to breathe: No windows. No doors to the outside. No escape. She should have known her mother would never have allowed herself to be held captive in a place like this for so long. Would have killed herself first.

"Where's the other one?"

"Staying with the vehicle."

"I'll take you to the security office, where there are some tools." Drake turned toward the stairwell. He lowered his voice. "They know Chaplin is dead, by the way. They know you're rogue."

Neko didn't feel afraid. She felt like she was living someone else's life. "I want you to take me to Layla Wei's apartment before we get the tools." She opened a satchel full of scratch and sun coins, a packet of heirloom tomato seeds.

He looked at her nervously, eyes darting. "Let's go to security first. Then I can call her and have her meet . . ."

Neko put her Glock to the back of his neck before he could finish. "I don't want to hurt anybody. I just need to talk to her."

WHEN THE APARTMENT DOOR OPENED, NEKO THOUGHT SHE HEARD music, faint and fast, a saxophone.

Aunt Layla turned from where she sat at her desk. First there was nothing, no real connection, but then a spark from her eyes—a luster, a recognition. "You're back." Her face held some new mystery.

Neko told Drake they wanted to be alone, and when Layla nodded, he said, "You probably won't have long," and left.

As soon as he was gone, Layla came in for a hug, surprising Neko, leaving her with nothing to do but to let it happen, to not laugh nervously but just accept it.

They walked farther into the small apartment. A paper calendar hung by a thumbtack: The photograph for December 2029 was of a snowy cabin, the paper bleached from years of light exposure. "Aunt Layla, how did you end up here? You still haven't told me."

Layla walked over to the corner and turned on a lamp—so quaint, so Old World. She motioned for Neko to sit beside her on the low bed.

"I grew up in New Mexico, did you know? I spent my adult life trying not to think about that place at all." Her voice was soft and buttery. "Now I only dream of arroyos after the rain."

"I know you're from New Mexico. But how did you end up *here*?" Neko almost asked: *Didn't you know that a cellar is just another name for a dungeon?*

"On my birthday, your mother used to make me guacamole. She would go into our neighborhood grocery and ask to see any avocados in the back—sometimes they threw them out still ripe.

The ones in the wooden crate up front were hard—it would take days before . . ." Layla looked up and seemed to notice Neko's expression. "But that's not what you asked."

She sighed. "At first, it was just a backup plan. Totally abstract. Then, when they called and told us to come during Frida, it was supposed to be temporary." She stood and walked to the stereo, turned it up a bit, some weird acid jazz. "I love this riff." She closed her eyes. "Anyway, I ultimately couldn't face it—when I saw what happened to the city. All the funerals, the evacuations. Buried my head in the sand rather literally."

Layla began to sway to the music. Slowly. Neko watched and tried to imagine what her mother would have looked like at Layla's age—rounder, surely, and softer, maybe. Neko longed for something soft. She thought about how you could try your best and still fail. How it happened all the time.

"I should have known she didn't mean it," said Layla, eyes still closed, "your mother."

At first Neko wasn't sure she'd heard correctly. Her brain buzzed, reached out as though to some collective intelligence that might link her with Aunt Layla. She went to the stereo and turned off the music. She needed to be sure. "Say that again?"

"I should have known she wouldn't have actually let them take her brain waves. She never truly bought into any of that stuff. I didn't want to think it through, but I should have known." Coarse, copious hair fell around her face.

Neko sensed motion inside the chambers of her heart, its thrum moving in time with her breath, metronomic. She welcomed a flash of wisdom, some mystical instruction about what to do now, but none came. "You've listened to the album. How? Where is it?"

"The mother is a positive cast of the master. So it can technically be played on a record player." She reached under her bed and pulled out the album. "We have one in the Control Room."

Neko automatically reached for the mother, but Layla retracted her arm so that it was out of reach.

"You have to understand." She raised her hands toward the ceiling. "I just wanted to staple us to the sky. Me and Jenny. Together."

Staple us to the sky. Neko considered this turn of phrase, the violence of it. Part of her understood how Aunt Layla could've been taken in by the charlatans promising plasmatic freedom. Because wouldn't it be nice to think you could be reunited with your best friend in a place where nothing could hurt you ever again? Where there was no pain and no limits? Neko realized she'd never really considered the word "span" in the term "lifespan." "Span," like a bridge. A bridge to what, exactly?

"Have you ever thought about why we spend so much time mourning the afterlife and not the beforelife? I mean, nobody spends insomniac nights mourning all the centuries they missed before they were born. You might be curious—like, wouldn't it be cool to have met Sappho or Coltrane? But not in that existential dread sort of way. Not in that banging-your-head-against-the-wall-of-nonexistence kind of way."

"I want the album. And I want you to come with me. It's not safe here."

"There's more I need to tell you first. Your mother wasn't going to leave you for Europe. I lied about that. Well, not entirely, but mostly. And even worse, I'm the reason she wasn't here, safe, during the storm. I'm the reason she's gone." She was shaking. "You asked me why I was obsessed with all this, and that's why."

"What are you talking about?"

"She called me that evening before Frida, saying this guy,

this CEO we'd met, was giving her a ride from Burning Man. I was already en route to the bunker and was about to tell her to come, too, come with me. To not go back to New York. But then she said she was pulling out of the Berlin project, even though the contract was already signed and everything. I was pissed, so I didn't invite her. I didn't send the extraction team for her."

Neko didn't want to hear any of this. None of it mattered anymore. But Layla kept talking.

"She reminded me about the CEO's project, consciousness in sound waves, and she said that her consciousness was on the album. She said I would understand when I heard it. And then later, after the storm, I thought: She was with Chance Morris. She must have used his technology to capture her brain waves in sound waves and put them on the album. This is how I can save her. This is how I can make things right."

"It wasn't your fault she died, Aunt Layla. She wouldn't have gone to the Cellar because she thought I might be in New York. You understand? It's *my* fault."

Neko's device began buzzing, and she looked down to see a message from Harriet. *The bees are swarming,* it said. *They're almost there. Queen Bee says they'll spare everyone if you let them in the doors.*

Neko felt the prickle and shift of flannel against her ribs and the fire of adrenaline in her veins. "We're out of time," she said to Layla. "Do you know how to open the outside bay doors?"

"Of course." She smiled. "Are your friends here? We're in need of some new blood."

"They will take over this place if you let them."

She shrugged. "Personally, I'm tired of being director of the future."

Layla directed them out of her door and down the hall.

When they got near the Control Room, she told the security guard, "I'm going to play that record again. This woman needs to hear it before she leaves."

He shrugged. He didn't care.

In the Control Room, Layla pointed to the screen showing what the camera picked up outside the doors. "We have to wait until we see them. When the outer doors are open, the chairman gets an alert."

"Do you have any weapons in here?"

Layla shook her head. "But there's tear gas in every room." She showed Neko a small insert in the corner wall by one of the large panels of buttons.

They waited. The calm before the storm.

"I wanted to ask you before, though I also kind of didn't want to: What happened to Max in the end? And Jesse. I know they survived the storm, but what happened then?"

"It's a long story."

Layla opened her palms.

Sighing, Neko told her about her father, speeding through the stations of the cross to get it over with: dementia, steep decline, Aimee, a nursing home. "Jesse, I don't know. The last time I saw him was when he came to visit us in Philly."

They'd almost never gotten visitors at the house, so she remembered that day with special clarity. The front yard was small and narrow with an old, gnarled box elder that Neko was fond of because of how it greeted guests like a butler, forcing people to duck beneath one branch as they came up the walkway.

Jesse arrived with a small bag of brown sugar, the way people used to bring bouquets of flowers. A gift, something special.

He soon realized that conversation with her father was almost impossible, the way he started and stopped stories, digressed and got distracted, stared intently at the spider plant hanging from the ceiling, which was somehow more interesting to him than a rare visit from his decades-long bandmate and friend. "Dad's disintegration was not exactly a secret, but it wasn't until I saw him through Jesse's obvious alarm that I fully realized, well, the extent of it. The fullness of his lost swagger, I guess."

Later, she heard Jesse arguing with Aimee in the kitchen, pushing for more medication or help or something, as though what was happening could be reversed. It was clear from the way they held their bodies that they didn't like each other, and as far as Neko knew, Jesse never visited again, though for a while he'd sent postcards in the mail.

Before he left that day, Jesse brought out a shiny harmonica painted with small purple flowers from the messenger bag always perched on his hip.

"Your mother's," he told Neko. "Borrowed it from her and never got the chance to return it."

Neko hadn't said anything, afraid that, if she did, she would start crying and never stop.

"I have something else of your mother's. Come visit me at my house, okay? I'll give it to you."

She nodded, but she never went to visit him. She watched Jesse leave through the crescent moon window in the front door. He stopped and leaned against the trunk of the box elder, like a bear or a drunk, almost flung himself against the jagged bark. And the tree held him for a moment.

When her father had finally been moved into a home, she'd left the harmonica by his bed because she wanted him to have something of her mother's with him.

"I regret that sometimes," Neko told Layla.

They sat there for a minute in silence.

"Where was he living then?"

"What?"

"Jesse?"

"Long Island."

"I wonder if the vinyl copy is still there?" She told Neko about how Jesse had pressed one vinyl from the master as a gift. One copy.

"Maybe that's what he meant by having one more thing of my mom's." Neko saw smudges suddenly appear on the monitor. She couldn't tell if Iggy was with them, but it was likely. "There. They're fifty yards away."

Layla walked over to the turntable. "Let's distract the root vegetables a little. Let's play this bad baby on the intercom system." She removed the mother from its sleeve.

"You can do that?"

"I can do that."

The needle dropped and immediately—slow, chiming cords building toward something.

Penelope waits for winter

The sounds from the album rose and fell, her mother's voice surrounding them as though electrified by the fourth state of matter. As though beauty was all that mattered in the end, and maybe that wasn't far from the truth. Maybe her mother had struggled to be both an artist and a mother, and maybe Neko struggled to be free and also a good person. Maybe all that mattered was that they'd tried.

"When I first heard the demo for *Wok Hei,* I loved it immediately." Layla was watching the album spin, as though hypnotized. "But I had no idea it would change my life." She looked at Neko. "The Nightjars' tour bus was never exactly famous as a party bus, at least not by the industry standard, but still, after you were born, we took to calling it the Tour Bus of Zen on the Highway of Screaming Babies." Layla's fingers fluttered. "Your crib was in the back, and above it were one thousand cranes connected by lines of filament, shimmying with each bump in the road, delighting you to no end."

As she tried to picture the scene, Neko opened her palms. "I wonder what she would think of . . ."

The music crescendoed into loud punk riffs shot through with crackling melodies, and Layla had to practically shout to be heard.

"You?" Layla considered it. "She would see you, see the world that made you, and it would make her sad. But she'd be proud of you. She was a survivor in her own way."

We mistook it for gold, let it out
Smoked a fag
As the floating island burned

Layla reached out a hand and tucked an escaped curl behind Neko's ear. "Jenny and Max used to dance like idiots for you under that flock of cranes. Dance like they would never cut each other to the bone." She smiled. "You, too. You were a fantastic dancer, a natural. You used to drive us all mad begging us to put on the Beatles, the Go-Go's, the Ramones, and dance. We all had to go along with whatever you wanted, the charmed child."

Neko's cheeks were wet, and she made no move to dry them. "I wonder what happened to her."

My daughter didn't cry
She asked if the cat spirit would get wet outside

As they listened and waited for what would come next, Neko couldn't help thinking about *The Odyssey*. So much of the original story was about the pain of waiting—Odysseus must wait before he can return, and Penelope and Telemachus must wait for him. They are burnished by the element of time, like copper oxidizing into the blue-green of a sea monster. *And yet they are supposedly the lucky ones,* thought Neko. *They are alive.*

Even if it were possible to bring her mother back in the ethereal way Aunt Layla had believed, would that be a life worth living? Her mother used to say that people who claimed to be color-blind, to not see race or gender, were liars. The body in which we moved through the world was not inconsequential. Neko looked down at her own body—a piece of each of her parents, a Venn diagram of Max and Jenny—and then ran her hand across the crisscrossing latticework of ink—the part that wasn't them at all. Her body. Her body. Her body.

It was like when her father had found her at Burning Man—exhausted, awash in the sunrise over the Esplanade—and Neko understood from the almost violent, possessive way he reached for her, searching her body for damage, the intensity of his love. The power of his attention and adoration, focused on her physical existence and nothing else. Not that she'd doubted his love before, but there, in that shimmery moment in that surreal desert, Neko saw, uncoiling from every part of *his* body, the naked need for her to be okay.

All these years she'd been consumed by her mother's dramatic exit from her life, and the guilt associated with it. But her father had slipped away slowly, a different sort of pain that layered inside her like geological strata. And weren't all Neko's sketches, her body ink, all of it ultimately an attempt to arrest that decay? To hope that no matter what happened to her mind, those pictures of her life would remind her who she was?

"They're almost here."

Layla nodded. "And when it's time for the doors to open, I'll need you to go up and run the elevator so it doesn't get locked. Understand?"

"You should do it. That way you're near the exit if things go sideways."

She laughed. "Things went sideways for me a long time ago."

Goldenrod
Gold band
Dark
Darkest
Darkness

"Go," said Layla. "It's time." She moved to the switchboard and toggled switches until there was a loud crack. On the screen, the dome doors opened with a groan, releasing the artificial darkness.

Neko stood there watching the people swarm the screen, and for a minute everything around her seemed to go quiet, as if the volume had been suddenly turned down on the world. As though she were peering into a story, watching the plot from outside. And then the world grew loud again. She looked to the beautiful, chiseled old woman standing beside her, but Layla had already turned away.

And what am I?
Just milk, mother, wolf

It would be almost six hours before Neko would learn that that beautiful old woman wouldn't make it out. That Layla had known she wouldn't make it out. It wasn't tear gas in the corner after all but something more deadly, and the chairman would use it to try to gain back the Control Room, though by that point it would be too late for him, too.

Neko didn't know any of this yet. She closed the door and began to jog down the corridor. The concrete was smooth and hard beneath the soles of her boots. And the music. The music bled. It curdled and screamed and ricocheted and spoke of love as though none of it would ever, ever end.

36

THE PAIN RODE ACROSS HER BACK. MOSTLY IT DIDN'T FEEL LIKE BEING pierced by needles, but rather like being ground down by a pestle pummeling the mortar of her bones.

Neko straddled a chair backward, forearms braced. She was positioned in front of Louise Bourgeois's Spider Woman, a print Chaplin had stolen from the Whitney that depicted a woman's face on a spider body encircled by a red oval. As the tattoo progressed, Neko focused on the image until it blurred.

The dark radio played headlines over the speakers: *Government says: Electric grid now stable . . . U.S. in dispute with Canada over cloud brightening . . . Border communities protest tighter enforcement . . . Government says: Laboratory meat is patriotic . . . Best Actor winner a no-show at the Oscars: Is he really an A.I.? . . . Government says: Sacrifice is patriotic . . .*

The phone rang.

The needle whirred to a stop, and the pain released its clutch.

Neko looked at her phone. "Sorry," she said to her partner. "I have to take this."

She stood and walked down the hall, pausing in front of a doorway that opened to several feet of black soil that Neko watered and raked twice weekly. A garden of nothing.

She picked up the call. "I told you the shipment was delayed." In the year since the Cellar had become the Hive's newest cell, Neko had managed to painstakingly re-create most, though not all, of Chaplin's underground networks. "Next week. Promise."

"I'm calling because I forgot to ask for another stack of visas," said Jules on the other end of the line. "We need to make a supply run to Fringetown."

"Those have gone up to a hundred apiece." It turned out Neko was good at business. At keeping the revolution stocked while also turning a respectable profit.

"That much?"

"Yes." Every time they spoke, it was the same. Jules was a tough customer. "And that's after my special discount for young insurgents."

"Seventy-five."

"Eighty."

Neko bent down, picked up some of the domesticated dirt from the other side of the plexiglass barrier, and rubbed it between her fingers. "And tell Iggy I threw in something special for him in your shipment."

There was a brief silence. "If he wasn't in the vegetable garden right now, I know he'd want to talk to you. Cabbages and rutabagas and all that."

Neko knew that Jules was lying, but she said, "Yes." She wished she could see his face when he received the painting—Kehinde Wiley's *Napoleon Leading the Army over the Alps,* still in its gold museum frame. A peace offering.

"And the gift you sent us last time," said Jules, her voice rounding with emotion. "I don't know how I'll keep them from playing it all day long." She was talking about the mother. *The Wreckage* had played over the intercoms during the siege of the Cellar and become the soundtrack of the revolution. But the mother wouldn't last forever, just a physical object that would decay with each play. But it was where it belonged.

"I'm glad."

"Maybe we'll find the other copy one of these days. Jesse's copy," Jules said before whisper-yelling at somebody on her end of the line.

"You never know." After hanging up, Neko stood for a moment. The silence of daytime in New York City. The garden of dirt. Rather grandiosely, she thought of herself as one of the lesser gods: Protector of emptiness and loss. Curator of the decay. Guard to the barely necessary.

She walked back into the office.

Government says: Neighborhood Watch groups should no longer be armed with automatic weapons . . . Communication blackout continues along the Breakwater, but for how much longer? . . . Government says: Everything will be okay . . .

Neko had discovered that waiting was its own fruit. She waited and grew plump and satisfied in the waiting. Not Penelope. No. Rather, like Circe, alone on her magical island, she let the prey come to her.

But not really alone.

"Do you want to finish this later?" asked Harriet from where she waited with the needle. Her black hair was looped on top of her head in a loose bun held together by a pencil.

Neko sat back down in the chair. "Let's finish it now."

The buzz started up again, the artist ready to continue the tale—one emblazoned on the walls and curves of the body. An axis of scars and ink and bone.

"You never answered me before. Why these notes on a staff? What's it the score to?"

Neko closed her eyes and smiled.

THE WRECKAGE

Track 11 (Secret Track): "Waiting Redux"

Fat rain droplets splattered the windshield as the black Lincoln Town Car slid through the empty streets of Manhattan. Air heavy with impending storm. Beside Jenny in the back seat, Chance Morris scrolled through his phone, its blue light giving his face an eerie cast.

Though it was technically morning now, neither Greta's nor Greta's mother's phone was turned on. At this point, Jenny had to hope that, if Neko had returned to New York, she was safe—sleeping over at Greta's or tucked into her own bed at their apartment.

As the driver exited the FDR, the East River a dark backdrop for the glittering Williamsburg Bridge, Chance Morris closed his phone and turned to Jenny. "Ms. Sweet, I want to say again that I hope you'll consider entrusting us with your zeta waves." He laughed. He'd had a few drinks on the jet from Burning Man and his cheeks were pink. "You will get to see your great-grandchildren grow up!"

Jenny tried to smile. "Maybe *see* is not the right word."

He looked confused.

"Since I won't have eyes."

"Yes, well."

The car pulled up in front of her building across from Tompkins Square Park. The rain was coming down in sheets now, and Jenny was drenched just walking the few feet from the car to the entrance.

As she closed the lobby door behind her, lightning struck nearby, momentarily freeze-framing the surprised look on the doorman's face where he sat behind the desk. Then, with a crash of thunder, the room fell into darkness.

"Shit," said Rick, the night doorman, fumbling around in a drawer. "I have a flashlight around here somewhere."

Once he found it, he lit the way.

Jenny followed him. "Have you seen Neko? Did she come home?"

"Not on my shift."

"Can you check the log?"

"Once the power comes back on."

"Should we be worried?" she asked, pointing at the sandbags lined up next to the door.

"Nah. Those are just in case some water comes up through the sewers like in Sandy. The fancy new storm doors should keep even the ground floor dry. You're lucky. They haven't finished the walls down in Jersey, and my brother says they've got megaphones out in the street telling folks to evacuate."

In the apartment, Jenny flung open the door to Neko's room and called her daughter's name.

She wasn't there.

The place was empty, just as they'd left it. Jenny's bag suddenly felt too heavy and she dropped it on the hardwood with a thud. It would be impossible to find a cab in the current deluge, and it was too far to walk to Greta's apartment. She couldn't even charge her phone with the electricity out.

Waiting.

Being a parent in the world meant being a magnet for platitudes: *Appreciate every moment,* they tell you. *You'll miss this later. The days are long but the years are short.* Often, too exhausted or bent out of shape or sick of having her experience narrated by condescending empty nesters, she had just wished they would shut the fuck up.

But every once in a while, she had recognized the fleeting, magical moment as it was happening. Like that day walking Neko to preschool. They'd just stopped at a coffee shop and Jenny was holding her thermos in one hand, Neko's hand in the other. They were just two people in step with each other, walking down the early morning sidewalk dressed in matching red sneakers. Alive and in love.

Maybe it was the tiny palm, like a tiny heart, sweaty against hers. Maybe it was because they walked so slowly, constrained by her daughter's short stride, like slow-motion film footage. Maybe it was how Neko stopped to stick her finger in the open mouth of a purple tulip in a garden-level window box. Whatever it was, Jenny knew the feeling had blossomed from her body pressing against this new, miniature body beside her. Being in a body. Jenny couldn't escape that the moments that made up her life, all the best ones, and all the other ones she hardly remembered, were inexorably linked to this organic life-form. This flesh and these bones.

Jenny sat on the sofa and stared at the eggplant-purple front door.

A few months earlier, Jenny and Max had stared at the other side of it. They were leaving Neko home alone in the evening without a sitter for the first time. Max kissed the fingertips of his left hand and placed them on the door, a gesture that broke Jenny's heart. They planned to tell Neko about their separation the following week on a trip to see a James Turrell light installation, but for now they lived together in a state of fiction, of performance art.

That night, exiting Brooklyn's Seventh Avenue station, which smelled even more strongly of piss than usual, they tried to re-create the Red Krayola's discography from memory.

"What was the first one they did after the original lineup disbanded? It had that super serious–sounding name." Max carried his Strat strapped to his back in a soft case embroidered with roses, and Jenny traced them with one finger as she walked behind him up the stairs.

"Soldier-Talk?"

"Good call." Max kept walking. "Now, *Coconut Hotel* wasn't actually released for years after . . . ?"

And they talked about music the whole way to avoid talking about anything else.

At first there was only a small group at Jesse's place, and Jenny actually enjoyed herself—the bite of the strings on her fingers, the reverb in her chest. They sat packed tight in an oval around the living room, attention evenly dispersed, everyone a decent musician giving and taking without ego. Building on one another's riffs, sometimes crushing them, but with an air of respect and good cheer.

As usual, Jenny was the only woman. Well, someone's wife or girlfriend stood in the corner and watched—she initially tried to snap them with her phone camera, but they all yelled at the poor woman: *No photos. Private party.*

Jenny was surprised when Max positioned himself next to her in the circle—ever since they'd made the decision to disband the Nightjars and separate, he usually kept his distance. But that night they achieved synergy: No audience. No recording equipment. It was like the early days, when they never expected to make it big, when they just fucked around. Jenny didn't need to look at him to feel him responding to her with his arpeggios.

It was true that Neko connected her and Max in a stronger way—the stranglehold of parenthood—but it was also a connection complicated by responsibility and anxiety and the hot flares of pure joy. Music connected them in a way that, when it worked, felt free and light and open-ended by comparison. When they'd had sex, they'd understood how to make each other's bodies respond, the way a surgeon knows the cuts. But there was nothing clinical about the way they played music together.

Before long, more people arrived, younger musicians with their own instruments and agendas filling up the apartment until it felt like the only fresh air to breathe was right up by the ceiling. Jenny slipped out of the circle and folded her body into the doorway of the kitchen. She drank a beer and wondered when cans had become fashionable again.

She searched for Max to tell him she was leaving and found him in the hallway being fawned over by a group of young people. He was laughing and seemed to be having a good time, so she was surprised when he said he would leave with her.

"I miss Neko," he said as they waited on the corner for their rideshare.

"She'll probably be asleep."

"I know." The look on his face told Jenny that he, too, was feeling grief in his own way.

She nodded. She thought about how, when Neko was a toddler, she would sit on Max's lap in front of the keyboard and he would use her hands to bang the keys in a guessing game he called "Neko or Debussy?" Jenny always guessed Debussy, and Max always said, "No! Original composition by Neko Sweet." And they laughed. Sometimes that was what a family had felt like.

Salt on the rim of a glass, scarf on the curve of a scapula, scalding hot baths competed against the unraveling, the crumbs, the rotting cabbage in the vegetable drawer of adulthood. She repeated in half bitterness, half awe: *It's a privilege, it's a privilege.*

She thought of the album Jesse had pressed. Her album.

Would Neko understand that it was a love letter to her?

The rain continued and the winds picked up. Tree branches in Tompkins Square Park whipped back and forth. Above a construction site in the distance a crane literally bent backward. Jenny was restless, wondering if Neko was warm and safe. Wondering if the girl missed her, if she felt regret. If she was scared.

Jenny put on her camping headlamp and took down Neko's box from the top of the closet. She ruffled through it until she found the black film of the sonograms. She ran her finger along the curve of the image. The beginning.

When she was pregnant, Max had liked to read on the Internet about what fetuses looked like, what they were doing—as big as an avocado; as big as a grapefruit; she was growing eyelashes, sipping amniotic fluid like a fancy cocktail.

The feeling of being pregnant returned to her now as she watched the streets outside her apartment fill with water, the whole world drowning. The whole city a womb. Car alarms and sirens sounded distant, muffled by the rain, the rush of runoff, and she pictured skyscrapers covered in sludge until they looked like mountains with no slopes.

She'd found one last apple in the fruit bowl, and, though she wasn't hungry, she used a paring knife to peel spirals from the skin and wear them like bracelets. Her body was rank, grains of sand abrasive in the tucks behind her knees, but she couldn't imagine putting in the effort to peel off the layers of clothes and wash herself in even more water. The heart-shaped leaves of the *Monstera deliciosa* in its pot of peat seemed to reach toward the largest window as though it wanted to partake in the deluge, thirsty to feel wetness drip through its fenestrations.

She propped her feet on the sill below where the glass streamed with rain and thought of Neko, and of floating. She thought of Odysseus by himself on the raft, watching the Wagon as it wheeled around Orion in the night sky.

Floating in bed: As the baby grew bigger, she turned inside Jenny like meat on a spit. The stiller and sleepier Jenny became, the more active the baby was, stretching and thumping at the door of Jenny's uterus. The low swoosh of the noise machine, the thrum of blood.

One night a storm materialized, loud and raucous, thunder toppling over itself, threads of lightning unspooling outside the window. Jenny and Max reached across the bed and touched palms, checking in. "Do you think she can hear it?" she asked.

"Oh, yes," he said, "this baby will love noise," as though saying it could make it true. Jenny had hoped the thunder thrilled the baby, moved her with possibility.

Floating in the hammock: When no chair was comfortable for her anymore, Max set up a hammock on the roof of their building. Jenny pulled the sides around her like an amniotic sac, rocking and peering through the green-and-blue vinyl webbing. Sometimes, Max would take a guitar up there, too—the Gibson Hummingbird that had belonged to his now-dead friend, James, and that they'd recently had restrung—and play Hank Williams and Janis Joplin, Smokey Robinson and Lightnin' Hopkins. Once he played "Puff the Magic Dragon," but they'd forgotten how sad the ending was, and they couldn't finish singing through their sobs.

Floating in the ocean: One Sunday, Jenny went for a swim off

Jesse's small fishing boat, the water still and salty and smoky blue, the sky cloudy. Through the snorkeling mask she watched tiny fish dart through seaweed down below, the sandy bottom. She flipped over, pregnant belly protruding from the water like a dolphin's back, rising and sinking with each breath. She wondered if giving birth to a baby was like having a song torn from your body. Like rock 'n' roll. Like how people can turn into light or sound or other people.

There she was
Waiting for summer
Here she is
Waiting for the quick-beating wing
Waiting for her life to change
Waiting for life
Waiting to show life what kind of mother she really is
Waiting

ACKNOWLEDGMENTS

THANK YOU TO MY WHIP-SMART (AND PATIENT) AGENT HALEY HEIDEMANN. So many thanks to Jesse Shuman, brain like a spinning galaxy, who saw this story's potential and pushed me to do more than I thought possible. Gratitude to the teams at WME and Penguin Random House, particularly Abdi Omer and Dan Denning, for their assistance and hard work throughout.

For various types of support across the years and drafts, thank you to my beta readers and writing group heroes: Dalia Azim, Jennifer duBois, Hillery Hugg, Jill Meyers, Maya Perez, Deb Olin Unferth, Amy Gentry, David Wright Faladé, Becka Oliver, Stacey Swann, Caroline Morris, Charlotte Gullick, Tyler Smith, and Amanda Eyre Ward. This novel is leaps and bounds better because of each of you. Thank you to St. Edward's University and San Ysidro Residency for material support during the writing of this novel.

Thank you to everyone who generously shared their expertise in so many realms (music, tattoos, origami, Burning Man, etc.): Lisa Smith, Jana Horn, Holden Rushing, Julian Solis, Tony Faia, Chris Zarate, Laura Meilander, and others. All mistakes are my own (probably). Thanks to the climate scientists, fighting the good fight. Thanks to Sasha West, for capturing so much beauty and truth in the poem "We've Not Long Come In," and to Michael Ondaatje, for the inspiration of the poem "Light." Thanks to Erin Hamilton, for, years ago, telling me I should write something set at Burning Man. At the time, I thought that was the worst idea, but look at me now.

The following resources were particularly useful in my research for this book: Lara Maiklem's *Mudlark: In Search of London's Past Along the River Thames,* Barbara Taub's *Desert to Dream,* Brian Doherty's *This Is Burning Man,* the National Park Service Submerged Resources Center, and Alan Weisman's *The World Without Us.* While I tried to mostly stay true to geography and facts, I did take liberties here and there.

While the character of Jenny Sweet is entirely fictional, I owe an invaluable debt to many real-life musicians (including Kim Gordon, Kathleen Hanna, Neko Case, and Carrie Brownstein) whose music and stories helped me to begin to understand that world.

Thank you to my teachers, students, friends, and family, without whom this would all be meaningless. (Hi, Mom and Dad!)

All my love to T, who somehow knows how to make everything better and always does.

To the Wolverwren, thank you for the privilege of a lifetime, letting me trail behind your wild sparkler as you make your way through this hard, glorious world.

And thanks to the mothers (any shape, any kind, including my own), especially those with rock 'n' roll in their hearts.

MUDLARK

A Novel

Mary Helen Specht

A BOOK CLUB GUIDE

A LETTER FROM THE AUTHOR

Dear Reader,

In a world of rampant technology and social media brain rot and enormous spider robots slithering across the Earth (maybe not yet, but soon), you are my hero. The librarians, the children using flashlights under the covers, the subway straphangers showing off their Toni Morrison cred, the book clubs scattered across the country keeping the publishing (and cheese and wine) industries alive. I may be biased, but readers are the best kind of people.

I tell my students that writing and reading fiction is not the same as keeping a diary. When you write or read fiction, it's not just for yourself. You're attempting to communicate across space and time. You're attempting to connect with another person, to try to understand what it means to be human.

I'm no different. I wrote this novel for so many reasons, only some of which I can articulate. I wrote it because an old friend told me I should write something set at Burning Man, to which I first responded, "Worst idea ever!" I wrote it because I always wanted to write a quest narrative. I wrote it because I had a baby and wondered what her future might hold on this crazy, complicated, warming planet. And I wrote this book because I never got to be a rock star myself. (There's always time, though, right?)

But, mostly, I wrote this book to feel less alone in a world that is changing too fast. I wrote this book to have something to hold onto and something to offer you. In case you wanted it. I hope you do.

Best,
MHS

QUESTIONS AND TOPICS FOR DISCUSSION

1. "In the eighteenth and nineteenth centuries, poor Londoners sold scraps they found on the foreshore to earn any money they could. They became known as mudlarks. . . . They were looking for lumps of coal, rope, bones, iron or copper—anything that could be sold. The treacherous mud and fast tides made it a dangerous activity" (London Museum). How has the author refashioned the term "mudlark" into something more contemporary? Consider the shift from mudlarking valuable materials like coal to ephemera and souvenirs, like what Neko and her team collect. What does this say about humanity in times of immense struggle, if they value their memories as much as their resources?

2. Imagine Hurricane Frida is heading toward you. In your rush to evacuate, what are the most meaningful items you have that you choose to bring with you? What would be hardest to leave behind?

3. What role does the theme of hope play in *Mudlark*? Are there moments where the characters find hope, despite their dire circumstances?

4. Discuss the symbolism throughout Jenny's solo album, *The Wreckage,* and the "Hades" bunker—in relation to Greek mythology, and in particular, to Homer's *The Odyssey*. How does each track reimagine the classic story? What are the similarities between Jenny's life story, and Odysseus's journey home? Neko's?

5. Analyze the various ideological factions at play in the world of *Mudlark*: the Hive, the Bunker, the remnants of the U.S. government, the cowboy church, Chaplin, Neko, and her team. What do they each believe when it comes to the correct way to rule? To live? How do you think society should be structured, and which faction do you most align with?

6. Discuss Neko and her tattoos. What does tattooing mean to her? What did it mean to her when she first discovered it as an art, and what does it mean to her later, as a mudlark?

7. Jenny Sweet struggled to be a mother and a wife, even as she succeeded at being a rock star. Do you think she was a good mother or a bad mother? Why? What do you think being a "good" mother means? How does one weigh their own ambitions against caring for their child, or sustaining their marriage? What is the impact of Jenny's ambivalence? Do you think she ever reconciled her feelings?

8. Do you think Neko's guilt about her mother's fate is warranted?

9. What did you make of the denizens of the bunker, and especially of Aunt Layla and her misguided quest to be with Jenny again? What is Neko really seeking from her?

10. What are the parallels between Neko's and Jenny's storylines? Do you believe that we can ever escape where we come from?

11. How do the interactions between the characters Neko, Iggy, Harriet, and Jules reflect the strains on human relationships in a collapsing society?

12. After finishing *Mudlark,* has your perspective changed at all on climate change and survival? How did it make you feel about the current state of things? Did this imagining of our future ring true to you? How so or how not?

13. Discuss the theme of *waiting*. What are each of the characters waiting for? Do they get what they want?

14. What is it about speculative fiction in particular that might allow authors to get closer to depicting the human condition?

MARY HELEN'S *MUDLARK* PLAYLIST

Blondshell, "What's Fair"

Liz Phair, "Divorce Song"

Arcade Fire,"Unconditional (Lookout Kid)"

Julie Ruin, "Radical or Pro-Parental"

Sonic Youth, "Little Trouble Girl"

The Flaming Lips, "Yoshimi Battles the Pink Robots"

Lauryn Hill, "Everything is Everything"

LP, "Switchblade"

Sharon Van Etten, "Seventeen"

Malia J, "Smells Like Teen Spirit"

Neko Case, "This Tornado Loves You"

Grace Jones, "Warm Leatherette"

The Walkmen, "Red Moon"

Kim Deal, "Are You Mine?"

David Bowie, "Blackstar"

Kate Bush, "This Woman's Work"

HOW TO SURVIVE IN THE WORLD OF *MUDLARK*

SHARE YOUR AIR DURING DIVES

When diving in a flooded Manhattan for resources, if you run out of air, share the regulator with a partner, passing it back and forth to ensure you can both breathe until you safely return to the surface.

They began to share air, handing the mouthpiece back and forth like a dance. They rose alongside their combined column of air bubbles. Breathe. Pull. Slow. Don't panic. (pg. 140)

NAVIGATE CURRENTS

When swimming against strong currents, move parallel to the shoreline to avoid being swept away. Do not panic. Focus on breathing slowly and steadily.

At the surface, Neko barely had time to take in one fierce gulp of air before being forced to swim hard against the water that threatened to push them toward open ocean. They moved parallel to the current, trying to avoid the eddies where nails and shards of glass and other debris gathered and swirled. (pg. 140)

PREPARE FOR THE WEATHER

Be prepared for sudden weather changes by carrying ponchos or other protective gear.

They secured the Land Rover and set out in the direction of the creek, bushwhacking their way through overgrown semi-marshland. As they walked, it began to rain again, and they pulled ponchos over their heads and kept moving. Neko marveled at how animals never showed any misery when it rained. (pg. 148)

COORDINATE WITH YOUR TEAM

Work in unison with your team, imitating movements to stay together and navigate challenging environments.

Beneath the surface, the crew allowed their belt weights to take them below the current. Like a flock of birds, they mimicked the person in front, turning and kicking in near unison, crossing over the crumbling remnants of a snaking coastal road, floating above the ravaged roofs of seafood shacks or whatever these buildings had once been, eventually swimming through the underwater bay doors and hauling themselves up onto the concrete steps in the center of the manufacturing plant. (pg. 138)

TAKE HEALTH PRECAUTIONS

Address health issues promptly, such as treating infections or ensuring proper hygiene.

"Because she has ringworm and God knows what else. Because you want me to call Richie and beg for a dangerous lark we have no business being on. Because I need to be alone, and because I asked you to" (pg. 93).

BE MENTALLY RESILIENT

Maintain your sanity by focusing on tasks and avoiding negative thoughts.

Neko made the wrinkled scrap paper into an origami crane. Crease, pinch, smooth. The one thing everyone in their line of work learned to endure: waiting. Fold, crease, fold, flip. With each turn, she made nothing into something. (pg. 19)

HAVE A PLAN

Have multiple emergency plans in place for different scenarios, ensuring everyone knows their role.

"We have three emergency plans for each family to ensure passage to the facility in the event of any *catastrophe."*

"Asteroid impact?" whispered Max. "Nuclear winter? Yeti attack?" (pg. 215–16)

Mary Helen Specht is the author of *Migratory Animals,* a *New York Times* Editors' Choice and winner of the Texas Institute of Letters Steven Turner Award for Best Work of First Fiction and the Writers' League of Texas Book Award for Fiction. Her writing has appeared in *The New York Times, Prairie Schooner,* and numerous other publications. A past Fulbright Scholar to Nigeria and Dobie Paisano Writing Fellow, Specht currently teaches creative writing at St. Edward's University in Austin, Texas, where she lives with her family.

maryhelenspecht.com
Instagram: @maryhelenspecht
Bluesky: @mhspecht